BROKEN PIECES

BY

RILEY HART

Copyright © 2014 by Riley Hart

All rights reserved. Printed in the United States of America.

No part of this book may be used or reproduced in any form or by any means electronic or mechanical, including photocopying, recording, or by any information storage and retrieval systems, without prior written permission of the author except where permitted by law.

Published by Riley Hart

The characters and events portrayed in this book are fictitious. Any similarity to real persons, living or dead is coincidental and not intended by the author.

Cover photo by jackson photografix

Dedication:

To Jessica. Thanks for being a great friend, for listening while I talk your ear off, and for loving so many of the same crazy things I do. And remember no matter what you're going through, you're strong and you have friends in your corner.

PART ONE: Josiah and Mateo

Chapter One

August

Josiah

The guy looked like he wanted to rip someone's head off.

"Josiah, this is Mateo. He's going to be staying with us." Mateo didn't look at Josiah as his foster mom introduced them. His arms were showing, long and muscular with a few tattoos here and there. Josiah didn't want to study them too much. He figured the best thing to do was not draw attention to himself where Mateo was concerned—not that he ever liked to draw attention to himself.

"Hi." So he didn't have to look at Mateo, Josiah studied Molly, the wall, the door, the bed he sat on but didn't call his own. He got shipped around too often to call anything *his*.

Mateo didn't reply, just ran a hand through his coal-black hair.

"You two are around the same age. Mateo, Josiah is sixteen. And Josiah, Mateo's seventeen. I bet you have a lot in common. I'm sure you'll love hanging out with each other."

Mateo groaned, the sound penetrating the armor Josiah fought so hard for. He still hadn't gotten the hang of not letting things in. He was good at not getting close to people. Being quiet came naturally, but he still felt things on the inside. He hated that about himself. Hated being vulnerable to the things others said and did.

"Mateo, Josiah is very sweet. I know the two of you will hit it off. Why don't you get to know each other a little before dinner?" Molly smiled as though she'd just said the greatest thing.

Yeah, because that's what he wanted Molly to call him in front of the guy who looked like he was probably a gang member. *Sweet.*

"Sure thing, *mamacita.*" Mateo winked at her.

Molly frowned. While Mateo paid attention to her, Josiah took a minute to let his eyes take the other guy in. Yeah, he was definitely stacked. And tall. Between his neck and shoulder, a thick, raised scar marred his brown skin.

Holy shit. This was bad. So, so bad. He'd seen kids like this—dangerous looking, who obviously hated the world. He'd lived with other kids like this, and they all made Josiah's life hell. Finally, things were okay with Molly and William. He'd been here all summer with no problems. They were nice and smiled and treated him well. If he could let himself feel safe and comfortable anywhere, it would be in this home.

Things were all going to change now.

"William and I expect certain behavior, Mateo," Molly told him. "One of our most important rules is respect. You must respect us, and we'll respect you in return. At dinner we'll talk more."

With that, Mateo walked into the room. Josiah's eyes never left the doorway as Molly stood there and smiled at him before she closed the door, leaving them alone.

"This is such fucking bullshit." Mateo fell onto the twin bed on the other side of their small room. Josiah figured it was hardly bigger than a dorm room in college would be, with a desk between their beds. Mateo picked at the blue blanket.

"They're nice people." On the one hand, Josiah regretted the words. The last thing he wanted was to piss this guy off, but then he thought about how kind Molly and William were to him and he didn't wish he could take them back.

Mateo laughed. "I bet they're real nice. Does Mama Molly sneak in the room at night and show you just how nice she is? Or maybe it's William. Gets his ass on the side because his wife won't give it up to him."

Josiah's stomach churned, nausea slamming into him. "They're not like that." He'd heard stories about homes that were that way, though. He'd been around some real assholes, but luckily he never had to deal with the kind of abuse Mateo spoke of.

Again, the other guy laughed. "Must be nice to live in the perfect world. You might not realize it now, kid, but everyone is some shade of fucked-up."

Annoyance snaked around Josiah that the guy would call him "kid" when they were so close in age.

"I wish I'd ever been lucky enough to see shit positive like that. Why you here?" Mateo asked.

Josiah wrung his hands together. He hadn't expected Mateo to ask him this—to ask him anything that mattered. "My parents…they died. Car wreck, when I was young. Don't have any family."

"Ah, then you're lucky. See, I know the truth. My dad didn't give a fuck about me. It's because of him I have this scar." He pointed to his neck. "Everyone lets you down at one point or another, pretty boy, and these people will, too. The sooner you learn that, the better off you'll be."

Mateo lay on his back, crossed his arms, and closed his eyes. Josiah hadn't known a lot of nice in his life but he refused to believe it was as bad as Mateo thought. What was the point in living if that was the case?

But he didn't say that. Didn't say a word. Just sat on his bed and watched Mateo sleep.

Chapter Two

Mateo

The kid watched him all the time. Every time Teo looked at him, Josiah's eyes would dart away, or he'd stumble, or look like he was gonna throw up or somethin'. The kid wouldn't make it a day in Teo's old neighborhood. It would eat him up.

The first few days, it took everything inside him not to put a fist in the kid's face and tell him to quit staring. But then... he actually started to feel sorry for him. He looked like he wanted to jump outta his skin most of the time. He hardly ever talked unless Molly or William spoke to him. Not that Mateo did a whole lotta talkin' around here, either, but it wasn't because he was scared. It was obvious the kid was.

If his dad were around, he'd call him weak for not beating Josiah's ass no matter how scared of everything he was. He was starin', he deserved to get taught a lesson. Mateo didn't see how taking someone out who was weaker than you made you a man.

But then, that probably made him a little bitch, too.

Just like the fact that it'd been two weeks since they'd sent him here and he hadn't bailed yet. His dad was in prison and he was expected to get his ass back to Brooklyn to take his rightful spot in Los Demonios. He was Ricky Sanchez's son, after all. His uncle Javier was in command, but it was always known Teo would be his second.

And Mateo would make it there—soon. He wasn't *loco* enough to try and make himself think he belonged in a place like this. It wasn't who he was, and he didn't deserve it after what he'd done, anyway.

He belonged on the streets, so he better get used to it now.

Even though he had ear buds in, Teo still heard the bedroom door open. Josiah looked at him before his eyes darted away. Mateo chuckled. This kid was so fucked if he ever got out of Yorktown.

He let his blond hair hang in his eyes, like he wanted it as some sort of shield between himself and Mateo.

Teo's hands itched to pull the goddamned things out of his ears and tell the kid to man-up. That he'd get his ass kicked every day of his life if he didn't even have the balls to look someone in the eye. He'd learned that lesson by the time he was five.

But he didn't do it. Teo just let the rap music play and pretended he gave a damn about it as he decided how he would go about getting the fuck out of Yorktown and back to hell. He'd already have to make excuses for not calling Javier and telling them exactly where he was so they could come and get him.

Chapter Three

Josiah

Mateo wasn't what he expected. It wasn't as if he was nice to Josiah or anything. The guy hardly talked to him, or even Molly and William for that matter, but he didn't give them crap, either.

He basically ignored Josiah, which was a whole lot better than the wisecracks about why he was so quiet, or so skinny, or whatever else people didn't like about him.

He and Mateo took turns doing dishes and taking out the trash. There had been a few times he got into it with Molly and William, but that had been more so in the first week.

But now it was the start of a new school year. Josiah hated going to a new school. He'd been to enough of them and they were always hell. People were assholes, and people his own age always worse.

Mateo looked tense as Molly drove them. For the first time since he'd moved in with them, he wore a baseball hat, backward. His thumbs drummed on his legs, almost as though he was…nervous, though that didn't make any sense. What did a guy like Mateo have to be worried about?

Josiah's mouth opened a million times to ask him but he never got the courage. Instead his focused on his own leg that bounced up and down, faster and faster the closer they got.

"If you have any problems, you know you can call me, right, Josiah?" Molly asked.

Mateo snapped out, "Don't baby him. He's a man. Treat him like it."

Josiah wasn't sure who to reply to first. His heart amped up, his eyes wide as he looked at Mateo next to him in the backseat. He'd defended Josiah. He didn't get why the guy would do that, and he wanted to know.

He settled on answering Molly first because it was easier than talking to Mateo. "He's right... I know I'm quiet, but it's not like I haven't been to high school before. I've been through a lot. I..." He looked out the window. "I can take care of myself. But thank you."

To a degree, Josiah realized that was a lie. He'd never been in a fight, and he got embarrassed easily, but damn did he *want* to be that guy. He wanted to be able to take care of himself, and if he couldn't, he'd go down fighting.

"That's not what I meant." Molly looked at them in the rearview mirror. "I don't doubt you, Josiah. And I know you're probably used to being on your own, both of you, but regardless, you're still boys. You deserve your childhood."

"What childhood?" Mateo asked. Josiah jerked his head in Mateo's direction only to have the guy lock eyes with him for a second before turning to watch the scenery go by like Josiah just had.

***

Josiah stumbled backward when the guy pushed him. His feet tangled and he fell. Everyone around them laughed as he struggled to get back to his feet. His heart collided with his ribs over and over. Three guys stood around him, blocking him.

"I don't know where you come from, but we don't like fags here. You keep your fucking eyes off me."

Josiah shook his head. "No…I wasn't…" He couldn't finish his sentence. He also couldn't say he wasn't gay because he was. Still, he hadn't been looking at the guy like that. "Please…"

"Aw, look. He even begs," one of the other guys sneered.

"Fucking faggots." The first guy came at Josiah again. For the second time, he stumbled, but now from trying to back away.

Just as he was about to grab Josiah, the guy tumbled backward, his friends trying to catch him as Mateo stepped between them. "You wanna fight, motherfucker? Fight me. I'm *begging* you to fucking fight me."

"Who the hell are you?" the guy asked.

"Someone you don't wanna fuck with but I'm really hoping you do it anyway."

The guy who pushed Josiah eyed Mateo up and down. Mateo's arms were stiff, muscles flexed, and even though Josiah couldn't see his face, he could tell the look there made his attacker pause. The guy backed up. "I don't have a problem with you. I have a problem with him.

The little fag's been watching me all day."

It was his fault. Josiah knew that. He'd always watched people, pretended he had their lives and dreamed about how he would live them. But it hadn't been because he wanted the boy.

Mateo didn't even pause. "You got a problem with him, you got one with me. And I'm telling you, you really don't wanna have a fucking problem with me, *pendejo*, cuz you're going to have it with a shit-ton of other people, too."

Josiah's stomach turned, *thank you* and *why* a tangled mess in his head. He was talking about a gang. He had to be.

"What's going on here?" A voice came from behind them, and then the principal was pushing his way through the crowd. Mateo didn't change his stance. Didn't back down or loosen up or even acknowledge that he'd spoken to them.

"Nothing," the first boy said. "Everything's cool." The whole crowd of people disappeared with him, but the principal and Mateo didn't move.

"Don't think I'm not aware you were causing some kind of trouble out here," he told Mateo.

Josiah stepped toward them. "No. He—"

"Has it exactly right. I was causin' shit. That's what I do. No reason to deny it." Mateo went around the principal. Josiah only paused for a few seconds before he went after him. He had no idea if it was the right thing to do, but it was instinct, and he wanted to be the type of guy who just went with his gut.

"Wait…Um…Mateo…"

"Not now, kid." He kept walking.

Thank you and *why* battled inside him again, yet Josiah didn't say either of them. But he let himself wish, wish he had the strength to stand up for himself, just like Mateo.

Chapter Four

Mateo

Teo bit down on the side of his cheek, trying to calm down. The kid sat in front with Molly on the way home, as though he realized Teo needed space. His whole body was hot, tight. He felt like he could explode at any minute.

Nausea crawled up his throat and he fought it back down. He closed his eyes, pictures of a man with his wrists tied together as he hung from the ceiling flashing in his head.

"Fucking hit him, Teo!"

He looked down at the chain wrapped around his hand, back to the man with blood running down his body, coloring the ropes red that tied around his feet.

"You are a Sanchez! Act like it. Hit him!"

So Teo had. He'd hit him over and over and over, with the thick chain still wrapped around his hand.

As soon as the car pulled into the driveway, Teo opened the door and ran out. He stumbled trying to get out of the moving vehicle before running to the side of the house. He heaved, his stomach purging itself of everything inside.

His throat burned. His eyes stung. Christ, he was such a fucking pussy. Why did he always lose it when shit got serious?

"Mateo?" Molly called to him from the front of the house in that sweet voice of hers. "Are you okay?"

No. "Go away."

Who the hell bugged someone after they just finished throwing up?

"He said he wasn't feeling well earlier. Guess he has a stomach bug." Mateo heard Josiah speaking to her.

"Oh…okay," she replied. "It would be better if you came in the house. I can get you some ginger ale."

Mateo ignored her. Didn't she get the fucking message? He leaned against the wall, puke at his feet, afraid to close his eyes. His father had been right. He was weak.

He heard a noise, grateful they were going to leave him alone, but then something out of the corner of his eye caught his attention. The kid walked around the side of the house, hands shoved into his pockets, his eyes cast down.

"She went inside. I…I told her I'd make sure you're okay."

"Don't need your help."

Teo watched as the kid actually made fucking eye contact with him and held it. Good for him.

"Yeah, but…but I need yours. And I don't want to. I mean, not just you, but anyone. I don't want people to see me and think they can do whatever they want. I don't want them to see me as weak."

For a second, Mateo wasn't sure what to say. Had he really heard this kid right? He didn't know whether to respect the hell out of him or tell him he was *loco*.

"I wanna be…more like you…" Josiah added.

Crazy won out. Mateo stepped toward him. Anger burned it's way though his insides. "You wanna be like me, kid? You wanna have blood on your hands and death on your conscience?"

At that, Josiah's green eyes widened. They were the wildest color, dark in the center with a lighter green on the outside. Teo pulled back, ripping his eyes away.

"Yeah, that's right. You heard me. You gonna tell Molly and William now? Sleep with a knife under your pillow or keep the fuck away from the dangerous guy who hurts people?"

Damned if something didn't draw Teo to Josiah's eyes again. How they looked at him differently…deeply, in a way the kid had never braved before. And they were almost sad. Mateo had never experienced someone looking at him like that. Maybe Molly and William, in their own way, but it was with pity. He fucking hated pity. He didn't deserve that Josiah's eyes looked like…almost like in some ways he felt what Mateo did. Like he somehow got it.

He grabbed his stomach so he didn't lose it again.

And then Josiah's eyes shot to the ground for the millionth time.

Thank you.

Josiah's shoulders lifted and fell again. "You didn't hurt *me*. You didn't have to but you stuck up for me…"

"That doesn't mean shit." Who the hell was this kid?

"It means something to me."

That stupid fucking hair went in his face again and Mateo had the urge to push it back. To see if it felt as soft as it looked because he hadn't had a whole lot of soft in his life. He'd never even wondered about the soft before. His fists tightened that he was now.

That kind of thinking, especially when it had to do with another dude, didn't belong in his world. Just like it hadn't when his dad made him fuck a girl at thirteen, to make sure he knew how to be a man.

For a second, Mateo let himself wonder what it would be like to be Josiah. He didn't know the kid's story besides the fact that his parents were dead, but there was something so fucking innocent about him. And Mateo wanted that. Wanted to protect it.

"You don't need to be like me, kid. I won't let anyone fuck with you. Not while I'm here."

Maybe…just maybe taking care of this kid would absolve him from some of his sins.

Chapter Five

Josiah

When they went back to school, Mateo was by Josiah's side every opportunity he had. Before school, after school, during lunch, he was always there, and it felt good to know someone had his back, that someone…he didn't want to think *cared* enough, because Mateo couldn't care about him. They didn't really know each other, and even though it made him feel like a jerk, he wasn't sure Mateo cared much about anything.

No, that was a lie. Mateo did—he just didn't like it. That didn't mean Josiah fell into that category.

Still, there was a part of him that resented it. Shame curled through his insides when he thought about the fact that Mateo *had* to protect him. That he was so weak that the guy who didn't want anything to do with people had to be Josiah's shadow.

And then, in some ways, nothing had changed at all. Yes, he had his self-appointed bodyguard, but that's all it was. They hardly spoke.

Mateo's eyes were hard every time they landed on Josiah, making that shame wrap him up even more until it started to suffocate him.

But still, no one bothered him. Not even in class, when Mateo wasn't there. He knew the reason was Mateo. He had no doubt they were right to fear him. Josiah did, too.

It was about a month after Mateo had put himself on babysitting duty when they were each sitting on their beds, Josiah with school books spread out in front of him. Every so often Mateo would make some sort of sound, or Josiah would *feel* eyes on him. When he'd look over, Mateo would turn away, or he'd stare for a second before his eyes eventually went the other direction.

He got this floaty feeling in his stomach because even though he knew Mateo wasn't seeing him the way Josiah saw Mateo, it made him smile to pretend.

When his hair fell into his face, Josiah pushed it out. It was only a couple inches long but gravitated down again. Most of the time he didn't mind it, but right now it blocked Mateo.

Mateo, with his dark, seeking eyes, and the muscle that always ticked in his jaw, but also, the couple times Josiah had seen him smile, looked like the happiest person in the world.

Peeking to the left, he risked a glance at him. Mateo didn't turn away, but Josiah couldn't stop his gaze from jerking the other direction. That's what had gotten him in trouble at school, when he hadn't even really been looking that time.

"Doesn't that bother you? The way your hair's always gettin' in your eyes?" Mateo huffed as though disgusted.

"I can't help it. It grows fast. I just got it cut a couple weeks go." Why did Mateo care about his hair anyway?

"Didn't mean nothin' by it. I was just... Never mind." Mateo reached for his headphones. Josiah's heart jumped, his brain going overtime wanting to think of something, *anything,* he could say to keep them talking. He wanted to know what he'd almost said but knew if he asked, Mateo would get pissed.

"Do you like that girl? The one with the red hair who was talking to you after school?" *What the heck. Did I really just ask him about a girl?*

"She was trying to talk to me. There's a difference." Mateo leaned against the wall. "She's not the kinda girl I'm used to."

It was stupid, but Josiah's hands suddenly got cold. He didn't know why they got like that when he was nervous. "Lots of girls watch you. I mean, not that I'm watching you. Or them, or anything like that. I just..." *Need to shut my mouth.*

Mateo chuckled. Josiah groaned. He always said stupid stuff. He scooted toward the edge of the bed to get up and walk out of the room when Mateo's words stopped him. "Nah. They're just wondering if they can piss off their parents with me or somethin'." He paused for a minute, then asked, "What about you? You want any of those girls?"

Holy shit. What was I thinking? He *really* didn't want to talk to Mateo about girls. "No." Josiah looked at his books again, hoping the conversation would end.

"Why not? They're like you, all good and shit. You ever fucked a girl?"

Josiah's face burned with the question. He wasn't surprised Mateo asked like that, but…what did he say? He rubbed his hands together to warm them up. Could he tell Mateo? Was he the type of guy who would freak out if he knew about Josiah? "No. I…never mind."

"You what?"

"Nothing." He bit his lip.

"Tell me. You're the one who started this shit. Can't back out now."

"I don't like girls, okay?" He shrugged, trying to pretend he didn't want to vomit. Trying to pretend his whole body wasn't waiting for Mateo to laugh at him or beat him up or something. When the silence went on for what felt like his whole life, Josiah risked a glance at Mateo, through his hair that had fallen in his face again.

Mateo shrugged. "Yeah. Okay. Whatever."

That was it? Josiah waited for more. Waited for him to say he didn't want to share a room with him or something, but he never did. Instead, he said, "Your hair's doin' that again. It's annoying as shit."

Josiah pushed it out of his face. When Mateo looked away from him, he suddenly needed something, *anything*, to say so he knew things were okay. "Where's your homework? I mean…why don't you do it? Like…ever?" *Great. I decide to insult him. Perfect thing to say.*

For the second time, Mateo didn't respond how he thought the guy would. He smiled. "You're really asking me why I'm not doin' homework?"

Even though every instinct in his body told Josiah to turn away, to say forget it or to leave the room, he made himself stay. Made his eyes continue to lock on Mateo's. "I…I'm pretty sure I just did, yeah. I don't think I've ever seen you do it."

Mateo's dark brows rose as if he was surprised by Josiah. A little burst of pride swelled in his chest at the thought. Mateo knew he liked boys, and it didn't make Josiah run away. He was…well, he was giving Mateo crap about his homework after. He felt like he could fly.

"I don't see the point." Mateo shrugged. "Hardly went before. Only did 'cause it's what my mama wanted before she died. Otherwise, my dad wouldn't have liked that it took me away from what was important."

Josiah tried not to let the shock show on his face. "School wasn't important?"

At that, Mateo let a loud laugh fall from his lips. As much as he tried not to, Josiah loved the sound.

"Not in my world, kid."

His pride deflated. Did he always have to put Josiah down? *The kid.* He didn't want to be some kid to Mateo. Just as he was about to turn away, Mateo said, "Didn't mean that in a bad way."

Now his heart started to race. The light, fluffy feeling came back. What if he was wrong about Mateo? Maybe he *had* been looking at Josiah the way Josiah tried not to look at him. Because even though Mateo was hard…there was something beautiful about him, too. And he knew, knew that Josiah was gay, and he hadn't said a word. No one had ever known about him before.

"Anyway, it's not like I'm gonna be 'round here forever."

"Where are you going?" Josiah asked.

Mateo paused before replying, "Brooklyn. The streets. Where I belong."

"You don't have to. This could be a fresh start." Josiah knew nothing about Mateo's history. Molly and William obviously did, but he'd never asked. He assumed gangs, and he'd obviously been in trouble, but it didn't feel right. Didn't feel like the guy who watched over him so he didn't get beat up every day.

When Mateo didn't reply, Josiah continued. "We could do it together. Homework, I mean."

"I'm not stupid. I don't need help."

"I know… I didn't mean… And not because I like…you know, either. I just thought we could help each other. Keep each other on track. Half the time I don't want to do it, either. I don't know. I guess it's stupid." Josiah turned his head to the side to block his heated face.

"I guess." Mateo mumbled. "Not like I have anything better to do."

Josiah's cheeks hurt his smile was so big.

Chapter Six

Mateo

Mateo grew up always being around people. His dad was the leader of one of Brooklyn's biggest gangs. They came to Ricky Sanchez for everything, and Teo was the son he groomed to be just like him. And when Ricky couldn't mold Mateo himself, his uncle Javier did it. He'd seen death and drugs and sex, and participated in most of it more than once. He hid the fear in his eyes and the vomit that crawled up his throat when it came to someone being hurt because there were always eyes on him. Someone was always watching, waiting for Ricky Sanchez's son to fuck up so they could take his place.

That didn't mean he liked being seen. Which was why it made his feet itch to run over the fact that he was letting this kid see pieces of him. Josiah had been there right after Teo vomited because of the argument at school, and for the past few weeks they were doing homework together. Josiah was talking more around him and Mateo realized he kind of liked it.

He had that voice in his head that told him to back away. That

Josiah was better than him. He'd been around drugs and shit his whole life. He'd witnessed people being hurt—or worse—and did nothing. They were different, and Javier was always there in the background. His father may be in prison but Javier wasn't, and they had expectations of him. By being here, he was abandoning his "family." He was turning his back on the gang. The more time that went by, the worse it was. It wasn't as though he was that far from home, or couldn't call. Because he hadn't been lying when he told Josiah that he wouldn't be here forever. This wasn't his life, but stepping foot in Brooklyn would be dangerous as hell for him. And he didn't even have an excuse for what to tell them, either.

Mateo leaned against the wall, on the side of the house. He didn't know why he sat out here from time to time. Gave him space, he guessed. It was so different being outside here than it was in the city. Trees, and houses, and so much fucking quiet you could hear the birds sing. This was the perfect kind of place for Josiah. Mateo didn't know why, but he wondered if the kid's parents had lived with him in a town like this.

This world was so screwed up. That someone like Josiah could've had his parents and the perfect life in a neighborhood like this one, only to have it taken away. Now he had to live with other people, go to different homes and deal with kids giving him shit. Screwed up wasn't strong enough a word for the world. It was shitty, brutal, and would eat you alive.

He deserved that. Not someone like Josiah.

I don't like girls, okay?

That had been so fucking stupid of him to just blurt that shit out to someone like Teo. Stupid, and brave as hell. Braver than Teo had ever been, because those words would never cross his lips. His dad made him fuck girls just for actin' soft, because it was one of the ways to prove he was a man. If he or anyone else knew that Mateo...*fuck*. They'd kill him. His dad would have killed him or beat him until that desire that Teo buried deep snuffed out.

Tires crunched on the gravel, telling him Molly and Josiah were home. They'd gone to the grocery store, asked Mateo if he wanted to go, too. What the point in a group trip to the grocery store was he didn't know, but once they'd left, he kind of wished he would've gone. Wished he hadn't told 'em he was going for a walk because he'd rather be alone.

Doors slammed and feet replaced the sound of tires, and then they were in the house. He flinched when the kitchen window, about three feet away from him, opened.

Water sounded, and he figured Molly was doing the dishes or getting dinner ready. They ate at almost the same time every day, and the house was always clean and William smiled when he got home. It was surreal. He'd seen shit like that on TV but honestly didn't think people really lived that life.

Mateo was about to walk away when Molly's voice spoke over the sound of the water. "Is Mateo here?" she asked.

Josiah must have left the room and come back because he answered with, "No. The door to our room is open and he's not in there."

His pulse actually started to jog, run, because he didn't want to hear what came next. And then he knew he had to. If he worried about hearing it was time for him to go, then he knew it really was.

"I planned to ask at the store but I wasn't sure if it was the best place, but…I wanted to ask you about him," Molly said.

Josiah was quiet. Teo held his breath, waiting for the answer. *Breathe. Walk away. Don't come back. It's what I should do.*

Teo took one step, then another, but stopped when Josiah spoke.

"What do you want to know? He's…he's my friend. It feels wrong to say something about him behind his back."

He's my friend. He's my friend. He's my friend.

The only friends he'd ever had were the gang, but they didn't give a shit about saying something behind your back. Guilt weighed heavy in his stomach. That was his family. He shouldn't be thinking things like that about them.

"This is our life, Teo. Our kingdom. No one will care for you like your family."

"No, no. That's not what I mean," Molly said. "It's that… he's quiet. He doesn't tell us anything. The principal said he almost started a fight the first day of—"

"It wasn't his fault." Josiah cut her off. "He was sticking up for *me*. He's nice. No one ever defended me like that before. And he's real smart, too. He's good at math. Helps me figure it out sometimes. I always hated math."

Blood rushed through Mateo's ears, so loudly he could hardly hear. His hands shook. *Weak. So fucking weak.*

Josiah's words shoved his dad's from his head. *"He's nice… And he's real smart, too…"*

The urge to scream hit him. To tell Josiah he didn't know him. That he wasn't nice. He'd watched men die and beat up a guy who couldn't defend himself and puked when his dad made him wrap up the body. That wasn't *nice*. It wasn't *smart*. It was weak. It was wrong. It was Teo.

"That's good. I'm happy to hear that," Molly said. The urge to tell her to shut up washed over him. He didn't want to hear her speak. He wanted to hear more of what Josiah said, because maybe somehow that would make it real. "I've seen you guys spending time together. That's very good. You look like you have fun when I see you both doing homework."

Yeah right. He doubted that. All it was was homework, and half the time Mateo was pissy 'bout it.

"Yeah." There was no sound. Mateo stepped closer, wondering if Josiah said something he couldn't hear.

"Yeah?" Molly prompted.

"I guess he makes me feel a little less lonely."

"You shouldn't feel alone, Josiah. You know we love having you here."

Her words became muffled sounds in Teo's ears. His stomach cramped. Josiah's words collided into each other in his head, falling off into quiet before surging up and sounding again.

He'd done so much shit. So much bad fucking shit. It was who he was. His dad told him so, and Javier told him. Teo knew that. Knew Josiah's words were wrong, but that didn't mean he didn't want them. Didn't want to hold them in his hands and tattoo them into his skin so he'd always have them.

Didn't mean he didn't wish they were true.

Suddenly it didn't matter that Javier would be waiting for him or that he'd probably get killed if he showed his face in Brooklyn again. That they'd think he spit on his dad's legacy by staying away. Whatever happened he'd deal with it, because he fucking wanted what Josiah said. Wanted to pretend he was that person. Wanted to keep Josiah from being alone.

Chapter Seven

November

Josiah

There was something different about the way Mateo acted. For weeks now he'd stood closer to Josiah, watching him and talking to him more frequently. But then he'd have these times when he was even quieter than he used to be—sad in a way that always lingered around Mateo—but somehow darker…lonelier.

Josiah didn't get it. Maybe he even imagined it because he wanted so much to really *know* someone. No, to really *know* Mateo in a way he never got close to anyone before. It was easier that way, but then, no one had really been worth the risk before.

Mateo was worth it. He knew it, felt it in that fluttering feeling in his gut he got every time they were together.

Even if Mateo didn't see him the same way. Didn't *feel* Josiah the way Josiah did him, deep inside. Because he couldn't. Not really.

But there were times he pretended Mateo saw him the way he saw Mateo. Like right now, when Josiah rolled over in bed, prying his eye open, even though he'd been lying here awake for at least half an hour.

When his eyes scanned the lump under the blue blanket on the other side of the room, he saw Mateo's eyes trained on him. And he didn't even have the urge to look away, because he wanted his eyes on Mateo. Wanted to see his secrets, and Mateo to look for his. He already knew the biggest one.

Josiah waited without speaking, expecting Mateo to look away. To make some smart-aleck comment, but it didn't happen. Their eyes just held each other, like Josiah couldn't look away even if he wanted to. Was it possible? Was there any way Teo could…he didn't know…like him, too? He knew Josiah liked boys, but he didn't treat Josiah any different. Still, he'd never said he liked them, too.

He got that tingle in his gut that Mateo always brought out in him and—oh crap, his dick was getting hard. If Mateo knew he was hard just looking at him he'd be disgusted. He'd hate him. It was one thing to know Josiah liked guys but another to know he got hard when he looked at Teo. That thought sent a blast of cold through Josiah's system.

"No one's ever looked at me the way you do. Like…I don't know." Mateo's voice was so soft he hardly heard him. But he had, and Josiah's face flamed with heat.

"Sorry. I didn't mean…" No other words would come so he started to roll over instead.

"No." Mateo's voice stopped him. "It makes me feel like I'm somethin'."

Josiah's heart thundered, rammed into his chest like a battering ram, over and over. "You are something."

"Yeah?" Mateo asked, what sounded like awe in his voice. How could he not know? He was strong and confident and hot. People feared and respected him. He was everything Josiah wished he could be.

Josiah jumped when someone knocked on the door. His mouth opened, wanting to tell whoever it was to go away. That they were talking and he needed Mateo to know how important he was. Before he got the nerve to speak, Mateo rolled over and turned his back to Josiah, leaving him to call out, "Come in."

The rest of the day, he wished he could get Mateo alone but it never happened. Molly or William always seemed to show up, Molly who was freaking out in a way Josiah had never seen from her.

"Are you sure you boys will be okay tonight? Mateo hasn't been here very long, and I'm not sure about leaving you." Molly looked down to where Mateo sat on the couch. He looked up at her and winked, so normal and natural Josiah wondered if he dreamt the morning up. How could he not be going crazy inside the way Josiah was?

"The party we planned will keep us busy," Mateo told her.

Molly sucked in a deep breath, but William chuckled beside her. "He's joking. It's only one night. They're sixteen and seventeen years old, and we trust them. They'll be fine."

The tone in William's voice, the way he stressed the word *trust*, made Josiah think he wasn't sure if he had faith in them or not. But he wanted to. And he wanted Josiah and Mateo to prove themselves.

"I won't do nothin'." All their eyes found Mateo.

"We know," William said, but Molly kneeled down in front of him.

"I know you won't, Mateo. It's me I'm worried about, not that you will do anything you're not supposed to, okay? It's my job to protect you guys, and I take that very seriously. I care about you both."

Josiah's heart raced as he watched and waited for Mateo's reply. *See,* he wanted to tell him. *You are someone. It's not only me who sees it.*

All Mateo did was nod, and a few minutes later, Molly hugged Josiah goodbye before she and William walked out the door, locking it behind them. Leaving Josiah and Mateo alone.

Mateo watched the TV, but it seemed to Josiah, he wasn't completely paying attention to it.

Nerves twisted and turned inside Josiah. What should he say? *Remember when we were talking this morning? I meant to tell you, you're something to me.*

That sounded stupid. He didn't know how to put it into words without sounding like an idiot.

You make me feel like something, too… No. You're my first real friend. Really, no. I like you. I might lo—

"I'm takin' a shower." Mateo words broke through Josiah's thoughts. Which was a good thing. He had no business thinking what he had been.

But he did. No matter how hard he tried not to, he couldn't stop thinking about Mateo.

Chapter Eight

Mateo

Mateo let the hot water wash over him, hoping it somehow helped him get his shit together. He needed to do it, and do it quick. The thing was, ever since he heard Josiah and Molly talkin' about him, it's all he could think about. Every time he looked at Josiah or walked with him in school or they did their homework together. When those big, trusting eyes would search around inside Mateo like no one ever did before.

Fuck.

This definitely wasn't getting his shit together. He would get out of his shower, get dressed, and man-up. They'd play video games or something and he'd forget what Josiah said to him this morning.

And that's exactly what he did. Well, most of it. They played some games on the Playstation, and Josiah ordered pizza with the twenty-five bucks Molly and William left them. "Want me to get you a drink?" Teo asked him as they stood at the counter. Their arms touched, sending a shockwave through Mateo, making him jerk away. "I'll get it." He didn't let Josiah answer.

They ate dinner and then watched a movie. Josiah was quieter than usual and Teo tried not to think about it, tried not to wonder if he'd done somethin' wrong. But then he got up and sat next to Mateo on the couch, saying he couldn't see from the chair. It somehow soothed him, made him feel like things were okay.

"What do you wanna do now?" Teo asked when the credits starting rolling, hoping Josiah would look at him like he did this morning. In Brooklyn he never had times like this. Where he was…free, comfortable. A quiet voice inside him hoped it could last.

"There's a chess set in the room. We can play that."

Mateo shrugged. "Don't know how." Who played chess? Not people like Teo.

"I could teach you. I mean, if you want. You don't have to. I know it's kind of a dorky game... It's my favorite."

"Yeah?" he asked. He didn't realize till this second he wanted to soak all these things in. Everything he could while he stayed here so he would always have the memories. "Think I could do it? I hear it's hard."

Josiah nodded his head, a big smile on his face. It made heat spread through Teo's chest. "I know you could."

They turned everything off in the living room and kitchen before making their way back to their room. Mateo closed the door behind them as Josiah pulled the game from the closet. He went over to Teo's bed and started to set the game out.

Mateo didn't know why but that made him smile, made more of that warmth fill him. They were both wearing sweats, T-shirts and socks. Mateo sat by the head of the bed, crossing his legs as Josiah crossed his, too.

Teo listened as Josiah explained the rules, told him what each of the pieces meant and what they could do. They sat on his bed for two hours straight, trying to work their way through a game of chess. It was confusing as hell, but the more time went by, the more Mateo started to get it. The more he could do things without asking Josiah questions.

"This is a long ass game." Teo stretched his arms. Josiah did the same, and his shirt pulled up, showing Mateo the pale skin of his stomach and a trail of hair, darker than what was on his head.

Teo jerked his eyes away, seeing that Josiah had seen him. He didn't let himself focus on that, though. All he could think about was that he hadn't wanted to turn away. He hadn't fucking wanted to, and that was wrong. That shit could get him killed in his world.

"We can put it on the desk and finish tomorrow."

Teo nodded. They both stood, carefully picking up the board so no pieces would fall and setting it on the desk between their beds. It was late now, sleep tuggin' at him, but Mateo ignored it.

And then they both stood there. Lead filled his feet and he couldn't move. Didn't know what to do. Josiah did the same. An eternity passed them by, Teo digging for something to say to cut through the tension in the room.

"You know I was going easy on you, right? I mean, I totally could have won. You did *not* come close to beating me your very first game." Sarcasm dripped from Josiah's words. It was just what Teo needed and so damn different than anything he'd ever heard from Josiah before.

A laugh tumbled out of Teo's mouth and he didn't hold it back. Second by second the tension eased out of him. And then Josiah was doing the same. They both stood there, holding their stomachs from laughing so hard.

When the laughter died down, Josiah spoke. "That was a lie, just so you know. There's a good chance you could beat me. You're good." And then his hand wrapped around Teo's arm.

It was warm and soft and now he realized he *really* liked that fucking softness. His breathing went faster, and he flexed his hands open and closed, wanting Josiah to hold on and let go at the same time. No, hold on, he decided, so when Josiah tried to pull back, Teo held his hand there with his own. "Thanks… for teachin' me. You're cool, Jay. I mean…" What the hell did he mean? And what the fuck was up with calling him Jay? It slipped out.

"You don't call me kid anymore." Teo let go and Josiah dropped his hand. "It's Jay, or Josiah."

Mateo's head pounded. He was hot all over. Embarrassed, angry at himself, and… "I didn't know you didn't like it. Kid, I mean. Which is stupid. Why the fuck would you like kid? I won't use it." He raised his hand, almost touching Josiah's hair, but jerked it back. Josiah's eyes followed the movement before their eyes locked.

They were just standing there one second and then the next, Josiah pushed up on his toes and pressed his lips to Teo's. Mateo froze, his insides cracking apart. His lips tingled. Wanted, needed, to kiss back, but instead he'd jerked away. "What the fuck was that?"

He was shaking. Holy shit, his whole body was shaking.

"I'm sorry. I'm so sorry. I didn't mean it. I don't know why I…" Josiah licked his lips. Closed his eyes and dropped his head forward. His hair fell in his face. "I'm sorry. I thought…"

A pull sorta took Mateo over. Luring him, easing him closer to Josiah. It started somewhere deep inside him, an urge he couldn't hold back. He'd hurt Josiah. Self-hatred rose up inside him. He never wanted to hurt him.

And he wanted to kiss him. Wanted it so bad, his whole fucking body ached with need.

Teo's hand shook as he lifted it. As he pushed Josiah's hair out of his face. As he hooked a finger under Josiah's chin and lifted. Mateo fingered his hair again. "It's soft."

Jay's chin trembled and Mateo brushed his thumb across it. Josiah's eyes went wide as Teo leaned forward. "It's okay. I won't hurt you. No matter what. Not you."

And then he closed his eyes and pressed his lips to Josiah's. His lips didn't move, so Teo kissed again. Over and over, until he earned Josiah's trust and he kissed back.

Electricity zipped through him. Fried him alive. Cupping both Josiah's cheeks in his hands, he kissed him harder, deeper, letting his tongue slide between his lips.

He froze when Josiah jerked back. "I'm sorry. I've never kissed…"

Teo smiled. "Yeah you have. You just did. And you had the balls to kiss me first."

When Josiah returned his smile, Mateo's heart started going crazy. They kissed again, and Josiah somehow even tasted innocent. He got closer, walked him backward until Jay went down on the bed. Teo climb on top of him, kissing him the whole time.

He touched Josiah's hair, let his lips trail down his neck. His whole body buzzed. Came a-fucking-live. It was more than just kissing a boy, when that's what he'd always wanted. It was kissing *this* one.

His erection grew, hardened with each press of lips, each sweep of tongues, until Teo made himself pull away.

"What's wrong?" Josiah asked.

"Nothin'." He'd never done right by anyone in his life, but he'd do right by Josiah.

Teo laid down next to him. Grabbed hold of his soft, blond hair. He should turn off the light, cover them up, but he was scared if he moved Josiah would disappear.

He smiled when a gentle, shaky hand wrapped around his other one. When Josiah's head rested on his arm.

When Josiah's breathing evened out and his body relaxed, Teo closed his eyes. *"Mi precioso,"* he whispered before joining him in sleep.

Chapter Nine

Josiah

Courage was a funny thing. There were still days that Josiah couldn't believe he'd had the guts to kiss Mateo. It had been a really stupid thing to do. Could have been a dangerous one. A guy shouldn't kiss another guy without knowing that's what they were into, but then, it had just happened and felt right and he couldn't imagine not having done it.

Yet weeks later, he hadn't gathered up the nerve to try it again. Mateo obviously wasn't doing it. He acted like nothing had happened at all, and Josiah was too scared to bring it up. Sometimes he wondered if it had been a dream, but he'd woken up in Mateo's bed that morning, with the scent of Mateo in his nose and the feel of him etched in Josiah's memory, where it still pulsed and *breathed* there. He thought about it all the time. The feel of Mateo's gentle yet hungry kiss. The weight of him pressing Josiah into the mattress.

A thrill of excitement raced up his spine at the thought.

Of course he'd thought about kissing guys before. He thought about a whole lot more than that, but those dreams were nothing on the aching burn Mateo had made him feel.

And he wanted it again.

On Thanksgiving, after they ate with Molly and William, they'd gone to their room to play another game of chess. He loved watching Mateo play. The way his forehead creased as he thought, or the way he cocked his head when he studied the board. Josiah wondered if he did little things like that, and if Mateo could ever like those things about him. If he ever noticed them and smiled at them and thought of them when he needed to feel good.

When the time came to put the game away, he reached out, brushed his finger over the top of Mateo's hand, wanting, *needing* to know if he thought about Josiah the way Josiah thought about him.

When Mateo jerked his hand back, making the chess board drop to the floor, Josiah's heart went with it. *Stupid. So freaking stupid.* "Sorry," he mumbled.

Josiah bent to pick up the mess but Mateo beat him to it. "No worries. I got it."

A quiet voice inside him yelled at Josiah to tell him no. That he'd do it. Not to keep his head down so Mateo couldn't see his face. *Look at me. Look at me,* he wanted to say, but just like always, he was too damn unsure to make himself spit it out.

But then his hands started to shake and his throat went dry, the words sticking there. Not knowing what else to do, Josiah walked out of the room.

His eyes burned. What a weak thing to do, to want to cry over something like that, but God, it had felt good to pretend. To think someone could really want him. Not like all the foster parents he'd had who shipped him away, or his parents who went out without him, or the friends he never really had.

He could deal with it, not having the rest of them, because deep inside he wanted Mateo more than anything else. He didn't know why and didn't understand it. All he knew was all those empty rooms inside him were somehow filled when Mateo was around.

Behind him, he closed the door to the bathroom, turned on the shower, and sat on the closed toilet. Maybe Mateo had been right from the beginning. He was nothing but a kid.

***

On December 1, Josiah turned seventeen. He woke up, got out of bed, and went to the bathroom to brush his teeth like he did every morning. His birthdays had never really meant much. Sometimes he got little gifts from whoever he was living with, others not. All the day usually did was make all those rooms inside him feel even emptier.

As he turned to head toward the bathroom, Mateo stepped out. He hadn't noticed Mateo was out of bed before him. It was probably the first time since he'd been here that it happened.

"We're making breakfast for ya. Me and Molly."

Josiah wanted to reply, but his mind raced thinking of what that kind of gesture meant, making it impossible to form words. They'd planned this. He didn't know how he knew it, but he did. Mateo had gotten up and out of bed early to help Molly do something for him. He smiled, loving the light feeling that returned to him.

"You look like you're going to throw up. I didn't fuck it up or anything. I can cook." He nudged Josiah with his arm.

He wanted the warmth of Mateo's skin back. Wished the already narrow hallway would shrink more so they had to stand even closer. "No. I wouldn't think that. Wouldn't think you'd mess it up."

Mateo nodded. "You ever had chorizo? It's really good. I used to make it. That's the only part I'm doin'."

He'd never had it but he suddenly wanted it really bad. "No. I've never had it."

"You'll like it," Mateo replied, then paused like he was going to do or say something else.

Touch me. Please. Josiah's hand itched to feel Mateo. To experience his warmth, just so he could make sure he was really there.

"Gotta go. Don't wanna burn it. See ya in a minute."

Josiah's chest deflated as Mateo went back into the kitchen. After cleaning up, he went to join them in the other room, just as Molly pulled plates out of the cabinets. Her face lit up when she saw him. She set the plates on the counter with a light *clank* before pulling Josiah into her arms. "Happy Birthday," she told him.

She smelled like vanilla. Her poofy, brown hair tickled his nose but he didn't mind. He imagined that his mom had been just like her.

"Thanks." Josiah smiled at her when she pulled away.

Mateo looked at him over his shoulder from where he stood at the stove. He had on sweats and a T-shirt. His boxers would be sticking out of the top of his pants. They always were. The scar on his neck peeked out from his shirt. Dark hair lined his jaw because he needed to shave.

"It's hot. You sure you can handle it?" Mateo asked.

He was hot. And Josiah suddenly felt hot, too.

Not realizing he was going crazy here, Molly started rambling about how they planned the breakfast and Mateo had asked for chorizo because he wanted to make it for him. Josiah opened his mouth, determined to push the words out this time—to answer Mateo's question. "I can handle it. I *want* to. What about you?" *Hear me. Hear what I'm saying,* he pleaded in his head. *Want me, too.*

Mateo's lips stretched into a smile—a different kind of smile than Josiah had ever seen from him before. It almost looked proud, only not of himself. Of Josiah.

***

William drove them, everyone refusing to tell Josiah where they were going. Nerves and excitement played tug-of-war inside him. He'd never had anyone surprise him for his birthday before.

When they pulled into the parking lot, and he saw the huge ice skating rink tucked inside a circular area of bushes, he smiled. "How did you know?" His voice wobbled slightly.

From the passenger seat, Molly said, "You mentioned it once. How you like ice skating but didn't get to go very often. We thought about going into the city, but—"

"I could have stayed home," Mateo interrupted.

"That's not what I was going to say," Molly said at the same time that Josiah said, "I wouldn't have wanted to come without you."

As soon as the words left his mouth, his cheeks started to burn. Why did he always say the stupidest, most embarrassing things?

Luckily no one called him on it. William mentioned something about not making the drive into the city, while Josiah fought the urge to look over at Mateo.

They climbed out of the car and bundled up in their jackets, hats and scarves that Molly and William had bought them. Mateo walked in front of him, his hands shoved into his pockets, his beanie pulled low.

They went into the building and rented skates. Mateo lingered while everyone else laced their skates up.

"Are you coming?" William asked as he grabbed Molly's hand.

"In a minute," Josiah replied before the two headed out to the ice.

"I'm going to bust my ass. I don't even know how to stand up in these fuckin' things." He looked up at Josiah from where he sat on the bench. "I mean, I'm not sayin' I won't go. I'm just sayin' I'm going to fuck up."

Josiah shrugged. "So?"

"I'm not used to shit like this, Jay. We didn't do family days out to the fuckin' ice skating rink. It feels like it's not me. I don't belong out here."

Josiah's heart sped up. Mateo hadn't called him Jay since the night they kissed. "Neither do I. Maybe we can…I don't know, both belong.

Both find a way to fit, or whatever. I just…I want you here." His eyes found the ground. "I can help, if you want me to. Skating or whatever."

"You belong," was Mateo's answer, before he worked his way to his feet. Josiah wanted to ask him what he meant. Ask where he fit, but before he had the chance, Mateo spoke. "Let's go. I'm gonna tear shit up out there."

They were hardly on the ice two seconds when Mateo went down. Josiah scrambled toward him, afraid he would be mad.

"Everyone falls the first time. Let me help you." He held his hand out to Mateo, and when he looked up at Josiah, he started laughing. Josiah couldn't help but laugh, too. Mateo reached out, and he could have sworn, even through their gloves, he felt Mateo's heat.

When he pulled, Josiah lost his footing and instead of pulling Mateo up, Josiah went down.

"Fuck," Mateo hissed out, making Josiah realize his elbow was in Mateo's stomach.

"Dude! I'm so sorry." He rolled off Mateo and onto the ice.

"No worries. How 'bout I help you up this time."

He watched as Mateo twisted, turned and pushed to his feet. He held his arms out, as though trying to keep his balance. His cheeks were pink. "Okay. I think I got it."

This time it was Mateo's hand coming out to help Josiah. They locked hands and Mateo helped him to his feet. As soon as he was up, Mateo let go of his hand but didn't move away. They were standing so close he felt Mateo's breath. Around them, people skated as though

Josiah wasn't experiencing the best day of his life.

"You good?" Mateo asked.

"Yeah. Remember, I've done this before."

Mateo winked. "Didn't stop you from ending up on your ass."

"Bet it won't happen again." Josiah grinned, proud of his comeback.

"Then let's do this."

Mateo fell at least five more times that day…but he laughed a lot, too. They ate lunch, and William and Molly bought them hot chocolate. When they went back home, they ordered pizza before Molly pulled out presents.

Josiah's hands were shaky as he opened the first package. Mateo stood on the opposite side of the room as everyone else, eyes on Josiah. He wanted Mateo to come sit by him, even to sit by William or Molly—someone just to be a part of this—but he knew not to ask.

He opened a video game first. Then, some new shoes. Afterward they had cake and ice cream, then watched a movie.

Long after he and Mateo had gone to bed, Josiah still laid there in the dark with his eyes open, wishing Mateo was doing the same. He never wanted this day to end.

Chapter Ten

Mateo

Mateo tightened his hand and rubbed his thumb over the top of the wood. It was stupid, holding it like this. The damn thing had been in his pocket all day. He and Josiah had been lying in their beds forever, and he squeezed it against his palm the whole time he should have been sleeping. It wasn't like it was that big a deal. Actually, he should probably throw it away. He wasn't even sure why he'd made it. It was such a pussy thing to do.

"Mateo?" He actually jumped a little at the sound of Josiah's voice in the dark.

"Yeah?"

"Thanks for going today."

Ice skating wasn't his thing. When Molly told him they were going, he wanted nothing to do with it. But nothing could have made him stay home, either. He wanted to go with them. He wanted to spend Josiah's birthday with him more than anything else.

"Wanted to go."

"You did?"

How could he not know that? "Yeah, Jay. Why wouldn't I? That was a stupid question." As soon as the words left his mouth, guilt rolled through him. "I'm a prick. I didn't mean that."

Josiah was quiet for a few minutes. Each second seemed to take longer and longer to tick by. He always said shit without thinking. It would serve him right if Josiah got pissed at him. "I didn't mean it." He wasn't sure what else to say.

"It's okay. Did you have fun? I think it was perfect. It almost feels like…I don't know. Like a real family—I mean, not us. Not that I don't want to be, but…well…"

Mateo couldn't help the chuckle that jumped out. Josiah made him laugh like that a lot. No one ever made Teo laugh besides Josiah. "Yeah… No offense, but I'm not thinking we should go for the brother thing. Not after that shit that happened the night Molly and William were gone."

Holy crap, what was it with him saying the stupidest stuff around Josiah? He hadn't meant to bring up their kiss. A part of him wanted to—wanted to do it again, but Josiah felt too *good* for him. Josiah deserved better. He'd realize that one day. Plus he was innocent, so damn innocent. Teo didn't want to take advantage of him.

"Why don't…I mean, that night. Why haven't we done it again?" Josiah asked.

Shit, the kid was brave. No, not the kid. Josiah. No one saw how fucking strong he was, how strong he could be. "Don't know if it's right."

"You don't want to?" Josiah whispered.

Heat seared him. Blood rushed through his veins. "I wanna do it. Believe me." He was already getting hard just thinking about it. "I'm just… I've done some fucked up shit. If you knew, you wouldn't want me anywhere near you. That's why it doesn't feel right. Not for you."

Josiah quieted, but Teo could hear him breathe. His heart felt like it stopped, waiting to hear what Josiah would say next. Wishing he would tell Teo he was wrong.

Finally he spoke. "Sometimes, I wonder what my parents would be like. What my life would be like if they didn't die. I usually do that on my birthday. Think about them. But this year all I can think is that if they were here, I wouldn't know you. It's probably a stupid thing to say, but I feel like I sort of need you. Like I would even if they were around."

Teo's heart was all but gone now. Shattered in the best way he had ever been hit. When Jay said shit like that? It made the bad shit not so bad. Or like maybe it was in the past and he could walk away from it. That he deserved to.

He rolled the piece of wood between his fingers. "You don't need me."

"Don't tell me what I need. The past doesn't matter. Molly says that. The past doesn't matter. Whatever you've done, I don't care."

"You don't even know me." But as true as the words were in some ways, they weren't in others. Josiah knew him enough to realize kissing him would be okay. He gave Teo time when he needed it and talked to him in ways no one else had.

So that's why he didn't let himself think about it as he pushed to his feet. As he walked over to Josiah's bed, because if he wanted Teo there, really wanted *him* and not who everyone thought he was, Mateo would be there. Maybe even more for himself than for Josiah.

He pulled the blanket back and climbed under. For a second he wondered if he should have asked, but then Josiah scooted over like he wanted Teo there.

"What about Molly?" Josiah's breath brushed across Mateo's cheek.

"She always knocks. And if she doesn't, I'll tell her it was my fault. That you were sleepin' or something and I just came over here."

The pillow moved as Josiah shook his head. "I don't want you to get in trouble for me. You're always trying to protect me. With the kids at school and—"

"That's all I have. All I know. I won't fuck that up. I wanna protect you."

Josiah rolled over so he faced him. Lights flickered from the window, making it so he could see Josiah. Mateo rolled over to look at him, too. After shoving his hand under the pillow and leaving his gift there, he ran his fingers through Josiah's hair. This time it was Mateo who leaned forward to start the kiss. Josiah's lips opened, and Teo slipped his tongue inside. He kissed him for what felt like forever and no time at all, too; his lips, his neck, shivered when Josiah's mouth pressed against the scar by Teo's throat.

His body was tight, sensitive, like any touch would make him break apart. When Josiah rolled to his back, Mateo went with him, lying on top of Josiah, between his legs. He pulled back, his blood running cold when the body beneath him froze. "Shit. I'm sorry. I thought..." Josiah always got stiff when he was nervous. Josiah's hand at his back stopped Teo from pulling away.

"It's okay. Don't go."

Slowly, Mateo leaned forward. He took his time teasing Josiah's lips with his, not wanting to push. He'd been with girls, even when he didn't want to be. He'd never really *wanted* to be. Josiah was the first guy and it felt so right that he wanted to have it *all* right now. That's how he was raised. His dad taught him that when he wanted something he had to take it, push for it, but Teo would never be like that with Josiah. He wouldn't screw this up by going too fast.

When they settled into a groove together, Teo moved his hips. Josiah did the same. Over and over, they kissed and rubbed against each other until pleasure burst inside Mateo. His body tensed as the best sensation he'd ever felt rolled through him.

Josiah groaned, and then he shuddered, breathing heavy. His grip on Teo tightened to the point it was almost painful as he followed Mateo over the edge. "That… Oh my God… Wow."

Mateo couldn't help but chuckle. He sounded like that was the first time or something. Leaning forward, he kissed Josiah again. "You jack off, don't you?"

"What?" Josiah tried to get out from under him, but Mateo didn't let him. A smile stretched across his face. He never felt as light as he did around Josiah.

"I didn't mean to embarrass you. Everyone does it."

"Obviously I do it. I just don't want to *talk* about it."

Teo laughed, burying his face in the pillow beside Josiah. The last thing they needed was to wake up Molly or William. "I'm sorry. Giving ya a hard time. You just sounded so…amazed or somethin'."

"It's different with someone else." Josiah pushed out from under him and Mateo let him go. Pinpricks stabbed into his body, worried he pushed too far.

"I'm sorry. Was just teasing ya." He stood up, too, turning on the small light next to Josiah's bed.

Josiah's cheeks were red when he looked at him. "I know." He shrugged. "Let's just get cleaned up."

Mateo nodded. They each pulled some clothes out of their dressers. One at a time they snuck to the bathroom, cleaned up, and changed. When Teo came back to the room, Josiah was sitting in his bed, twisting the hand-carved chess piece in his hands. Teo's stomach twisted with it. Fuck, he hated his weak-ass stomach.

"What's this?" Josiah asked. "I mean, it's obvious what it is, but where'd it come from?"

Teo shrugged, hoping it would look like this wasn't a big deal to him. "I'm good with a knife. Spent a lotta time carving stuff. Didn't have any money to get you anything for your birthday, so I made that. Reminds me of you."

Josiah looked down, watching the chess piece as he ran his fingers over it. "I remind you of the queen?" There was laugher in his voice, but it almost sounded forced. Like he wanted to pretend this wasn't a big deal when it was.

"Not like *that*." Teo took a step closer, then another one. "Just 'cuz it's the strongest piece in the game."

Josiah's head jerked up, so he looked at Mateo. It felt too close for him, so Mateo kept talking. "Sanded it as best I could. William has a buncha shit like that in the shed. Got the stain out there, too. I know it's not the best but—"

"Yeah it is," Josiah whispered. "It's the best gift I've ever gotten." He palmed it tightly in his hand before lying down. He kept it there as he scooted toward the wall. Mateo ignored the ache in his gut and climbed into bed beside him before turning off the light.

Josiah scooted closer to him. "Goodnight."

"Happy birthday." He wrapped an arm around Josiah and went to sleep.

Chapter Eleven

Josiah

Night was Josiah's favorite time of day. Mateo slept in his bed every night. Right after his birthday they started setting the alarm for a little earlier than they usually got up for school so they didn't risk getting caught. Teo would turn it off before stumbling out of bed and into his own. Josiah never slept after Mateo went back to his side of the room. He always lay there for that last half hour before he woke Mateo up again so they could get ready for school.

Weekends were the worst. They didn't have to get up early for school, and Mateo could sleep *forever*. Josiah would lie around for a little while, then get up and hang out with Molly or William before he'd sneak back to the room and wake Mateo up. Every time, Mateo would pretend to be annoyed but then he'd always touch Josiah's hair and smile.

Months went by and it was always the same routine. Any time they were alone, they would kiss and touch. Sometimes Mateo just held his hand. Or Josiah would sit with his head in Mateo's lap and he'd run his fingers through Josiah's hair. That was his favorite. All those rooms inside him were full, packed and overflowing with boards and locks on all the doors. When he was with Mateo, he knew those rooms would never be emptied again.

Josiah sat on the couch with Mateo, playing video games, when Molly walked in the room, drying her hand on a towel. "Are you guys going to spend your whole spring break playing on that thing?"

Mateo looked at her. One of his eyebrows quirked up as though that was a stupid question. "Do you see this shit—I mean, stuff? It's awesome. We'd have to be crazy *not* to wanna play."

Molly smiled at Mateo. He could tell she was thinking the same thing Josiah was: He'd changed. He was lighter…more comfortable. The changes made it impossible not to be happy when he was around Mateo.

"It's a very nice game." Molly set the hand towel on the coffee table. "But I still think you boys should get out of the house. What if I drop you off at the mall for a couple hours? The weather's getting warm. I'm sure you need some new shorts."

Josiah pushed to his feet, his pulse going haywire. He definitely wanted to get out of the house with Mateo. Wanted to be alone with him. To hear him call him Jay and maybe they could even find a place to sneak away to without eyes on them.

"Nah, that's okay," Mateo replied. And there went Josiah's pulse, slowing back down again.

"You don't want to go?" Josiah asked. Mateo looked up at him.

"We can go. That's cool. Just don't need any more clothes." He stood up and walked over to turn off the game.

He should have known that's why Mateo wouldn't want to go. He didn't like to take anything extra from Molly and William. It wasn't that Josiah particularly liked it, either, but he was more used to it.

"I'll be right back. Gonna go grab my shoes from the room."

As soon as Mateo left the room, Josiah looked at Molly. "I'll talk to him."

She reached out and touched his hand, where his arms were crossed over his chest. "You're a good friend to him, Josiah. I'm glad you guys are so close."

He's more than a friend... I love him. As much as those words were true, he couldn't say them. Not just because of their living situation. What if they made one of them leave?

It made it hard to breathe when he thought about telling Mateo, though. He was always careful...so careful not to do anything that could push Mateo away. Not to freak him out or make him think Josiah was getting clingy.

"Thanks," he told Molly as she handed him some money. "He's..." But then it didn't feel right to talk about Mateo to anyone, so he ended it there.

Once Mateo came back into the room, they left. It wasn't a long drive to the mall. Molly dropped them off, telling them what time she would pick them up again.

They went to the game store and looked around. Mateo always talked so much more when there weren't other people around them. He showed Josiah all the games he liked and then they had lunch.

After they ate they were walking through the mall. People were all around them, taking advantage of spring break by shopping. There was laughter and talking, coming from every direction. Josiah soaked it all in, watching everyone around them.

From beside him, Mateo nudged him with his arm. "You're being quiet, Jay. Just say whatever you wanna say."

He nudged back but really just to stall. "How do you know I have something I want to talk about?"

Mateo shrugged. Someone brushed past them, making Mateo lean closer to Josiah. A wishful thought surged through him. He wished he could reach out and grab Mateo's hand. Or that Mateo would grab his. He knew that would never happen, though.

"I don't know, man. I can just tell. You're actin' nervous, and you don't usually act nervous around me anymore."

This crazy urge to hug Mateo washed over him. Right there in the middle of the mall. His arm tingled but Josiah held back. "That's because…" He looked away.

"Don't. Don't do that no more. You can look at me when you talk to me now."

He was right. Josiah raised his eyes and let them lock on Mateo's. "You should let Molly and William buy you new clothes. I know you don't like to but they like doing it. It's important to them."

Mateo huffed and rolled his eyes. "Why would somethin' like that be important to them?"

"Because they care about us."

This time he shook his head. "They care about you, maybe, but not me."

Josiah grabbed Mateo's arm and pulled. He backed up until they got out of the way of all the people. "They care about you. How can someone not care about you?" His eyes widened as the words slipped out of his mouth, but to his surprise, Mateo's did the same. Not in an uncomfortable way or like he thought Josiah was childish, but as though Mateo had some of those empty rooms inside him, too. And maybe Josiah's words had somehow filled some of them.

Mateo lifted his arm, letting some of Josiah's hair slide between his fingers. "No one's ever said the kinda shit to me that you do. Not shit. I didn't mean it like that—"

"I know," Josiah interrupted him. "I like how you talk."

Someone bumped into Mateo from behind. He jerked back, and Josiah did, too. Holy crap, they needed to be careful. Getting close like that in the middle of the mall was stupid.

Mateo nodded his head toward the crowd and started walking. Josiah stepped up to his side and asked, "So the shorts… Are you going to do it?"

"Will it make you stop being mopey if I do?"

Josiah laughed. "I'm not moping, but yeah. I'll be happy if you do."

So they did. Each of them picked out three new pairs of shorts. Josiah even picked one of Mateo's out for him. Once they bought everything they still had an hour before Molly would pick them up.

"We can call her to come early?" Josiah asked but Mateo just shook his head.

"Follow me." Mateo led the way out of the mall. They took the far exit. Once outside, he went to the left, toward the back of the building.

"Where are we going?"

"I saw an alley back here when she brought us."

Josiah looked around, wondering how Mateo could have seen it. There was a small walkway close to the building that led to the deserted alley, empty street, or whatever it was. He didn't think cars really came back here seeing as it was blocked off by bushes.

"How'd you see this?" Josiah asked. There was a little hill running the length of the alley. Mateo plopped down on it, out of the view of the parking lot.

"Pay attention to your surroundings, Jay. Always. My dad taught me that shit. Always fucking pay attention. You should know where you're gonna run if you have to."

Josiah's heart dropped at that. Mateo didn't talk very often about his past but when he did, it was never something good.

"Don't look at me like that. Don't feel sorry for me. Just come sit by me."

That he could do. Josiah walked over and sat beside him on the hill. As soon as he did, Mateo cupped his cheek and said, "Haven't got to kiss you all day. Can I?"

Josiah's body temperature went up. "You don't have to ask."

Anticipation pulsed through him. Mateo leaned closer. Right before his lips pressed against Josiah's, Mateo jerked back. It wasn't until then that Josiah heard the noise behind them. Mateo was already scrambling to his feet.

"I saw you faggots in the mall. What the fuck makes you think it's okay to touch each other like that? Like we want to see that shit." One of the three guys stepped toward them. He had red hair and was even taller than Mateo.

Josiah's hearing went foggy, his pulse slamming in his ears. "We didn't do anything."

"You jealous, pretty boy? Mad I'd rather fuck him than any of you?"

Josiah stumbled backward at the harshness in Mateo's voice. He'd never heard him talk like that, not even with the near fight at school.

"Fuck you," the bald guy said.

"Aww, don't worry. There's enough of me to go around. Leave the kid out of it and step the fuck up if you think you can take me." But it was Mateo who moved toward them as he spoke.

Josiah's heart slammed against his chest, trying to break free. "Mateo, come on. Let's just go. We don't want any trouble."

"You think you can take us? What do you guys call each other? *Vato*, or something like that?" This from Red.

"Try me, *vato*. I didn't think pretty boys like you could fight. If that's really what you came back here for."

"Mateo." Josiah headed toward him. As he did, Mateo glanced over his shoulder.

"Stay back." Before he could face forward again, the red head slammed into him. Mateo hit the ground. As soon as he did, he was able to punch the guy who'd tackled him in the face. "That all you got? See, I knew I wouldn't even need my boy's help to take you guys."

"Queer motherfucker!" The guy tried to grab Mateo but he made it to his feet.

"If I'm such a queer, then show me what's up. Beat my ass. Bet the three of you can't fucking take me." His fists were balled tight.

"You're a stupid bastard." All three of the guys went at Mateo. Josiah ran to him, when the guy added, "Grab the kid."

"You fucking hurt him and you die, you hear me? And it won't just be me doing it. You'll have the streets on your ass before you know what hits you."

"Mateo, don't." But before Josiah could reach him, the shortest guy, but the biggest around, grabbed him. He fought, kicked, pulled trying to get out of the guy's grasp, but he outweighed Josiah by probably sixty pounds.

Mateo's fist flew through the air. It slammed into one of the guys but the other kicked him in the stomach. Mateo almost lost his balance but it didn't matter. He caught himself and punched the dark-haired guy. Blood gushed from his nose. It didn't stop Mateo. He hit him again, then elbowed Red in the face.

He was winning. Holy crap, Mateo was beating up both of these guys.

That's when they both ran at him at the same time. Mateo stumbled backward. His head bounced off the wall with a crack. He stumbled again, visibly shaken as he tried to gain his balance, but they didn't give him a chance. Both of the guys were on him again.

Josiah's eyes burned, his skin raw from where he tried to pull away from the guy who held him. "Don't! Leave him alone! We didn't do anything!"

Fists rained down on Mateo. "Body shots!" one of them yelled, and that's mostly where they hit him.

"Don't! Stop. Leave him alone!" He was crying now. He hated those stupid tears. The guy holding him laughed.

"Aww, don't cry. You're the girl, aren't you? You let the gangbanging motherfucker fuck you in the ass, don't you?"

A fist hit the side of Mateo's head. Another in his stomach. Somehow he was still landing them, too. One of the guys grabbed his head as though he was about to slam it into the building.

"NO!" Josiah yelled, just as someone came around the corner.

"Hey! What's going on here?"

The arms around him dropped away, and the guy took off running. The other two did the same as Mateo hit the ground. Josiah flew over and fell beside him. "Mateo. Oh my God. Mateo, are you okay?"

He grabbed for him, but Mateo was trying to push to his feet. "What are you doing?" he asked at the same time the man who broke up the fight said, "I'll call the police."

"No. Don't." Mateo's voice broke.

"Those guys were beating the crap out of you. I'm calling the cops," he replied.

Heart racing, Josiah reached for Mateo, helping him stand. His hands were shaking. He fought it, trying for once to be strong for Mateo. The back of his head was wet with blood.

"Mind your own fucking business, man," Mateo said to the guy, standing up straight. He winced as he did.

"Fine by me. Sounds like you deserved it, you little prick." And then he disappeared. As soon as he did, Mateo leaned against the building, grabbing his ribs.

"Fuck!" he groaned. "What the hell is wrong with me? I should have known those guys were following us. I fucked up, Jay. I'm so fucking sorry, I screwed up. They could have hurt you."

Josiah's chest ached. His heart broke for him. If he had ever doubted it before, he knew at that moment he was in love with Mateo.

Chapter Twelve

Mateo

Mateo closed his eyes when both of Josiah's hands cupped his face. He fucked up so bad. He couldn't believe he almost let Josiah get hurt. He could handle shit like this, not Josiah. This was the one thing he had, the only thing he could do for Josiah. Protect him.

"It wasn't your fault. Don't do that again. Don't try to protect me and get yourself hurt worse."

"I told you I'd protect you. I *want* to. I won't let anything happen to you." He pulled away. "Come on. We need to get out of here." Pain shot through him but he tried to ignore it.

"You're hurt. We need to call the cops. And Molly. You should go to the hospital."

Fear overpowered the pain. "No. No cops, Jay. You gotta promise me that. No matter what, no fucking cops." He'd never had any good experience with cops.

"Well, then Molly. You need to see a doctor."

Mateo shook his head. "No. You can't tell her, either." Under the radar. He just wanted to float under the radar. If he started causing problems, they might send him away. Send him away from Josiah.

"What if you're hurt?"

"I'm fine. You think I haven't had worse than this before? Get real, Josiah. This is fucking nothin'."

When Josiah flinched, guilt spread through him like a disease. Like *he* was the disease. "I'm sorry." He made himself pull his hand away from his side and wrap it around Josiah's neck. "I'm sorry. I don't wanna take it out on you. Let's just go, okay? And you gotta promise me. Promise you won't tell Molly or William."

It took a minute, but then Josiah nodded.

"I'm okay. It'll be okay. Can you grab the bags with our clothes over there?" *Dios,* his whole body ached. His head throbbed but he tried to ignore it.

Josiah grabbed their bags and went back to Mateo. He scanned the parking lot on the other side of the bushes but didn't see anything. When he remembered the gas station he'd seen on the other side of the parking lot, he said, "Come on."

Josiah tried to wrap an arm around him to help but Mateo shook him off. "I'm okay. Gotta try and look like I'm not hurt, okay? We don't want to call attention to ourselves. Just walk slow. We're gonna go to the gas station."

Josiah nodded, his eyes toward the ground. Mateo fucking hated that. Hated that he'd scared Jay. But he also didn't want to risk any trouble.

It took a long time to get to the gas station. Mateo felt like a punching bag, his whole upper body aching. His stomach cramped for a whole different reason and he hated it. When they got to the building, he leaned against the wall. "How does my face look?" he asked.

Josiah still didn't look at him. "There's a bruise on the side of your head."

He nodded. "Do you have any money left?" Another nod. "Can you go inside for me? See if they have any kinda hat or some shit. Whatever you can find. And grab the key to the bathroom."

He was jittery the whole time Josiah was gone. His body didn't want to stop moving, but every time he moved, he hurt. Molly and William were so good. He knew they wouldn't be down with fighting. And even if they did believe it wasn't his fault, they'd want to bring him to the doctor and call the police—all the shit Teo couldn't deal with.

Josiah came back a few minutes later. "They only had a beanie."

He nodded and took it from Josiah. "Come in the bathroom with me." There was no way he'd let Josiah stand out here alone. It was one thing to go into the gas station with Mateo waiting right outside. That was all he'd risk.

The bathroom was on the side of the building. Josiah opened the door for them. As soon as he did, Mateo ran into the stall and emptied his stomach. He cramped as he puked, wishing like hell Josiah wasn't out there hearing.

"Teo? Are...are you okay?"

The first thought that hit him was that was the first time Josiah had called him anything other than Mateo. Before he could speak, another wave of nausea hit him and he puked some more. He hated this shit. Despised the fact that he got sick all the time like a fucking pussy.

When nothing else would come up, Mateo struggled to his feet and flushed the toilet. Josiah grabbed ahold of his arm and helped him to the sink, where Mateo rinsed his mouth out. He threw water on his face. "Can you clean the back of my head for me?"

Josiah nodded before wetting paper towels. His head stung like hell with every touch. When he finished, Teo grabbed the beanie from Josiah and pushed it down on his head.

He knew their time was running short before Molly would be there to pick them up. "We need to hurry and go meet Molly. Remember, you promised you wouldn't say anything."

"I don't want to be quiet if you could be hurt!" Josiah's voice rose. "They slammed your head into the wall."

Mateo sighed. "I'm trouble, Jay. They know that." *They'll send me away from you.*

"No they don't. They care about you."

He'd give anything to be that innocent. It was such a precious fucking gift. "Maybe they do in their own way, but they know I don't belong with you guys just as much as I do. I don't want them to send me away. They're not gonna want me to cause problems for you. Fuck, they're probably right, but—"

"No. You're the only person who's always been there for me. I'd make sure they knew that."

Mateo shrugged. "Maybe, but I don't wanna risk it, okay? Just trust me. Everyone has their price. Even when people don't look like it, they're out for themselves. We gotta be smart. If she says anything, I'm gonna say I don't feel good. When we get home, don't come right back to the room with me, okay? Eat dinner with them or whatever the fuck else. I'll be okay. But if she wants to check on me, you do it. Can you do that for me, Jay?"

When Josiah nodded, Mateo licked his lips, wishing like hell that he could kiss him. Since he just puked his guts up, he didn't figure that was such a good idea.

The walk back to where they were supposed to meet Molly was killer. It hurt to breathe. Just like his dad had taught him, Mateo didn't let the pain show, shoved it to the side because he had more important things to deal with right now.

When Molly's white Toyota pulled up to the curb, Mateo forced himself to smile at her. His head fucking killed him. He held his breath as he opened the door and slid into the backseat.

"Did you guys have fun?" she asked once Mateo and Josiah were both in the car.

"Yep. Got some shorts. I'm not feelin' too hot, though."

"Oh no. What is it?" She turned to look at him. Mateo tilted his head down.

"My stomach. I think my lunch is messin' with me or somethin'."

"I'm sorry. What about you, Josiah? Did you eat the same thing?"

Without answering, he shook his head from the passenger seat. He never should have gone outside with Josiah like that. Never should have touched his hair when they were in the mall, or tried to kiss him in the alley. He definitely should have been watching what the hell was going on so those guys wouldn't have gotten the drop on them. He owed Josiah more than that.

It felt like forever until they were home. In the bathroom, Teo cleaned his head again, stuffing the dirty rag into one pocket and grabbing a clean one to keep between his wound and the beanie in case it started bleeding again. After brushing his teeth, he told them he was taking a nap before disappearing into his room. "Oh, fuck." Mateo winced, grabbing his side as he tried to lift his shirt up. There were black and blue bruises all over his torso.

What if those guys would have done that to Josiah? Rage gnawed through him, eating him alive.

Mateo kicked out of his shoes, managed to pull his pants off, and then fell into the bed. Stabbing pain pierced him as he pulled the blanket up and over him. He wished he had been able to climb into Josiah's bed instead of his. Mateo trusted Josiah to keep Molly out, but he had to be sure.

When his eyes fluttered open again, the room was dark, all except for a sliver of light from the door closing. "Jay?" His voice cracked. Hell, he couldn't believe he'd fallen asleep.

"Yeah…yeah, it's me. I kept checking on you, but you were sleeping. I didn't want to disturb you, but then I kept freaking out because of your head. Didn't mean to wake you up again."

Mateo got this strange flutter in his chest, the pain briefly subsiding because it felt so damn good that Josiah cared about him. "Again?" he asked.

"I was scared you had a concussion or something. I woke you up. You don't remember?"

He shook his head, but then remembered Josiah couldn't see him in the dark. "Come here. Come lay with me."

The sound of Josiah's moving across the room made him smile.

"Pull the blanket back. I don't wanna move."

"I got you some painkillers."

His eyes stung when the bedside light came on. He took three of the pills Josiah gave him, swallowed them down with the glass of water he had, too, before falling back into the pillows. Josiah wore a pair of basketball shorts and a T-shirt, obviously ready for bed. "Molly and William?" Teo asked.

"Going to sleep right now."

Mateo's fingers itched to touch his hair. To feel Josiah next to him, so he knew he was okay. "Come here… I…"

But before he could finish, Josiah was climbing under the blanket with him. "I don't want to hurt you. How should I lay?"

"Close." It was a pussy reply, showing how much he needed Josiah like that, but he didn't care.

Josiah curled up next to him, his hair where Teo could touch it.

"I'm sorry. So fucking sorry that happened," he told Josiah again.

"It's not your fault. I don't want it to be like that, though. I don't want you taking everyone on for me."

He paused for a minute before replying. "Takin' care of you is all I have. The only good thing I have."

Josiah wiped his eye before touching Mateo's hair like Mateo so often did to him. They were both on their sides, facing each other. It was the only place Teo had ever felt like home.

"Teo? I mean, Mateo."

"You can call me that. Call me whatever you want."

He nodded. "Why do you throw up? You did it when you almost got in the fight at school, and then again tonight."

You're too weak! You have to be strong, Mateo. You're a leader. Weak men are dead men.

Teo tried to block out his dad's words. Tried to focus on Josiah, because he was all that really mattered, anyway. "Because I'm weak… Hurting people makes me sick."

Josiah leaned up on his elbow, looking down at him. "That doesn't make you weak. It makes you incredible."

He wanted that to be true. Wanted it so fucking much. "I've hurt people, Jay. Hurt 'em bad. I beat a guy who was tied up with a fucking chain. Then I watched as my dad shot him in the head." He closed his eyes as though that would somehow block the memory of the bruises and cuts he'd put on the man's body. Of the blood and brains that his father blew out of the guy's head. "That doesn't make me incredible. It makes me nothin'."

Josiah gasped. He leaned away from Mateo, which was exactly what he should do. Teo was poison for someone like Josiah. But damn, he didn't want to be.

"Your dad made you do that?"

"I didn't want to do it, Jay. I swear. He made me. If I didn't, he'd hurt me. I shoulda let him. I shouldn't have put my life over that guy's, but I didn't know what to do." He didn't realize tears were coming out of his eyes until they landed on Josiah's hand. Mateo tried to wipe them away, but Josiah stopped him.

"You don't hurt people now. You take care of them." He cocked his head. "Has anyone ever taken care of you?"

He thought about his mom. She wanted to. She tried but the streets took her. "Not since my mom died."

Josiah sat up. Mateo reached for him, groaning when pain slammed into him again, but he didn't care. He'd go crazy if Josiah left him.

But then Jay's hand went to Mateo's side. Slowly his fingers slid Teo's shirt up. He sucked in a deep breath as he looked at the bruises there.

Mateo couldn't move, couldn't breathe, scared if he did, it would be over.

"I want to take care of you, the way you take care of me." Leaning forward, he kissed Mateo's side. Kissed all the bruises there. Each time his lips touched Mateo, pleasure shot through him, comfort, in a way he'd never felt. Josiah moved to his neck, tracing the scar with his lips, before he pressed his mouth to the bruise on Mateo's head, too.

His body sizzled under Josiah's touch. Every part of him wished it could last forever. His chest was tight, but it had nothing to do with the fight and everything to do with Josiah.

"I want to take care of you, too," he said again.

"Why?" Mateo's heart stopped as he waited for an answer.

Josiah turned off the light, lay back down, and covered them up again. "Because…I love you."

Josiah's words landed right in his chest, taking all the pain away. Mateo vowed right there that he would work hard to deserve Josiah's love. That he would do any-fucking-thing in his power to make sure no one ever tried to take Josiah away from him.

"Te amo, mi precioso."

"What's that?" Josiah asked.

"The truth. Who you are." Mateo kissed his forehead. "Everything about you is so fucking pure. I'm gonna deserve that. That precious fucking gift."

He kissed Josiah again, lowered his mouth to his ear. "I love you. It means what you are to me. Precious."

Chapter Thirteen

Josiah

It was a few weeks after the fight that Josiah went to Molly. Mateo had gone for a walk, being in one of his moods where he wanted to be alone. Even though his stomach was a mess, Josiah knew he wouldn't get another time like this to talk to her.

She had her back to him, standing in front of the fridge, when he walked into the kitchen. "Molly…hey. Can I talk to you for a second?"

She closed the door and walked to the table. "Of course. What's on your mind?"

They both sat down. Nerves gnawed at him but he ignored it. This wasn't betraying Mateo, it was doing what Mateo did for him all the time. Taking care of him.

"I wanted to talk to you about Teo."

She sat up straighter, frowning. "Is something wrong? Did he do something?"

Josiah's jaw tightened as he fisted his hands. "What? No. Why would you think that?"

Her body slumped. "You're right. I shouldn't have assumed the worst. I don't even know why I did. He hasn't caused any problems since he's been here and that wasn't fair. Chalk it up to my not feeling so good lately."

"It's okay." But still his body didn't let go of the anger. It wasn't fair the way everyone assumed the worst about Mateo. He wavered a little, unsure if he should go forward with what he planned to do. Maybe they could just run away together. It could be for the best. All he knew was he wouldn't lose Mateo. Not for anything.

Which was exactly why he thought it best to take what Teo had confided in him and share it with Molly. Give them a chance to stay together without having to run away. *Because I know he wouldn't let me go… No matter how much I wanted to, he wouldn't take me away from a home.*

"Is Mateo okay?" Molly asked. Josiah nodded.

"I just… I wanted to talk to you about his birthday. I didn't know if you knew it's in July. That's only two and a half months till he turns eighteen." He wrung his hands together. "I know you don't have any responsibility to him after that or anything, and I know you guys have already done so much to help us, but he has no place else to go. We wouldn't cause any problems or anything. And once I turn eighteen, we could move out if you want."

Molly sighed. "Josiah, I know you and Mateo are very close, but I have to say, all those 'we's' make me a little nervous. When you turn eighteen you'll still be in high school. I'd hate to think you're planning to live somewhere with him while you're still in school." She took a deep breath. "Is there anything you want to tell me?"

Panic choked him. If she found out about him and Mateo… What if she sent Teo away? He cleared his throat, trying to find his voice. "No." Josiah shook his head. "He's a good friend. Sort of like a brother. I just feel bad for him. I know he doesn't want to go back to Brooklyn, and he doesn't have anyone except for me—*us*."

Smiling, Molly said, "I'm glad you guys have each other. And honestly, I've already spoken to William about it. We just weren't sure how Mateo would take it. I worried he'd think we feel sorry for him. I know he has a hard time accepting help."

"He'll stay. If you say he can, I know he'll stay." Josiah fought to bite down his excitement.

Molly covered his hand with hers and smiled. "He can stay."

***

Josiah moved against Teo as he lay on top of him. He rotated his hips, feeling Mateo's erection rub against his. His whole body sizzled. He loved the way Mateo felt. Loved touching him and being kissed by him, the feel of his hand wrapped around his erection.

He groaned when Mateo pulled away.

"Shh," Teo whispered, laughter in his voice. "They're gonna hear you."

"Sorry, I can't help it."

Mateo moved lower. "Don't apologize for that. And I'm not goin' anywhere. Wanna try somethin'."

They were always nervous to do too much, afraid that Molly or William would hear them. Since Molly stayed home, they almost never had time to do much exploring. Kisses, touches, were about it. Not that those weren't okay with Josiah. He never thought he'd have even this with someone. To have it with Mateo… "Oh My God."

He melted into the mattress at the feel of Mateo's mouth on him.

"Shh," Mateo said again, before tossing a pillow to him.

Josiah got the message, biting down on it as Mateo used his mouth on him. Embarrassment flooded him when what was probably no more than thirty seconds later he lost control, his orgasm slamming into him. Josiah slumped into the bed, feeling like someone had taken all the bones out of his body.

"I never… It felt…" What he wanted to say was that he couldn't believe Mateo had gone down on him.

Mateo slid next to him again, taking away the pillow that now sat on his chest. "This is the only time I like you speechless. I like that I made ya feel so good."

"You always make me feel good," he said between breaths. Josiah paused for a minute, trying to gather his thoughts. He wanted to do the same thing to Teo that he'd done to him. But he also knew he needed to tell him he talked to Molly today. It didn't feel right until he made sure Mateo wasn't mad at him.

Teo's hand slipped under his shirt, rubbing Josiah's stomach.

"I talked to Molly today."

Mateo's hand froze. "Talked to her about what? Please don't tell me you told her, Jay. They'll send me away. They'll—"

"I didn't tell her about that. Just talked to her about your birthday… Asked her if you could stay. And you can. She said yes, Teo. She said she already talked to William about it *before* I even asked her!"

Silence greeted him. In the black of the room, he couldn't see Mateo's face, but the quiet said everything. "Maybe I shouldn't have done it without talking to you, but I won't be sorry for it. They said you could stay, Teo. It's what we want. No one is going to separate us. Don't be mad at me for that—"

"You think I'm mad at you?" he asked. "I'm…"

And that's when Josiah got it. He was grateful, surprised, that Josiah had done that for Mateo. For them. He still struggled sometimes, being the one to touch Mateo first, to talk to him without getting shy, but right now he forced all of those fears away. Wrapped a hand around the back of Mateo's neck. "I told you, it wasn't just you who had to take care of me. We'll take care of each other. You and me. Together."

"You and me. Together." When Mateo finished kissing him, Josiah moved down the bed to pleasure Teo, the same way Teo had done with him.

Chapter Fourteen

Mateo

"I'm sorry, but the position has been filled."

Mateo fought everything inside him not to hang up the phone. "Okay, thanks. Keep me in mind for anything else." The man on the other end of the line said he would before hanging up.

Yeah fucking right. Mateo knew better than that. They didn't want to hire him just like all the other places he'd applied in the past month didn't. He'd filled out apps everywhere. The fact that he was a young Mexican kid with no work experience, no car, and who they probably took one look at and knew he had some kind of gang affiliation, didn't make it easy. He wore the evidence of his lifestyle in his clothes, and probably in his stance, too.

"Any luck?" Josiah asked him as he leaned against the back of the couch. Teo shook his head before grabbing Josiah and pulling him close. Josiah wrapped his arms around him, squeezing as he kissed the scar on his neck.

Molly and William were out. He drove her to a doctor's

appointment or something like that, so he took advantage, holding Jay while he could.

"They didn't say you had to get a job. You don't have to be in such a rush."

Mateo huffed. "Yeah, I do. I'm not stayin' here if I can't pay my way. It's not right. I owe them more than that, and they don't owe me shit. It's not fair to them."

They bought Mateo all sorts of stuff for his graduation last week—he still couldn't get over that shit. He'd actually graduated fucking high school. Now he had nothing, though; no job…and in just a few weeks he'd be eighteen. Their obligation to him was over, no matter what he said. If he didn't figure out how to pay his own way, he had no choice but to leave. Turning eighteen meant Molly and William lost the money the foster system paid them. They'd done too much for him already, and he couldn't let them pay his way, too.

His throat squeezed up at the thought. Shit, he needed to figure this out. Needed to find a way to stay with Josiah. It wasn't like he couldn't handle the streets. Maybe he'd just stay around here, seeing Josiah when he could till he graduated.

Mateo stood straight, pulling away from Josiah. "I'm gonna go sit outside for a while, okay?"

Josiah nodded, obviously knowing Teo was a moody motherfucker and needed some space. He went to this spot on the side of the house and sat in the gravel, arms around his legs. What kind of man could he be for Josiah if he couldn't even get a fucking job? College was out. He knew that. It wasn't his thing. Plus, that didn't solve how the hell he would help Molly and William.

He groaned when he heard a car pull into the driveway. They were home sooner than he thought they would be.

Mateo turned his head when he heard the creak of the porch swing, wondering why they weren't going inside. He tensed up when he heard Molly crying.

"It's okay, honey. We'll beat this. We can beat anything," William told her.

"You heard what they said just as much as I did. It's too far progressed."

A brick landed on Teo's chest. Molly was sick?

"I should have gone in earlier. I think I knew, Will. I think a part of me knew and I was scared to find out." She started crying again. William talked to her and told her he loved her. Guilt added more weight to Teo's chest. He shouldn't be hearing this conversation, but if he moved, they'd know he'd already heard some of it.

When the crying finally slowed down, William spoke again. "We need to think about the boys. We're going to have a lot going on with your treatments. And our insurance isn't the best, honey. It's going to cost money and—"

"No, it's not right. I won't send them away."

"How are we going to support Mateo, too? You know I care about him just as much as you do, but he'll be eighteen next month. And if I'm being honest, I'm not sure I think he's the best influence on Josiah. I can't put my finger on it, but something isn't right with them."

More tears from Molly, then, "Let's wait until after his birthday. He deserves that, at least."

Blood rushing through his ears blocked out the rest of the conversation. They were right. They didn't need Mateo hanging around here when they would be dealing with Molly being sick.

He fought the urge to vomit, rocking back and forth to try and calm himself. It felt like an earthquake shook his insides, cracking him apart. He should have known. Should have fucking known it was all too good to be true. He didn't belong here. He'd have to leave Josiah.

***

Two days after he heard Molly and William talking on the porch, Teo had a job selling drugs. Shit like that was easy to find, and they didn't care if you had references, experience, or looked like you belonged behind bars.

He needed money and he needed it fast. He couldn't think of another option besides selling.

It made his skin crawl. Made him feel like the man he hated—like his father. But what if he could save enough? Find a way to get a little place or something like that so he could stay close to Josiah.

He wouldn't take drugs into Molly and William's house. Didn't want them around Josiah, either, but if he could get a place close, maybe it would buy him more time to get a real job.

Or at least help him if he had to go back into the city. Which, if he was being honest, he knew that's what he needed to do. All he'd been doing was biding his time here, dreaming and wishing stuff he had no business thinking about.

He should go now. Just get it over with, but…was it so fucking bad to want to spend his birthday with Josiah? To pretend they could have what they dreamed of?

So, that's what he did. Depression hit everyone in the house, so no one noticed how hard a time Teo was having. They didn't know he'd heard Molly and William talking. That he was leaving.

Josiah struggled, big time, scared of losing Molly. He didn't think of Teo having to leave, or if he did, he didn't bring it up. That was Josiah, though. His mind wouldn't think of Mateo having to go because he didn't look for bad shit the way Mateo did. Plus, he had enough bad worry about Molly.

By the time his birthday came around, Molly already started chemo. She put on the brave face, trying to make plans for Teo's birthday, but he told her not to worry about it. Just to get well.

That night he lay in bed with Josiah. Jay had his head on Mateo's chest as he lay on his back. Teo had his arm around Josiah, a hand in his hair.

"I wanted to make you something for your birthday, something like the queen you made me, but I'm not good at anything like that." There was a soft sadness in Josiah's voice that Teo wanted to wipe away.

"Just being with you's all I want. I don't need nothin' else."

"I wrote you a letter. It's under the pillow on your bed. Don't read it when you're with me, though."

Electricity zapped through him. Everything about Josiah made him feel like that. He needed to tell him that he'd have to go soon, but he didn't want to ruin this night. Or the life he could have. So, fuck NYC. He was staying close to Josiah even if he had to sleep on the streets every night.

"I won't open it, but then, you gotta talk to me till you fall asleep. I wanna know everything about you."

Josiah chuckled. "You already do."

"Not your future. Tell me that." He squeezed tighter.

"*Our* future. Where do you want to go?" Josiah asked.

"This is your story. You tell me. I'll go wherever you want."

Josiah thought for a minute. "California. I've always wanted to go there. I read about Fisherman's Warf in San Francisco. I want…. I think I'd like to work in, like, a coffee shop or something down there."

"No." Teo shook his head. "This is your dream, *mi precioso*. You're not going to work there. You own that shit."

"Yeah…yeah I do. And we'll walk to the ocean every day and feed the birds. Then you'll go to work and I'll go to the shop. People will come in to drink coffee, eat pastries, and listen to music. We'll have a stage in the front and we can do open mic nights or something like that. What do you think?"

Dios, his fucking eyes started to sting. None of that was his thing, but he wanted it. Wanted it so fucking bad he could hardly stand it. "It sounds perfect." And then the urge to tell Josiah something hit him. Just a little something that was a piece of his happiness, too. "There's this park in NYC, it's little as shit and not in the best area. It's called

Creekside. It wasn't the fucking ocean like your dream, but my mom and I used to walk by that creek before she died. I loved it there."

Josiah kissed his chest. "Maybe I can see it one day."

Mateo didn't tell him that he didn't want him to, that if he did that meant he'd be closer to Brooklyn, the last place Teo wanted him.

They talked for a little while longer before Josiah whispered, "Good night. Happy birthday."

Teo didn't move, laid perfectly still until he was sure Josiah was asleep. He tried like hell to fall asleep but it wouldn't come. When he couldn't just lie there any longer, he quietly slipped out of bed, grabbing the letter to take with him. The paper burned a hole through his hand he wanted to read it so badly.

Teo went into the kitchen and turned on the light above the stove. He set the note down, only seeing the **For Mateo, with love, Josiah,** before he went to grab a glass of juice out of the fridge. He had just pulled the door open when the kitchen light came on.

"Couldn't sleep?" William's voice sounded from behind him, holding a harsh edge to it.

"No." Mateo's eyes shot to the letter. His pulse went crazy when William walked toward it, to the cabinet that held the glasses.

Don't let him see it. Please don't let him fucking see it.

William opened the cabinet. Paused. Then tossed something to the counter right by the letter.

Game fucking over.

"I'm having a hard time sleeping, too, with Molly being sick. I went out to my shed tonight. I never go out there, but I was…hell, I don't know. I guess I was thinking I could find something to keep me busy out there. Found this."

Mateo didn't speak. What the fuck could he say with five ounces of weed sitting on the counter?

William didn't say anything, either, but then his eyes looked down at the counter, at the letter. Body stiff, he looked over his shoulder. "What are you doing with that kid?"

Teo shook his head. "Nothin'. Don't know what you're talkin' about. Don't worry about the drugs. I'll go."

William seemed to have forgotten about those. "What is this?" He grabbed the paper. "I knew it. I could tell something wasn't right. I told Molly."

Panic seized him. He didn't know what to do, and the truth came tumbling out in a moment of weakness. Weak, just like his father said he was. "I'd never hurt him. I love him."

William's features hardened even more. "He's young. Insecure. Oh my God, what have you been doing to him? In our house? After everything we've done for you, you're not only hiding drugs at my house but you're messing with that kid?"

Teo took a step toward him. "It's not like that. We haven't done nothin'."

"Then what is this?" William threw the letter at him. Mateo grabbed it. "That kid just wants to be loved. He'd grab onto anyone who showed him that. You might not realize it, you might not want to, but you're going to hurt him. He flinches at his own damn shadow." William shook his head. "It's not right. I can't have it. Not *that* in my house. Not that or the drugs."

Anger shoved its way to the surface. He didn't care if William thought he was a druggie, but he did care what he thought of Josiah. "He's stronger than you think. Don't push that weak bullshit off on him. Blame me all you want, but don't call him weak in front of me again."

William sighed. "I can't deal with this. My wife is sick. I won't deal with drugs in my house. I can't deal with the two of you guys, too."

Those last words slammed into Mateo. *You guys, too…* "Don't. Don't fucking take this out on Josiah. It's not his fault." He couldn't get Jay kicked out of here. He loved it here. Loved Molly and William. He'd never forgive himself if he got Josiah sent to another home.

"You need to watch your language when you talk to me."

"Fuck my language! I care about him! Don't hurt him because of me."

His face hardened, his fist coming down on the counter. "Don't raise your voice! You're going to wake Molly. This will kill her. We have too much going on to deal with this. You're out of here. Tomorrow. I don't want to see you around Molly."

Mateo knew he couldn't wait until tomorrow. If he did, he'd have to say goodbye to Josiah. If he did, Josiah would try to go with him. "You'll be good to him? He didn't know about this shit, and the other thing was my fault, too. I'm the one who pushed him into it."

William shook his head, whispering that he knew it. "Then just go. This is already going to kill Molly. I don't want her to lose Josiah, too."

Mateo's gut clenched because he was going to lose Josiah. *Dios,* he was really going to lose Josiah. Because he couldn't stay here. If William found out Mateo was around, he could screw up Josiah having a home.

"I'll be outta here. You won't have to see me again."

He didn't even go to his room to grab any of his shit. He had his letter and that's all the really mattered. Mateo shoved his feet into the shoes that were by the door.

"Te amo," he whispered one last time. Mateo grabbed the doorknob, slowly pulling it open.

As soon as he hit the street, Mateo went to a streetlight and pulled the letter out.

Teo,

Sometimes I feel like the only thing I have to give you are words. I can't protect you, and I don't always know the right thing to do like you do. I want to give you everything, so that's what I decided to do. I know it's not much, but everything I am, everything I have, is yours. Because that's what you do with me. I know you don't see it, but you do. You give me everything you are, and that's all I need. You. You said to me once that I make you feel like something, but you do that to me, too. You make me feel like someone for the first time in my life. Even without me, you'd be something, Teo.

Happy Birthday.

Love,

Josiah

Josiah was wrong. Mateo wasn't something, as Josiah had said in his letter.

Without letting himself look back, he walked away from Heaven and headed back toward Hell.

Chapter Fifteen

Josiah

Molly cried all day, upset that Mateo had disappeared. William told them he caught him leaving, and that he'd wanted to go. Mateo was old enough that they couldn't do anything about it.

Josiah didn't believe that for a second. Still, he sat with his arm around her, comforting her, but he didn't shed a tear of his own. He knew he would see Mateo again. He wasn't losing him. He refused to.

When Molly laid down for a late afternoon nap, William approached him. "I know about you two. I know this is hard on you, but it's for the best. It was wrong of him to take advantage of you like that."

Josiah saw red, his heart exploding in his chest. "What? Teo didn't take advantage of me. He would never hurt me."

William sighed. "Did you know he's doing drugs? Doing them or selling them, I don't know, but he hid drugs at our home, Josiah."

Josiah flinched at that, but still it didn't matter. If Mateo had drugs here, it was for a reason. He closed his eyes the second it hit him... He couldn't get a job. He did the only thing he knew how to do to make money. "Fine. Whatever." Josiah walked away, trying not to show he was upset as he was. Trying not to tip his hand.

When the house was dark, everyone in bed for the night, he grabbed the two backpacks he'd filled with his and Mateo's things. Grabbed his queen and put it into his pocket. He didn't know how he'd do it, but somehow he'd find Mateo.

***

Josiah wrapped his arms around his legs, hiding himself behind some bushes. Four days and three nights he'd spent in Creekside park, not knowing what else to do. Mateo would come here. He knew it.

A sound came from the distance, making him jump. He tucked himself deeper, hoping like hell whoever it was didn't see him. There'd been a fight in the park his second night here, and someone had pulled out a knife. The days were okay, but he didn't know if he could do it… didn't know how many more nights he could take. Alone.

Teo, where are you?

Sleepiness made his eyes droop before he popped them open again. He couldn't go to sleep, couldn't risk being passed out if someone found him.

***

Two days later he sat by the creek when he heard footsteps behind him. The only time he'd left this park since he got here was to get food. His stomach growled because he didn't have enough of it, his eyes grainy and in pain from lack of sleep, his movements slow as he turned around. That's when he saw him.

Teo.

"*Dios,* Josiah. What the fuck are you doing here?" Mateo ran over to him, surprising Josiah by pulling him close. He melted into Teo's arms. *Finally.*

"I couldn't stay. Not without you."

"Shit. You shouldn't have done that, Jay. You shouldn't have fucking left. It's not right. You don't belong here. You belong with them."

Josiah pulled back. "I belong with you."

Josiah tried to keep the hurt from his face but knew he didn't succeed when Teo said, "I wanna be with you, but it's not right. You shouldn't be here. What do I have to give you? I don't have shit."

Josiah's body went hot. "Fuck you, Teo."

Mateo's eyes widened. "I think that's the first time you've cussed at me."

Josiah didn't laugh. Mateo didn't get to change the subject on this. "It's not about what we have or don't have. It's about *us*. Ever since my parents died, no one ever loved me, not *really* loved me and *wanted* me until you. That's all that matters, and I'm staying. I'm not letting you push me away."

"It's not that I want to push you away! I don't even have a real fucking place to stay."

"So? You can handle it but I can't?"

"No, it's not that you can't. You shouldn't *have* to."

Josiah pulled his hand away. "Don't do this. You said. The first day of school, you told Molly not to baby me. Don't you do it, either. I don't deserve anything more than you do. I can handle it if you can."

Mateo closed his eyes, letting out a deep breath. Josiah wracked his brain, trying to think of anything he could say or do to change Mateo's mind. Panic burned through him. He couldn't do this. Couldn't lose Mateo. He'd do whatever it took to make that happen.

"You promised. You said you'd take care of me. I can't do this without you. If you really want to protect me, to take care of me, I need to be *with* you, Teo." The words, though true, were like acid on his tongue. No matter what, it felt wrong to manipulate Mateo like this.

Mateo reached for him. "Jay, don't do this. Don't let me drag you down. It's not right. They'll let you go back. It'll kill me if somethin' happens to you."

"You won't let it. I trust you. We'll be okay, as long as we're together."

"Josiah." He ran his hand through Josiah's hair and cupped the back of his head before letting it fall. Mateo dropped his forehead to Josiah's.

"I need you."

"Do you know what you're saying? You're a runaway. We'll be on the streets, Jay. I've been selling drugs for a month just to have money. That'll be our life."

He shook his head, panic shoving words out of his mouth. "Not forever. Just for six months. When I turn eighteen, we won't have to hide anymore. We can do this. We'll do it together."

"Then you can go back to Yorktown for six months. We'll see each other when we can, and then when you graduate next year, we can go to California. Maybe you could go to school out there or something. I'll save money for us until then."

Josiah's stomach dropped out. This wasn't going to work. Mateo was going to leave him. He had this voice in his head, this piece of knowledge that he didn't know the origin of, that told him it wouldn't work. That if they weren't together, Mateo wouldn't be able to deal.

How could he go back and stay in a nice house every night and sleep in his comfortable bed while Mateo was on the streets? Or living in some crap place selling drugs to eat? He couldn't do that.

"Together. We're in this together, Teo. I won't be without you. If you go, I go. I won't go back without you, even if I have to stay here alone." That was the truth. "I've never stood up for myself in my life, not really, but I'm doing it now. You…you mean too much to me not to. I love you, Teo."

Josiah's heart started beating again when Mateo's lips pressed to his. "Fuck, I don't know. I don't know if I'm doing the right thing by you." But then he grabbed the bags from Josiah's hands and said, "Come on. Let's get the fuck outta here."

***

Mateo said they had to stay out of Brooklyn. That he'd been staying out of that borough, so hopefully he wouldn't see anyone he knew. He wore his beanie all the time, trying to blend in with everyone.

They slept on the streets. Well, he did, at least. Mateo hardly ever slept, always trying to keep an eye on him.

He bought a knife off some guy that he kept in his pocket all the time. Josiah held onto the queen that Mateo had carved for him. But no matter how hard it was, how much he shook from nerves or how fast his heart beat when they saw a cop or when noises woke him up at night, this was right. Being with Mateo was *right*.

About two weeks after they got into New York City, Mateo brought him to a different park. "Here." He slipped his hand into Josiah's pocket. He didn't have to feel it to know it was the knife.

"What? No. I don't want that."

"And I'm not leaving you without it. You keep that fucking thing in your hand, and if anyone gives you shit, you use it, Jay. You hear me?" He scanned their surroundings.

Josiah's nails dug into Teo's arm he held him so tightly. "What? Where are you going?"

"I'm gonna figure some shit out for us today, okay? It's not good for you to be with me. We're in a safe area, so you'll be fine. Pretend you're a tourist or some shit. I'll be back before dark. I promise."

Before Josiah could say anything, Mateo disappeared. He closed his eyes and steadied his breathing. *I can do this, I can do this, I can do this.* He would do it for Mateo. He wouldn't make this harder on Teo than it already was. He'd prove to Mateo he was right when he said they could both take care of each other, not just Teo taking care of him.

So he did. He walked around all day, pretending like he belonged here. He stayed off the main paths, trying to steer clear of cops. Every so often he made his way back to the tree where Mateo had left him. It was dusk when he found his boyfriend there.

"Holy fuck, I've been freaking the hell out." Mateo pulled him into a hug.

"You told me to walk around. That's what I was doing. You worry like you're a girl or something."

Mateo laughed. It was the first time since they'd been here that he'd seen Mateo laugh.

"Come on. I got us a place to stay." He nodded his head in the other direction and started walking.

Josiah's heart soared. "What? Where? Like, a real place?"

"Don't get too excited." Mateo shook his head. "It's a piece of shit. One room and that's all. A downstairs apartment in a shitty neighborhood from the kinda guy who doesn't care that I don't have a real job and who will break my neck if I don't have rent."

Josiah's feet rooted to the ground. "Umm…what?"

"That's all we can do right now, Jay. I told you that. I need somewhere to stay where they won't think twice about seeing you. Where they're not gonna care if they do find out you're a runaway. I can't get a real job because if I do, they'll know where I am. They have to be looking for me, knowing you're with me."

This time it was Josiah who almost vomited. He hadn't thought about all that. The kind of trouble Mateo could maybe get into because of him.

"I don't want you sleepin' on the streets anymore. It'll be okay.

Trust me." He started walking again, giving Josiah no choice but to do the same.

"What about rent? How are we going to pay?"

"First month's taken care of. Once I know you're safe there, I'll go out and find a way to get us some more money."

Fear clogged Josiah's throat. He didn't want to ask how Mateo got the money for this month, or what he'd be doing to get the rest of it. Instead, he followed Mateo. Together. They were together. That's all that mattered.

Chapter Sixteen

October

Mateo

Nothing he did for money was on the up and up. Mateo did the dirty work for the guy they got the apartment from and for another street player he found. Mostly drugs and weapons. Even though he hated it, all he had to do was sell. He didn't come home to Josiah with blood on his hands, and the money took care of them. That's all that mattered to Mateo.

Months passed by. He felt like shit because Josiah didn't get out a whole lot. He couldn't do the kind of work Mateo did, but he couldn't get a real job, either. Not being a seventeen-year-old runaway.

He'd get excited when he found some crazy piece of furniture, or something for their apartment at this hole-in-the-wall used store. And they bought a chessboard, too, and played every night.

Things were hard, and a day didn't go by that he hated letting Josiah live this way…but they were happy, too. They were together, and Josiah smiled a lot, which often made Teo do the same. How could he *not* be happy when he had Josiah with him? Josiah had said it before, and even though he'd argued, he agreed: As long as they were together, things were okay.

At about nine o'clock, after one of the longest days of his life, Mateo unlocked the door to their apartment and went inside. The couch bed, which was what they slept on, had already been pulled out. The chessboard sat in the middle of it, but Josiah was nowhere in sight.

"Jay?" Mateo called, realizing their whole apartment smelled like a coffee shop.

"Hey!" Josiah pushed the bathroom door open and came out. "Check this out." He had this huge ass smile on his face that Mateo couldn't help but return.

Teo followed him to the kitchen.

"It's an espresso machine. I got it at that secondhand store down the street. I made us some."

Mateo bit back his words. It made him nervous when Josiah went out too much on his own, but he also couldn't expect him to stay locked up in their dingy apartment all day, either. "Smells good. I drink that shit and I'm gonna be up all night, though."

"So?" Josiah shrugged. "I'm making it, so you have to drink it." His eyes were firmly planted on Mateo. They were most of the time now. They warmed his skin. Made him forget about all the bad shit because he had Josiah. He never thought he'd be so lucky.

"Okay." But before Josiah could do anything, Mateo pulled him closer and kissed him. Holy shit, he'd never get tired of kissing him.

Josiah pushed closer to him, went up on this toes as he kept Mateo's body between his and the counter.

Teo let him take over the kiss. Let Josiah take the lead as his tongue slipped into Mateo's mouth. Josiah tasted like coffee, telling him he'd already had a drink or two.

After pressing two more kisses to Josiah's lips, Teo let him pull away so Josiah could make him his drink. Mateo changed into a pair of sweats. Ignoring the loud music from other apartments, and the sounds from the crazy streets outside, they sat in the middle of the bed and played a game of chess, drinking their espressos.

His life felt so *normal* at times like this, when he'd never had normal before. Shit was broken and fucked up, but they were broken together, and that meant something to him. Teo wouldn't let anyone take this away from them.

"You're being quiet," Josiah said to him as he moved the chessboard to the floor.

"Are you happy?" Mateo asked. "I know it's not your dream. I want that for you, and we'll get it one day. And the apartment, it's shitty, and my job…Fuck. Was that a stupid question? When I start thinkin' about all the stuff you don't have…"

"I have you. The other stuff doesn't matter. I love you, Teo. That's all I need to be happy."

Mateo shook his head. "You're too easy." But then he threaded his fingers through the hair at the back of Josiah's head and pulled him forward.

"Te amo."

Josiah crawled closer. When Mateo tried to kiss him, he pulled back, but then climbed onto Mateo's lap, straddling him. "I wanna…you know. I want to *be* with you." Shyly, his eyes darted away.

All the blood rushed to Mateo's crotch. He wanted that, too. Wanted it so fucking bad. It wasn't that they didn't mess around, because they did. It just didn't feel right going all the way with Josiah. He deserved better than that. Better than some fifty-year-old couch mattress with drug dealers and gangbangers outside their apartment. Hell, he deserved better than having a drug dealer inside him.

Mateo tried to laugh it off. "You can't even say it. That should tell us it's not time."

He tried to get up but Josiah wrapped his arms around Mateo's neck, his voice strengthening. "I want to have sex with you. I want to make love with you."

Mateo groaned, suddenly feeling like he sat in an oven. "You think I don't want that, Jay? I just…doin' right by you is all I've ever wanted. The only thing I wanna get right. This," he pointed around the room. "You deserve better than this shit. When I…" Mateo closed his eyes and took a deep breath. He wrapped his arms around Josiah, as Josiah buried his face in Mateo's neck.

"You wanna know how I lost my virginity, Jay? In a dirty-ass room just like this one, I fucked a girl while my dad watched. The next day I fucked another one, and another one, 'til he believed it was what I wanted. That he'd never find another magazine with guys in it hidden in my room. I was only thirteen years old."

Mateo shivered, his neck cold because of Josiah's tears. "I want it to be better for you."

Josiah's head jerked away from him. "We *are* better than that. You love me and I love you. And maybe I want more for you, too. You're always talking about what you want for me, and how I deserve better, but you do, too. You deserve better. We can take away those memories with *us*."

He tasted salt on his tongue when Josiah kissed him. All Mateo's reservations melted away with each sweep of Josiah's tongue, each time it brushed against his.

He wanted that, too. Wanted to wipe away all his bad memories and replace them with Josiah.

Mateo pulled back enough so his eyes could meet Josiah's.

"Please, Teo. Please."

They'd gone over this before. Mateo always stopped before they went all the way. They'd had their mouths on each other, and showered together, but he never let it go too far. Always wanted Josiah to have an out if he needed it, but this time, he couldn't say no.

Mateo pulled Jay's shirt off and dropped it on the bed. Then he took off his own before rolling them so Josiah lay beneath him. His smaller body felt so good, so right, against him.

"I um… I got the stuff while I was out today." Josiah's finger brushed over his scar.

"What?" Mateo couldn't stop from grinning down at him. "You put a lot of thought into this."

"I was freaked out. I thought they'd want some ID or something but they didn't." His cheeks turned red. Mateo kissed one, then the other. Josiah told him where he'd hidden the condoms and lube, and Teo went to grab it. His heart beat a million miles an hour the whole time.

He went back to the bed and kissed Jay again. They took off each other's clothes, touching and kissing the whole time. He spread lube on his fingers before gently probing Josiah. He went slow, sliding one finger in and out, as he kissed him.

Josiah winced when he added another.

Mateo took his time. He did everything he could to get Josiah ready for him, wanting him to love this as much as Teo knew he would.

He looked down at Josiah, hard as he'd ever been in his whole life, and kind of felt like this was his first time, too. Like the others somehow didn't count.

Josiah squeezed him tightly, breathed heavy and hard as Mateo worked his way in. "*Lo siento, mi precioso.* I'm sorry..." Hurting Josiah was a kick to Mateo's gut.

But then Josiah moved against him. The sounds whispering past his lips changed—less pain, more pleasure. They moved together. Together, like he always wanted them to be.

"Teo..." Josiah whispered.

"*Estoy aquí. Siempre aquí. Soy tuyo.* I'm here. Always here. I'm yours." Mateo wrapped a hand around Josiah, wanting him to feel all the pleasure he did. He stroked his hand up and down Josiah's erection. They climbed higher and higher, the pressure building stronger. A slow burn started inside him, getting hotter and hotter.

"Teo…" Josiah tensed. The second he stepped over that ledge, Mateo was right there with him. Together.

As they lay there afterward, Teo asked, "Do you want me to run a shower for you? If we had a bath, that would be better. We don't even have a fucking bath." He shook his head and tried to get out of bed but Josiah held onto him.

"Just want you."

Teo just wanted him as well. Only him. "Let me get rid of this stuff." Once he disposed of the condom, Teo wet a washcloth then turned off the light. He cleaned Josiah off before wrapping around him in the bed.

"What happened to your neck, Teo? I want to know."

He knew he couldn't avoid the question this time. Wasn't even sure he wanted to. "My dad did it when he found the magazine. He hadn't meant to, I don't think. He fought me, made me fight him. There was a broken bottle and I came out with the scar. The girls came after. They were older, didn't give a shit that they were fucking a thirteen-year-old kid. Only cared they were making dad happy. Ricky Sanchez's son couldn't be a fag." He shook his head.

Josiah squeezed him tighter. "No one will hurt us anymore. Not while we're together."

He sure as hell hoped not.

"I love you, Mateo."

"Te amo."

There was a pause and then Josiah said, "Please tell me we get to keep doing that now."

A laugh jumped out of Mateo's mouth, quickly followed by Josiah doing the same. They lay in bed, talking and laughing the rest of the night.

Chapter Seventeen

December

Josiah

"I'm not doing anything, Teo. It's not right for you to have to be out there doing all the stuff you hate every day to support us while I do nothing." Josiah paced the room, searching for the right words to make Mateo understand. "I'm eighteen now. If they find me, does it really matter that I ran away six months ago?"

Teo shook his head. "I don't know how it all works, but if they find you, they find me. We don't know what Molly and William told 'em. I'm sure they said you ran away with me, which means they could be lookin' for me. You were seventeen. I don't think I can get into trouble for anything now, but I don't really wanna risk it, either. Cops and me aren't really a good combo, Jay."

Logically, he knew Mateo was right. They didn't need cops breathing down their necks, especially with what Mateo did for money. But then, if Josiah worked, too, maybe they could actually save and get out of here. *And maybe I won't risk him getting tired of taking care of me...* "Can't you... I don't know, find me some kind of job like you do? Something so I can make some money, too?"

Mateo actually laughed. "Hell no. Fuck no. You're not dirtying your hands with this shit."

"But *you* can? I don't need you to be my hero. I love you for it, but you've got to let me learn how to take care of myself, too!"

Mateo shook his head and leaned against the counter in their kitchen. "I'm not saying this to be a dick, but you're not cut out for what I do."

"And you are? You hate it."

"But I know how to hide that. You couldn't, *mi precioso*. You just couldn't. You're too *good*. People would see you and know they could take advantage of you."

Josiah turned away from him and grabbed his backpack. "Awesome, Teo. Thanks for the vote of confidence. People see me and know they can take advantage of me. So glad you have faith in me."

He wasn't surprised when he felt Mateo come up behind him. When Mateo's arms wrapped around him. When Josiah automatically leaned into him.

"I'm sorry. I didn't mean it like that. You're the strongest person I know. It's just not you. Be glad this life isn't you, okay? Gimme some time. I'll figure somethin' out. I know it's not fair to you."

Josiah nodded. He believed in Mateo. If he said he'd figure it out, he would. "Thanks. I'm going to spend the day with Charlie."

Charlie worked at the secondhand store Josiah went to. He was even smaller than Josiah was, a little Asian guy who loved video games. The past few months, they'd become friends. He was the only real friend Josiah had. He was only a few years older than Josiah. His parents owned the store, but Charlie was the one who was always there. They sat around and played video games most of the day.

"Okay. It's almost four. I shouldn't be late tonight. You'll only be gone a few hours?" Mateo asked.

Frustrated, even though he knew he shouldn't be mad at Mateo, he said, "I don't know. They close at five, but Charlie said we can hang out after they lock up. I think we're going to get some coffee or something."

Mateo tensed, probably worried about him again. "Okay… How about I meet you there at about seven? We can walk home together."

"You can walk me home, you mean?"

Mateo groaned. "I have to get out of here. I don't have the time to fight right now, Jay. I'll be there around seven. Don't leave without me." Mateo stepped out, slamming the door behind him. The urge to run after him hit Josiah. He got it. He did. He was smaller and weaker than Mateo. He didn't know how to fight like Teo did. They lived in a bad neighborhood, and Teo had seen so much more than he had. But he needed this, too. Needed to start learning how to do things himself. Needed to be able to take care of himself so it didn't put so much stress on Mateo. So he could take care of Mateo as well as Mateo took care of him.

Ignoring the rock that landed in his stomach, Josiah left. He and Mateo hardly ever fought. He should go find him, call him and apologize, but he didn't. Even though that rock got heavier and heavier by the second, this was important. He needed Teo to take it seriously.

Josiah weaved his way through the crowded street until he got to Charlie's. He usually went once a week, looking for new things for their apartment. He saw Charlie there a lot.

They didn't become friends until after Charlie asked him out. No one had ever asked him on a date. He'd only ever been with Mateo, and it wasn't like they asked each other out on dates or anything. They'd lived together their whole relationship.

Josiah'd told Charlie he had a boyfriend, of course. MJ was what Teo told him to tell people his name was.

For weeks after Charlie asked Josiah out, Teo had gone with him every time he went to Charlie's. He smiled at the thought, at how strongly he knew Teo loved him. It just made that rock gain a few more pounds.

It didn't take him long to get to Charlie's. For a second he felt guilty going inside. It wasn't Charlie that necessarily made him come back…it was just knowing *someone*. Being friends with *someone*. He sat in the apartment every day while Teo was gone—but Teo would rather be with him. He knew that. He did what he did for them.

The door opened and Charlie stuck his head out. "Hey! You're late. I didn't think you were coming."

Shaking off his discomfort, Josiah went inside. Mateo said not to tell anyone where they lived so he always came here.

They played games for a while, Charlie going off to work every time someone came in. When it was time for the shop to close, they ran next door and grabbed some coffee before going back inside to hang out a while longer.

At about five till seven, Josiah told Charlie he had to go.

"Oh, wait. I wanted to give you this new game I bought. It's in my car in the back alley. Come check it out real quick." Charlie stood up.

"I can't. Ma—MJ is meeting me outside at seven. I don't want him to wonder where I am."

Charlie shrugged. "No problem. I have to count down the register and take care of a few things in here before I go. I'll let you out."

After unlocking the door, Charlie told him goodbye. Josiah pulled his hoodie up over his head, put on his gloves, and leaned against the building to wait for Teo. Light flakes of snow fell, the streets not as busy as usual as he huddled, trying to keep warm.

What felt like every other minute, Josiah looked at his watch, waiting for Mateo. At fifteen after seven, his heart sped up a little. If Mateo said he'd be there at seven, he always was. Josiah pulled the prepaid cell out of his pocket and called. Teo didn't answer. Palming the queen Teo gave him a year ago, he rubbed his thumb over the crown, wondering why he didn't answer. Teo always kept his phone with him.

By seven thirty, his heart raced, his foot tapping on the ground as though that would do anything. When his prepaid cell phone vibrated in his pocket, a relieved breath escaped his lungs.

"Hey," Teo said as soon as he picked up. "I'll be there in 'bout ten or fifteen. Some shit went down. Sorry I'm late."

And there went his heart, going all crazy again. "Are you okay?"

"Yeah…yeah, I'm good. Is Charlie still there? It's cold. See if you can go back inside. I'll be right there. And…sorry. 'Bout earlier, I mean."

Josiah shook his head. "No, don't be. It's just hard. I know it's not your fault. I want to help you, Teo. I want to get out of here."

When Mateo spoke again, his voice was low. "We will. I promise you. You won't be stuck in this city forever. Shit, I gotta go. See you in a few minutes." Then the line went dead.

Josiah rubbed his gloved hands together, trying to fight off the cold. He should go back inside like Mateo said, but he didn't get a chance because Charlie came out. "Oh. I didn't know you were still here. Wanna go get that game real quick?"

Josiah looked down the street. Teo was nowhere in sight. He said it would still be a few minutes until he showed up… "Yeah. Let's make it quick, though. My boyfriend will be here any minute."

"He won't let you walk home without him, or what? He seems a little possessive." They turned down the side alley on the far side of the store.

"He's not. Mat—*MJ* would do anything for me. Don't talk about him." The urge to turn and walk away pulled at him, but then he didn't want Charlie to think himself right. That Josiah had to run back up there to wait for Teo.

"Sorry. Didn't mean anything by it."

They made another turn after that, the alley behind the building completely deserted. There were two lights, one of them out, making it darker than it should be. A sound came from his right. Josiah flinched. A paper cup rolled by, making the tension in his body ease. *Chill out. If I ever want to be able to help Mateo, I need to learn to chill out.*

Charlie walked to the only car in the alley. Something made Josiah's feet stop moving, keeping close to the corner of the two alleys.

Josiah froze when a hand wrapped around his mouth from behind him. It only lasted a second before he tried to jerk away. To scream. To kick. Whatever he could to get free.

His bag dropped out of his hand. His eyes landed on Charlie, hoping for help. Frozen, he stared wide-eyed at them.

"You think anyone's gonna come if they hear you scream 'round here? Think again, white boy."

The guy shoved Josiah against the wall, and pain shot through him. Tears blurred his eyes. He didn't let it stop him from trying to get out of the guy's grasp.

That's when another dark figure stepped out from around the corner. "Get the fuck out of here," he yelled to Charlie.

"I'm sorry. I'm… sorry." Charlie's voice cracked, but then he jumped in the car and pulled away.

"Wait! Don't go!" Josiah's scream came out as a muffle from behind the hand that held him. "Help!" The guy holding him laughed.

"I love it when they fight. Keep going. All it does it get my dick hard." Josiah cried harder, fought more, his whole body shaking like crazy when an erection rubbed against his butt.

"No!" He managed to jerk one of his arms free and tried to elbow his captor, but the second guy grabbed him.

"That's it. Fight for us." His breath was hot on Josiah's cheek, the scent of cigarettes making him almost puke.

The first guy jerked Josiah toward him as the second slammed his fist into Josiah's stomach. He gasped, then accidentally bit down on his own tongue. The bitter taste of blood filled his mouth.

No no no. This couldn't happen.

Cloth was shoved into his mouth, keeping him from screaming. Pain hit him again as he was shoved against concrete stairs, bent over, weight heavy on his back.

"You're going to be fun. Keep fightin'. It'll only hurt more."

Josiah couldn't see past the tears in his eyes. Kept fighting as someone ripped his pants down. *No… Help… Teo, I'm sorry.* Mateo filled his thoughts. He should be able to fight back for Mateo. Be as strong as Mateo. This would kill him.

Through the echo of blood pulsing through his ears, he heard someone say, "Hold his hands."

Weight still on his back.

Someone kneeled beside him.

His legs shoved open.

Mateo… I love you…

Chapter Eighteen

Mateo

His whole fucking body went tight when he knocked on the locked door and no one opened it. All the lights were off inside. He walked around, looked inside the building but didn't see anyone. Mateo fought the burn of vomit in his stomach. Fought the rapid beating of his heart. None of that would help him find Josiah.

He took a few steps toward home, but then something made him turn around. Teo jogged to the other side of the building. Maybe he waited there. After Charlie left, he could have wanted to keep away from people. His blood went cold when he saw a bag on the ground toward the end of the alley.

Instincts took over.

He ran.

Pulled his knife out of his pocket. Took the corner. Red flashed in front of his eyes. His heart fucking gone as he ran toward Josiah. Josiah on his stomach, bent over some stairs. Josiah with his pants down. Josiah with a man on his back. Josiah with another guy holding him down.

The guy looked up. "Ah, fuck, Mateo." The guy scrambled to his feet but Mateo didn't give a shit about him. Didn't care about anyone but the guy on Josiah.

No thought. No reservations. He grabbed the guy by the hair, pulled his head back with his gloved hands, and slit his throat. Hot liquid slid down his arm, under his sweatshirt, and hit his bare skin. Still he sliced into Josiah's attacker's throat, more blood spraying into the air.

Mateo shoved the guy away. Shoved him off Josiah. *Dios, they'd hurt Josiah. I let them hurt Josiah.*

He turned for the other guy, the one *who'd said his fucking name*, but he was gone.

A strangled cry came out of Josiah as he pulled something out of his mouth. "Mateo...I'm sorry. I'm so sorry. I tried."

Mateo fell to the ground with him. His eyes went blurry at the guy's blood on the back of Josiah's shirt. "Shh. It's okay. I'm here. Don't apologize. Don't you fucking apologize, you hear me? This wasn't your fault."

His hands shook like crazy as he grabbed for Josiah. Tears streaked down his ghost-white face as he wrapped his arms around Mateo's neck. "I'm sorry, I'm sorry, I'm sorry."

Everything in him wanted to do nothing but hold Josiah. To take this shit from here. Bear all the pain for him. But whoever the fuck that was knew his goddamned name. They had to get out of here.

"Josiah." He grabbed his face so Jay looked at him. "Did he...?" He hadn't meant to ask that.

Josiah shook his head. "No. Almost. You got here in time."

No, he so fucking didn't. He should have been here a long ass time ago. Should have never let Josiah stay in this fucking city. "I need you to listen to me, Jay. We need to go. That guy said my name. We gotta fucking go." Mateo already struggled to pull Josiah's pants back up. When he couldn't, he stood and pulled Josiah up with him.

Once they stood, he got Josiah's pants up. "You did what I said, right? There's nothing in the apartment with our names on it?"

Josiah shook his head. "No…nothing."

"You have your money on you?"

"Yeah…"

"Okay, good." He went to the body on the ground. He shoved his hands in the guy's pocket and pulled out a wad of cash. No ID on him. "Stay right there. Don't step in the blood." Mateo shoved his arms under the guy's armpits and drug him toward the dumpster.

This would be a shit-ton easier if Josiah could help, but he'd never let him do something like this. Teo struggled, lifting the guy while trying not to get any blood on him. It took three tries before he got him in the dumpster and shut the lid.

He pulled his sweatshirt off, leaving himself in just a T-shirt. "I need your hoodie, Jay. There's blood on it." When Josiah didn't move, Mateo pushed it up and over Josiah's head. He wiped his hands on it, then ran over and grabbed Josiah's bag, shoving them both inside. Then he grabbed the cloth that had been shoved in Jay's mouth, ripped the gloves from his hands, and put them in the bag, too.

"We gotta go. Come on, *mi precioso*. Let's go." Josiah shook like crazy, his face red with tears. "Fuck, I am so sorry this happened, but I need you to try and pull it together. We gotta get out of here."

Josiah shook his head. "I'm trying…I'm trying. He wanted…" He shook his head again. "I don't know if I can do it, Teo."

Mateo closed his eyes and pulled Josiah to him. He fucked up so bad, letting him get hurt like this. It was too much. "Okay, we'll find a hotel for tonight, and then we'll decide where we want to go tomorrow. I'll figure it out somehow, and we'll get the fuck outta here, Jay. Somewhere safe."

Mateo slid his arm through Josiah's and started to walk. "Just try to act as normal as you can. I'll get us somewhere we can stay tonight."

His eyes didn't stop scanning their surroundings as they went. Teo tried to walk fast, hoping to put as much distance as he could between them and cops, or whoever else could come back.

"Come on, Jay. You can do this. We're almost there."

Mateo found a shitty hotel, half of the bulbs out on the letters, where he knew they wouldn't worry about credit cards or anything like that.

Five minutes later, they were in a room. He pulled Josiah over with him and checked the window to make sure it was locked before leading him to the bathroom. Everything inside Mateo called out for him to hold Josiah, to find a way to get him out of here tonight, but he knew Jay couldn't make it.

Kneeling in front of him, he cupped Josiah's face with his hands. "You did so good tonight, *mi precioso*. So fucking good. I'm so proud of you, but I need you to do something else. You're going to have to stay here for a few minutes. I won't be gone long, but I have to get rid of our clothes." His fingers shook as he untied Josiah's shoes.

"No!" Jay shook his head. "I want to go with you."

Mateo just pulled his shoe off before going to the other one. "You can't. You'll draw too much attention to us. I'll be gone forty-five minutes, tops. I got you. Don't worry. I'll be back. I promise."

Josiah shivered as Mateo finished undressing him. He shoved everything in the bag. "Take a shower while I'm gone, yeah? I'll be back by the time you get out."

He didn't wait for Josiah to reply before washing his hands and going out the door. It didn't take long for him to find some piece of shit clothing store, where he got them both pants, boxer-briefs, T-shirts, hoodies, gloves, shoes and beanies. He found an alley to change in before taking the bag down to where the homeless hung out and burning all their shit in a trash barrel.

He kept his face down the whole time, but knew that might not matter. His heart hadn't slowed down since he saw the lights out at Charlie's. He fought to keep his breathing steady, knowing if he lost it, Josiah would be right behind him.

When Teo got back to the room, Josiah sat on the bed, his hair wet and a blanket wrapped around him. He had his arms around his knees, his eyes wide and frantic until he realized it was Teo.

A scream fought to jerk out of him. The urge to kill anyone who stood in the path to keeping Josiah safe kept his heart beating and his blood flowing.

Mateo went straight to the bed, crawling in with Josiah and wrapping his arms around him. "I got you, *mi precioso.* No one will ever hurt you again. I promise." Self-hatred burned like acid through all his vital organs as Josiah shook in his arms.

"We're gonna get out of here, Jay. I'm going to get you somewhere safe. If we go far enough, and since it's been so long, I don't think anyone will be lookin' for me." Which was a lie. He'd said the opposite just this afternoon. "We'll find us a place and you can get your GED. I want that for you. Promise me you'll get it."

Shakily, Josiah whispered, "I promise."

The sound of his voice almost cracked the last of Teo's resolve, but he stayed strong for Josiah. "Once you get that, then you can go to school. You'll be real good at college, and you can work in your coffee shop till you graduate."

The shaking started to slow. "What about you?"

What the fuck was he good at? He couldn't even keep Josiah safe. "Don't know. What do you think? What should I do?"

Josiah paused for a second before speaking. "You can go to school with me. Or work at the coffee house with me. You can do whatever you want."

"Yeah…yeah, I like the sound of that." Mateo kept talking. Kept telling Josiah about the future he wanted more than anything but knew in his heart would never be. He told him everything they would do and what he wanted for Jay until he finally fell asleep.

When he did, Teo laid him down before quietly getting out of the bed. He got the bathroom door closed but hardly made it to the toilet before he violently purged everything out of him. His stomach cramped and his throat burned but it kept on coming.

Mateo's hand slapped down on the handle as he flushed the toilet. He crawled over to the sink and fumbled with the faucet to rinse his mouth out. And then he went down on the bathroom floor, curled into a ball.

And fucking cried. Rocking back and forth, he let the tears fall. For Josiah and all the ways he'd been hurt. For all the ways Mateo had fucked up with him. For his mom who got killed because she stayed with his gangbanging dad. All he wanted to do was love Josiah, to be with him and protect him. Was that too much to fucking ask? He cried until he didn't have any tears left.

He didn't flinch when he heard the bathroom door open. Curled into Josiah when he lay on the floor with him. They wrapped their arms around each other, Teo holding on with everything he had, to the only thing in his life that mattered.

They didn't get up till morning.

He didn't say much as he tossed the clothes at Jay and told him to get dressed. Teo took a shower and then got dressed again, too.

"Where are we going?" Josiah asked.

"William and Molly's."

"What? What if you get into trouble? What if Molly is…"

"William will still help you. It's the only thing we can do, Jay. You're going to go there and tell them you don't know where I am. That you haven't seen me for a while. They had your birth certificate, your social security card and all that shit."

Josiah shook his head. "I should have thought to take it when I ran."

"Be glad you didn't. You don't want that kind of shit to come natural to you. Anyway, this is the best opportunity we have. If they don't have that stuff anymore, they can help you get it. You tell them I forced you to come with me if you have to, okay? I'll be okay. I won't leave Yorktown without you, but that's the only way we have of findin' out what happened after we left, so we'll know if people are looking for us. It's the only way, for you to resurface without me. Make 'em think we're not together anymore. Then we'll get on a bus and go. Wherever you want."

He pulled the backpack on.

"Together?" Josiah grabbed Teo's arm. "We'll go together?"

That question and the need in his voice had the power to take some of the bad shit away. *Dios,* he fucking loved Josiah. "Yeah… Together." Because as broken as they both were, together they made something better.

Teo opened the door, and in that second everything changed. Fear cemented his insides as Javier smiled and stepped into the room.

Chapter Nineteen

Josiah

Everything had changed in the month since Javier showed up. They were now living in Brownsville, part of the borough Mateo told them they could never go to. Teo worked with Javier.

Josiah watched as Mateo came in the door and went straight into the bathroom. The water turned on, but it wasn't enough to cover the sounds as he vomited. Josiah paced the apartment that was slightly better than the first one they had, wringing his hands together as he waited for Mateo to come out.

When he did, he went straight to the kitchen and downed a whole glass of water, without a word to Josiah. Mateo washed his hands, even though he knew he'd done it in the bathroom, too, before he walked over and pulled Josiah to him.

"Hey." Mateo pushed a hand through Josiah's hair and pressed a kiss to his lips. "I missed you."

"Missed the kid, huh?" As soon as the words left Josiah's mouth, he wanted them back. He had no right to take any of this out on Mateo. Not after everything he did for Josiah. "I'm sorry."

Teo shook his head. "Don't be. I fucking hate it, too, but they can't know what's going on with us. I had to tell them somethin'."

Josiah had turned into a favor that Mateo owed someone, an obligation. He secretly feared really being an obligation to Mateo. He knew Mateo loved him, but having Josiah around made things more difficult. Teo had everything harder. He knew that, and he hated it.

"I know. I'm sorry." He laid his head on Teo's shoulder. "Why can't we run? Just get a bus ticket and go?"

Mateo sighed. "We *will*, but I have to be smart about it. Javier's watchin' me. I gave him a bullshit excuse for not comin' back, but who knows if he believes me. He's testing me, Jay. And…" he shrugged. "Now I owe him. He took care of the body for me."

A rival gang, Javier had told Mateo. Enemies of his dad who had somehow found out Mateo was in the city. Word traveled, which was how Javier heard Teo was back, too, but he hadn't made it to Mateo in time.

"I hate being here. Hate having you here. But he's protection, and I'm makin' money, both of which we need right now."

Josiah pulled back. "If you don't kill yourself from puking up your insides every day or end up in prison. I don't want you to do this for me. I don't care about the other guy who attacked me."

Mateo groaned, frustration obvious in the way his jaw tightened. He grabbed Josiah's hand, ran his thumb over the nails that Josiah chewed so much they bled.

"You gotta stop doin' that. No one's gonna hurt me, and I'm not going to prison. Not when I have you here waiting for me."

The tension didn't leave the room as Josiah wrapped his arms around Mateo. It was there all the time now. They were both always on edge, always fighting.

"You up for another lesson?" Mateo asked him. He was determined that Josiah learn to fight now. He'd bought him a knife, and taught him how to shoot a gun. Josiah hated guns. Wanted nothing to do with them, but he did it for Mateo; and because he didn't want to be helpless again. For Mateo to always have to come to his rescue.

"No." He shook his head. Heat zipped through him. He needed to find that piece of them they'd lost recently. "I want to be with you. I just want you, Teo."

They hadn't had sex at all since he was attacked. Mateo refused to, and automatically shook his head now. "No. It's too soon."

This time Josiah wouldn't take no for an answer. He pulled Mateo toward the bedroom. "Please, Teo. I need to feel close to you. Need you to take the bad memories away."

With that, he didn't have to pull anymore. Mateo just went with him. They lay on the bed and took off each other's clothes. He kissed Josiah so perfect. Tasted his skin everywhere. When Josiah tried to reach for him, Mateo shook him off. He grabbed Josiah's erection, taking it deeply into his mouth.

"Teo…" he whispered.

Mateo went from there to his balls, licking and sucking on those, too, before spreading Josiah's legs wide.

"I love having my mouth on you. Love it so fucking much."

Chills raced through him when Mateo's tongue traced his hole, only to quickly be replaced by heat.

"More."

Mateo gave him more, lashing his tongue over the most intimate part of Josiah's body.

"I want you inside me."

"Yes…" He moaned when a finger pushed into him before Teo's mouth covered his erection again. His finger pumped in and out as he sucked Josiah.

"More. I want you inside me, Teo."

"I want that, too, Jay. Would live inside you if I could."

He grabbed a condom, ripping it open and rolling it down his shaft.

"I don't have any lube, Jay. Fuck, I didn't even think of that."

Josiah pulled him down so their lips met again. He took the kiss deep, his body moving against Josiah's, sending shockwaves of pleasure though him.

"Fuck, I gotta be inside you." He spit on his hand, rubbing it on his erection, and then did the same thing to Josiah's entrance.

When he pushed inside, everything felt okay again. They'd make it out of this. They had to.

Their bodies found a familiar rhythm together. Josiah stroked his own cock as Mateo pumped in and out of him.

The orgasm slammed into him, semen pooling on his belly. Mateo groaned above him, going rigid as he came, too.

With little rests in between, they made love twice before crawling under the blankets, his body tucked against Mateo's.

"We're gonna get out of here. You're right. We should just go."

Josiah looked up at him, his heart running wild. "Really?"

"Yeah. Lemme figure some shit out tomorrow. You get everything packed. We'll go tomorrow night."

Josiah's mouth came down hard on his. Finally they were going to get out of NYC. "I love you, Mateo."

"Te amo."

Chapter Twenty

Mateo

"Sit down, *hermano*. Have a drink with me. You're always in such a fucking hurry to get out of here. I'm beginning to think you don't like me." Javier laughed, making Mateo's skin crawl. Brothers. Yeah, right. They weren't anything close to that. But he also couldn't disrespect Javier, especially in his own home.

"I need to get back and check on the kid." The name tasted like bile on his tongue.

"The kid, huh?" Javier shook his head.

Josiah. His name is Josiah. I love him and I'm getting him the fuck out of here. "That's what I said, yeah." Teo crossed his arms. He glanced at Javier, his black hair slicked back, and watched as his eyes narrowed.

"Sit the fuck down, Mateo."

Icicles froze inside him, but he had no choice but to sit down. This time when Javier spoke, every word was in Spanish. "You must think I'm a fucking idiot."

Mateo struggled to steel his emotions. Not to wipe the sweat from his forehead. "Whatever you have to say, spit it out," he replied in

Spanish.

"You think I don't know what that little white boy is to you? You're a disgrace. A disgrace to your father and to all of us."

Mateo pushed to his feet. But sat back down when Javier set a gun on the table in front of himself. "We came for you because you're Ricky Sanchez's son, my nephew. We protect you out of loyalty to your father, even though you deserve nothing more than a bullet in your head."

Teo squeezed the arms of the chair. Javier was going to fucking kill him. Who would take care of Josiah?

"You abandoned your family, yet I saved your ass when I heard you were in town. You're a dick to everyone here, running back to your fucking *boy* like you're better than the rest of us, yet I put up with it, for your father. That won't last, Mateo. You need to decide where your loyalty lies, and do it now. You're either with us, or you're the enemy. You're dead." He ran his hand over the barrel of the gun. "I wonder what would happen to your boy then."

Mateo shoved to his feet so hard that the chair fell over backward, hitting the ground. "No one fucking touches him. No one looks at him wrong. I don't give a fuck who it is. They do and they're dead."

Javier's black eyes looked at him and then he smiled. "Protective. You know I don't want to hurt him, Teo. I don't even want to hurt you. You're more than my nephew. You're like a son to me. A brother. I'm your godfather. Ricky wanted you to be my second. It's time you wake the fuck up and be the man your father raised you to be."

Teo's jaw hurt he held it so tight. He was too fucking late. He'd fucked up again. Why the hell didn't he leave with Josiah that first night?

Or any night over the past month? Or hell, never stayed here in the first place?

"You know you're never really alone, don't you? I have eyes on you all the time. If you're thinking of running, you won't get far. Won't even see the bullet coming."

Those words were the nail in the coffin. He couldn't risk Josiah like that. It was over. "What do you want?"

"What your father wanted. What he *wants*. You, here where you belong."

He threw his hands in the air. "Where the fuck does it look like I am?"

Javier grabbed the gun and aimed it at Mateo. "This is the last time I tell you to watch your mouth." He was quiet for a minute, his eyes never leaving Mateo. "I remember when your mother died. It killed your father. Killed you. I told Ricky, to love her was a liability. In our world, he was asking for her to get hurt. She was his weakness, and she died because of it."

Mateo's stomach bottomed out. As much as he hated it, Javier was right. His dad's lifestyle got his mom killed, just like he would do to Josiah. Staying with him, *being* with him, was like hanging a target on his back. Even from Javier. That's what he was telling Teo right now. Even if Josiah stayed, they were at risk.

He bit back the urge to puke. "I'll take care of it. I need 10 G's for him."

"What do I get in return?" Javier smiled.

Mateo hung a noose around his neck with his words. "I'll owe you."

Javier nodded, opened the drawer next to him and pulled out a stack of cash. He tossed it to the table. Teo picked it up and shoved it in his pocket. "Don't fuck up. We'll be watching."

Mateo shook his head. He wouldn't. Not this time.

He puked two times on the way to his apartment. Outside the door, he opened and closed his hands, trying to get them not to shake. Ignored the rapid beat of his heart that wanted nothing more than Josiah.

He pushed the door open. Josiah smiled at him with his big ass, happy smile. Ready to leave with Mateo. Expecting Mateo to keep his word to him, even though he never had.

"You packed?"

"Yeah, I got your stuff together, too. Everything's okay? We're really going?"

A knife dug into his gut, twisting and turning. "You are." He walked past Josiah and grabbed his two bags.

"What do you mean? We're going together, Teo. You said." He grabbed Mateo's arm but Teo shook him off.

"I changed my mind." *Lo siento. I'm sorry...*

"Teo?"

Mateo made the mistake of looking at him, Jay's green eyes, round and scared. The knife shoved in deeper. Another one went into his chest. "I can't do this anymore. I tried but I can't fucking do it. It's... it's too hard to take care of you all the time. I have my own shit to deal with."

Holy shit, this was killing him. Each word he spoke stabbed another knife into him, but he knew he had to do it. Knew if he didn't make Josiah think he didn't want him anymore that he wouldn't go. That he wouldn't move on.

"Here." Mateo pushed the money into his hand. "I got this for you. You should be able to figure out how to get yourself somewhere." He closed his eyes, trying to hold in the warmth of Josiah's skin. To engrave it into him so he'd never forget it.

Josiah shook his head. Tears pooled in his desperate eyes. "I love you, Teo, and I know you love me. Why are you doing this? Did he make you? Did he say he'd hurt me? I don't care. I'll risk it. We'll run together. Right now. *Let's go.*"

He wanted that. Wanted it so fucking much he could hardly breathe. "It's this! This right here that I can't fucking stand anymore. I have to do everything for you. I don't want to do that shit anymore, kid. I don't want you." Out of everything he'd ever done, this felt the worst—these lies were the worst.

Josiah gasped. His bag fell out of his hand.

Teo walked over and opened the door. "Look at all the shit I've had to deal with since I met you—taking care of you at school, the fight at the mall, everything that's gone down here. I'm tired of it. It's too much of a fucking obligation."

"Teo...I..." Josiah couldn't get his words out past his tears.

"Get the fuck outta here!" Mateo yelled. "There's a cab for you outside. See if you can take some of that shit I taught you and take care of yourself." *The knife should be in his pocket. I told him to always keep it on him.*

Josiah still didn't move.

"You won't fucking go? Then I will. Be gone when I get back, kid."

He took a step out the door and paused. "All that shit you were supposed to do? Do it now. Go to school and get your coffee shop. You don't belong here. You don't belong with me."

With one last look at the man he loved, Mateo walked away.

He never could have deserved Josiah anyway. All they'd been doing the past year and a half was pretending. He belonged here, and Jay belonged out there. With each step Mateo transformed into the man he was always supposed to be. Josiah's Mateo disappeared. He became his dad, and Javier. The real Mateo Sanchez.

Goodbye, mi precioso. Te amo.

PART TWO: Josiah and Tristan
San Francisco, CA

Chapter One

Two years after Mateo

Josiah

Josiah stood in his small apartment, staring down at the wobbling piece of paper in his hand. No matter how hard he tried to steady the limb, it wouldn't quit trembling.

Words jumped out at him from the shaking paper.

Josiah Evans.

General.

Education.

Diploma.

 He'd promised Mateo he'd get it one day, and he did. Stupidly, he somehow thought that would bring Teo back to him. That he'd magically know and find him. Tell him he still wanted Josiah. That it had been a lie. That he really did love him. That someone loved him.

But it had been two years since Mateo sent him away. Two years that he'd been alone.

If Mateo wanted me, he'd be here.

He'd made sure Teo could always find him. He couldn't afford to live in Fisherman's Warf, but he worked at a coffee shop there. Traveled to the other side of the city daily to be there. He walked by the water every morning and fed the birds, just like he told Teo he would.

He hadn't come. He wouldn't come. He didn't want Josiah.

After all this time, a strangled cry still surged up his windpipe. Fat drops fell from his eyes, hitting the paper, that ache that hadn't left his chest in two years still there.

Josiah's hair fell in his face, making anger pump through him. That stupid, blond hair that Mateo had loved so much.

Dropping the paper to the floor, he went into the bathroom. Ripped open the cabinet and jerked out an electric razor.

His hand still shook as he plugged it in. Turned it on. Ran it over his head. Watched as the blond strands fell into the sink.

Josiah looked at his red eyes in the mirror. Watched the tick in his jaw. Saw his shaved head, the hair Mateo loved, gone.

It didn't take that ache away. Didn't remove the need. The loneliness. Worry. Fear. Regret.

Love.

Mateo sent him away, but Josiah still couldn't cut him from his heart.

Just like always, he wasn't as strong as he wanted to be.

Chapter Two

Three years after Mateo

Josiah

"Do you go to school or anything? I'm studying psychology." Elliot, Josiah thought his name was, smiled at him. He was new to Fisherman's Roast Coffee House, and today was Josiah's day to train him. Elliot pushed his dark hair out of his face, making Josiah miss his own. It was stupid to keep his head shaved. Stupid to think something like that would hurt Mateo, who would never know about it, but Josiah had to do something. He couldn't think of anything else.

"Hello? College? I didn't mean to make you feel bad. It's not like I think everyone our age has to go to school or something. What are you? Twenty? Twenty-one?"

Josiah studied him, squinted his eyes a little trying to figure him out. Warning bells played through his head. Charlie had been nice like this. Charlie had run away while two guys tried to rape him.

He turned, running a rag over the table to wipe it clean.

"Oh-kay," Elliot mumbled.

"Don't take it personally. Josiah hardly talks to anyone. Always keeps to himself." Larson pretended Josiah wasn't even there while he spoke and Josiah let him. "Anyway, I'm out of here. He'll help when it comes to work. All he cares about is this coffee house." And then Larson was gone, leaving Josiah alone with Elliot.

"Wow. He's kind of a dick. So anyway, school?" he asked again. "You look about my age."

Didn't he get it? Josiah couldn't just *be* friends with someone. Not after everything he lost. That's all he did was lose. His parents, William and Molly…Mateo. When he'd gone back to William after Mateo sent him away, William had done the same. He'd said it hurt too much after losing Molly.

Josiah ignored the question.

The only time he talked during their six hour shift was to explain something to Elliot or talk to a customer. When it was time to leave, Elliot looked at him and said, "Thanks. I learned more with you today than I did with Larson yesterday." And then he smiled.

Nice… He seemed really nice. Words bubbled up in his throat and Josiah opened his mouth to let them out. "Thanks. And I'm twenty-one. No, I don't go to college."

That was as much as he could give.

Chapter Three

Five and a half years after Mateo

"I'm thinking about staying in tonight." Josiah swapped the phone from one hand to the other. He kicked his feet up on the antique coffee table he found at a garage sale.

"No, you said you were going to hang out, and you're going to hang out. I just got my bachelor's degree. If that's not a good reason for you to hang out with a friend, I don't know what is." Elliot let out a heavy breath.

A few months after Elliot started working at Fisherman's Roast, Josiah realized he was one of the most determined people he knew. Why the guy wanted to be friends with him so bad, Josiah didn't know. But he hadn't given up, kept pushing and talking to Josiah until words just started tumbling out of Josiah's mouth, too. Until he started asking Elliot questions first and listening to him talk about girls, his family, or whatever else.

Sometimes they'd have lunch together, or Elliot would go to thrift stores with him, and once they even went on a tour of Alcatraz. Growing up here, Elliot had been before, but he didn't mind going again with Josiah.

It took a while, but he finally realized Elliot wasn't Charlie. Josiah actually trusted him, and didn't believe Elliot would ever betray him. In fact, he seemed to really like having Josiah around.

"You're going back for your Master's next year."

"So? That doesn't mean I can't celebrate now. Come on, Jay."

Frost bit at Josiah's insides. "Can you not call me that?"

Elliot sighed. "Another one of those things that you won't tell me about, have probably never told anyone about, that will eventually eat you alive, huh?"

Josiah couldn't help but crack a grin. "Shut up."

"Come on, Josiah. It's not a big party or anything. Just a few friends. You never know, you might even *like* some of them. I know I'm a great guy, but you might find you actually enjoy having friends other than me."

This time Josiah let out a real laugh. A voice in his head told him Elliot was right. He needed to do this. "Yeah…okay. Sure. I'll be there soon."

The bus showed up a little late, so it took Josiah longer to get to

Elliot's than he planned. His stomach rolled with nerves but he made himself ignore them. It would be a night out with a friend, and nothing more.

About two seconds after he knocked, Elliot jerked the door open. "I thought you changed your mind."

"Nah. The bus was late." Josiah shook his head, slowly stepping inside the apartment. His eyes traveled the room, wanting to get a good look at everyone who was there. It was something Mateo would have done. *Always pay attention*. He tried to do that all the time now.

There were twelve people here not counting Josiah and Elliot. Elliot walked him around the room, introducing him to everyone there. He stood in the corner while everyone talked and laughed. Music played in the background. He wasn't sure of the song, but still Josiah focused on the beat, needed the steady sound to keep him distracted.

This wasn't him. He didn't feel right around all these people his age, joking around and drinking because they just graduated college.

What would it have been like to have one of their lives? To have grown up with friends, and his own parents? To have gone to school?

"Josiah, I want you to meet my brother, Dylan. Dylan, this is Josiah." Elliot smiled at him and winked. Josiah immediately felt his cheeks warm.

"Hey, nice to finally meet you. Elliot's told me a lot about you." Dylan grinned at him. Dylan, with big, blue eyes. Dylan, with a happy smile. Dylan, who Josiah knew was also gay.

"Yeah…you, too."

"Oh, I have to go talk to Lacey real quick. I'll be right back." Elliot disappeared before Josiah could say a word.

Dylan laughed. "My little brother's real smooth. No one would ever guess he's trying to play matchmaker. You work with him at the coffee house, right?" Dylan moved closer to the wall so he stood next to Josiah. When he did, his arm brushed against him.

"Yeah…" Why would Elliot do this to him? He knew Josiah didn't want to meet anyone. His heart began to drum.

"What do you like to do? For fun?" Dylan asked.

Then all he saw were dark brown eyes. Smooth, brown skin. Felt a hand on his head, though it wasn't right because he didn't have hair anymore.

And because Mateo wasn't really there. "I have to go."

Josiah took a step, but then Dylan's hand landed on his shoulder. He flinched, and almost ran, before focusing on the room and realizing he wasn't in that alley.

"Did I do something wrong?"

Josiah shook his head. "No. I just… I have to go."

Dylan's hand fell as Josiah walked away. His heart didn't slow down until he was locked in his apartment. He didn't want to meet anyone. Ever. Not when he'd only lose them.

His heart would always belong to Teo, anyway.

Chapter Four

Tristan

"I'm going to have to call you back." Tristan Croft didn't bother with hello. The voice on the other end of the line laughed.

"What are you even doing up this early? I expected to leave a message," Ben said. "Never mind. This is Tristan I'm talking to. I don't know what I was thinking. If I remember correctly, you never sleep. Moving out West didn't help your workaholic tendencies, did it?"

"I have to go." Despite the sun having just risen a few minutes ago, Tristan had been awake for hours. Ben was right about that.

"I don't suppose you'd tell me why? You know, now that we're not fucking, live on opposite sides of the US, and are supposed to be friends? It might be easier to talk to a friend rather than a boyfriend. You can let some of whatever you're always holding in off your chest."

Tristan pulled his BMW into a parking spot and killed the engine. After giving Ben a humorless laugh, he said, "Now come on, Ben. You know we were never boyfriends."

"Bastard." Ben laughed.

"You got that right." Tristan hung up the phone, knowing he'd been an asshole to who was probably his only real friend. The only person who didn't want something from him. He knew a lot of people, but he didn't call any of them friends.

He slammed the car door harder than he needed to before slipping his phone into his suit pocket.

"Mr. Croft." The doorman nodded as Tristan walked into the building. He returned the nod before taking the elevator to the eleventh floor. Using his key, he unlocked the door before stepping into the immaculately clean apartment. On the far side of the room, in front of the window, he saw her sitting in a chair and staring out.

He bit back the anger that surged to the surface.

"I woke up to go to the restroom and she was just sitting there, staring out the window," Isabel whispered, stepping up beside him. "I asked her if she needed anything but she only shook her head. That's the only response I've gotten out of her. I've offered her food, drink, if she wanted to go back to bed, or if she wanted me to call you. Nothing. She didn't have the blanket when I woke up, but it's cold, so I wrapped it around her. Still nothing."

Tristan bit the inside of his cheek. Shoved his fisted hands into his pockets. "Thank you, Isabel. I'll take care of it from here." Without another word, she went to her room and closed the door.

Tristan walked over and stood next to her. "What are you looking at, Mom?"

Silence greeted him. Tristan forced himself to continue talking. "Did you sleep at all last night?"

Nothing.

From standing over her, Tristan could see her eyes wide, lost in he had no idea what. The busy streets of San Francisco were below, but she didn't seem to be focused on them.

"Isabel called me. She's worried. She's great, don't you think? She takes incredible care of you."

His mom loved Isabel. She wasn't the first caregiver he'd hired to live with his mother, but by far the best. When his mom felt well, she always tried to marry them off. Said she loved Isabel like the daughter she never had and knew she could make Tristan happy.

He never told her that no one could do that for him. He accepted that, and was okay with it. He had his career, and she was taken care of. That's all that mattered to him.

When she didn't reply about Isabel, worry burned deeper through him. She hadn't had an episode like this in so long.

"Mom." He set his hand on her shoulder. "I need you to speak to me. Do you hear me? I need you to pull out of it. Come back." Lightly, he squeezed her shoulder. The anger fought to take control again. *Damn it. God-fucking-damn it. Hadn't she been through enough?*

"Tristan?" She turned and looked at his hand. "I'm sorry. I didn't hear you come in."

He allowed himself to breathe again. "I'm here. What were you doing?"

It took her at least a minute to reply. "I'm…I'm not sure. I couldn't sleep. My mind wouldn't stop going, so I came out here. I guess I fell asleep or something."

Or something. He hated it when she got lost in her head like that, felt out of control. Neither of them had much control over their world when he was younger. He damn sure did everything he could to make sure they had it now.

"That's okay. Are you taking your medication?"

"Yes. You know Isabel gives it to me every day." She looked up at him with dark eyes like his. Dark brown hair like his.

"Did something happen? Did I do something?" Her voice rose, panic making it shake.

"No." Tristan shook his head. "You're fine."

She grabbed his hand and kissed it. "You're such a good boy. Isabel…she's good too. She—"

"Isn't a man." It wasn't the first time he'd said it. "And a relationship is the last thing I want." Ever.

"Well that's just silly. Everyone wants to be loved, Tristan, and if it's a man that will make you happy, then find one. I don't care who makes you happy, as long as you are."

Everyone wanted to be loved? Not him. That need in her had caused her nothing but pain.

"I'm happy."

She smiled. When she did, it was easy to forget she was clinically depressed. That she lost herself sometimes. "And I'm hungry. They have the most incredible berry scones at the Warf. Fisherman's Roast. Isabel gets them for us often. Do you have time to go for me? We can have a scone and chat."

The muscles in his legs suddenly wanted to move. Twitched and pulsed. Jesus, he was a horrible son, because he wanted nothing more than to get out of here, so they wouldn't have to talk.

"I don't know," Tristan said.

"It's early."

"True. Let me go grab the scones. I'll see what time it is when I get back."

After calling Isabel out of her room, Tristan left. His mom lived close to the Warf, so instead of getting in his car, he walked down the block to Fisherman's Roast. As he crossed the street, his eyes caught a man down by the water, tossing something into the air that the birds swooped in and caught.

Over and over he threw food for them, which they attacked with frenzy. If he turned to the right, it would lead him straight to the coffee house, but Tristan moved toward the water instead. It was an asshole thing to do—to stall so that he wouldn't have time to talk to his own mom, but he did it anyway. Curious why someone would be out here at six in the morning feeding birds.

Tristan didn't approach him, instead sitting on a bench, twenty or thirty feet behind the man. From the back he looked young, shaved head (he'd never get why men did that), a good four inches shorter than Tristan's six feet, two inches. He wore old-looking blue jeans and a sweatshirt, without the hood pulled up. Every couple tosses or so, he'd bend, grabbing food from the bag at his feet and throwing it for the birds again.

And then he stopped, his shoulders slumped as he looked out at the ocean. Sadness radiated off him, riding the wind, twisting and turning around Tristan.

The boy shook his head. Bent it forward and then lifted the hood up and onto his head. For a good five minutes, he just stood there. And Tristan sat. Sat and watched, though he didn't know why. He looked the way Tristan felt, the way he wanted to be. Alone.

When the guy turned around, he flinched as though Tristan had scared him. Not that he didn't get it. He probably looked strange, sitting here watching him. Still, he didn't turn away.

"Sorry...I didn't know anyone was here."

He started to walk away when Tristan spoke. "That's an odd thing to be sorry for. You shouldn't take responsibility for things you have no control over. Why is it your fault? You didn't know I was here. I'm the one who came up behind you. I'm the one who sat down. None of which you are to blame for."

He narrowed his eyes a little, as though he couldn't figure Tristan out. Most people couldn't.

"I didn't...that's not..."

"People who aren't responsible always try to take responsibility, yet those who are never do. I don't understand that. Don't apologize for things you shouldn't. Let other people own their own mistakes. If you're like most of us, I'm sure you have enough of your own."

Tristan shrugged, not moving from the bench. He wasn't quite sure why he'd just said what he did, but he wouldn't take it back, either. His business or not, it was true. It made it much easier for people to take advantage of you.

Without replying, the man standing in front of him let his eyes travel the length of Tristan. Interest. There was definitely interest there. Confusion, too. Straight boy attracted to a man for the first time? No, he didn't think so.

He read people well. Always had, and it definitely came in handy as an attorney.

"You're eating me alive with your eyes, much like those birds devoured your food."

His eyes widened in shock as red flooded his cheeks. The boy was pretty. Young, but pretty.

"I'm not. I didn't mean…I don't."

Tristan smiled. This he was good at—playing this game. He'd done it enough. Even when he was fucking Ben, they hadn't been exclusive. Sex he could do very well. It was the other things he wanted nothing to do with.

"It's okay. There's nothing wrong with it. How old are you?"

He looked at the ground. "Twenty-three."

Thank God. He'd thought younger. That was good, at least. An eight year age difference wasn't bad. Maybe coming down here hadn't been a bad idea. He could use a distraction.

"What would you say if I asked you to meet me tonight?" Tristan stood, slowly walking toward the other man. He took a step backward when Tristan moved forward. Tristan stopped, and when he did, something fell from the man's hand.

Guilt slammed into Tristan from all different directions. His first thought was the guy wasn't interested, but his wide-eyed expression said differently. Damn it. Maybe he was in the closet? But it looked like more than that, too. He had this innocent expression on his face, as though he wasn't sure what to make of Tristan. "Fuck. Let's forget I said that. I didn't mean to scare you."

Tristan bent to pick up what he dropped. As he did, the other guy spoke louder than Tristan had heard him speak yet. "I need that back." He held out his hand and stood tall, eying Tristan as though he wanted to steal what looked like a homemade chess piece. It was the most secure Tristan had seen him since they started speaking. He had the feeling the younger man would attack before he'd let Tristan leave with the chess piece.

Tristan held out his hand, watching as he snatched it back and then turned, walking briskly toward the businesses with his head down and the wooden piece enclosed in a tight fist.

Shaking his head, Tristan went back to the bench and sat down.

Chapter Five

Josiah

Josiah went straight to Fisherman's Roast, shoved his way behind the counter and to the employee bathroom. He jerked his work shirt out of his bag, ripping it over his head before turning on the water and splashing his face.

Putting his hands flat on the sink, he leaned forward, trying to catch his breath. Trying to figure out why he was so angry.

"Josiah? You okay in there?" Elliot knocked on the door. He still filled in for them when they were shorthanded, but who knew how long that would last.

"No," he snapped. Gripping the doorknob tightly, he ripped the door open. Heat flooded his body, and he still hadn't stopped squeezing the doorknob.

"What happened?"

It was on the tip of his tongue to tell Elliot nothing, the way he always did. He didn't think he would ever be able to talk to anyone about his past. But then, he wanted to as well. Wanted to share something—*this*—with someone. "Some guy just asked me out," he blurted, fumbling for his words. "Or maybe *not* out. I think… I think he was asking me to have sex with him tonight."

Elliot sighed. "Don't take this the wrong way, bro, but aren't you gay? I mean, you said you were, but the way you ran from my brother last weekend… And if you are gay, that makes this kind of a good thing, right? I know if some chick asked me to have sex with her it would be."

Josiah shook his head, closed the lid to the toilet, and plopped down. How could he expect Elliot to understand something like this?

"Um… this is weird, but let's just… I'm sure you don't want everyone to hear our conversation, so I'm just going to come in and close the door."

A foreign kind of smile appeared on Josiah's face for some reason. He really was lucky he'd met Elliot.

"So, what? They guy was ugly or something?"

Josiah thought back to the suit that had hugged each and every muscle on his body. The strong jawline with dark stubble. His short, black hair. Dark eyes. He was… sophisticated, and as far from ugly as Josiah could imagine. "No…" He looked at the ground. "Definitely not ugly."

"So what gives?"

He wasn't Mateo.

Besides the dark hair and eyes, he was opposite Mateo in every way. He'd never imagined being with someone other than Teo. And what would a guy like that see in Josiah, anyway?

"I have an ex-boyfriend." What could he say other than that? It wasn't like he could give Elliot the whole story.

"Again, what's the problem? I have ex-girlfriends, too. Unless, you're still in love with him? If you ask me, that's even more reason to get laid." Elliot laughed.

Josiah's elbows rested on his knees and he buried his face in his hands. *I've never been with anyone but him. I don't want to be with anyone other than him.*

He doesn't want me. He sent me away...

"I haven't...you know..."

"Oh...*oh*... Like, ever? I mean, not that it's my business, but you're twenty-three. Maybe it's time to remedy that."

"I did with Mateo." He'd said his name to someone. That was the first time Josiah had said his name to anyone in over five years.

Elliot bent down. "I'm not going to pretend this isn't kind of weird. I have no idea what to say here. It's obvious... Well, I don't mean to sound like an asshole when I say this, but it's obvious you've been through a lot. You're dealing with a lot. But whatever you're doing right now isn't working. My dad taught me that—if something's not working, you fix it. You change it. Hell, I don't know if you should go out with this guy or not, but it wouldn't hurt. You might have some fun.

"Your ex... It seems like you're waiting on him, and it doesn't look like he's coming back. Sounds to me like you need to move on. Even if it's not with this guy, or Dylan, at least with your life. Stop running. We've been friends for a while now, and this is the first time I've even heard about your ex."

"No." Josiah shook his head. He didn't know how to move on from Mateo.

"Elliot!" Larson yelled. "I need your help out here!"

"I better go." Elliot stood, nudged Josiah and grinned. "Maybe we should come out of the bathroom one at a time so people don't realize we were in here together." He smiled again showing Josiah he wanted to lighten the mood. "And I'm here. If you ever want to talk or anything, okay?" Then he walked out. Josiah didn't move, Elliot's words playing over and over in his head.

Mateo wasn't coming back.

Not.

Coming.

Back.

It had been over five years. With the lifestyle Teo lived, he might not even be alive. Josiah slammed the door on those thoughts. He wouldn't believe that.

Anger like he felt that first time he'd shaved his head rumbled through him again, but it wasn't at Mateo... It was at himself. All he wanted was a life—a real life—yet he wasn't letting himself have it. All he did was run. And he was alone. He always would be if he kept doing what he did now.

Mateo was strong. Josiah had always wanted to be like him. Didn't want to need someone taking care of him, yet that's exactly how he lived his life. That guy offered for him to not feel alone, even if it was only for one night. And he wanted that. Wanted it so bad he could taste it.

He didn't want to be the kind of guy who always apologized for things that weren't his fault.

Josiah grabbed his bag and rushed out of the bathroom, the same way he'd rushed in. He heard Larson ask him where he was going when he headed for the door. Josiah ignored him. Sure the guy probably wasn't out there still, but he intended to try. To show himself he could move on. It was time. He didn't need Mateo.

As soon as the door closed, he looked up. In front of him was the guy in the black suit, carrying a folded-down Fisherman's Roast bag.

Josiah's heart went crazy. "Hey. Umm... Hey."

The guy turned around, but didn't smile. *Please smile. I need you to smile.*

"My name... It's Josiah... What's yours?"

The guy looked at his watch, sighed, and walked closer to Josiah. "Tristan. Listen, I have to go. I need to get this scone to someone, and then I'm heading to work. Did you need something?"

Josiah's stomach twisted, turned. Ached. "What you said... Or what you asked. I want to. Meet you. Tonight."

Tristan closed his eyes briefly and shook his head. "That was a mistake. I shouldn't have asked you."

All the courage he'd built up evaporated into nothing. "Oh. I'm sorry."

He turned to walk away but Tristan grabbed his arm. "You're sorry I spoke too soon? That I asked you an inappropriate question? That you're just replying to my question? Which of *my* actions are you sorry for?"

Two minutes ago he'd acknowledged he didn't want to do this, and he already had again. "None. I take it back. I'm not sorry." He crossed his arms and stood up straight.

Tristan cocked his head a little, studying him. "Why do you feed the birds?" His forehead wrinkled as though the question surprised him as much as it did Josiah.

Because it was part of our dream… Because I told Teo we would… But then, that wasn't all of it, was it? It had been his idea to feed them in the first place. There had to be a reason he said it to begin with.

"They might be hungry. Or even if they're not, maybe it's a gift, a treat. I kind of think we all deserve that. Someone to do something special for us." Josiah took a deep breath. "And I don't think it was a mistake. To ask me, I mean. I want to meet you tonight."

Tristan's hand came up and cupped Josiah's cheek. He brushed his thumb over the bone there, and Josiah let himself lean into it. Lean into the touch and feel close to someone.

"Jesus, that blush is sexy. As much as I would enjoy taking you home with me, it's not going to happen. It was a mistake, because I'm the wrong kind of man for someone like you. I was looking for a fuck.

That's all."

Josiah squared his shoulders, even though he felt like melting into the concrete. "That's all I want, too."

"I'm an asshole, but not that big an asshole. You don't belong in my bed, Josiah." Tristan dropped his hand and walked away. He stopped again, about ten feet away. Josiah realized then he held his breath. "Do you do that every day? Feed the birds?"

Josiah nodded.

Without another word, he disappeared into the crowd.

Chapter Six

Tristan

Tristan gave up on sleep hours before. He'd always suffered from insomnia, and taught himself to function on about four hours of sleep per night. When he was young, he taught himself to be a light sleeper. It was the least he could do for his mother—keep an ear out in case she needed him. Not get hours of sleep when she spent ninety percent of her time trying to support them.

The actual insomnia didn't start until college. His Masters in Law, plus the time he spent studying and learning stocks, fueled him better than sleep ever could. Burned a fire beneath his feet that kept him from ever slowing down. Not to mention *how* he learned so much about stocks. Or the way he earned money back then, not only to invest, but to take care of his mom. Thoughts about that time in his life made him squeeze the pencil in his hand, breaking it.

If there was one thing Tristan would always be able to do, it would be to financially support himself.

Around five a.m. his cell rang. With a steady hand, he reached out and picked it up from the desk in his home office.

Ben, again. Much better than it being Isabel, though.

"Why are you calling me so early again?" he said in place of hello.

"I'm in New York. It's not early for me."

"Yes, but it's early for me."

Ben chuckled. "I may never have been your boyfriend, but I am your friend. I know you, Tristan, and I know the only time I can reach you. You can't tell me you weren't awake." He paused before continuing. "I can call you that, right? Friendship doesn't create too many ties for you, does it?"

Sighing, Tristan leaned back in his chair. "If you don't want me to hang up on you, I'd change the direction this conversation is going very quickly." He held a finger to the pulse in his wrist, concentrating on the beat.

"It's been two weeks since you were supposed to call me back. I decided if I kept waiting, it would never happen."

One, two, three, four, five...

"I'll be out west in a week. It's a quick trip. Only a few days, but only one of them is taken with business. What's your schedule like?"

Another man would offer his friend a place to stay. Maybe clear his schedule for a visit from the only person he still talked to from college.

But that wasn't Tristan. The thought of someone else sleeping in his home made the beats in his wrist speed up. Even when they'd been sleeping together back in New York, they always stayed in Ben's dorm, and then his apartment.

A lunch. What kind of man didn't have lunch with his friend when he came to town? But he knew Ben. Seeing him always came with questions, with worry, when Tristan didn't like either.

"I won't get in your business. I promise. Even though you're an asshole, you're a friend, man. It's been too long since we've seen each other."

Friend? What did Tristan even know about the word? Business he understood. Money he understood. Ben knew him probably better than anyone, other than his mother, yet Ben didn't even know Tristan's mom was alive, least of all anything about her or Tristan's past.

"I'll see what I can do."

Ben sighed, and he had a feeling the other man knew that meant no.

"I've known you for years, Tristan. We studied for our LSATS together. I probably wouldn't be where I am without you. You're really not going to make time in your day to have lunch with me?"

Billows of guilt blew through him. "I said I'd see what I could do."

They hung up the phone right after that. Tristan went straight for the shower. Afterward he dressed in a black suit, packed his briefcase, and went out to his BMW.

One, two, three, four, five.

He pretended to count the beats of his pulse, even though he couldn't while he was driving. Morning just started to settle into the city. Too early to go to work, yet he'd known that when he left.

As though it had a mind of his own, his car led him toward his mom's, though he knew he wouldn't go in and see her. He parked at her building, where he had a permanent parking spot, before heading to the Warf.

A million times he almost turned around, fire blazing through his veins that he even came this way at all. He didn't know what he was doing here. All he'd known was he couldn't be home, and he suddenly thought about those stupid birds. He hated birds. Always had. Yet that didn't stop him from heading toward the water.

As soon as Tristan got close, he saw him. Mornings in June were still cool in San Francisco, so like that day two weeks ago, the younger man wore a hooded sweatshirt.

He could easily walk away. Go the other direction, or sit on the bench, but he didn't do any of those things. Tristan kept walking until he stepped up beside Josiah. He threw a quick glance at him.

"I heard you coming. I didn't know it was you, though."

"Would you have walked away if you had?" Tristan asked.

Josiah shook his head. "No. I just like to listen. That's why I was surprised I didn't hear you the other day. Mat—someone I know taught me to pay attention. To always know who's around me."

Tristan crossed his arms and looked at him. There were only a few reasons someone would try to teach a lesson like that. He should have adopted it himself years ago. "It's smart. You never know."

He watched as Josiah stuck his hand into a bag, throwing food in front of him, which the birds devoured.

"What are you doing here?" This time when Josiah spoke, he didn't look at him.

Still, he shrugged. "I don't know. Needed to walk, I guess."

Josiah turned his way and smiled. "You want to feed the birds?"

The palm of Tristan's hand tingled but he didn't hold it out. "No. Just came to walk."

His answer made wrinkles form on Josiah's forehead. It hadn't been what he wanted to hear.

But when Tristan put one foot in front of the other, walking down the walkway in front of the water, Josiah stepped in beside him.

They didn't talk. Just walked. And somehow his thoughts weren't as loud on that walk. Somehow, the air and ocean, or maybe even the birds, made him feel free, even if only for a little while.

Chapter Seven

Josiah

Josiah let his eyes dart toward Tristan. This was their third day walking in near silence. He'd come those first two days in a row, then a week between those visits and today. Like the other two times, Tristan refused his offer to feed the birds. He had no idea why Tristan continued to come since they hardly spoke, but he did, and Josiah found that he was glad. He always felt more alone on his morning walks, emptier. He was supposed to share this with Mateo and he never had. For these few minutes, those empty rooms that filled him again after Teo sent him away didn't feel so bare.

"What do you do?" Josiah finally asked near the end of their third walk.

"I'm an attorney. You?" Tristan replied without looking Josiah's way.

He closed his eyes, wondering why out of all the questions he could ask, he chose that one. "Fisherman's Roast. I work there."

That was the end of their conversation for that day, but on their fourth walk, a week later, Tristan asked him, "Do you go to college?"

Josiah shook his head. *Don't ask why, don't ask why, don't ask why.* He wasn't sure the reason he didn't want Tristan to ask him that question. Probably since he wasn't going because Mateo wanted him to, which he knew was stupid.

But Tristan didn't ask. And then, he suddenly wished he had.

Tristan
August

He'd never been attracted to a man with a buzzed head before, yet multiple times Tristan found himself wanting to run a hand over Josiah's. To feel the brush against his skin. He gritted his teeth, trying to curb some of those desires.

"Why the Warf? There are hundreds of other places to walk in the city. Some better. Why do you come here every day?" The question had plagued Tristan for a while now. Sure people loved it here, but he had a feeling Josiah had been walking this same path for a very long time.

The fact that he wanted to know made Tristan's muscles spasm. "Forget I asked. It's your business."

To his surprise, Josiah said, "I don't... I don't mind that you ask me questions. I just won't answer them all. There are something things that are mine, I guess. Some things that will always only belong to me."

Tristan pressed two fingers into his wrist. *One, two, three, four, five.* "You remind me of myself. Especially when I was younger."

Josiah huffed and gave a small laugh. It was the first one he'd heard from him.

"Great. Just what a guy wants to hear. I remind you of a younger version of yourself."

He realized then what Josiah meant. So he was as attracted to Tristan as Tristan was to Josiah. Not that he couldn't tell by the blush that often colored his cheeks, or the quick glances pointed in Tristan's direction. Things he liked more than he should.

Josiah went on. "I mean, not that I thought these walks meant anything. I know you said it was a mistake when you asked me to go home with you, and I'm not dumb enough to think you changed your mind."

Tristan stopped walking and grabbed Josiah's arm. His skin was warm to the touch, sending that same warmth up Tristan's arm. Immediately he pulled his hand back. "It wouldn't make you dumb to wonder, but the truth is, though I enjoy our walks, that's all they'll ever be." The words bounced around inside him, ricocheting around as though they waited for him to grab them back. It would never happen, though damn he wanted to. He craved a night of skin-to-skin, because fucking someone was the only way he let himself get close to anyone.

"I get it. And, it's better, anyway. I know that."

Tristan almost asked why, but instead started walking again. "Good.

I'll never push you to talk about anything you don't want. People are always trying to take things from someone that they don't want to give. That's not me."

"Okay." Josiah scratched his arm before looking over. "So, we'll just talk, and if one of us asks something the other doesn't want to answer, we don't."

Light red colored his cheeks. Tristan couldn't tell if it was from embarrassment or not. He found himself nodding.

He hadn't been lying when he said Josiah reminded him of himself. Quiet, private. He wondered if there were as many stories inside Josiah as there were in him.

Josiah pushed a hand into his worn blue jeans before tossing some food for the birds with his other.

In those ways, they were the same. But in most ways, they were incredibly different. He wondered why he continued to come back, but knew he would.

Josiah
September

"How old are you?" Josiah asked Tristan on walk number... he couldn't even remember anymore. It got harder to count because of the week's Tristan would show up multiple times.

"Why do you ask?"

Josiah shrugged. "I don't know. Is this a veto?"

"No, it's not. I'm thirty-one."

Wow…young. In some ways he wasn't shocked. Tristan had smooth skin, a muscled body, and, when he did smile, he looked young. Not *young* young, but as though he wasn't too much older than Josiah. But then the suits, the career, sometimes the tiredness Josiah saw in his eyes, made him think older.

"Do you have family around here?"

Tristan tensed a little beside him, and Josiah knew what the answer would be before he said it.

"Veto." Tristan took a deep breath. "School. Why didn't you go? It's not that I think college is for everyone, but you often ask me what it was like. There's interest in your eyes. Curiosity."

Josiah's mouth went dry, making it hard to open it. "You'd think I was crazy if I told you."

"Try me."

He took a few deep breaths. He could do this, right? He could talk about Mateo without *really* saying anything?

"Someone… someone wanted me to. I don't think he ever planned to do it for himself, but he wanted it for me. It made me believe things that weren't true." Josiah bit his lip, thought about Mateo and how all those things made him believe so much that Teo loved him.

And he had to have. A part of Josiah knew that, but like so many things in his life, Mateo's love had gone away.

"You're right. I do think that's crazy."

A laugh jumped out of Josiah's mouth. He whipped his head toward

Tristan as though he could somehow explain how Josiah could be laughing—*laughing* after he was thinking about Teo not loving him.

Tristan stopped them with a hand on Josiah's shoulder. It was warm, and even though the air around them was as well, Josiah craved it. Wanted to nuzzle himself into the heat of another person.

"Don't let people have that kind of power over you. I've seen what power does. When people love so much they put someone else above themselves. Or equal to themselves. All it does is hand power to them. Keep that for yourself. No one else deserves it."

Josiah opened his mouth, not expecting the words that came out. "Love equals power? So, you'll never love because you never want to hand over the power?" The thought made Josiah kind of sad. It was so…cynical, and so true.

Tristan sighed, making his reply obvious. "Veto."

Tristan
October

Cool, fall air drifted over him, the sky gray and hazy.

Josiah trembled, burying his hands in his pockets. He had his hood up, the morning air colder than it had been yet. The pocket edges were frayed. A little hole had ripped in the arm, the black faded from what no doubt had been hundreds of washes.

"We can go. The weather's getting cooler."

Josiah shook his head. "This isn't cold. Plus, I walk all year. It doesn't matter the season."

"Why?"

Josiah quirked an eyebrow at him, a sign of comfort that hadn't been there when they started their walks. "Veto." Then he nodded toward Tristan. "I noticed... I don't know why I want to know, but you press your first two fingers to your pulse in your wrist a lot. Why?"

Tristan fought to keep himself from doing it now. It was something he'd done since he was a kid, when he needed something to focus on to block out his surroundings. No one had ever noticed him do it before. But then... it didn't surprise him that Josiah did. Maybe that's why he said, "To keep me steady," rather than veto.

Josiah's cheeks flushed as he looked up at him and smiled. Tristan fought the urge to touch him. To brush his thumb over Josiah's cheek like he had done that first day all those months ago.

Josiah
November

Josiah stepped up to Tristan, at their spot by the water where they always met. "Here, I brought you a scone. It's the berry one you always get."

A couple times a month, Tristan came in and bought himself a berry scone. He never ate it there, but Josiah figured he had to really like them if he bought them so often.

"It doesn't mean anything. It's in exchange for the hoodie, I guess. You wouldn't let me say no, so I'm not letting you, either. I know it's not the same, but take it."

Tristan smiled at him before raising his hand. His fingers brushed Josiah's as he grabbed the bag, making shivers that had nothing to do with the weather rush through him. They walked again. Every few minutes, Josiah's eyes darted toward Tristan. He wore a nice trench coat that probably cost more than anything Josiah owned. They probably looked ridiculous walking together. For the millionth time he wondered why they were. Why Tristan continued to meet him.

But he was glad Tristan did.

It was the end of the walk, Tristan turning to go back to his car when something made Josiah say, "Wait."

"Yes?" Tristan asked.

"School. I… I think you're right. I want to go. I don't know if I'll be able to, if I can figure it all out, but I don't want to hold myself back anymore." And it was him. He could blame Mateo all he wanted, but Josiah controlled his own actions. "So, yeah… That's my goal. To figure out how I can go to college next year. I'll be twenty-four on December first. It's time… I just…" he was rambling. Why couldn't he stop rambling? "I wanted you to know. It's partially because of you, and—"

His words were cut off by the feel of Tristan's mouth coming down hard on his. His tongue slipped between Josiah's lips, and he let it, savored it, while a voice in his head couldn't help but think how different it was from his first kiss with Mateo. Teo had gone slow, eased him into it, while Tristan pulled Josiah tight against him. His hand slid under the back of Josiah's sweatshirt, landing on his bare skin.

It was hungry and urgent. Josiah found himself wrapping his arms around Tristan's neck. Pushing closer, soaking in the feel of another body against his after so long.

He instantly went hard—felt Tristan's erection, too.

Tristan wanted him. He wanted *Josiah*.

But then he pulled away. The foot between them felt like miles. "I haven't kissed anyone in almost six years. Not since Teo."

He wanted the words back. His body froze and felt numb at the same time. That was stupid. So damn ridiculous. He shouldn't have brought up Teo. Not after the kiss.

It felt like his insides were being ripped apart. Pulled two directions—the one who wanted to grab Tristan and kiss him again, to explore his body, and the one who missed Mateo. Who would always miss Mateo.

Tristan's stare went blank, his eyes concentrative in a way Josiah didn't understand.

"I'm…" He didn't have a chance to reply before Tristan walked away.

Tristan
December 1st

"I asked for the files to be on my desk when I got to work. Can you explain to me why they're not here?" He squeezed the phone tightly.

"I'm sorry, Mr. Croft. I got a little behind this morning. I'll bring them right now—"

Tristan hung up the phone so he didn't throw it across the room. When Annie brought the file in, he found it in himself to apologize, knowing it wasn't her fault they were busy and he was being an ass.

It's just the walks, he told himself. They'd loosened him up somehow, been the perfect way to start the day, but he hadn't been in three and a half weeks. Not since the day he kissed Josiah.

Jesus, what had he been thinking? He knew he wasn't the type of man Josiah should be with. They'd gone over that. But he hadn't been able to hold himself back. He wanted to taste him, wanted his tongue in Josiah's mouth and to feel his body wrapped around him.

Big fucking mistake. If he hadn't known it before, he definitely did the second Josiah'd admitted he hadn't even kissed a man in almost six years.

Tristan was on edge all day. His pulse was going haywire every time he touched it.

He stayed at the office until almost eight p.m., working in the empty building. Work was supposed to help. It always did, but it wasn't now. Damn Josiah and the walks. What had they done to him?

After work he didn't go home. Spent an hour driving around the city before he found himself parking at his mom's. Before he found himself walking over to Fisherman's Roast. He needed to get those goddamned walks back. He wasn't sure what they did to him, but it was something. The only way was to talk to Josiah. Explain to him that the kiss had been a mistake, and try to find whatever it was they'd discovered the past few months.

He snuck inside the small coffee house. It was obvious they were about to close for the evening. He looked around, hoping to spot Josiah. There were two men working. With Josiah nowhere in sight, he headed for the door again.

"Hey! Are you looking for Josiah?" A blond man walked over to him.

"Yes. I thought he worked today, but I guess not." He tried to sound as though he and Josiah were close. In a way, they were—or they had been.

"The boss always gives people the day off for their birthday."

The reminder kicked a rock into his gut. He'd wanted to see Josiah for his birthday. That's what part of this was about.

"Thank you."

"No problem. I'm his friend Elliot. I wanted to thank you for letting him stay with you. I can't believe his asshole landlord kicked him out with no notice. I told him he could stay with me, but my place is small so he figured it would be better to stay with you."

One, two, three, four, five.

"No problem. If you'll excuse me. I need to go."

Tristan shoved the door open, almost hitting someone as they walked by. He didn't stop. Kept heading toward the water.

Josiah had been kicked out? He told his friend he was staying with Tristan. Where the fuck was he staying if he had to lie to Elliot about it? That wasn't Josiah. He couldn't see him lying about anything. Not answering, yes. A direct lie, no.

It wasn't his business, and he didn't want it to be his business, but that didn't stop him from needing to find Josiah. Needing it in a way he wasn't familiar with.

Rain started to come down but Tristan kept walking. Kept going down the path they'd walked on a hundred times. Farther and farther from Fisherman's Roast, through the dark night.

In the distance, he made out a figure sitting on the bench. It was Josiah. His worry deflated the closer he got. Tristan didn't stop until he got to him. Josiah wore his hood over his head, his arms wrapped around his knees as he sat there in the pouring rain.

He looked up as Tristan reached him. No doubt he had tears mixed with the rain sliding down his face. "It's my birthday," he whispered. "That's when he gave me the queen. He said it's because I was the strongest person he knew."

Tristan's heart ached like it hadn't since he was a kid. Without a word, or thought, he wrapped his arms around Josiah and picked him up. Settled a little into his touch when Josiah's arms wrapped around his neck.

"Where are we going?" Josiah shook as he spoke.

"Home." Then he walked through the dark and rain, hoping for the first time that something had the power to cleanse them both from their pasts. And that he was making the right decision with this friendship, mutual care, whatever it was.

Chapter Eight

Josiah

Cold shook him bone deep. His eyes couldn't focus, blurred with moisture and seeing double as his body trembled.

Josiah tried to look around Tristan's house as he led him, by the hand, but it was no use.

"This way. You need to get into a warm shower." Tristan's voice was steady, but clipped.

Josiah followed as he brought him to a bathroom that was at least three times bigger than any bathroom he'd ever had. Cold rocketed through him again, making him reach for the counter to keep his balance.

"Sorry...sorry...sorry..." His mind realized he kept repeating the word, but he couldn't seem to make himself stop.

"Later." Another short reply from Tristan.

He jumped when he felt Tristan pushing his sweatshirt up. Wanted to tell him he could do it himself, but couldn't.

The sweatshirt was gone.

Then his shirt.

Shoes.

Socks.

Pants.

Underwear.

Oh God, what's wrong with me. I can't even take care of myself. Can't undress myself. Shame ballooned inside him. *I'm sorry,* he tried to say again, but the words wouldn't come out. He was a mess, such a mess. The knowledge made the cold inside him multiply.

Glass shower doors opened. Tristan pushed him inside, the warm water like fire on his skin. Still, his thoughts overpowered the burn. *Weak, weak, weak. I'm even weaker than I've ever been…*

Tristan stood outside the shower, his arm on Josiah. Words were still lost in his head, so he tried to let the heat warm him. Tristan turned it off after what felt like only a few minutes, but because of his pruned hands, and the cooling temperature, he knew it had to be longer.

A white, thick towel was wrapped around him. Josiah sank into it.

"Tris—tan…"

He shook his head. "Tomorrow."

The word was issued as a command Josiah felt compelled to follow. He went with Tristan to another room.

"I'll be back with clothes."

He watched as Tristan walked away, his dark suit wet and molding to his body. Josiah's heart sped up.

"You're…you're wet, too." The words were like peanut butter in his mouth.

"I won't be for long."

And then the towel was gone, a flannel shirt placed in his hand. It clicked in his mind that he was naked in front of Tristan. Had been for a while now. He waited for the embarrassment but instead started to warm up faster, hotter, from the inside out.

He wanted that, he realized. Wanted Tristan.

Josiah met his eyes, hoping to see the same thing reflected there, but they were dark—closed off. He let his eyes wander down, landing on the thick bulge in Tristan's pants. Tristan wanted him, too.

"It's not going to happen. Get dressed," Tristan told him.

The desire deflated as his fingers fumbled with the buttons on the shirt. He didn't look at Tristan as he took the matching pants and slid them on as well.

"Thank you. I don't know," he shook his head. "I don't know what I was thinking."

For the first time since they got there, Tristan's features seemed to soften, if only the slightest bit. "Not tonight, Josiah. I can't talk about it tonight." He took a step backward, then another. "Get into bed. Go to sleep. We'll talk tomorrow."

Josiah watched the door close. Memorized the sound of the click. Fought to keep himself from following. If that's what Tristan needed, he'd find a way to make himself stay away.

***

Josiah woke up, warm and in a bed unlike any he'd ever slept in. The sheets caressed his skin, comforting and safe. The mattress molded to his body like a hug. He drowned in the clothes he wore because he was so much smaller than Tristan. The man was muscular, though in a different way than Mateo had been. Teo was longer, leaner, but cut and defined. Tristan wasn't overly bulky, that was for sure. And he was taller than Josiah as well, but Tristan's bone structure was larger, too. His shoulders wider, something he hadn't realized until he'd been in Tristan's arms the night before.

Fragmented, blurred memories of the night before became spotted vision in his mind.

Tristan undressing him, putting him in the shower, giving him clothes.

His stomach cramped with memories of sitting on that bench. Letting the rain drown him, hoping it really could.

Acid burned through him, making him want to vomit. But then he thought of Teo, and how Teo always puked. He fought it, trying to vanquish thoughts of Mateo from his mind. Trying to shove the love he felt for him so deep that it couldn't claw its way to the surface again.

He loved Teo. He always would. But he was letting that love kill him, letting it make him weak. Sure, he had a job, and Elliot, and even Tristan as a friend, but he was dead, and using Teo's love, Teo leaving him, for an excuse.

No matter how things had gone down between them, he knew it had been real. At least some of the time it had been real, and what they shared had been too beautiful for Josiah to continue suffocating on memories of it.

He and Mateo didn't deserve that. Not after all they'd been to each other. And Josiah alone didn't deserve it, either.

A determined fire blazed inside him—something he hadn't felt since he told Teo he didn't want to have to be taken care of anymore. Stronger even than the feeling he'd had then.

Josiah stumbled as he pushed out of the bed. He ignored his weak legs and headed straight for the door and into Tristan's long hallway. Doors were closed on each side. He went past each one, somehow knowing Tristan wasn't behind any of them.

The hallway led to stairs, which he took down and into a large room with tiled floors and sparse furniture. A couch, a chair, a large flat screen on the wall. An elliptical by one of the oversized windows along one of the walls.

He kept going through the room, past a small, square kitchen table behind the couch. To the left and through a dining room with a longer, rectangular table with modern, silver lights hanging above it.

And finally to the kitchen, with more silver lights, steel appliances, and Tristan. Tristan sitting at yet another table, this one round. His bare back faced Josiah. His eyes traveled down to see Tristan wore a pair of sweats and nothing else. His back glistened slightly, maybe water droplets from a shower? But then, his hair would be wet, and it wasn't.

Josiah's breath caught as he took in the sight.

"Coffee's in the pot. Cream in the fridge. I called your work to see if you were supposed to go in today, but I guess you're off." Without turning around, he lifted a glass of orange juice to his lips and took a drink.

"Thanks. I appreciate that." Josiah walked over to the coffee pot. He almost asked Tristan where the cups were but decided just to open the cabinet above to check. They were there, so he pulled out a black coffee cup, filled it, and put two scoops of sugar in before going to the fridge for cream.

When he finished, he sat across the table from Tristan, ignoring the rapid beat of his heart. "Thanks for bringing me here last night."

"You didn't give me much choice."

Josiah's eyes flashed to Tristan's face as he raised one of his dark brows. He hadn't really thought about it like that. He guessed a part of him had hoped Tristan brought him here because he wanted to. But that's not what came out when he opened his mouth. Somehow, "There's always a choice," tumbled free.

Surprise sparked in him when Tristan smiled. "I guess that's true. Just like you had the choice whether to sit in the rain or not. To lie to your friend about staying with me."

Shit. He took a drink of his coffee before replying. He'd hoped Tristan didn't know about that. "I didn't want him to feel like he had to let me stay with him. That he had to take care of me."

"So you decided to put yourself in the position to need to be taken care of?"

Josiah fought to meet his eyes. "Regardless of what I did, I'm not a child. So please, don't talk to me like I am one."

Tristan stared at him, with what Josiah could have sworn looked like respect. Josiah let his eyes travel down, to the cut pectorals of Tristan's chest. The light dusting of dark hair in the middle. Holy shit, he had a nice body. Josiah's dick started to stir.

"You can't look at me like that. When you do, it's damn near impossible to keep my control." Tristan pushed to his feet, went to the sink and dumped out the rest of his juice before setting the glass down and leaning against the counter.

For once, Josiah wanted to just speak. To talk and let whatever he wanted come out of his mouth. He hadn't done that since… "Why do you have to? Keep your control, I mean. Maybe I don't want you to."

Tristan groaned…or growled? Was there a difference, really? He wasn't sure.

"Why don't we start with you. Are you living on the streets?" There was a sharp edge to his voice when he said streets.

"No. I'm staying at a hotel."

"And it didn't cross your mind to go there last night?" he snapped.

How could he explain to Tristan how he felt? That he was empty. He'd always had emptiness inside him, but then someone had come and filled him, only to leave Josiah more alone than when he'd found him. That he couldn't be inside that small room, which reminded him of the small apartment they'd shared? That it hadn't just been the past haunting him but their kiss, and Tristan walking away? Being forever alone?

He couldn't. "It was a mistake. Or…mistake isn't the right word. A lapse in judgment, something I'm tired of doing. Something I won't do anymore. Just like you won't tell me why you count your pulse or who you visit by my work, I can't talk about this. But, I'm ready to get past it." *To let go…*

Tristan crossed his arms. Josiah hurried to continue before he could reply. "I'm ready to move on." He looked down at his coffee, feeling his words but still struggling to be that guy. To be like Tristan or Teo or even Elliot, who were all confident enough in who they were to always look someone in the eye. To have faith in the decisions they made.

"I'm going to try and go to college. There has to be financial aid or loans or something I can do. I want to know how to run my own business. It was our dream—*my* dream—to own a place like Fisherman's Roast. I know it's not much to some people, but it would be everything to me."

Tristan watched him carefully before speaking. "How other people feel doesn't matter. The only thing that does is what you want. And that you can take care of yourself. I was there last night, Josiah. There won't always be someone there. You shouldn't want someone there. All you have in this world is yourself."

Truth sounded off each syllable of his words. He knew Tristan was right, but in a way, wished he wasn't. He wanted to live in a world where he and Teo could have had each other—always had each other. Not to depend on, but lean on. A world where maybe now he could be there for Tristan, the way Tristan had been there for him last night.

Josiah nodded.

"I learned that lesson young. Too young." Tristan ran a hand over his face. "Jesus, how did I fucking get here?" he said to himself, before walking over and stopping right in front of Josiah. His line of sight met the top of Tristan's jeans. He let it go up…up until it landed on his face.

"You'll stay here. If you want to get your life together, you'll stay here, but I'm telling you right now, there will be rules."

Josiah couldn't move. Couldn't talk, couldn't think. Tristan was asking him to stay here.

Chapter Nine

Tristan

Pull back. I have no business letting him stay here. Not with the hunger in his eyes right now. Not with the matching craving inside me.

But damn, he couldn't take the words back. Probably knew last night he would utter them. He saw something in Josiah, though he couldn't nail down exactly what it was. Yes, he was beautiful, with his soft features and even softer eyes. With days' growth of hair on his jaw and a determined curve of his plump lips. Lips Tristan very much wanted to take possession of.

It was that thought that made the blood run cold through him. That thought that again reminded him that if he was going to help Josiah, that's all it would be. He wouldn't wield power over Josiah, and let him repay Tristan sexually.

"There are things you want, Tristan. Things I can help you get.

You're a smart young man. I wouldn't offer to take you under my wing if I didn't think you had it in you to succeed, but what about me? All the hard work and money I'm putting toward you. I know you're taking care of your mom, too. Nothing comes for free. Don't pretend you don't know."

Nausea rolled through Tristan's gut. Nothing comes for free. He'd heard that before. Seen it before, with his mom. When she did what she had to do to support them—the way he would do now…

Tristan dropped to his knees in front of Wilson.

"That's it. I knew you'd understand. You give me what I want, and I'll give you what you need."

Wilson was exactly right. Tristan needed this. Needed to be able to take care of himself so no one could take anything from them again.

With steady hands, he pulled Wilson's zipper down…

Tristan jerked himself from the past. He bit down so hard, for so long, his jaw hurt. Two fingers pressed to his pulse. *One, two, three, four, five….*

"That. Right there." He didn't take a step back, but put a hand under Josiah's chin so he couldn't look away. "The way you're looking at me right now. You need to know that nothing will happen. If you're staying here, it's to help you get on your feet. I have space, so you're welcome to use it while you're getting your life in order, but I won't fuck you. The men I take to bed know we'll share it once and then I'm done. And I won't fall in love with you, either, so don't try to romance me. I don't do relationships, and if you're thinking this is the start of one, it isn't." Tristan let his hand fall. Josiah didn't react right away.

The only person Tristan had taken to bed more than once who he'd actually wanted there was Ben. But they'd both always known the score. During the crazy days of law school, it had been easier for Tristan to fuck him than to make time to find someone else. Ben was one of the few people he could stand.

Josiah paused. His tongue snuck out and licked those damn lips again, but Tristan fought to hold his ground. Giving in meant he couldn't handle this craving for Josiah, and he damn well would make sure he could.

"Why?" Josiah finally asked.

It was such a simple question but pierced Tristan's armor as he realized that months ago, Josiah wouldn't have asked it. Which meant he felt comfortable enough around Tristan to speak more openly. The knowledge was equal parts humbling and frustrating. "Any of my personal relationships with men or family are a permanent veto."

"No." Josiah shook his head. "I meant, why would you let me stay here? Why would you offer to help me?"

Tristan took a second to study him. To really see the younger man. His cheeks were pink, though he doubted Josiah knew it. Determination set in his jaw, and kindness danced in his expressive eyes. There was something so very…innocent, and genuine, about him. Even the way he was with feeding the birds. Tristan had never known anyone like that.

Because you deserve it. Because if I don't, someone else might try to, might snuff out the kindness in your eyes. "I don't know. Because I can?" And then he decided Josiah deserved at least a partial truth. "I want to. I was never exactly like you, was never so caring, but I was closer than I am now. I don't want you to lose it."

Those words made everything too much. Suddenly needing a little space, he turned and headed toward the other room. "I have some work to do. Make yourself at home. We'll talk more when I'm done."

If Josiah answered, Tristan didn't hear it. He took the steps two at a time, going straight to his office and closing the door behind him.

***

Tristan spent almost two hours going over case notes he already had memorized by heart. The whole time, he waited for the tension to ease out of his muscles the way it usually did when he worked but it never happened.

It wasn't often that he let himself think about Wilson and the things he'd done during those years of his life. The things he had allowed to be done to him for the security he now had. But then, his mother hadn't had much of a choice when she'd sold herself. When she'd lose a job and have no other way to put food in their mouths except for letting men use her body.

And he'd been too young to do much of anything to help.

Fingers. Pulse. *One, two, three, four, five.*

No one would make him helpless again. At least he'd known what he was getting into. At least he'd had a choice.

Buzz!

Tristan's hand slapped down on his cell, picking it off the table and pressing it to his ear. "Croft."

"No shit." Ben laughed.

"Christ, not you. This isn't a good time."

"When is it ever a good time with you? Do you have any fun out there in California? You sound like you're in a worse mood every time I speak to you. Maybe I could have helped if you would've let me see you when I was in town a few months ago. Those California boys must not know what they're doing."

"Or maybe we don't all think with our dicks the way you do."

Another laugh from Ben. "That's a shame, Tristan. If I remember correctly, you were very good with yours."

Tristan sighed and propped his elbows on this desk. Words teased the tip of his tongue. *What do I do? There's a boy here I want that I can't have. I'm in over my head.* Hell, maybe Ben was right. Maybe he did need to go out and get laid.

"What's wrong with you, Croft? You just passed up a prime opportunity to give me hell, or to hang up on me, and you didn't take it."

The truth was, he wouldn't do any of the things he thought of. He wouldn't talk to Ben, and he probably wouldn't go get laid. "Nothing. I'm busy. Do you ever work? I—"

"Tristan?" Josiah knocked on his office door.

"Shit." He held a hand over the phone and put it in his lap. "I'll be out in a minute."

Ben was already speaking when Tristan put the phone back to his ear. "There's someone there with you…" His voice trailed off as though he tried to make sense of it. "You have a man in your house, Tristan, don't you? And I swear to God, if you hang up on me, I will jump on a plane today."

Tristan dropped his head back. "The only reason I'm humoring you is because I have no doubt you'll show up. It's not what you're thinking, so put it out of your mind."

"And you didn't hang up on me. You really don't want me to come."

Ben paused and Tristan took advantage. He kept his voice low and spoke. "I said it's not what you think. He's a kid. Twenty-four years old. I'm helping him out. It's nothing more than that."

Ben sighed. "He's in your home, Tris. I've never been there, and I'm the only person you care about, even though you pretend you don't. Lie to yourself all you want, but you can't lie to me."

Tristan closed his eyes, trying to bury Ben's words so deep inside him he wouldn't have to hear them. Yes, he did care about Ben. He was the only person he ever really cared about besides his mother. Yet, Ben didn't even know about her, didn't know to add her to his sentence. Somehow, that knowledge gutted him.

"I have to go."

Ben was quiet. Tristan gave him a little while to speak. Ben always had something to say, but when half a minute passed by with nothing but silence, he ended the call.

Tristan stood and shoved the phone into his pocket. It was never out of reach in case his mom or work needed him. After grabbing a T-shirt from the chair in the corner, he slid it on before opening the door. Josiah waited on the other side, still wearing Tristan's clothes.

Jesus, there was something sexy about seeing Josiah in his clothes.

"You said to make myself at home, so I hope you don't mind, but I made us some lunch. You've been working for a while, so I thought you might be hungry. It's okay if you're not, and I'll replace the food. I wanted to do something nice for you."

Tristan felt a kick of guilt. Sure, he'd brought him home, but he'd also been an asshole to him this morning. He'd walked away from him with no real excuse and left him alone for two hours, yet Josiah had still made him lunch. It was a small thing. It wasn't as though a man had never cooked for him, or as though there weren't men who would do anything to be in Tristan's home right now. The difference was, they wanted something from him. As far as he could tell, Josiah didn't.

"You didn't have to do that," Tristan told him.

Josiah shrugged. "I wanted to. It's not a big deal. Just some ham and grilled cheese sandwiches, and a salad."

Tristan gave him a simple nod before holding out his hand and telling Josiah to go on. He did, and Tristan walked behind him down the stairs. He had the food on the table, with silverware next to the plates and dressing in the middle.

"I didn't know what you'd want to drink."

Tristan chuckled, his own ears shocked at the sound. "I think I'm going to need wine. A lot of wine. What do you prefer?" He headed for the wine fridge.

"I don't know. I don't know much about wines."

Tristan looked over his shoulder at Josiah and wrinkled his

forehead. "We're going to have to do something about that. Sit. I'll pick something good."

Tristan let his fingers ghost along the bottles until he found what he wanted.

Josiah sat at the table facing away from him. He watched as Josiah's shoulders jerked when he popped the cork. Tristan grabbed two wine glasses from the cabinet and set them on the table, filling first Josiah's glass and then his own. He placed the bottle down, and then sat across the table.

"What do you think?" he asked Josiah, who then picked up his glass and took a small drink.

"It's good. Sweeter than I would have thought."

Tristan didn't know why that made him smile. "I'm glad you like it." He took in the man sitting across from him in clothes that were too big on him as they drank wine that cost nearly three hundred dollars a bottle. It made him smile again.

"You don't do that often." Josiah took another drink.

"What?"

"Smile. Oh, there it goes. I shouldn't have mentioned it because you're frowning now."

Was he? He guessed he was. Tristan ignored the comment. "I have an extra laptop you can use to look up whatever information you'll need—"

"I can't do that. I decided while you were working. I can't stay here. Can't put my problems off on you. It's not right."

He respected Josiah for those words, while at the same time making him frown deeper. "You're not putting your problems off on me. Your responsibilities are still your own. The only thing I'm doing is giving you a free place to stay. And a small loan, if need be. You'll pay me back." He didn't want Josiah's money, but knew he would insist on it, as most men would.

"No," Josiah shook his head. "It's not right. It would be years before I could repay you. I have to earn my keep."

Ah, the things he could say to that. But he wouldn't. Not after his past.

Tristan's eyes drifted down to his plate. "So, you'll cook for us. I hate to do it. I'm too busy to be bothered, and most of the time I order out."

"It's not enough."

Tristan set his glass down and let out a heavy breath. The tips of his first two fingers tingled but he held them still. His chest felt heavy at the thought of Josiah walking back out to the streets. "I don't typically ask things of people. I'm asking you to do this. It's important to me. The why of it doesn't matter. It's a good opportunity. This is your life, Josiah. It would be stupid to pass it up."

He picked up his sandwich and took a bite. Josiah didn't reply. They both ate in silence. When Tristan was finished, he poured himself another glass of wine and waited.

Finally, Josiah spoke. "I'll…I'll do it."

"Look at me when you say it. I want to see your eyes." He really shouldn't fucking want that, but he did. Wanted to take in their unique light and dark shades of green. So damn sexy.

"I'll do it. But I'm paying you back. And I'll clean the house, too, not just cook. I'll do whatever you need."

Tristan gave him a simple nod before standing. "I'm taking a shower, and then we can go get your things. I washed and dried your clothes. I'll grab them for you."

The eyes he'd just been admiring went wide. "My stuff. I had something in the pocket. It's... It's important to me."

Why? he almost asked, but didn't. "Your queen. I remember. It's safe."

When Tristan walked out of the room, he saw nothing but the homemade chess piece, and wondered about who had given it to Josiah, and what he'd meant to him.

Chapter Ten

April

Josiah

Half of the time, Josiah didn't know how to act. Tristan was gone a lot. When he was home, he spent hours at a time in his office. There were days that even though they lived together, Josiah didn't see him for more than fifteen minutes while they ate dinner.

And there were days where even that didn't happen.

Guilt gnawed at him daily. This was Tristan's home, and he shouldn't feel uncomfortable in it. It was obvious he did, but whenever Josiah brought it up, Tristan told him he was being ridiculous and the subject would be dropped.

It didn't make the guilt go away, so he threw himself into getting his life together—making sure this wasn't for nothing. He'd registered to start school in January, taking as many classes that were available to him. He applied for financial aid, and saved every dollar that he could from working at Fisherman's Roast. Each payday, he left fifty dollars for Tristan to go toward the laptop he'd given him, and though he could tell Tristan didn't like it, he never said a word. He just took the money, opened a bottle of wine, and then he and Josiah would sit at the table in near silence.

The house was always clean, and even when Tristan didn't come home, Josiah cooked. It was all he could do, and he wanted to do it well.

There were times Tristan got phone calls and suddenly left. Once, Josiah asked him about it, and all Tristan did was mutter a, "veto." Like so many conversations, it ended before it really began.

Classes started, and he got into a routine of school, work and paying his way by keeping up with the house. And of course, there were his walks. He still went every day. Took the bus across town, because even though he tried to lock his past away with the wooden queen stuffed in the pouch of the backpack he always carried, he couldn't leave the walks behind. And the queen was no longer in the pocket of his jeans. Even though it was a small step, to Josiah, it was something.

But what he did miss was Tristan taking those walks with him. He thought maybe Tristan would join him again, but he still never had. No matter how much he wanted to, Josiah didn't have the courage to ask him.

"Hey," Elliot said one day after work. "Do you want to hang out or something when our shift is over? Seems like you're crazy busy now that you're going to school."

Josiah smiled. "Like you aren't?"

"Yeah, that's true. But I'm not tonight, so let's go see a movie or something." He leaned against the counter in the break room.

Josiah shook his head. "I have homework to do, and Tristan's working on a big case. I want to make sure he has dinner when he gets home."

Elliot shook his head. "This whole thing is so crazy. I mean, cool for you, but crazy. You're a twenty-four-year-old guy who just started college, works at a coffee house, yet you're with one of the top prosecutors in the state. Wish I could find a woman like that."

Josiah grabbed his backpack. "I'm not with him. How many times do I have to tell you that? He's…" Josiah shrugged. "Helping me out. I don't have the money to do much else. Cooking's all I got."

"And you also didn't see his face a few months back when he came in here looking for you. He doesn't know you, but he let you live in his house. He wants you, man."

A slow heat rolled through Josiah, making his skin burn. The thought of Tristan wanting him made the ache, the desire he felt around Tristan, multiply. He'd give anything for Tristan to want him.

"I have to go." Josiah went for the door, but Elliot's voice stopped him.

"Go for it, man. Can't hurt. Make a move or some shit. Try to be happy."

That word swam around inside him. Happy. He'd dreamed of that his whole life. He found it briefly with Teo. Things had been hard—

scary—but despite it all, having Teo had made him happy. What he wouldn't give to be happy again. Really happy. Forever happy.

He nodded at Elliot, unsure if it really meant anything or not, if he'd really *do* anything before walking out.

Josiah looked at his cell phone on the way home. It was five thirty. Tristan had said he'd be home at seven.

The closer the bus got to Tristan's neighborhood, the faster his heartbeat. Could he do this? Did he want to? Hell yeah, he wanted to. That was a no-brainer. The only thing he had to do was figure out if he *could* do something about it or not.

He'd kissed Mateo first, told Tristan he wanted to go home with him the first day they met. And Josiah didn't want a relationship, he wanted pleasure. For once, just pleasure, and maybe the only way to get it was to show Tristan he wanted it.

Yes...he could do this. He *would.* For once he just wanted to react and not think about the consequences.

Josiah started dinner as soon as he got home. He sautéed chicken in red wine Tristan had bought for cooking. Chopped vegetables and rice before mixing them all together. Josiah put it in the oven before heading to the shower.

It wasn't like he had anything nice to wear like Tristan. Didn't have a different suit for every day. That didn't bother him, though, because...well, because suits weren't really him. Josiah slid on a pair of the nicest jeans he had and a shirt before he went back down to wait for Tristan.

Searching the wine fridge, he looked for Tristan's favorite kind. At seven he set it on the table and made them both plates, the whole time thinking, *holy shit, I'm going to try and sleep with Tristan Croft.*

At seven thirty he put the wine back in the fridge so it didn't get warm. At eight he checked his phone for missed calls or a text. Then at eight thirty. And again at nine.

Nothing. "I am so stupid."

What had he been thinking? Yeah, he knew Tristan didn't owe him anything. If he wasn't here, it was because he was busy, or disappearing to wherever he refused to tell Josiah he went. Very likely with another man. And he had every right. That didn't mean Josiah didn't wonder why it couldn't be him.

Josiah scraped the food off his plate and into the trash before washing it. He covered Tristan's plate and set it in the fridge for him before turning off all the lights and going to his room.

He studied, and read a bit. Fought with himself on whether or not to Google Mateo Sanchez. Everything in him begged for Josiah to do it, but he managed to hold off again. Nothing he found online could soothe him.

At ten thirty, there was a soft knock on his door.

"Come in," he called, and Tristan slowly opened the door. His tie was undone, as were the top buttons on his shirt. Desire sliced through him.

"Dinner was good. Thank you."

"No problem."

Tristan's eyes skated around the room. Even from ten feet away, he saw Tristan's jaw flex, the way he did when he was frustrated by something.

"You've been here over four months. Why aren't you completely unpacked?"

Josiah shrugged. "My clothes are put away."

"But your other things are boxed up."

He almost held back his honesty, but he was tired of that. "Because it's easier when you have to pick up and leave. I might live here, but the house isn't mine." Just like the bed he'd had at Molly and William's hadn't been his. The apartment with Mateo and the one he got when he moved here had been the only places he ever fully unpacked.

Tristan crossed his arms. "Fair enough. You're angry at me, though. I see it. Do you want to explain that?"

Josiah shook his head, but then realized Tristan probably thought that meant he didn't want to explain it. "I'm not mad at you. More mad at myself." He paused a minute and took a deep breath. "Things haven't really changed for me. Not since I've been here. I'm going to school, I decided I wanted to move forward, which in a way I am, but, not completely."

Elliot had told him to be happy, and even though Elliot had meant with Tristan, it hadn't even crossed his mind to try to be happy with himself first. "I want to try and be happy, I think."

Another pause. Tristan's almond-shaped eyes never left Josiah. Finally, after what felt like an eternity, he replied, "Good for you."

The door closed quietly behind him as he walked out. Josiah turned off the computer, then the light. Took off his pants, and then climbed into bed.

He was moving on.

He would try to be happy, for himself, *with* himself.

And there was something else he could do, too. If he wanted pleasure, he could give himself that, too. It wasn't that he'd never jacked off before, but it had been a long time. He hadn't wanted it. Well, that was a lie. His body had, but the rest of him had never been into it. Now, he was.

Josiah pushed a hand under his boxer-briefs and then decided they were too confining. He kicked out of them. Wrapped a hand around his cock, which was already hard. Twice he stroked up and down his shaft, but it just wasn't right. He pumped some lotion into his hand and rubbed it down his length before he pumped his hand again. Slow strokes, fast strokes. He squeezed tighter as he jerked himself. With his other hand, he reached down and cupped his balls, remembered the way Mateo played with them, thought of the way he wished Tristan would, but then shoved both men out of his head.

He rolled them the way he liked. Tugged a little, shocked that the slight pain made a pleasurable sensation shoot through. He did it again as he kept those quick, tight strokes on his cock.

Josiah shivered. Why had he waited so long for this? Why didn't he pleasure himself more often?

It wasn't long before his balls started to ache. His body went taut with the first burst of come that shot out of him. He kept going, kept working himself, as another ribbon of semen flew up and landed on his stomach.

A laugh tumbled out of his mouth. It was crazy, and if Tristan could hear him, he probably sounded ridiculous. Josiah didn't care because he felt good, and he'd just given himself pleasure. He'd just done something he wanted for himself, and it had felt incredible.

He couldn't wait to do it again.

Chapter Eleven

July—the following year

Tristan

Tristan walked downstairs to see Josiah standing in the doorway, with it partially closed. Outside stood another guy who looked to be a little younger than Josiah. Neither man saw him as they talked. He wasn't sure what made him do it but he stopped, leaned against the wall at the bottom of the stairs, and watched.

Josiah pushed the dark blond hair that he started to grow a few months after moving in out of his face. It had been long for a little over a year now, the perfect length to grab on to. And he wanted that. Wanted it since before Josiah moved in, and the year and a half that he'd been here had only made the desire, the *craving,* grow more and more, until it threatened to eat him alive.

Josiah shifted, muscles constricted that wouldn't have been

noticeable a year and a half ago. It wasn't as though he was big, still shorter and leaner than Tristan, but more defined since he started using Tristan's workout equipment almost daily. At first he'd thought Tristan didn't know—he always exercised when Tristan was at work—but he'd known from the first day. He's smelled Josiah on his things, and the obsessive-compulsiveness in him knew they had been touched.

"We're all getting together down by the water. I thought you might want to come with me." The other man stepped closer to Josiah.

A fuse sparked, overheated, and blew inside him. Tristan fought to contain it. Josiah was free to go out with whomever he wanted, especially since Tristan knew he would never let himself fuck him.

"No, I can't. I want to get started on a presentation I have to do."

The guy shook his head. "I forgot you take summer classes."

Tristan automatically smiled at that. He'd done the same thing all through school.

"I want to graduate early. If I keep up the way I'm going, I can get my degree in three years instead of four."

"It's just one night." The guy reached out and ran his hand up Josiah's arm. "I like you. I want to get to know you better."

Even from behind, Tristan knew Josiah would be blushing. Sure, things had changed. He was more self-confident than he'd been, and he had a few more friends besides his buddy who used to work at the coffee house with him, but he was still Josiah. Still so damn innocent. So sweet.

His cock stirred. Fuck, Tristan wanted him.

"Yeah?" he asked, all shock in his voice. He didn't know how desirable he was.

"Yeah. What do you say?" The man's hand moved to Josiah's hair, and he let his fingers run through it. Josiah's head snapped back, forcing the other man's hands from him. He had a thing with his hair. Tristan had noticed that. He didn't like anyone touching it.

Josiah pushed it behind his ear. "Not today. I have some stuff I need to take care of. But, soon. I think I'd like to get to know you, too."

"Great, I'll call you."

Josiah closed the door when the guy walked away. He turned, and jumped a little when his eyes landed on Tristan. "Shit, I didn't know you were home. You scared me to death."

Tristan didn't uncross his arms. Didn't move from where he leaned against the wall, but cocked an eyebrow at him. "New boyfriend?"

Josiah bit his lip, stalled, before saying, "You wouldn't have asked me that a year ago."

"Don't remind me." Tristan shook his head. "And you wouldn't have called me on it. I miss the old Josiah." He didn't, really. And Josiah was right, too. Even though things had started off rocky, they'd fallen into this strange, almost comfortable life. Tristan stayed away from home longer than he needed to, missing being alone, just himself and the four walls surrounding him. He kept his distance. There were so many things Josiah didn't know about him, and never would. They still didn't walk together, even though Josiah still always went. But they were…friends. He was the first person other than Ben Tristan had ever called that, even though it still felt different than things with Ben.

Probably because Tristan had enjoyed fucking Ben, and he couldn't do that with Josiah.

"No, you don't."

It took Tristan a moment to remember what they'd been talking about. When he realized Josiah meant he didn't miss the way things used to be, Tristan gave him a small nod before pushing away from the wall.

"I'm going to my office."

He took one step when Josiah's voice stopped him. "Don't."

Tristan let out a deep breath and turned around to face him again. The look in his wide eyes had changed. Gone dark, and a little sad. He pushed his hand in his pocket and Tristan wondered if he still kept the queen there. If he was holding it right now.

An unexpected ache spidered through his chest.

"Let's have dinner. Maybe we could watch a movie or something."

The bottoms of his feet tingled, telling him to walk up the stairs, to lock himself in his office for the rest of the night, but he didn't. Not when he saw the way Josiah's eyes pleaded with him. For some reason, he didn't want to be alone. With anyone else, that would have made Tristan walk away. But not with Josiah. The urge to protect him, to fix whatever ailed him, sprouted. No, it had always been there, but it just grew, rooted deep into him.

Josiah should never have to be alone if he didn't want it, because he knew that Josiah was the kind of person who would never let someone else feel that way. He would never leave someone who cared about him, never walk away. That kind of roughness just wasn't inside him. Even though he didn't know it, he made Tristan feel less alone.

"I'll help you."

Josiah nodded, walking to the kitchen behind him. He took his backpack off and set it by the kitchen door.

They washed their hands, and then Josiah pulled ingredients out. He noticed right away what they were making—the pasta and sun-dried tomatoes—but he didn't comment on it. Josiah handed him vegetables and told him to chop them. Tristan got started on washing them while Josiah busied himself with other things.

Once they were clean, he started to chop. The room was silent except for Josiah's footsteps as he moved around the room, and then a laugh in Tristan's ear. "What are you doing? You're pulverizing it."

Tristan looked down at the small squares he cut. "You said to chop them."

"You've eaten before, right? These are squash and zucchini. When have you seen them cut so small? They're going to turn into mush." He laughed again before stepping up beside Tristan. "Like this." He pushed some of the smaller pieces aside before starting with a new squash, and much bigger chunks.

"Where'd you learn to cook?" Tristan found himself asking Josiah.

He shrugged. "Don't really know. I used to cook a little with Molly, my last foster mom, but not a whole lot. Then... well, cooking was something I could do for us. One of the only things, so I did it."

Who is us? He wanted to ask, but really, he knew. The man who'd given him the queen, whoever he was. Tristan swallowed down the sudden burn in his throat.

When Josiah stepped away, he finished the vegetables. They cooked, Josiah doing the most work, and laughed. Dinner came next, but they didn't eat in the kitchen like they normally did. They took their plates and a bottle of wine to the living room. Josiah put a movie on that they didn't really watch.

"Where do you go when you disappear?" Josiah asked, surprising him. It reminded him of the questions they'd ask when they used to walk. The word *veto* played on his tongue but Tristan bit it back. Maybe it was the alcohol. Tristan wasn't sure. All he knew was he couldn't give him everything, but he owed Josiah a little something.

"To see my mom."

Josiah's eyebrows squeezed together as if to ask how, after living with Tristan for a year and a half, he could have a mom Josiah had never heard of.

"Why doesn't she ever come here?"

Because she can't. She doesn't leave her apartment, and she loses herself in her head. "Veto." Tristan pushed his plate away from him. "How did you know that this is my favorite meal?"

It was a long time before Josiah replied. They both took a drink of their wine. Tristan ran his finger around the rim of the glass. Josiah bit his lip. "I pay attention, I guess. It's the only way to learn anything about you."

Tristan kept up the movement, finger to glass, trying to figure out what to say. Trying to ignore the blood pumping through his veins, and how it all seemed to head for his cock.

"Why did you make it?"

He blinked a couple times, looking unsure. "Because I wanted you to be happy. It's something small, but you're never happy. You knew I didn't want to be alone today, and you stayed for me. I wanted to do something nice for you." He took a drink. Eyed Tristan.

Fuck, he was so incredibly screwed right now. Especially when Josiah kept talking in that somber, soothing voice of his.

"I still don't want to, you know… Be alone. I can, though. That's the difference between now and before. I know I can, but tonight, I don't want to."

"Josiah—"

"I'm not asking for a relationship with you. I'm twenty-five years old, and I know what I can handle. This has been a bad day, and I want to forget. I want to lose myself in another person. Is that too much to ask?"

Did he know how incredibly brave he was? Somehow, Tristan doubted it. "Maybe."

"Why? It might just be physical, but I know you want me, too. And you know that's hard for me to say. Tell me why. Why is it too much? It's just sex." He looked down after he said it, that delicious red spreading over his face.

Sex. Josiah was right. It wasn't that he didn't use sex not to feel alone. It wasn't even like he hadn't had it since Josiah moved in. But then, he knew it would be more than that with Josiah, when he'd never had more than just sex with anyone.

"Look at me, Josiah." Tristan didn't move. Josiah did. He looked up at Tristan.

"Tell me why it's too much."

Tristan shook his head. He wouldn't do that. Couldn't. No one knew that he'd sold himself to Wilson. Sold himself the way his mom used to so she could support them. The way he'd sometimes hear as he sat in the closet, counting his pulse as though that would make it go away.

He didn't want Josiah to ever see him through those eyes. To know how weak Tristan had been. Josiah was far too good for that. He would never sink that low.

"No."

Josiah shook his head and turned away.

"I asked you to look at me, Josiah."

Josiah looked back at him. "And I'm asking you not to leave me alone tonight. I'm asking you to help me forget. To let me try and do the same for you."

Tristan's cock pressed against the zipper on his jeans. Hard. Painful. He pushed to his feet. Took four steps and stopped in front of Josiah. He touched Josiah's hair, and like he had earlier with the guy at the door, he pulled away. It bothered him—seeing someone else touch Josiah. The floodgates shattered, Tristan unable to hold back his lust any longer.

"Not my hair. He used to love my hair."

Tristan gave a quick, short nod. Fair enough. So instead, he touched Josiah's face. Cupped his cheek. Rubbed his thumb across Josiah's skin. "Do you have any idea what I want to do to you? Look at me. Look at how hard I am for you."

Josiah's head tilted down, landing on the bulge in Tristan's pants.

"Tell me you know you don't have to do this."

At that, Josiah's head snapped upward again. "What? Why—"

"Just tell me."

"I know I don't have to do this. I want to. I want you."

Tristan moaned. His cock jerked. "Hearing things like that come out of that sweet little mouth of yours... That's my favorite thing about you, Josiah. Everything about you is so damn sweet. Even your mouth. I remember that, you know. And I want to taste it again." Tristan dropped his hand from Josiah's cheek.

"Come here."

Without hesitation, or fear, cheeks flushed with desire, he stood.

For tonight, Tristan would make Josiah his.

Chapter Twelve

Josiah

Heat pooled low in Josiah's belly. He was hard, so hard that he feared one touch from Tristan would push him over the edge. But no, he would make this last. Feel, and touch, and have as much of Tristan as he could. Give as much as Tristan wanted, because they both needed it—release, pleasure, to forget. He wasn't sure how he knew that about Tristan, but he did.

He opened his lips as Tristan's came down on his. Tristan's tongue dipped into his mouth, sweeping, tasting, touching. All Josiah could think was, *Yes. Yes.*

"So sweet," Tristan whispered before his mouth came down again, urgent this time. Tongue probing. Josiah's did the same, wanting inside, wanting to know Tristan, too.

"Upstairs." By the time the word left Tristan's mouth, Josiah was already heading for the stairs. He took them two at a time, with Tristan right behind him. He wasn't sure why he started to pass his room, just assumed Tristan would want to be in his own since he knew it was bigger, as was the bed, but instead he grabbed Josiah's wrist to stop him. "In here."

Josiah pushed the door open and Tristan closed it behind them. The second it clicked, Tristan's hands were gripping the bottom of his shirt, pulling it over Josiah's head. He tossed it to the floor as he buried his face into Josiah's neck, sucking on the place where his neck met his shoulder.

"You unpacked," Tristan said against his skin.

"Six months go." But he didn't want to talk about that. Just wanted to feel. Wanted the heat of another man's body for the first time in seven years. Skin to skin. No, more than that—Josiah to Tristan, because even though touch was what he craved, he wanted it to be with Tristan. Someone he trusted.

Josiah pushed his hands under Tristan's shirt, feeling each defined muscle in his back.

Tristan moved away, ripping his own shirt off. His fingers went for Josiah's jeans. Unbuttoning. Unzipping. Shoving them down his legs. "Step out of them. Take your underwear off, too."

The demand made shivers race the length of Josiah's body. He worked quickly, doing exactly what Tristan told him to do.

"Jesus, you are so fucking sexy." Tristan ran his hands down Josiah's chest. Brushed his thumb through the hair that trailed his stomach and down to his erection.

Josiah hissed when Tristan's hand wrapped around him. "Oh, God. Please… I want." Everything. Wanted to feel everything, when he'd felt nothing for so long.

That's when Tristan dropped down to his knees. Josiah's heart raced, seeing this strong, confident man on his knees in front of him. Seeing Tristan there, it flipped a switch inside him. Showed him an almost vulnerable side to Tristan he'd never seen. It made Josiah's heart stutter.

Leaning forward, Tristan nuzzled his face in Josiah's crotch. Inhaled. Then sucked one of Josiah's balls into his mouth.

"Tristan..." His knees almost gave out.

"Shh," he replied before taking Josiah's length into this mouth, deep, and pulling off again.

His sac burned. Fire spread through his whole body. "That feels so good, but I want..." He wanted Tristan inside him. Wanted to feel full, instead of empty and alone.

"I don't go down on someone unless I really want to. I'm not going anywhere. Don't worry. I'll fuck you, too."

Those words cracked, broke through the armor around Josiah. The piece of him that desired something strictly physical. There was a need in Tristan's voice he'd never heard. A need for Josiah.

Then he took Josiah to the back of his throat again. His warm, wet mouth stroked Josiah's prick. The room spun. He had nothing to hold onto except for Tristan, so he did just that. Bent his head forward and watched the sexy man as he sucked Josiah off.

It wasn't as if Tristan wasn't always gorgeous, but there was something so...beautiful about seeing him let go. Because he was. Josiah saw that in the way he lavished him. The way his eyes closed and his body shuddered. It was the first time Josiah has really seen Tristan free, and it rocked him to his core.

Each time he pulled off, he swirled his tongue around the head before taking him deep again. Josiah's balls tightened. His release right there and begging to burst free, but wanting this to last forever, too. But then Tristan pulled off. Squeezed the base of Josiah's cock. "No. Don't come. I want to taste you. Want to know if you're just as sweet as you are everywhere else, but I want to be inside you when you come."

Josiah jumped when Tristan smacked his ass and said, "Get on the bed." He took that slap, hoping it would pull him out of whatever he'd started to slip into. The part of him who started seeing Tristan differently.

Josiah did as he was told. Tristan pulled out his wallet and grabbed a condom from inside before unbuttoning his pants and letting them drop to the floor. His boxer-briefs went next. He stood in front of Josiah, long, thick and hard. The head of his cock purple-ish. Veins ran the length of it. Josiah's breath caught.

"Lube?" Tristan asked.

"Drawer." He barely managed to push the word past his lips. His body felt like it was on fire. Needy and urgent and ready to explode.

Tristan grabbed the lube and tossed it along with the condom onto the bed. "Open your legs."

Josiah did and Tristan went between them. He squirted some of the lube onto his finger before rubbing it on Josiah's hole. It was cold and he flinched, while his body begged for more at the same time.

"How long has it been for you?" Tristan asked.

He didn't want to, but finally admitted, "Over seven years."

Tristan just stared at him. If Josiah knew him, he was thinking about the fact that Josiah hadn't been with anyone since he was eighteen. Even now that he was in school and people asked him out, he still hadn't had sex with anyone. The knowledge started taunting him, too. He hadn't wanted anyone. He'd said no, but maybe…maybe this had been what he waited for. Tristan. Josiah couldn't give himself to just anyone. Fear began to push its way through. Not wanting Tristan to change his mind, he said, "I want you. Please."

The familiarity of the words threatened to drag him to the past, but Josiah didn't let them. He moved his body toward Tristan, who gave his signature nod and slowly pushed a finger inside. Past the ring of muscles. Josiah's body automatically tensed up.

Tristan's finger pressed in deeper. His mouth came down on Josiah's at the same time. In and out, he worked his finger as his tongue did the same to Josiah's mouth.

He took his mouth away and said, "That's it. Relax for me." He twisted his finger as he worked him. Another squirt of lube, and then Josiah tensed again as Tristan used two fingers to stretch him this time.

"Tristan…" But he was moving against Tristan's hand now, too. Twist. In. Out. Tristan rotated movements, preparing Josiah's body for what would come next.

"You're so tight. I'm going to hate hurting you, but Christ, I can't wait to fuck you, either. I'll make it good for you."

And then, more than just his body exploded. Emotions, too, at the sound of Tristan's voice and the part of him Josiah knew never would want to hurt him in any way. His eyes closed as he moved his body along with Tristan's hand, trying to focus on the physical. "I know," he whispered. There had only been one other person in his life he knew truly never wanted to hurt him… But then, he had. He had.

"You're disappearing on me. Come back." Another slow and sensual kiss. Josiah's whole body buzzed with electricity. Felt sensitive. Even the sound of Tristan's breathing threatened to make him spiral out of control.

Reaching out, he wrapped a hand around Tristan's erection. Pumped it up and down. Hot. He was so hot and hard.

"Fuck, I need inside you." Tristan pulled back, and his fingers were gone. Josiah watched as he slid the condom down his thick rod. "Turn over."

Josiah paused, but then Tristan added, "I told you I'd make it good for you. Trust me."

He rested on his stomach, and then Tristan was at his back. More cold lube on his hole. His body went taut, and then a kiss to one of his ass cheeks. Then his lower back. Shoulder blade. Tristan's arms went under his then wrapped around so he held Josiah's shoulders. Pain shot through him as Tristan started to push inside.

Josiah moaned.

"Relax, Josiah. Let me in." His breath on Josiah's neck made him shiver, but then he pressed a kiss there. And another, and another. His teeth bit into Josiah's skin as he kept pressing forward. Pushing inside.

Josiah's breathing sped up. When Tristan filled him, the reaction was automatic. He moved back, trying to get closer. Wanting Tristan to move. To fuck him. But that's not what this felt like, was it? It was more. Unexpected. And he was drowning in it.

Tristan's nails dug into his shoulders as he pulled out then slammed forward again. Slow and smooth, but with strength, too.

"So fucking good. You're going to be the death of me, Josiah. You know that, don't you?"

He nodded, though he wasn't sure why. He didn't want to be the death of Tristan… but he wanted him. Wanted him more than he realized before. Knew emotions twirled and built inside him that he shouldn't feel. That Tristan wouldn't want.

With each thrust, his nails bit deeper. He pushed Josiah's body so he met each of Tristan's pumps. Skin to skin. Tristan to Josiah. Just like he wanted.

Over and over, Tristan filled him. Fucked him. Made love to him. It felt incredible. Made him happy, even though he knew he was in over his head. But still… Josiah's eyes burned. Wetness dripped onto his hand that rested under his head, unsure how to feel. He was sure it would make Tristan pull away. Walk away. He almost turned his head to face the pillow, rather than sideways, but then Tristan's lips pressed to a spot beneath his eye. They had to have come back wet, but he kept going. Didn't slow his movements as Josiah's pleasure built higher and higher. As the water rose higher and higher and Josiah sunk deeper and deeper.

Sadness and happiness blended together. Teo. Teo had been the only other person who'd ever been inside him. The only one he'd wanted there, and feeling this made Josiah miss him more. But he wanted Tristan here, too. Wanted it over and over, because he'd changed something inside Josiah. Made him want again. Made him feel something besides emptiness again. He had a life now, and knew he was strong enough to give himself a future, too, but this? Feeling connected, being together with someone. He craved that, too. Had craved it from Mateo, and now with Tristan.

Tristan's body slapped against his. His shoulder stung where Tristan held him, but it just added to the pleasure surging through him. Their bodies moved together. Josiah's cock rubbed against the blanket, creating a friction that added to the feel of Tristan inside him.

"I'm going to come, Josiah. You're so fucking good. So tight, squeezing my cock." And then one of his hands went down, under Josiah, and wrapped around his erection. He thrust harder, faster, stroking him at the same time.

That was all it took. Josiah's insides exploded. His body went rigid as he came, hot semen pulsing out of him in waves. Tristan kept up his movements. Stroking and pumping.

Josiah felt Tristan's cock jerk inside him. Felt Tristan stiffen on his back. Heard him quietly whisper, "Josiah…" That simple word—his name that he'd heard millions of times in his life made him shiver. *Again,* he almost asked. *Say my name again…*

And then Tristan was gone. Pulled out. Stood up. Fear raced up Josiah's spine. He should let him walk out. It's what Tristan would expect and what he'd agreed to, but suddenly not what he wanted. "Don't go. Not yet."

A small nod. "Okay." He pulled the condom off and tossed it into the trashcan before lying next to him again. The bed was so small they hardly fit, but that was okay. Twin bed, two bodies. He'd done that before.

It was forever until Tristan spoke. "What's today?"

The thought of lying didn't even occur to him. "His birthday."

"And he left you? That's how you ended up here?"

Veto, veto, veto. "He saved me first. Saved me many times. But yes. He left me in the end."

Josiah melted into Tristan when he felt an arm wrap around him. *Thank you.*

He hadn't expected this. Hadn't expected to need it, either, but he did.

"And you wanted me to help you forget him?"

Josiah turned to face him. Looked him in the eyes. "Partially. But more than that, I wanted you. *Want* you. I never thought I could want someone other than Mateo, but you gave me that back. That…desire. I never thought I would care about someone again, but you gave me that, too."

Josiah waited for him to get up. To tell Josiah he was crazy. That he'd told him he didn't do relationships and this was just a fuck. But Tristan didn't move.

"You still love him."

It wasn't a question, but Josiah answered anyway. "A part of me will always love him. There's… we went through a lot. Being with you helps." He wanted to say more but knew he couldn't. He should have known his emotions would get involved, but he could be strong.

"There are things I've done I will probably never be able to tell you," Tristan said. "I had a hard childhood. We lived on the streets sometimes. Even when we had a home, that's all we had. My mom sold her body and was hurt by men. I saw it and couldn't save her. But I know in a way I had no control over those things. The things I did after, when I was older, were my choice. My mistakes, but I wouldn't take those back, either, because they gave me what I have now. Control over myself and my world."

Somehow, Josiah knew what he was saying. And shocked that Tristan opened up to him. "And loving someone would make you lose that control."

Tristan didn't answer that. "I can't give you what he did. I can't give you everything you deserve. But pretending I don't want you, that I can handle not having you, isn't something I can do anymore, either. I can give you my body, if you haven't gotten your fill. Not because I have to, but because I want to, if you want to continue to give me yours. I can give you my home—"

"Your friendship." Because he did. Tristan gave him that.

He nodded. "Yes, that, too." And then he paused before speaking again. "There's something so addicting about you." He touched Josiah's hair, but then pulled back and ran a hand down his back instead. "Something so good and kind."

Josiah fought to snuff out, to extinguish, the spark that Tristan lit inside him. Friends. Friendship and sex. He could handle that. He had to.

Chapter Thirteen

Tristan

"Tristan, I want you to meet someone. This is Oliver. Can you say hi for me?"

Tristan eyed his mom. Eyed the tall man standing next to her with the expensive looking coat. Watched as he latched hands with his mom, something he'd never seen before.

"Tristan?" his mom asked.

"Hi," he mumbled.

His mom let go of Oliver's hand and kneeled in front of Tristan. His eyes didn't leave Oliver as the man smiled and backed away, as if to give them space. And then he winked at Tristan, who didn't know what that meant. It made his skin feel tight.

"Sweetheart, Oliver is mommy's friend. He's been coming to the restaurant to see me every night. I love him, Tris. And he loves me, too. Can you believe that? He's going to save us. Oliver is going to save us."

Tristan jerked himself out of the dream and sat up in his bed. He glanced at the clock to see he'd only left Josiah's room about an hour before.

He didn't try to go back to sleep. It never worked, anyway. He didn't attempt to close down his mind, either.

"How…how can you ask me to do that, Oliver?"

"I don't want you to. Don't you see that, beautiful? Not you. I want you all to myself… but I'm taking care of you, and your son, too. And you know I have my parents and sister I'm helping out as well. Things at work are slowing down. It'll just be a few times. I couldn't handle to share you more than that. And you're so beautiful. Everyone will want you. My beautiful Rhonda. Don't let me down, Rhonda. You know I hate asking you this. I just want to take care of you…"

"Okay. I'll do it for you. For us."

Tristan stood outside the room, not knowing what was happening, but knowing it was wrong.

Tristan pushed out of bed and headed straight for his shower. When he got out it was three thirty. Despite the early hour, he dressed for work. Tristan could always find something to do when it came to work. When he got downstairs, he heard movement in the kitchen. His skin pricked with awareness, which he immediately tried to stamp down. Eagerness at seeing Josiah made no sense. He'd only left his bed two hours ago.

Tristan made a stop in the kitchen, where Josiah stood, pulling his bag onto his shoulders. Him and that damned bag.

"What are you doing up?" he asked.

Josiah whipped around to face him. "You're always able to sneak up on me. Mateo used to tell me I had to be more aware of my surroundings. I try to do that, but it never works with you."

Tristan opened his mouth, but instead of speaking, he touched his tongue behind his teeth. Curiosity tugged at him. Why would he need to be so aware? But then, in a way, he knew. Knew Josiah had lived some form of darkness the same way Tristan had growing up. Asking only opened wounds. Made him vulnerable, when he couldn't allow himself to be. He'd inadvertently given that to Josiah last night when he'd sworn he would never leave himself vulnerable to a human being the way his mom had.

Josiah obviously realized Tristan wasn't going to reply. "I work at five this morning. You couldn't sleep?"

"I never sleep. And God forbid you miss a morning of walking or feeding your birds. You're very loyal."

Josiah shrugged. "I do it because I want to, not because I have to. They depend on it now, and I won't let them down."

The whole time he considered what he was about to do, Tristan cursed himself. His dream reminded him of where he stood in life, yet he still stepped forward and cupped Josiah's cheek. "The way you've been let down?"

No hesitation. Just wide, honest eyes when he said, "Yes. But I've had loyalty, too. Not often, but from a few people, so I can't really complain."

Finger to wrist. *One, two, three, four, five.* Jesus, this man would really kill him. Tristan stepped away, but Josiah reached out, grabbing the sleeve of his jacket. "Will you go with me?" he asked.

Tristan closed his eyes, and replied, "Yes."

That was the beginning of their morning walks again. Tristan couldn't go every day, but he went when he could. And missed it when he couldn't.

Still, he kept the dream in his mind. Kept the past present in his head, because he wanted Josiah, when the only times he'd been with people in his past, even Ben, it had been because he wanted sex. His mother had wanted Oliver, and he turned her onto the streets. He gave her drugs that she hardly escaped from. Tristan could never give himself to someone like that.

But they still walked. And talked. And ate dinner together at night.

It took three months for the question to come from Josiah. They stood together at the counter, after dinner. "I want you again…" Tristan silenced Josiah with his mouth. That one statement had been all it took. The whole time, a quiet voice in the back of Tristan's mind whispered, *"why did it take you so long to ask?"*

Time passed, and it went from three months to two. Then monthly, biweekly. Now, a week didn't go by that Tristan didn't visit Josiah's bed at least once, sometimes more. He fucked him and held him and talked to him in a way he'd never done with anyone. But always, *always,* he ended the night with a kiss to Josiah's lips before going to his own bed.

And there had been no one else since he stared fucking Josiah. No one came to see Josiah, either, except his friend Elliot. Those were things Tristan pretended he didn't notice.

The weather had already turned cold and started to warm up again, the days and months flying by.

Josiah shivered as they walked by the water, the sun yellow in the distance. "How are you cold?" Tristan asked him.

"Because it's six in the morning, during spring in San Francisco," he laughed. The wind kicked up and blew his hair into his face. Tristan almost pushed it back but remembered Josiah got uncomfortable when people touched his hair.

"You're from New York. That's cold. Not this."

"You're from there, too!" Josiah countered.

"Yet, I'm not cold."

It was Josiah who pushed his own hair from his face this time. "I like it. I'm glad you grew it," Tristan found himself saying. He didn't let himself focus on that, just waited for Josiah's reply.

"It used to be blonder. I didn't expect it to grow in so much darker."

A burn landed in his chest. He rubbed his hand there, wishing he had an antacid. His hair was another thing that had to do with Josiah's ex-lover. He didn't need Josiah to tell him to know it.

His phone cut off any chance of a reply. Tristan pulled it from his pocket, groaning when he saw Ben's name show up. He hit ignore before pushing it into his pocket again.

"Who was that?" Josiah asked.

"And old friend," he replied. There was no reason he couldn't tell Josiah about Ben, and wasn't sure why he didn't.

Ben was fascinated by Josiah, though.

Because he's lived with me for nearly two and a half years. Because he could tell Tristan was fucking him. Because he saw Josiah was different to him.

"Are you going to see your mom before work?" Josiah asked, changing the subject. He knew Tristan's mom was here. Knew he helped take care of her, but that was all Tristan could bring himself to tell him.

"Yes." They both stopped walking, Josiah looking up at him, his eyes probing, searching like they always did. *What do you want? You already have more of me than anyone ever has.*

"Have a good day," he said.

Tristan nodded. "Thanks." And then he turned away. Walked, before he kissed him goodbye. It was one thing when he left Josiah's bed. In public would be totally different.

Behind him, Josiah spoke again. "Miss you…"

Tristan didn't stop, didn't tell him, even though he'd miss Josiah, too.

***

"What's it like? How does the weather feel?" Tristan's mom asked when he sat beside her at the window.

"You can go out, if you want. I'll go with you. We don't have to go far." He waited, hoped her answer would be different than it was any other time he'd asked.

"You know I can't, Tris. In my head, I know, I *get* that it's crazy, but… I'm safe in here. I wasn't safe out there."

The heartburn came back. This time, his body somehow felt frozen at the same time. As though he couldn't move.

"I get myself in trouble out there," she whispered.

"No." He shook his head. "It was never your fault. People took advantage of you. Abused *you*. It was never your fault."

"If I had been stronger… I was your mom. I should have known better. I made so many mistakes, Tristan."

Ice and fire. All he felt was ice and fire. "You did the best you could. We're good now. No one will hurt you again."

At that, she smiled. "Sorry. I'm being a downer. It's been a bad day."

"What happened?"

"Nothing. I don't want to talk about it. I want to talk about you. You were smiling when you came in, Tristan. You do that more lately."

One, two, three, four, five.

"I'm the same as I've always been." But he knew that wasn't true. In some ways he was, but he didn't feel as alone anymore. Not with the walks and sharing dinner with someone else every day.

"You're different and you know it. I'd like to meet him, whoever he is."

The thought of bringing Josiah here, of introducing him to his mom, of Josiah seeing what Tristan allowed to happen, made him nauseous. "There is no one. And I thought you were determined it would be a she?"

"I wanted there to be *someone*. If you haven't noticed, I don't get out much. Isabel is the only person I know."

His mom smiled, but Tristan didn't. That wasn't funny at all.

"Humor me for a second, will you? I'll believe there is no one, but tell me… if there was, what would he be like? You're my son. I want to pretend you can be happy. That I didn't screw everything up."

Tristan looked down at his wrist. Tried to find his pulse with his eyes rather than with his finger. *Slam, slam, slam, slam.* He closed the door on all his thoughts. Just spoke…and felt. "He would be kind, loyal. Stronger than he realized. Braver than most people thought. He'd like coffee and cooking. He'd like to walk, and he'd always feed the birds."

His mom reached over and grabbed his hand. "That sounds nice. He sounds nice."

Tristan squeezed her hand back. "He would be."

Chapter Fourteen

Josiah

A soft buzzing sound pulled Josiah out of sleep. He pulled a pillow over his head, trying to ignore it, but the buzz continued. He could tell it was a cell phone, but his wasn't on vibrate, and Tristan always had his with him.

Buzz.

Sitting up, Josiah felt around the mattress, his fingers wrapping around Tristan's cell.

"Josiah, I can't walk with you this morning." Tristan's hand had cupped his face before dawn. *"I won't be home until late, either. I'm in court, and it's an important case."*

Josiah remembered Tristan bending to kiss him before he'd gone ahead and flipped back the blankets to get up. They'd kissed before Tristan left, Josiah went for his walk, and then came back home to nap before class.

Tristan would lose it when he realized he'd dropped his phone.

It stopped ringing, and Josiah got up to get dressed. Maybe he could get ahold of someone at Tristan's office and drop the cell off there.

Immediately it started to ring again, from the same number. He let it go to voicemail, but the person called right back.

Nerves bundled in his stomach. He knew Tristan valued his privacy, and didn't want to do anything to betray that, but then, what if it was important? What if something was wrong?

With shaky fingers, he answered. "Hello?"

"Who is this?" A soft, female voice asked.

"Josiah. I'm a friend of Tristan's." Thoughts began to spout in his head. This was Tristan's mom. Josiah didn't have a doubt in his mind.

"Is Tristan there? He didn't answer. He always answers his phone, and I was worried."

"He's fine. He's at work. I think he must have dropped his phone. I can't get ahold of him because he's in court today, but I'm going to head down to his office and see if they have a way to get it to him."

There was a pause on the other end of the line that stretched on uncomfortably.

"Is something wrong?" Josiah finally asked. "I can find him if you need me to. I know he would want me to. He's already going to be angry at himself that he left his phone."

Another pause. "You're him, aren't you? The one who likes to walk and feed the birds?"

Josiah's heart sped up, a racecar circling a track in his chest. Tristan had told his mom about him? The knowledge didn't compute. Didn't feel like something Tristan would ever do. Questions begged to break free. He wanted to know exactly what Tristan had said about him, and how it had come up, but to ask almost put a sour feeling in his stomach. It almost wouldn't matter knowing if Tristan didn't make the decision to tell him.

"I do walk, every day.... Is there something I can do for you? Something I can tell Tristan?"

He heard movement on the other end of the line before she spoke. "I was just lonely and hoped Tristan could stop by today. Isabel is out, and...I just missed him." She sighed again. "Just ignore me. It's one of those days. He's at work, and I know I can't interrupt him there. It's not fun being alone."

Josiah shook his head as though she could see him. He had firsthand experience with being alone. "No. No, it's not." And he also knew that if Tristan got this phone call, he would have gone to see his mom. He'd find a way to work it out so he could give her what she needed.

"You sound familiar with the emotion."

"Not as much as I used to be."

"Because of Tristan?" she asked.

Josiah sat back down on his bed and leaned against the wall. "Yeah."

"How did you meet?"

Josiah told her how he'd been walking by the water, then stopped to feed the birds, and turned to find Tristan there. He shared about his daily walks and his job at the coffee house. He talked about school and how, if he kept going at the rate he was, he only had a little over a year left. That he'd have his four year degree, something he never expected to get, and that he'd get it in less time, too.

They both asked questions and talked about Tristan. Neither let the conversation go too deep, not letting it veer into topics they both knew Tristan wouldn't want to share. It was like an unspoken vow that they both accepted, because it wouldn't be fair to Tristan.

Time passed by, and Josiah just kept talking to her. He made lunch while on the phone. Ignored the time, even though he knew he should be in class. When the cell started to die, he plugged it in and let her keep talking. She asked about his family and apologized when he told her he'd lost both his parents.

At close to five, she quieted for a few seconds. "Tristan was right. You're very kind."

With the back of his hand, Josiah brushed it over his own cheek, as though he could feel Tristan that way. Tristan, who was so serious most of the time but could make him laugh, too. Tristan, who gave him a place to stay and talked to him. Who made love to him as though to him, it really was more than sex. "So is he."

"I have to go. Thank you for talking with me today. I was having a harder day then I let on. Now I'm…hopeful."

A burst of pride swelled inside him. "I'm glad it helped."

When they got off the phone, Josiah went downstairs to start dinner. Even though Tristan wouldn't be home until late, he wanted to make sure he had food waiting. The roast and potatoes had only been in the oven about thirty minutes when he heard the front door.

Josiah headed for the door of the kitchen, but Tristan somehow made it there before him. He blocked the doorway, his tie undone like it so often was when he got off work.

"Hey. I thought you were going to be late?" Josiah asked, but Tristan didn't reply. He just studied Josiah intensely, as though he'd never seen him before. The hairs on the back of his neck rose. He leaned against the counter because he couldn't make himself stay still. "Is everything okay?"

He couldn't help the fear that ate away at the happiness he'd started to feel—living here, being with Tristan, falling in love with him. To have him come home almost just like Mateo did before he'd walked away. That's the way it went for him. When he felt secure or comfortable, when he found someone to love, even if Tristan couldn't feel the same about him, he lost it. He'd lose Tristan the way he did Mateo. The wild look in Tristan's expressive eyes told him that.

And then he cocked his head a little bit. A slight smile tugged at Tristan's lips. "You talked to her. This was the first day of college you missed, and it was because you spoke with her all day on the phone."

The fear eating at him started to ease back. Josiah shrugged, but still wondered how he knew. Did he look for his phone at the end of the day and call her? Stop by? "I'm sorry I answered your phone, but she kept calling, and I was worried. She was lonely, and I knew you were in court. I didn't want her to feel alone."

Tristan took a step forward, and then another one. "You cared how she felt and you don't even know her. Her parents didn't care when they kicked her out for not aborting me, and my father didn't care when he told her he didn't want to be a dad and walked away. Men used her because she had a big heart and didn't care if they hurt her, and others used her for her body, when she only wanted to take care of her son."

Closer and closer he got, until he stood right in front of Josiah and looked down at him. He fought to breathe around the ball in his throat. This was Tristan giving him more bits and pieces of his life that he kept locked so far inside of him.

"No one cared enough about her. People she thought loved her turned her into a prostitute and fed her drugs. They let people hurt her, until she became too afraid to leave our apartment. I didn't…" Tristan shook his head, pain darkening all of his features. Though everything inside of Josiah wanted to know more, he wanted to take away Tristan's pain even more. To make him forget the same way Tristan had done for him the first time they were together.

"It wasn't your fault." Josiah pushed up and covered Tristan's mouth with his. He let his tongue dip inside and tangle with Tristan's. His body began to overheat, his erection pressing against the zipper of his pants.

Tristan's arm wrapped around him, pressed his lower back so Josiah didn't have a choice but to mold his body against Tristan's.

It wasn't as though he wanted to fight him away.

And then Josiah's mouth was the one invaded as Tristan fought his way inside, licking and tasting. Owning. His hands slid up and cupped Josiah's face as his kisses slowed but were no less hungry.

When he pulled away, Josiah leaned in again, needing more, but Tristan didn't let go of his face and didn't let him move.

"I want you in my bed. I'm going to fuck you all night, Josiah."

His erection throbbed with need. "I want you, too." But then, he always did. Wanted him in every way.

"Go." Tristan nodded for the kitchen door. Josiah didn't argue, just started to move, and Tristan turned off the oven. He took the stairs with Tristan right behind him. Tried to walk into his room, but stopped with a firm grip on his arm. "No. I said *my* bed."

Neither man moved. Josiah's body thrummed to life, his erection impossibly hard. But it was more than that, and this time, he knew it was more to Tristan, too.

Chapter Fifteen

Tristan

Tristan watched Josiah as he slowly walked into his bedroom and turned to face him. He concentrated on his dark blond hair and the curve of his lips. On the shadow of hair on his jaw, and the way his throat moved when he swallowed. He concentrated on the rapid beat of his own heart, needing all of those things to drown out the voice in his head that told him to walk away. The one who told him to force Josiah out of his room and to board up his heart so he could stop finding his way in.

Then, as if Josiah knew he was losing Tristan, he pulled off Tristan's tie. Slowly worked the buttons on his shirt, one by one. Tristan's body was set in stone, unable to move, but then, he didn't have to. Josiah pushed his shirt off his shoulders and ran his hands over Tristan's chest, down his stomach, before he took care of Tristan's pants, too.

"Has anyone ever taken care of you?" Josiah asked as he led Tristan to the bed.

Take control! Don't give him power over you. But Tristan just kept walking. He sat on the edge of the bed and said, "I've never let a lover take care of me. I never wanted them to."

"Will you let me?"

Christ, Josiah was so dangerous to him. He was more than just the kind man with the big heart. He was brave, and went after what he wanted. Tristan balanced on the edge, almost slipping over. Almost saying yes, but he caught himself before making the plunge. "Take off your clothes for me, Josiah. I want to see you."

Josiah's eyes drifted closed, and Tristan knew he'd let him down. All he'd had to do was mutter yes, and hand over the reins, but he couldn't do it. The only man who ever had power over him had been Wilson, and he would never give that away again.

Gripping the bottom of his shirt, Josiah pulled it up and dropped it to the floor. He stepped out of his pants, his body firm, defined. He had a little mole above his heart. The hair that trailed down his stomach, darker than that on his head. His cock hard, and long, the tip swollen and leaking.

Tristan craved Josiah's taste on his tongue.

"Come here. I want you in my mouth."

"I wanted to take care of you."

You already do. You might not know it, but you do. "Not right now. Lie on the bed, Josiah. I need to call the shots." He wasn't dominant, not really, Tristan just needed to set the pace. He couldn't deal with someone else running the show.

Josiah gave him a small nod before lying on the bed. Tristan moved to hover over him, looked down at Josiah laid out for him, his skin a contrast to the black bedspread. His chest got tight and his heart sped. He almost wished he could take back what he said. That he could let Josiah lavish him however he wanted. But damned if he didn't want to do the same thing to Josiah. "You are so damn sexy," he whispered before sucking Josiah's cock all the way to the back of his throat.

There was a slight tug when Josiah buried his hand in Tristan's hair and pulled. Just as quickly as it happened, it was gone. "You're okay. Don't let go."

And then the hand was back. Not directing Tristan's head, just there, as Tristan's mouth slid down Josiah's length again.

"Tristan... More, I need more."

And so, he gave it to him. Tristan laid between Josiah's legs, pushing them open for him. He sucked one ball, then the other, into his mouth. Josiah moaned. Tristan wanted to bottle that sound so he could replay Josiah taking his pleasure whenever he wanted.

Pushing Josiah's legs up farther, Tristan lashed Josiah's hole over and over with his tongue. "So fucking good. I could have my mouth on you all night."

"More... I need you inside me, Tristan."

"I'm getting there," he smiled, unsure if he'd ever smiled in bed with someone before. "Grab the lube and a condom from the drawer," Tristan instructed.

Josiah's body twisted slightly as he pulled open the bedside drawer. Tristan let his teeth dig into Josiah's thigh, first one, then the other, making Josiah's body quake.

"I love the taste of you. Everywhere." Tristan sucked on his finger before pushing it inside Josiah.

The bottle of lube fell from his hand. "Holy shit. More. Give me more. Please."

It was the *please* that did it. Tristan replaced his finger with his tongue, fucking his lover with it. He used his hand to stroke Josiah's cock. He noticed the tightness in Josiah's body. Felt the way he started to thrust and knew he was about to lose it. Quickly, he covered Josiah's dick with his own mouth just as a jet of hot come shot in the back of this throat. And then another one. Tristan swallowed them both down.

Electricity sizzled beneath his skin, his cock already ready to explode.

He ripped open the condom with his teeth before sheathing himself. With fumbling hands, he managed to open the lube, coating himself and then lying down behind Josiah. He positioned him on his back, slightly rolled up onto his side. "Give me your leg."

Josiah lifted it and Tristan wrapped an arm around it, holding it up before pushing into Josiah from behind. "Christ, you feel so good. I love fucking you." He pulled almost all the way out before slamming forward again.

Josiah tilted his head toward Tristan, looking over his shoulder, before kissing him. Their tongues battled it out, taking and receiving, as Tristan thrust into him. He kept his arm under Josiah's leg but reached up to grab his cock, discovering it was hard again—or still, he didn't know.

"Want you to come again with me." And then they were kissing again. Kissing and fucking as Tristan jacked him off. That electric feeling started to take him over. Started to burn him alive, and he knew he wasn't going to last much longer.

"Come with me, Josiah." He squeezed tighter, pumped faster, and then dug his teeth into Josiah's shoulder. His body thrashed beneath him, come slipping through Tristan's fingers. That was all it took before his own body let loose—tensed, came un-fucking-done, as he filled the condom with his own jizz.

Tristan lay back on the bed, looking up at the ceiling. Josiah didn't roll over to look at him, and damned if he didn't want that. Suddenly need it.

After pulling the condom off and tossing it into the trash, he said, "Come here, Josiah."

Josiah rolled his direction, come dripping down his stomach. Tristan reached out and rubbed it in. "Next time, I'm going to come on you. That way, it's my spunk I get to rub into your skin." The thought made the blood start rushing to his cock again.

"That sounds good," Josiah smiled at him.

Words played on Tristan's tongue, but he couldn't push them free. The truth was, this thing between them meant more to Tristan than pretty much anything ever had. He'd been feeling it for a while, but after talking with his mom, hearing that Josiah had been there for her when he hadn't, a woman he didn't know, well…that meant something to him. It meant more because he knew Josiah hadn't done it for him, he'd done it because that's the kind of man he was. Good.

And it made Tristan even more of an asshole, because he still couldn't let Josiah all the way in.

"Can I ask you something?" Josiah laid a hand on his chest and Tristan nodded. "The only time you've ever let me go down on you is when you told me to. I wanted that, Tristan. Tonight. I wanted to take care of you."

Tristan's body froze up. How could he tell Josiah what he'd done? That he'd let someone use his body—let someone control and dominate him for money? That he'd been a whore for another man through college, despite the fact that his mom had been manipulated with the same thing? That he'd seen it break her?

The truth was, he couldn't. Couldn't lose Josiah's respect, because he was the only one he gave a shit about.

Silence stretched on, one minute, two, three, four. He counted the seconds, then flinched when Josiah picked up his wrist and pressed his fingers to Tristan's pulse.

"If I could completely give myself to anyone, it would be you. If I deserved anyone to take care of me, I would want it to be you." That was the realest truth he could give Josiah.

Josiah paused. "Emotionally or physically?"

"Both." Because he couldn't completely give up control physically. Could never let someone inside him the way only Wilson had been.

"Because of what happened to your mom?"

"That's the emotional part," was all he could say. Couldn't tell him the physical had to do with Wilson. "She gave her heart to my father, and then to another man, and it destroyed her. I can't do that, Josiah, but damned if you don't make me want to."

With that, Josiah pressed his lips to Tristan's. Tristan opened his mouth and dipped his tongue into Josiah's, the kiss so sweet he couldn't regret his honesty.

He pulled Josiah on top of him. "You were there for her, Josiah. The way I was raised…we never had anyone who was there for us, yet you were. I want you to know that means the world to me."

The room was silent for what felt like an eternity. "I know what it's like to feel like you have no one. I'll always be here for you."

Tristan squeezed him, trying to tell him with his body that he would be there for Josiah, too. "And you weren't alone anymore after him?" Jealousy took over his bloodstream, rushing through his whole body.

"No."

"Tell me." The word almost stuck in his throat. The last thing he wanted to talk about was the man Josiah loved, but he needed to know, too. Their story was a part of Josiah, which made it a part of them.

Josiah grabbed his wrist again, placing his fingers at Tristan's pulse. "I was sixteen when I met him. The first time he walked into the room, I thought he would kill me…but he didn't. He saved me. He loved me."

Tristan held Josiah while he talked about Mateo. As he told him how the man had protected him, more than once, in every way possible. He heard about Mateo's fights and learning to play chess, and the day he gave Josiah the queen. About Mateo getting sent away and Josiah going to him. He listened as Josiah told him about the apartment they shared and Mateo's work and how he always got sick. Tristan's blood ran cold, his whole body aching as Josiah told him he was attacked, and that Mateo had saved him then, too.

He didn't go into details, which Tristan was thankful for. Rules were important to him, laws were, but there was a part of him that respected the hell out of Mateo, too. He'd done whatever he had to to protect someone he loved.

He wanted to hate the bastard. And he did, in a way…but then he thought of Josiah. About what he'd dealt with before Mateo, and how Mateo'd kept him safe. And for that, he couldn't completely despise the man.

"He's worthy, then…worthy of your love," Tristan said when Josiah finished. He'd given Josiah something Tristan couldn't willingly hand over: His heart.

Josiah leaned up and looked at Tristan, eyes full of emotion. "So are you. I love you, too."

The words knocked the breath out of him. Tristan waited for the urge to flee, but it didn't come. Opened his mouth to return the words, but damned if he could make them come out, no matter how true they would be.

Instead he leaned over and opened the drawer beside his bed, pulling out the carved bird from inside. "I saw this a few months ago, and it made me think of you. I didn't make it, but—"

"It's incredible." Josiah plucked it out of his hand.

Tristan cupped his face and pressed a kiss to his lips. "Stay in here with me tonight." There were so many things he couldn't give Josiah—words, promises—but he wanted to give him what he could. Wanted to hold him at night and pretend he had it in him to tell Josiah he wanted Josiah to be his.

Chapter Sixteen

Josiah

Even though he kept his things in his room, Josiah never slept there anymore. It started out slowly, the night they made love. Tristan would invite him into his room, and then ask him to stay. As the months went on, he stayed there more and more, until one night when Tristan shrugged and said, "There's no reason to go to your bed anymore when you almost always end up in mine."

So, he hadn't. In a lot of ways, that was the only thing that changed. Tristan still didn't sleep well. Even though Josiah woke early to walk, it was rare Tristan didn't make it out of bed before he did. And it was rare that Tristan didn't walk with him, too. The few times Josiah had told him he loved him, he still never returned the words, but he would smile, or kiss him, showing Josiah he was important to him.

Josiah walked through their living room on one of his rare days off from both school and work. With graduation approaching, he was crazy busy. His cell rang on the way to the kitchen, and he smiled when Tristan's name lit up the screen.

"Hey, aren't you supposed to be saving the world in court today?" he teased.

"Very funny. Court date got postponed. I have about an hour left here, and then I'm going to stop by my mom's for a little while. What do you want me to get for dinner on the way home?"

Home. The word still comforted him. As did the fact that a man like Tristan shared it with him. That he called to bring home dinner to someone like Josiah. That even though Tristan couldn't admit it, he was Josiah's as much as Josiah was his.

"I can cook." Josiah opened the cabinet to see what they had.

"I told you I don't want you cooking every night. That was the deal before."

He never said what the "now" was as compared to before. Was it because Josiah meant more to him than he originally thought? That they were now in a real relationship, whether Tristan would admit it or not? "Okay, then you can cook for me."

Tristan laughed. "Would you like me to cook something from the Thai restaurant or the Italian place?"

Before Josiah could reply, the doorbell rang. "Someone's at the door. Hold on a second." Josiah walked over with the phone in his hand and pulled it open to see a blond man in a suit. "Can I help you?"

"You must be Josiah. I'm Tristan's friend, Ben." Ben, who obviously knew who Josiah was even though Josiah'd never heard of him.

"Shit," Tristan groaned into the phone. Josiah just stared at the man.

"Yeah. Hi. I'm Josiah."

Ben reached out and shook his hand. "Is that Tristan on the phone?"

"Yes." Josiah's hand tightened on the cell, not wanting to give it to the man.

"Let me talk to him." Tristan growled into his ear and Josiah handed it over.

"Surprise!" Ben laughed into the phone, paused as though he was listening to Tristan before laughing again.

"Is that any way to treat your only friend? Well, maybe not only one now." He raised a brow at Josiah before adding, "but your oldest."

Another pause. "You're stuck with me now, Tristan. I'm here."

Josiah watched the whole thing play out, wondering if Tristan laughed on the other end of the line. Wondering how this man knew him when Josiah didn't know who he was. He couldn't help but wonder what he meant to Tristan.

A minute later Ben ended the call without Josiah speaking with Tristan again.

"He said to tell you he's skipping out on his plans after work and will be home as soon as he's done there."

He doesn't know about Tristan's mom, Josiah realized. He may be someone in Tristan's life who Josiah had never heard of, but he didn't know about the most important person in Tristan's world.

"Come in." Josiah stepped out of the way.

They sat in the living room, on opposite couches. Josiah couldn't help but take in the sight of him—blond hair, smart eyes, a body that said he spent as much time as Tristan did keeping in shape. His suit hugged him the same way Tristan's did. They looked like a match, the two of them. Like they belonged in each other's worlds in a way Josiah feared he would never belong in Tristan's.

It was those thoughts that kept him quiet. He had no idea why the other man didn't speak. Josiah excused himself upstairs, though he didn't really have anything to do there. He waited a few minutes before coming down again, only to have silence between them again. It was minutes later before spoke.

"Have you and Tristan known each other long?" Josiah asked.

Ben leaned back on the couch, all confidence, and yeah, he was gorgeous and he obviously knew it. "Since college. We were in law school together, too."

He wasn't sure why that surprised him. Maybe because he'd been living with Tristan for almost three and a half years, yet he'd never met one of Tristan's friends. He was like this fortress that nobody could penetrate. No one completely made it past his walls, yet Tristan had been friends with this man for years. In Josiah's mind, that was huge.

"Never mentioned me, did he?" Ben laughed it off. "The bastard. I'm not surprised. The only time he talks to me is before dawn. The man sleeps less than anyone I know."

Jealousy bled through him that Ben knew these things about Tristan. Knew his sleeping patterns. He couldn't help the challenge that seeped into his tone. "Yeah, he's out of bed before me every morning, though I think it's getting better."

Ben cocked a brow at him. "You don't have to try and stake your claim. I know you're sleeping with him."

There was a part of Josiah who liked hearing that. His storm calmed, because Tristan told Ben that they were together. If there wasn't more between them, he wouldn't have shared it. But to Ben, they were just sleeping together. In the grand scheme of things, that meant nothing. Sex was sex, and Tristan had had it a lot and none of those men were still around.

But Ben was.

"You want something to drink?" Josiah stood.

"No thanks." Ben pushed to his feet as well and walked over to the large window on the far wall. He ran a finger over Tristan's elliptical as he went and snickered.

Josiah went to the kitchen and grabbed himself some water before lingering there a few minutes. When he made it back to the living room, Ben spoke again. "I have to admit, I've been curious about you."

"Why?" Josiah crossed his arms. "You know more about me than I do you."

"And you've lived with Tristan for three years." His voice was lower than before. Before Josiah could reply, the front door opened and Tristan walked in, obviously having left work as soon as they'd gotten off the phone.

"I'm going to kick your ass, Ben." Tristan strode across the room and Ben smiled.

"No, you won't. You're secretly happy to see me, even though you'll never admit it. Don't you realize I know how you work by now? You'll tell me not to come but be glad that I did." Ben opened his arms in invitation for an embrace.

The familiarity between them burned a hole through Josiah's gut.

"You think too highly of yourself, and you think you know more than you do." There was a slight edge to Tristan's voice, but he still briefly returned Ben's hug. Tristan pulled away and glanced over at Josiah. "I assume you two have met?"

"Yes," Josiah said at the same time Ben said, "I feel like I knew him already."

Tristan's eyes jerked away from Josiah. "Ben."

Josiah wondered if Ben heard the warning in his voice. Wondered why Tristan felt he needed to use it. His first question was answered when Ben raised his hands in the air as if surrendering. "I get it, I get it. I'll be good. I promise." Laughing, he winked at Josiah. Tristan groaned.

There was an ease between them Josiah had never seen Tristan have with anyone else. Ben came at Tristan in a way no one else did. In a way he never could.

A couple hours later, the three of them sat around the kitchen table eating Thai that Tristan had ordered. Josiah hardly spoke, and though Tristan didn't start many conversations, he always had a reply for whatever Ben said. And Ben talked enough for both of them. College, law school, study sessions. He had so many memories with Tristan. And they'd slept together, too. Ben alluded to that more than once, though Tristan ended the conversation each time.

"Where are you staying tonight?" Tristan asked later that evening.

Ben's eyebrows rose again. He did that often, Josiah noticed. He did it each time he tried to get under Tristan's skin. It always worked.

"There are plenty of hotels for you to choose from," Tristan told him.

"Is that any way to treat an old friend?" Ben replied.

"He's right." Josiah hated the truth in the words, but he was. There was no reason for him to put out the money on a hotel when Tristan had space here. Not that he doubted Ben couldn't afford it.

Slowly, Tristan turned to Josiah. His eyes studied him. His jaw set the way he did when Tristan tried to see deeper than what someone was showing him.

He gave Josiah a simple nod before facing Ben. "One night."

Once Ben disappeared into the room that held Josiah's things, the two of them went to Tristan's. They were quiet as they brushed their teeth and got ready for bed. Josiah turned out the lights and climbed into bed behind Tristan.

"Why don't you ever talk about him?" he asked. Was there more between them than Tristan could admit? The thought made him nauseous, but did he really have that right? Yes, he loved Tristan, even though Tristan couldn't say the same to him, but then, a piece of his heart would always belong to Mateo, too. It had faded farther to the background now, but it still hid there.

"I don't talk about anything if I don't have to, Josiah. You know that."

"But you talk to him about me?" That had to mean something.

"No, he's a nosey bastard who pushes until I give in."

Or not. Still, when Tristan kissed him, Josiah let him. When he stripped off all Josiah's clothes, he let him do that, too. Hunger rose through him. The need to feel like Tristan was really his, without the words.

Josiah tilted his head back as Tristan's mouth kissed down it. "I want you," Josiah whispered.

"I'm right here."

He ran one hand through Tristan's hair, the other down his back. "No… I *want* you. I want to know what it's like to be inside you. To make your world shatter, the way you do with me."

Tristan's lips stopped moving. His body shivered. "Why? Because Ben is here? You've never wanted to fuck me before."

"I might not have asked, but of course I wanted to. I told you, I want to take care of you, too." *Give me that. Give me something to hold on to.*

Tristan scooted off him. "No. And don't pretend this is about something it's not. If you want to fuck me, make it about wanting me, and not out of jealousy."

His fear came out of hiding, running through him. Josiah grabbed Tristan's arm when he tried to get out of bed. "I'm not going to lie and say I'm not jealous, but you have to know this is about you. That I want all of you."

Tristan sighed and pulled his arm free. Josiah thought he would walk away, but he paused a moment before sitting on the bed. "I can't give you that, Josiah."

The tone of his voice and the hard expression on his face made Josiah's skin crawl. "Tristan?"

"Drop it, Josiah. If you don't, I'll pull away."

The honesty in his words stabbed a hole through Josiah's heart. But then, he'd said them. He'd said them because he didn't want to walk away.

"Let's go to bed."

Tristan lay down and pulled Josiah to him. Josiah rested his head on Tristan's chest. "I'm sorry."

It took a lifetime for Tristan to answer. "I'm sorry I can't give you the things you deserve."

"I love you."

Tristan squeezed him tighter and didn't let go all night.

Chapter Seventeen

Tristan

The next couple months, Tristan tried to keep that night from his head. Tried to forget Josiah's question and the knowledge in his voice and the knowledge in Tristan's head. Because there were things he couldn't give Josiah, and maybe would never be able to.

The thought of anyone inside him filled him with rage. Made him feel like the man who sold his body to get where he was. But he'd done what he had to. He could now care for his mom, and no one would ever be able to take that away from him, but he sold it for the price of his dignity. Of his pride. And even though Josiah made him want to push those things aside, he couldn't.

So he couldn't let Josiah fuck him. Couldn't tell Josiah he loved him. What did he have to give?

Josiah never mentioned it again. He still shared Tristan's bed and still offered his body. They cooked together and walked together, but Tristan always had the knowledge in the back of his head. The truth he'd somehow let himself forget. They were different. Tristan could play the game, but he never fully gave himself to anyone.

He groaned when his cell rang. Tristan almost ignored it, but knowing Ben, the asshole would jump on another plane and come back to California. "I don't have time to talk."

"Oh yeah. Your guy gets his degree today, right?"

"Don't say it like that. And yes, he does. What do you want?"

Ben was quiet. He was almost never quiet. "It's more than just fucking with this kid, isn't it? I guess I knew, but I thought you'd deny it."

"He's not a kid. He's twenty-seven years old. He's been through more life than both of us in some ways."

"Not the point. You didn't deny it, Tristan. You said not to say it like that, not that he wasn't yours."

Unlike with Ben, Tristan's silence was typical.

"Even before I came, I knew it. Hell, that's why I was there. Three fucking years, Tris. I waited three fucking years, wondering when you'd push him away, but you never did."

Tristan imagined his hand on his pulse. Imagined the beats he could count. "No, I haven't."

Another pause from Ben. "Why him?" he finally asked. "I've waited for you since our freshman year at college. You have to know that. I figured eventually you'd come around, but I've lost you, haven't I?"

Tristan tried to make words come out, but none would. He didn't know why he'd never seen it coming but he hadn't. Or maybe he hadn't wanted to. "I didn't know."

"You're a shitty liar."

"I'm sorry."

Ben chuckled. "You've never apologized to me in your life. Don't start now. It's not who you are."

"Can I tell you, you're my only friend?"

Another laugh. "I've always known that. You just never would admit it. And a year or two ago, you wouldn't have. You've changed, Tristan. Because of Josiah, I'm guessing."

Tristan shook his head as though Ben could see him. He hadn't changed. Not enough. "I can't talk to you about this."

"Do you talk to him?"

"I try," was all he could get out. He gave Josiah everything he could.

"Try harder." Ben hung up the phone.

Tristan let his eyes drift closed as he thought about his friend and how he'd treated him over the years. He'd fucked Ben, but never slept in the same bed with him all night. Hell, he didn't even let the man come see him very often, yet he'd always been there for him. Even now.

Jesus, he was fucked up. Broken in so many ways.

Pushing to his feet, Tristan left his office, heading toward Josiah's room. Josiah had his back to him as Tristan stood in the doorway. As Tristan watched him pick up Mateo's queen and put it in one pocket. Then the bird Tristan gave him, putting it in the other.

"Do you carry them both with you all the time?"

Josiah whipped around at the sound of his voice. "Shit. I didn't hear you walk up." And then he touched his pockets. "Only on important days. I know it's crazy…"

After all these years, Josiah still carried the queen. Still carried a part of Mateo with him. Still loved him, the way Ben had apparently loved Tristan for years, too.

"I know I should get rid of the queen…"

"Not if it's important to you." If Josiah could get rid of that, then he could eventually do the same to Tristan. It was the fear he kept buried so deep he could forget it was there.

"You're important to me."

He nodded at that because he knew the words to be true. There wasn't a part of him that doubted Josiah loved him. Or that he would always love Mateo. And that Mateo had given Josiah things he didn't.

"We should go."

Tristan drove Josiah to the graduation ceremony. It put him there early but he worked in his car until it was time to go in. He met Elliot by the gates, and they sat together as they watched Josiah get his degree.

"You've been good for Josiah. I was nervous at first, but you've helped him a lot. He wouldn't be here without you," Elliot told him.

"He would have. Even if it took him a little longer, he would have done it." There was no doubt in his mind about that.

"Still, you've changed him in other ways. He's more sure of himself."

"Is that the psychologist in you speaking?" Tristan teased.

"No." He shook his head. "The friend."

Tristan continued to record the ceremony for his mom. The place was packed, but somehow Josiah managed to find them easily afterward.

"Congrats, man." Elliot gave Josiah a hug.

"Thanks." No matter how much Josiah tried to hide the smile, he couldn't. It made Tristan do the same.

He wrapped an arm around Josiah and pulled him close. With his mouth close to Josiah's ear, he said, "Did I ever tell you I have a fantasy about fucking someone in their cap and gown?" Which was a lie, but he had one now.

Josiah fisted his shirt. "We can do that."

Tristan waited as Josiah and Elliot made plans for lunch later in the week and then they headed back to the car. "So what do you want to do? Dinner?" Tristan asked.

"Can we go for a walk first?"

"Sure." Tristan drove to the Warf. Josiah pulled off his gown and tossed it into the seat, wearing a pair of cargo shorts and a T-shirt. Tristan couldn't help but look down at his slacks and chuckle.

"What?"

"Nothing. Let's go."

They took the same path they took every day, only this time with no food. It was a cool, June evening with a light breeze.

"You're happy," Tristan said as they walked.

"I'm ecstatic. I did it, Tristan. I never thought I would, but I did."

"I asked my realtor to look around for buildings. There's a lot you're going to have to look into before opening up your own business, but—"

Josiah stopped walking.

"What?" Tristan asked.

"I don't have the money to open a coffee house, Tristan."

"You don't? I thought you had thousands of dollars waiting."

"That's not funny. I can't let you do that. I won't."

And he'd expected that. Respected the hell out of him for it. "You're right. It's none of my business. I have no doubt you'll figure it out."

Josiah locked his fingers with Tristan's. "Everything about me could be your business if you want."

Jesus, he wanted that. Wanted it so damn much. He didn't want to be alone. Didn't want to waste time the way Ben had wasted time loving him. Didn't want Josiah to do it, either.

Still, the words were lodged in his throat. He wasn't sure how to say it.

"I don't want to push you, Tristan. I know there are reasons you still can't share, but—"

Push. Tristan opened his mouth to tell Josiah to push, when he felt him tense. His face went pale as he stared over Tristan's shoulder, a wave of white starting at his forehead and flooding down. His grip on

Tristan's hand tightened, but that was the only movement he made.

"What's wrong?" Tristan asked, but Josiah didn't reply.

Turning his head, Tristan looked behind him, searching for what held Josiah's eyes.

He stiffened, too, emotions battering him hard and fast. He knew. Knew when he saw the dark-skinned man standing twenty-five feet away from them. Knew before Josiah said a word. Still, he pulled his hand away. Found that spot on his wrist and lost himself *one, two, three, four, five* as one word slipped past Josiah's lips. "Teo…"

PART THREE: Josiah, Mateo, & Tristan

Chapter One

Mateo

I knew he'd come…

He told himself when he came to walk by the water that it was to say goodbye. That it was better to bail before he screwed things up for Josiah. That Josiah had a life now that was a whole hell of a lot better than anything he'd had with Mateo, but that didn't stop the tension from seeping from his aching muscles when he saw Josiah walking his way. Didn't stop the heavy breath from deflating his lungs.

"Teo?"

Mateo turned to see Josiah taking slow steps toward him like he didn't know if Mateo was really there or not. His man walked right behind him, his body looking as tight as Teo's felt. The other man's eyes narrowed, anger stabbing straight from them and into Mateo. He bit down to keep from telling the bastard to back the hell off. That he'd never hurt Josiah. But that was a fucking lie. The reasons he sent Josiah away didn't matter, because it had hurt him regardless.

He saw that in Josiah, but something else was there, too—confusion; and damn, he thought he saw want as well.

"Guess I owe you a congratulations. Knew you could do it, Jay."

Josiah stopped in front of Mateo, his hair a darker shade of blond than it used to be. His body was wider with muscles he didn't have when Mateo pushed him away. But he knew that. Knew it because this wasn't the first time he'd seen Josiah.

Teo watched his former lover, not veering toward the man who looked like a fucking accountant or something.

Josiah's eyes took him in, the wild mix of dark and light green that he missed so much.

His skin sizzled beneath Josiah's stare. He felt a pull from inside him, like someone stuck magnets all through him and each and every one of them fought to be nearer to Josiah. To feel him, and touch him, after a fucking lifetime.

But it was obvious Josiah wasn't going to move. Bracing himself in case the suit came at him, Mateo reached out his hand. "We'll deal with the rest later. Just…com 'ere, Jay."

Mateo fought the automatic urge to ball his fists, ignored the pain that slammed into his chest when Josiah turned to look at the motherfucker in the suit. Who in the hell walked by the water in a fucking suit, anyway?

The guy didn't move an inch. Didn't change his expression, yet they must have been speaking in a silent language that only they knew, because Josiah's head turned back to him and he stepped into Mateo's arms.

Teo squeezed him so fucking tight, he thought he would break him, but then the man in his arms was a whole hell of a lot different than the one he held all those years ago. He was bigger, more muscular, solid. There was a hint of cologne on his skin that Teo wanted gone. He wanted nothing more than the scent of Josiah.

Josiah was trembling as he fisted Mateo's shirt and buried his face in Teo's neck. "You're here. I can't believe you're here."

And he probably shouldn't be but he was, and now that he had Jay in his arms again, he didn't know how he'd let him go. "I'm right here."

Josiah pulled back, but didn't go far, only leaving a few inches of space between them. "I'm right here, Jay," he said again as he ran a hand through Josiah's hair. "It's darker now. Jesus, I fucking missed touchin' your hair."

Mateo felt Josiah's body stiffen. Felt the air around them change, a blast of cold freezing him out.

His head snapped to the right when Josiah's fist slammed into it. The bitter taste of blood met his tongue when Teo ran it over his lip. If anyone else would have hit him, nothing would have held him back from retaliating—from being the one to end what someone else started. But fuck, he couldn't help the feeling of respect that burned through him along with the sting to his lip. Josiah wasn't going to lie down and let Teo slip easily back into his life. It was the right decision, and Mateo was proud as hell of him for it.

"Good for you. Don't take anyone's shit, Jay. Even mine." He wiped the blood from his mouth with a thumb.

"Don't." Josiah shook his head. "You don't get to do this. You don't get to walk out of my life and then show up after nine years with no explanation. You don't get to just touch me and tell me you miss me. You left, Teo. You!"

And as much as he'd wanted to come back, that hadn't been what this was about. Okay, that was a lie. At first it had been, but not when he saw Josiah had a good life. That he had someone in it. He'd known then he didn't belong.

Mateo's eyes darted to the suit when he stepped close to Josiah. "I know." He wouldn't give Josiah bullshit excuses. He wanted to protect Josiah, always had, but that didn't mean he didn't know he'd fucked up in too many ways to count.

"Wasn't going to see you." Mateo shook his head. "You think I want this? Want to fucking hurt you again?"

"And you think that makes it okay? That you didn't want to hurt me? Or that you didn't want to see me?" He yelled before dropping his eyes to the ground. "That makes it worse."

"That's bullshit. I didn't say I didn't want to see you. I said I wasn't going to. You know me better than that." Anger at himself, pain because of Josiah, and need, so much fucking need, created a tornado of emotions inside him. What had he been thinking coming back here? *Why did I have to walk away in the first place?*

But Jesus, after all the shit he'd done, and looking at Josiah now, knowing he just got a degree today, and seeing the man beside him; even if Mateo had deserved him back then, he definitely didn't now. He'd always known he was different than Josiah, but he'd never felt the wall separating them that did now. He didn't fit in this life with the man he loved anymore.

"I don't know you anymore. I used to think I did." Josiah's expressive eyes stared at him unflinchingly. "I used to think I was the luckiest man in the world because I got to know you, but did I? I don't know if I ever really knew you, Teo."

The words stabbed him like a knife. It was worse than any physical pain he'd ever felt. Worse than the hole in his shoulder where he'd taken a bullet. *You're the only person who's ever known me.*

He didn't say that, though. Didn't say a word as Josiah turned away. Didn't say a word as the bastard in the suit wrapped an arm around Josiah. Didn't say a word when they stopped less than ten feet away from him.

Mateo watched Josiah slip a hand in his pocket. Reflex made his hands shoot out to catch the thing that Josiah tossed his way.

His finger brushed over the edges at the top of the queen until Josiah disappeared from sight.

***

Mateo lay on the bed in the rundown hotel where he'd been staying. He glanced at the small kitchen but didn't feel like eating. He held the queen in his hand, rolling it between his fingers like he'd been doing for hours.

He still had it. Josiah not only kept the queen, but he carried it with him. Everything inside him wanted to take that as proof that Josiah was still his. Or fuck, that he belonged to Jay. He didn't give a shit as long as he could claim him in one way or another. But what the hell did he have to offer him? He was fresh out of prison. An ex-gang member who'd done things he'd never forgive himself for, and didn't even know where his life was going.

He should have known better than to go down by the water. No, that was a bullshit thing to even think because he knew it was a lie. He could say he went there to say goodbye, but he went because he knew Josiah would go. When he left the graduation, he'd gone straight there. When important shit happened, Josiah wanted to be somewhere that was close to his heart.

He wondered if that suit knew shit like that about Jay. If he knew him the way Mateo did. *He probably knows him better…*

Fuck that. Mateo wouldn't let himself believe that.

He squeezed the queen in his hand. He also knew it was bullshit to tell himself he could just walk away. Not after having Josiah in his arms again. He had to be near him, no matter how much it would hurt to see him with another man. Teo couldn't stay away.

Chapter Two

Tristan

Tristan watched Josiah as he lay naked in their bed. He had his eyes closed, yet Tristan knew he was awake. It was after eight on a Saturday morning and his lover had yet to get out of bed once.

"I hope the birds aren't starving." He brushed his finger back and forth across Josiah's collarbone.

He slid his eyes open and looked up at Tristan. "They're birds. They'll find food."

"Would you have said that a week ago?" Tristan cocked one of his brows. They both knew the answer to that question, so he wasn't surprised when Josiah didn't reply. He hadn't been to the water once in the week since they'd seen Mateo.

"I have to go to the bathroom." Tristan's arm flopped to the bed when the body beneath it pulled away. He watched as Josiah disappeared behind the door.

Pushing to his feet, Tristan pulled on a pair of sweats and went straight to his office. The ache in his gut didn't go away as he collapsed into his desk chair. The image from Josiah's graduation day played in his head for the millionth time. Seeing Mateo there. Knowing who he was. Fighting the—hell, he didn't even want to think about the emotions he'd been holding back as he watched Josiah step into the man's arms.

And seeing the way they both relaxed into each other.

He picked up a pencil, rolling it through his fingers until suddenly the damn thing snapped. He was hard on his pencils.

Nine years apart, and a connection was still between them, visible even to Tristan's eyes. And the knowledge there, in the back of his head, that Mateo would give Josiah the things Tristan couldn't.

There were things Tristan *could* give: Help with his business, a home…but the emotional pieces were trapped inside him. Probably always would be.

Leaning forward, he hit the button to turn on his computer. He counted the hours as they passed. Tristan buried himself in his work like he always did, trying to lose himself in definites. He needed facts that were written in stone—things he could control—and emotions weren't that. No, he couldn't control every aspect of his job, but work was tied with facts. Tied to how hard he worked, and what he could prove, not to his heart.

Josiah didn't knock on Tristan's office door all day, and Tristan didn't come out. Around five, he leaned back in his chair when he heard a soft rap on the door. "Tristan? I made some dinner."

Standing, Tristan pushed a piece of paper into his pocket. Josiah leaned against the wall when he opened the door. "I told you I don't want you to have to cook for me anymore."

"No one said I had to. I wanted to. And I don't do it every day now."

Tristan nodded as he followed Josiah down the hall. He'd managed to get dressed today, wearing a pair of jeans and a button-up, short-sleeved shirt, while Tristan still only wore his sweats.

"Italian. It smells good. I'll open a bottle of wine."

"Okay," Josiah replied.

They sat at the table together, eating the baked ziti Josiah had made. They were quiet for most of the meal. No matter how good the food was, it didn't sit right in Tristan's stomach. He ached and cramped in a way he wasn't familiar with. Because Josiah affected him. He'd known that, of course, but feeling the space between them tied him in unexpected knots.

When they finished eating, Tristan went to the sink. "I have the dishes."

"Okay." Josiah sat back down. Tristan felt his eyes following him as he cleaned the kitchen. They warmed his skin, and Christ, did he want to strip Josiah and take him right there on the table. To make Josiah *his*, because sex was the only way Tristan knew how to do that. No, it was the only way he chose to do it. The fault was on him.

He dried his hands after washing the last dish but didn't turn around. He closed his eyes when he felt Josiah's body behind him. Felt lips on his shoulder. "I'm sorry, Tristan. I know I'm not being fair to you. I'll get better. It's just—"

"You love him," Tristan finished for him. And it hurt...but not as badly as he would have thought. The words weren't as bitter as they could be because he'd always known Josiah loved Mateo. And as much as he had to hold himself back from hitting Mateo, from trying to make him hurt even a fraction as much as Mateo had hurt Josiah, there was a piece of him that knew that was wrong. That had always wondered about Mateo, having only seen him through Josiah's eyes, but then had seen firsthand how much Josiah meant to the other man. Seen the fire there—the strength of it, knowing that Mateo would do anything if he thought it would protect Josiah.

Picturing it through stories Josiah told and seeing it were two different things. And somehow, he had seen it.

"I love you," Josiah whispered.

Tristan turned around, placing his hand behind Josiah's neck as his head rested on Tristan's chest. "I do. I love you, Tristan. I don't understand it. How I can love you both so much. How you both are so connected to me. But you are. I love you," he said again, his lips pressing to Tristan's chest.

Tristan's fingers went to his pulse, but Josiah separated his hands. Turned his head so his ear lay over Tristan's heart. "I'll count them for you."

He squeezed his eyes shut. Jesus, he loved Josiah, but still the words lodged in his throat, especially now that another man was threatening what they had. He may not be able to say it, but he loved him enough to do anything for him, the way Mateo had.

"I know you love me. I've never wanted anyone to love me besides you, and I know you do." He slowly eased Josiah's head from his chest.

Cupped his cheeks in both hands as he tilted Josiah's face upward. Tristan kissed the corner of his mouth, sick about what he was about to say. Still, he knew he had to. Knew that if he didn't, the what-ifs would ruin them anyway. That Josiah needed to say goodbye…or be given the option of choosing Mateo…something he wouldn't do without Tristan insisting. "I know you love me… But you need to go to him. Go to him tonight."

Josiah stiffened. "What?"

Tristan held Josiah's eyes with his own. "Go to him. If you don't things will be even more fucked up between us than they would be if you do. Even if it's just to say goodbye and get closure, you need to go."

Josiah laid a hand on Tristan's stomach, breathing deeply. "I don't know if I can tell him goodbye, but I can't walk away from you, either."

Mateo's words from that day by the water filled Tristan's ears. "We'll deal with the rest of it later."

Because he knew Josiah had to do this. Knew he had to let him. He replayed the image of Josiah in Mateo's arms. On the one hand, he'd hated it… but on the other, there was this part of him who thought they were beautiful together. The way they contrasted each other in every way—dark and light. Anger and love. Rough and smooth. Bitter and sweet. But yes, they'd been beautiful, too.

"It's not right." Josiah shook his head, but Tristan heard it in his voice. As much as this ate him up, he wanted it, too.

"I've shared you with him ever since I've known you. If it wasn't for him, you wouldn't be here right now. He's always been a part of you, Josiah." Which in a way meant he'd always been a part of *them*.

"No." Josiah tried to shake his head again but stopped when Tristan kissed him. When he let his tongue slide between Josiah's lips. Turned them, pressing Josiah against the counter as he devoured his mouth. Their tongues battled, savored. His cock went hard and he rubbed it against Josiah's, as he let Josiah lead the kiss for just a second. But then it was Tristan's game again, tasting him deeply.

"You're still mine," he said when they parted.

A crease formed in Josiah's forehead, and Tristan realized that was probably the first time he'd ever said something like that to him.

"I'm not giving you away. You go to him, and then come back to me. You have to, or everything will crumble around us. It's the only way for you to know what you truly want. It's the only way to make peace with it."

"I don't even know where he's staying or if he's even still here."

Tristan pulled the piece of paper from his pocket and placed it in Josiah's sweaty palm. One of the perks of having the kind of connections he did.

Josiah's fist balled.

"Go," he said.

"I love you," Josiah replied. And then he did what Tristan told him to. He went.

Chapter Three

Josiah

Josiah ignored the nerves taking over his gut and brought his knuckles down heavily on the door to Mateo's hotel room. He waited just a few seconds before banging again. Teo was in there. He didn't know how he knew that, but he did.

"Teo…open the door." The last word had hardly passed his lips when Mateo jerked the door open. They stood there, Josiah in the hallway and Teo in his room, staring at each other. He didn't have a shirt on, just a pair of sweats, the exact same way as Tristan when Josiah'd left home.

Their looks were so different, though. The light dusting of hair on Mateo's chest, though dark like Tristan's, wasn't as thick. A couple of tribal-looking tattoos decorated parts of his chest, but there was one, one tattoo, that Josiah knew exactly what it meant. It was the sign of his gang. They both had the same abs, firm with ridges between each muscle. Teo's skin was darker, rougher. They were both incredible, just in different ways.

Comparing them made Tristan storm into his head again. It was wrong, walking out the way he did. He—"Don't let me lose you. Whatever you're thinking right now, come back to me, Jay. You're here. *Dios,* I can't fuckin' believe you're here."

He reached out his hand for Josiah, and Josiah let him take it. Let Mateo pull him into the room and close the door behind them. He spotted a camera on the bedside table, training his eyes there because it felt safe. Words. There were so many words and questions in his head. He needed to get them all out, but his body craved Mateo, too. Needed him in ways he hadn't even needed him all those years ago.

Like he always could, Teo seemed to read Josiah's thoughts, pulling him so close, it was like they were one. He pushed a hand through Josiah's hair, and then Teo's lips covered his.

Josiah went weak against him as Mateo's tongue stroked his—familiar yet foreign, but never forgotten.

Finally, finally, finally, echoed throughout his head.

Mateo's lips trailed down his neck. Josiah tilted his head back to give him better access.

"I should have gotten a better room in case you came. All these years later, and I still can't give you what you deserve."

Josiah grabbed on to Teo's side, running his hand up and down Mateo's hot skin. "It won't kill me, Teo. Just like it didn't then."

The lips on his neck stopped moving. "You deserve better. I'm sure the suit—"

Josiah's body iced over. "Tristan. His name is Tristan."

The muscles in Mateo's side tightened beneath his hand. "Don't let me lose you," Josiah repeated Mateo's words. "Whatever you're thinking right now, come back to me, Teo."

And he did. Slowly he backed Josiah up until the backs of his legs touched the bed. His fingers fumbled with the buttons on Josiah's shirt until he muttered, "Fuck it," and just ripped it open. Josiah's pants were next, Mateo's calloused fingers pushing them down his legs.

Josiah knew what they needed to do was talk, but one look at Teo and he was lost in sensations. He needed to feel him. He missed every part of him so much, and this was the easiest to tackle.

His mouth trailed down Josiah's stomach, ripples of pleasure drifting out from where lips met skin. "I wanna go slow with you, Jay." Mateo lashed his tongue over one of Josiah's nipples. "Wanna savor you, but fuck, I need you so goddamned bad right now. I wanna taste you everywhere."

Josiah's erection was so hard it hurt. "Me, too. I want you, too." He fell backward when Mateo pushed him down, his legs hanging off the bed.

"You look so different." Mateo went down on his knees, running a hand over Josiah's chest. "You're bigger."

Mateo's simple touch almost drove Josiah over the edge. He felt it everywhere. Never wanted it to stop. "I…*Damn it*," he added when Mateo pinched both of his nipples. "I work out now."

"And your hair. I miss it lighter, but you're still fucking gorgeous."

He savored the feel of Mateo's hands in his hair. "I shaved it…when I was mad at you. For years." Maybe he shouldn't have said that, but he wanted Teo to know.

"I deserve worse than that."

Before Josiah could reply, Mateo's mouth slid all the way down his erection, sucking him to the back of his throat. Josiah couldn't stop his hips from thrusting forward. *Oh, God.* His whole body shuddered, pleasure ripping through it.

Teo ran his tongue from the base of Josiah's shaft to the tip. "I missed this. Missed you so fucking much." He ran his tongue down the seam of Josiah's sac. Sucked one of his balls into this mouth, then the other. "Wanna taste you everywhere. Lie back."

Heat took Josiah over, his cock achingly hard. He did as Mateo said. Then let Teo lift his feet so they were flat on the bed, his ass on the edge. His erection jumped, bounced against his stomach, when Mateo's tongue flicked his hole. "Teo!" He pushed down, trying to get closer to Mateo's face.

"Wanna love every part of you, *mi precioso.*"

The name made the past slam into him. Josiah fought his way through it, trying to stay in the present as Mateo alternated between sucking him and letting his tongue play with his ass.

When his mouth covered Josiah's shaft again, he felt his orgasm pushing closer and closer to the surface. He didn't want to come yet. Couldn't, because he wanted every part of Mateo, too.

"I want to taste you, too." He softly tugged at Mateo's arm. Dark brown eyes met his from his spot kneeling between Josiah's legs.

"*Dios,* I missed you."

Josiah sat up, capturing Mateo's mouth with his. He ignored the dizziness taking him over, wanting to think, feel, and know nothing but Mateo right now. Josiah pulled him to his feet, Teo going easily.

He hated that his hands shook slightly as he started to pull down Mateo's sweats.

"I love this." Teo touched his hand. "Love that you want me as much as I want you. I never stopped, Jay. I never stopped—"

"No." He shook his head. "Not now." He knew once they started talking, all the touching would end. There was so much time and pain between them. And Tristan. Tristan was still there, the thought making Josiah freeze up.

"I'm not giving you away. You go to him and then come back to me. You have to or everything will crumble around us."

So Josiah kept stripping Mateo. Watched as his dark erection sprung free. Hunger exploded inside him.

Mateo moaned, threading a hand through Josiah's hair when he sucked Teo into his mouth. He tasted salt—like masculine skin that Josiah loved so much.

"I'm not going to last very long if you keep doing that, Jay."

Josiah slowly dragged his mouth to the tip of Mateo's cock before letting his tongue circle the head. His heart ran wild. Having Mateo here like this, he could almost forget about all the pain. It was just love. Love and passion that had always been between them.

Mateo tilted his head up, much like Tristan had done with him not long ago. "I want you, Jay."

And he wanted that, too. Wanted it so badly… But *he* also wanted Mateo. Wanted to make him his, as though that would change things. As though that would make it so Teo never could have sent him away and he'd never have to lose him again. As if he could have both Mateo and Tristan… "I'm still with him." He wanted Mateo to know that. Teo frowned but nodded as if he understood what was going on even though he didn't.

Josiah pushed to his feet, his body skin-to-skin with Mateo's.

"Dios, you're trembling.*"* He ran his hands down Josiah's body. "Why are you shaking?"

"Because I want you, Teo. I want to be the one to make love to you."

Mateo didn't move. Didn't reply, pinning Josiah with his stare. It wasn't something he'd ever asked when they were together before, and it wasn't something Tristan could give. It wasn't even something Josiah would want all the time, but he did crave it.

"You can have whatever you want from me." Mateo's voice was low. Without another word, he turned and walked over to a suitcase. He pulled lube and a condom from inside before going back over to the bed.

Still, it was Mateo who laid Josiah down on the bed. Mateo who covered Josiah's body with this. Mateo who kissed Josiah deeply. Mateo who thrust his hips so that his erection rubbed against Josiah's.

After pressing one more soft kiss to Josiah's lips, he rolled off of him and onto his stomach on the bed.

"No." Josiah turned his way. "I want to look at you."

This time Teo rolled onto his back, opening his legs. Lust burst inside him, making Josiah crack at the seams. He was really here. Teo was really with him again.

"Has anyone ever had you?" he asked, not sure why he needed to know.

"No."

The rest went both in slow motion and overdrive at the same time. Josiah opened the lube, coating his fingers. He lay on top of Teo, kissing him as he pushed a finger inside.

Mateo tensed up beneath him.

"Teo…Please. It's just me."

The words were the right ones to use because Mateo's body slackened beneath him. Josiah moved his finger in and out, his tongue doing the same to Teo's mouth, and he figured maybe this was the way it was supposed to be. Maybe he was supposed to be the one to make love to Teo, the way Teo had been the first to make love to him.

Soon it was two fingers and more lube to stretch him.

"Get inside me, Jay. Fuck me."

Live wires snapped and popped at Teo's words. Josiah ripped the condom open before rolling it down his erection. Fear pooled inside him. How was he supposed to do this? How was he supposed to make love to Mateo and then walk away? But he couldn't walk away from Tristan, either. Losing either of them would shatter him.

"Jay, come on. I'm giving myself to you."

And he knew right then that Teo meant completely. When he'd seen

Mateo last week, he'd been sure he'd walk away from Josiah again. That he would leave. But the conviction in his voice, in his eyes, told him he wasn't. Teo wasn't leaving him again. And he wanted that. Wanted Teo *and* Tristan but knew he couldn't have both.

"I'm the one here with you right now, *mi precioso.* You stay here with *me.* You're going back to him, but right now, you're mine."

You're mine. The same words Tristan had used. Add to that that Teo somehow knew, knew that he wasn't—*couldn't*—leave Tristan, and Josiah almost lost it right there.

But he didn't. He was so damn tired of that. Instead he pushed forward, slowly easing into Mateo's body.

Oh God. The need to orgasm slammed into him but he held it off. It was tight, so tight, as he pushed himself inside of Mateo.

"Oh, fuck. That's it. *Dios,* I want you."

Josiah slammed his hips forward, burying himself inside Mateo. They were both still. He was scared if he moved, he'd come. But then Teo's nails dug into his ass. Josiah pulled out before thrusting forward again. Over and over, he made love to Mateo. Having a part of Mateo no one ever had. Knowing that he'd always had parts of Teo no one would ever have.

His eyes took Mateo in as he moved beneath him. Saw the scar on his neck, and a new one that wasn't there before, on his shoulder. As if he knew what Josiah saw, Teo said, "I'm fine. It doesn't matter."

But it really did matter. Seeing that bullet wound made it all more real to him. Mateo had been through things he couldn't imagine. He knew none of the details and feared they'd slay him. No matter what he'd been through, he knew it wasn't nearly as bad as what Mateo had.

Mateo wrapped a hand around his own shaft, stroking it while Josiah pumped in and out of him. He felt a tingle start at the base of his spine. A heavy ache started to build in his balls that he wasn't sure he could hold off much longer.

He changed the position of his hips, trying to hit Mateo's prostate. He hit the spongy spot right as white fluid shot out of Mateo's cock. With that, Josiah let go, letting his orgasm pull him under. He kept pumping as he filled the condom before he fell on top of Mateo, resting his head on the bullet scar he would give anything to take away. And through the bliss…all he could concentrate on was the fact that he was lost. He would have to lose one of the men he loved.

Chapter Four

Mateo

Mateo watched as Josiah walked naked to the bathroom to toss the condom. Watched as he made it halfway back before stopping, as if to decide if he wanted to climb back into bed with him or walk away.

Before Mateo had the chance to ask him to come back, Josiah slowly made his way over and sat next to him.

"*Dios.*" Mateo ran his fingers over Jay's shoulder and down his arm. "You are so fuckin' sexy."

A calmness Mateo hadn't felt in years washed through him when Josiah's cheeks reddened. That blush always drove him wild.

Reaching out, Josiah touched Mateo's bottom lip with his thumb. "I hit you."

Mateo grinned. "Don't feel bad."

"Who said I do?"

"You don't have to say it. I know you. And you know I deserved it. Plus, it was fuckin' hot…seeing you take control like that. You wouldn't have done it nine years ago." As much as those words were true, and as much as it made him proud as hell of Josiah, it made his chest ache, too. Those were changes he made while with Tristan. Changes that the other man could have had a hand in.

Josiah pulled back and looked away. "We need to talk, Teo."

"You're still with him," he confirmed. He knew it made him an asshole for pushing for more information from Josiah, but he needed it. Needed every piece of him he could have, even if he didn't like the answer.

"Yeah."

"But you're here."

"Tristan knows where I am. He knows I'm going home to him."

The urge to throw up hit him. His skin suddenly felt too tight. He had no right to feel that way. No right to let the anger and jealousy burn through him like acid. He'd walked away. And the fact was, even though he couldn't walk away from Josiah again, that didn't mean he'd never be forced to. And even though the words hurt, he was proud of Josiah for saying them, for not letting Mateo steamroll back into his life so easily.

That didn't make it easy to swallow, though. "So he let you come to fuck me out of your system?" The words stabbed him in the chest.

Josiah rose to his feet. "Don't do that. It's not fair. You're the one who pushed me away. I didn't see you for nine years, and then you show up and I still don't have any answers."

Guilt added more sourness to his gut. Mateo sighed. "Come 'ere."

Thank fuck Josiah came without him needing to say anything else.

Without him needing to say he couldn't talk about this without Josiah next to him. Jay crawled into bed and lay on his side, facing Mateo.

He had so many excuses on the tip of his tongue, real reasons, but still just excuses. He'd done it to protect Josiah. He hadn't wanted this lifestyle for Josiah. He never thought he was good enough. Again, all true, but they didn't excuse the way Mateo had hurt him. They didn't change anything.

"I don't know what you want me to say. That I was fuckin' stupid? We both know that." When Josiah tried to get up, Teo thread his fingers through Josiah's hair, making him stop. "I made so many mistakes with you, Jay. I was just a stupid, fucking kid. For once I wanted to try and do what was right by you. To *really* protect you. That doesn't mean I ever stopped wantin' you. It doesn't mean I ever stopped loving you."

His heart collided with his chest so hard, he wondered if Josiah could feel it. He'd never been as real with anyone in his life as he was with Jay.

Josiah sighed. Closed his eyes, then muttered, "That's not good enough, Teo." And then he pushed from the bed.

Mateo scrambled up behind him, the ache inside him already threatening to swallow him whole again.

Josiah grabbed his underwear from the floor and pulled them on before reaching for his pants.

"I can't fully regret it, man." He shook his head, Josiah reaching for his shirt.

"When I came to find you and I saw you with him. Saw you with normal fuckin' friends and going to school…I couldn't really regret it.

You wouldn't have had that shit if you stayed with me." Mateo dropped his head forward and leaned his arms on his thighs. "You've been with him a long time. He's good to you?"

The movement in the room stopped. Mateo looked up to see Josiah's feet firmly planted, his back still to Mateo. The room was silent. Teo heard nothing but the sound of his own pulse in his ears.

The palms of his hands started to sweat as he waited, trying to let Josiah do whatever it was he needed to do.

"How long?" he asked without turning around.

"For what?"

"You said you saw us together and then mentioned I've been with Tristan for a long time. How long ago did you come?"

Mateo ran both his hands through his hair, letting them rest on the back of his neck. "What does it matter?"

"How long ago?" Josiah said, louder this time.

"Almost five years."

Josiah shook his head, slowly turning around. "Let me guess, you saw us walking?" After a nod from Mateo, he continued. "We weren't together then."

He started to pace the room. "You came for me. All this time I thought you forgot about me, but you *came,* Teo. You came and I didn't know. You came when I wasn't even with Tristan and I don't even know how in the hell to feel about that!"

His voice got louder and louder as he continued. "I've loved you since I was sixteen, but now I love Tristan, too. I can't wish I didn't have him, but you *came back* for me."

Mateo stood up, walking toward him. "Jay—"

"No. Stay the hell away from me. What happened next? Where did you go next?"

He stopped a few feet away from Josiah, wishing he could tell him to fucking forget about Tristan. That he belonged with Mateo.

But then it was Josiah who stepped toward him. "What happened next, Teo?"

Dios, he hated this part. His throat tried to close so he couldn't get the words out. So he didn't have to let Josiah now how big a piece of shit he really was. Mateo grabbed his pants and pulled them on. "Prison." He crossed his arms as if they were a barrier, a wall between them. "Just a couple years. Not like that fuckin' matters, but yeah. I was locked up for a couple years. Came here almost as soon as I got out."

Mateo's hands fisted but he silently counted backward from ten, trying to calm himself down.

Josiah didn't turn away. He sighed before asking, "What for?"

"Drugs." But then, because he couldn't hold the words back, couldn't keep himself from reminding Josiah just what a bastard he was, he added, "But you know that's not the worst thing I've done."

"And I also know you never wanted to do those things."

Thank you. He shrugged. "But I did." And since he was a dickhead, he might as well do it thoroughly. "I came here to say goodbye to you for real, *mi precioso.* I just wanted to make sure you were okay and then I was gonna walk away. Disappear." *Where no one could find me.* "I didn't mean for you to see me but now that you did, fuck, I don't even know what the hell is gonna happen with me. I can't fucking walk away from you again. Even if I only get a week with you that's better than nothin'."

"And I'm with Tristan." Josiah spoke low, but with conviction.

Not for the first time today, Josiah carved out his heart. It's like he'd put it back in, giving Mateo hope, and then sliced it out again. "The suit. He's good to you?" he asked again.

Josiah paused before replying. "He's not perfect but I know he loves me. Things haven't been easy for him, either. If it wasn't for him, I wouldn't be here right now. He's the one who found out where you were today."

Mateo dropped back down to sit on the bed. "Am I supposed to thank him? I can't do that shit."

"No, you're just... I can't do this. I have to go." He picked up his shoes and didn't bother putting them back on. "Give me my queen. I want it back."

Mateo opened the drawer by the bed, pulled it out and tossed it to him. "You kept it with you, Jay. All these years, and you still carried it with you." He took out a worn piece of paper next. "All the shit I've been through, and I still have the letter, too. Always. I read it a million times while we were apart. I kept you with me, too."

Josiah didn't respond. For the second time in a week, Mateo didn't stop him as he walked away. He hardly made it to the bathroom before he vomited until there was nothing left.

Chapter Five

Tristan

Tristan hadn't slept in three days. Four if you counted the last night Josiah was here with him. When he knew that he would have to let Josiah go to Mateo.

So he had.

And he hadn't seen him since.

He'd gone to work and ran on his elliptical for hours on end. Worked, went to visit his mother, yet none of it cured the loneliness spreading throughout him more each day.

He'd never really been lonely before because he never let himself emotionally connect enough. But now he did, and it multiplied inside him like a deadly, fast-moving cancer.

He wasn't sure how he felt about it. Anger braided together with the loneliness, and through that a strand of love. Yes, he'd known he loved Josiah. He'd told Josiah that he expected him to come home to him. He wanted that, but he also thought that if Josiah chose Mateo, he would be able to let him go.

A fucking delusion is what that thought had been.

He wasn't with Mateo. He knew that. He might have promised Josiah that he'd stay away, but he also made sure he knew where Josiah was.

Tristan scrolled through his few text messages from Josiah.

I don't know what to do.

I can't deal with this.

Don't find me… not yet.

I'm safe.

Tristan squeezed the cell until he heard a cracking noise and stopped before he broke it.

If Mateo had done something to hurt him, he'd kill the man.

Yet, as much as it would be easier if something like that were true, he knew it wasn't. He didn't have to know Mateo to recognize how much the man loved Josiah. They were together in that.

Shoving out of his desk chair, Tristan headed straight for the door. He didn't even know where in the hell he was going, he just knew he needed something.

***

In the distance, Tristan saw a figure walking his way. From the build and smooth, brown skin, he knew exactly who it was. He kept going, fingers on wrist.

The other man looked up and noticed him but didn't stop coming. And stopping wasn't a consideration in Tristan's head, either.

Tristan and Mateo stood face to face as a humorless chuckle threatened to tumble from his lips. He should have figured they would both come to Josiah's favorite spot—where he'd come to walk and feed the birds for years.

"He here with you?" Mateo stared hard as he crossed his arms.

Tristan fought himself not to state the obvious, considering Josiah wasn't standing next to him. "I haven't seen him since he went to you." His words sat heavy in the air. As heavy as the ache in his gut at having said that. *Since he went to you...*

Mateo's eyes seemed to widen with panic. "What the fuck do you mean? Do you know where he is? If he's okay?" Without letting Tristan answer, Mateo pushed past him. He felt Mateo stiffen when he reached out and grabbed the man's arm. "If I were you, I'd get your hand off me. Now."

"You still think you have to protect him," Tristan said simply. Mateo's jaw locked so tight, he thought it would break.

"You don't know shit about me."

"I would venture to guess I know more about you than you know about me."

Anger darkened Mateo's features. Tristan watched as his look transformed to sadness. Damned if the pain in his eyes didn't make Tristan loosen his grip. He was surprised he'd held him that long. Surprised Mateo let him. But then instead of his hand connecting them, it was as if the chains that kept Tristan locked down, kept him closed off, didn't somehow wrap around Mateo, too. They'd seen a lot, the two of them. Josiah had, too, but not to the same extent as Mateo and himself. There was a darkness in Mateo's eyes that matched the one he tried to keep hidden in his own.

It was that connection, and how they both felt about the same man that made him say, "Let's walk."

Tristan took a couple steps, Mateo not moving but watching Tristan, as though he wanted to figure him out. Then, without a word, he stepped in line with him. It was a few minutes before Tristan spoke. "He's at a hotel. He asked me not to come yet, so I've respected that. Still, like you, I wanted to be sure he was okay, so I did a little digging to find out where he was."

Mateo cursed under his breath.

"He's trying to figure out what to do, I think. He doesn't know how to deal with *this*."

Mateo nodded as they kept walking. "I shouldn't have fuckin' come. The last thing I've ever wanted to do was hurt, Jay."

The nickname made Tristan flinch. Even though it was only a shortened version of his name, it was intimate in a way he'd never let himself become with Josiah. That wasn't fair to Josiah. *It's not fair to me…*

Tristan sighed, wishing the words swimming around in his head weren't true. It would make this a whole hell of a lot easier. "I know that. Even before I met you, I knew that. I see it in the way you look at him, too."

"Bet that makes you want to take me out, doesn't it?" Mateo

chuckled.

Tristan was surprised when he did the same. He wouldn't lie and pretend he wouldn't like to at least get a few hits in on him. "More than you'll ever know."

Mateo scratched his chest. When he did his shirt moved, showing Tristan the edge of a tattoo. Dark stubble covered his jaw, midnight just like the hair on his head. He squeezed his lips together as if deep in thought and it added a softness to his hardened features. He was a beautiful man. He almost scratched the word, thinking it too sweet for a man like him, but somehow it fit.

"You loved him enough to let him walk away, knowin' he was coming to me. I don't know if I could've done it."

He shook his head at that. He got what Mateo tried to do there. He wanted to give Tristan something in return for what he said, only Tristan didn't agree. "Maybe it means I didn't love him enough. Maybe it was the wrong way to show him how I feel."

"He would have resented you if you hadn't, and you both would have always wondered why he was with you. If it was just 'cause he didn't have a choice."

Tristan's head jerked in Mateo's direction, feeling as though another chain wrapped around the two of them. It was as if Mateo had plucked those words from his head. Before he could reply, not that he knew what he would say, Mateo spoke again. "And he will choose you. I fuckin' hate it, but I know he will. And I know he should."

Those words should have made Tristan ecstatic. In a way, they did...but they also hollowed him out. Made that emptiness take over again. "And I also know the decision will kill him. A part of him will always belong to you."

"I shot that all to hell when I walked away from him. You think it'll kill him to choose you, but it'll do the same fuckin' thing to him if he chose me. I can't give him the shit you can."

"*Stuff!*" Tristan yelled before lowering his voice. "I can give him *stuff.* I have never told him I love him. I've never given…" He shook his head, not able to go there.

"And I've come to him with blood on my hands. I've left him. I'm an ex-con. I know all that shit, yet I'm still here. I can't walk away from him again unless he tells me to go."

Tristan stopped walking, and so did Mateo. They faced each other, different in so many ways. Tristan wore a suit, Mateo low-slung jeans. He had his ear pierced, tattoos, while Tristan had to go to his high-rise office soon, prosecuting people who did many of the things he knew Mateo had done.

But then, they both loved the same man. Both had done things that were very wrong, and against the law. And he respected the hell out of Mateo in some ways because he'd been strong enough to do things Tristan never had. He didn't need details to know it. Mateo would and probably had manned up to protect what was his, rather than plugging his ears and pretending nothing happened. His mom kept herself locked in her apartment, scared of the outside world because he hadn't protected her the way he should.

"We've both failed him," he told Mateo.

Mateo nodded and took a step backward, then another, obviously knowing their conversation was over. Before he left, he asked, "What time did he used to come feed the birds?"

"He won't be here."

"I know."

Tristan told him what time and hesitated, but then just let himself speak. "I'll see you in the morning."

Mateo nodded before walking away.

Chapter Six

Josiah

Josiah was lost.

He lay on the bed in his dingy room, remembering the time years ago he stayed in the same hotel. Only then, he'd been more than lost. He'd been broken. Which he guessed in a way he still was. He, Mateo, and Tristan were all broken in one way or another. Mateo had mended so many of his pieces all those years ago before shattering them again. Then it had been Tristan who handed him the glue to put himself together. Tristan, who was always there for him, yet had never told Josiah he loved him. Still, he might not use words, but Josiah knew Tristan wouldn't walk away from him, either.

Josiah stood, walked over to the desk, and looked at his bird and queen, pleaded with them to give him the answers like Tristan and Teo always did.

He scooped them both into his hand.

He couldn't make sense of anything. Doubted everything, but still had knowledge of the things he doubted cemented inside him. Confusion made it hard to sort through how he felt and what he knew. Mateo and Tristan were both in his life. He loved both of them, and he *did* know they loved him. He made it all these years without Mateo, but seeing him again fused them back together. But then there was Tristan. Tristan made him feel strong in a way he never had before, and he would always love him for that. He couldn't lose Tristan, either.

Josiah let his queen and his bird roll around in his hand. He made them touch and flip over each other, wishing they could somehow be a part of one another. That his queen could protect the bird. Be strong for it and take care of it. The bird in return nurturing and loving the queen. Or that he could do something for them. What did he do for them besides fall apart? Be the broken piece they'd both had to put together?

No, he was tired of waiting for others to take care of things for him.

Josiah pushed off the bed and slipped his feet into shoes. He hadn't left this room for days, drifting away like he had when he was a kid, alone in San Francisco for the first time. He wasn't eighteen years old anymore. He'd grown since then, and it was time he acted like it.

Josiah climbed onto a bus, silently riding it across town. His first stop was the bank. He picked up the paperwork he needed to apply for a start-up business loan and made an appointment with their loan specialist.

Next he went to talk to a realtor about spaces he could rent. Even if the loan did work out, he knew he wouldn't get a lot. He wasn't stupid, and knew he wouldn't be able to afford much, but none of that mattered. He just wanted something that was *his.* And he wanted to do it for himself.

When he was done, he stopped by Fisherman's Roast to make out the schedule for the next two weeks. There was stuff to be done, and he'd do it. No more falling apart. That didn't mean he felt any less broken. It didn't mean Tristan or Mateo ever left his mind. They were always with him.

Chapter Seven

Mateo

When Mateo walked away from the busy street and toward the sidewalk close to the water, he saw Tristan already standing there. He was next to a faded bench, his back to Mateo. He almost turned around and left. It was probably the smart thing to do. What in the hell was he doing spending time with the man, anyway? It didn't make any sense. He'd always known him and Jay were nothing alike. It was like that times a hundred when it came to Josiah's pretty boy.

But then, he didn't want to walk away, either. He was curious about Josiah's guy. He got what Jay saw in him. He was sexy and put together. Yeah, he definitely got the attraction part of it, but his interest in Tristan didn't go any farther than that, except where Josiah was concerned. Or maybe he really meant his interest *shouldn't* have gone further.

He didn't know what it was, but he'd almost felt comfortable walking with him yesterday. Mateo had never felt comfortable with anyone in his life other than Josiah. But then, Tristan and Josiah were together. He was Mateo's connection to Jay, so in a fucked up way, it made sense.

Mateo drummed his hand on his legs as he continued going.

"What's up?" He nodded at Tristan as he stepped up to the man.

"Hello. I wasn't sure you would come."

He realized how close they stood, near enough that he smelled a light scent of cologne. Mateo took a step backward. "Do you wish I didn't?"

Tristan stared off as if in thought before replying. "No, which I don't understand."

Tristan's thoughts mirrored his. "Maybe it's 'cause we both know something about him that the other doesn't. I know his past, and you got his present." Fuck, those words killed him. Strangled him and stabbed through him and every other fucking thing he'd lived with all combined into one. He ran a hand through his hair. "What the hell am I doin'? I'm getting outta here."

He turned and took a couple steps when Tristan spoke, his voice steady and strong. "Running away like you did when you left him?"

Mateo whipped around, his body going hot. "Fuck you. You don't know shit about me or what I did." His jaw hurt he pressed his teeth together so tightly, his hands balled into fists.

"Why did you send him away?" Tristan cocked his head a little as though he was really curious, then seemed to snap out of it. "You're right. This isn't…" He shook his head and somehow Mateo got what he meant. The way Tristan stood, and the far-off look on his face, in his eyes, was…distant. It was almost like looking in a mirror. He didn't talk to people any better than Mateo did. At least not about shit that mattered.

"Come on." Mateo nodded his head and started walking. It was a few seconds before Tristan stepped up beside him. Mateo let out a deep breath, unsure why. "Where'd you meet him?" he asked.

"Here. Walking. He came every day. There isn't a day that goes by that Josiah doesn't come here to feed the birds."

Until now, at least. Still, hearing that did something to him. Filled him up in a way only Jay ever had. This was supposed to be their thing. He imagined how it would have felt to have been out here with Josiah, and wondered if Josiah thought about being out here with him. But then, he'd been with Tristan. As much as that made him want to set the whole fucking world on fire, he was glad Jay hadn't been alone.

Mateo glanced at him. "We were in the same foster home for a while." As soon as he said it, he realized Tristan probably already knew that. Josiah probably told him everything.

Tristan didn't call him on it though and Mateo found himself continuing. "He was so fuckin' shy. I see it in him now but it's not the same. He's not the same." And that both hurt and made him smile, too. No matter what went down between them, Jay did good for himself.

"You protected him, he told me. Took care of him."

Mateo shook his head. "He always saw it like that. That's how Jay is. He's so damn *good* that he only sees things from one side. That's not how it was. Not in the ways that counted."

There was movement from the corner of his eye. Mateo looked over to see Tristan holding his wrist, his body tense in a way that surprised him.

His voice was low, hoarse, when he said, "You were there when he needed you. You saved him when it mattered. That counts."

Automatically, his body moved closer to Tristan's. "Even if it means you're walking with a murderer?" It was stupid to say that. Tristan was a prosecutor, but really what the fuck could he do? It wasn't like he hadn't been to prison. If he was going to get locked up again for something, at least it should be for something he didn't regret. Saving Josiah that night was one of the few things he was really proud of.

"It means I'm walking with someone who protected the person they loved. That's what I see. And maybe I shouldn't. It's my job to put people behind bars, and I believe in what I do. If the system hadn't let us down, then maybe my family wouldn't have gone through what we did. You took care of him for years. I failed those I loved. That's what I see."

Some of the heaviness, the self-hatred, in his chest lightened at that. Yes, he believed in what he did for Josiah. Always had, but that was way fucking different than hearing it from a man like Tristan. A man he shouldn't give a shit about what he thought, and he hadn't realized he did until this second.

Mateo's feet stopped moving. He didn't try to keep his hand from reaching out for Tristan's arm. For turning to face him, and still holding on while Tristan did the same. *Dios,* this was crazy shit. He didn't understand it, but as he looked into Tristan's dark eyes, he saw more pieces of himself. Pieces he never expected to see in the man. Pieces he hadn't see in anyone else.

He spent time around so many fucking bastards. Murderers and drug dealers. People who had done some of the same things as him. But they thrived on it. It was a part of them, while Mateo tried to vomit it up every time he had to hurt someone, like he could really fucking purge it out of his system. He suddenly wondered if Tristan did the same. If he tried to expel his regrets.

He wasn't sure exactly what Tristan had gone through. He didn't know if Tristan meant going to the extent that Mateo had, not that he knew all the details. Still, he knew enough, and everything Mateo did from the drugs on up wasn't easy. "It's hard livin' with taking action sometimes, too. You don't escape the pain either way."

He took a small step closer to Mateo, his body relaxing a little. "Then we both suffer, only in different ways. You saved Josiah and I allowed things to happen to my mother."

Ice crystalized his insides. Fuck, he hadn't expected to hear that. Didn't quite understand why Tristan told him. Though he guessed that wasn't true, either. Like Tristan said, they both suffered with it. It was something they shared that most people could never imagine.

Words hung on the tip of Mateo's tongue, begging to be let free. Did Tristan still see his mistakes when he closed his eyes, the way Mateo did? Did he wake up a night, wet with sweat, heart hammering?

He wouldn't insult Tristan by telling him it wasn't his fault. Not that Mateo thought it was, but he also knew Tristan wouldn't want to hear it. That it would only piss him off, because Teo felt that way, too. He might have made it in time but Jay had been out there because of him. He had a hand in every bad thing that had happened to Josiah since he'd been sixteen years old.

So instead of saying any of that, he tried to give Tristan a piece of what he'd offered to Mateo. "Do you take care of her now?"

"Yes."

"That counts. That's what I see." He let go of Tristan's arm, but let his hand slide down instead of immediately breaking contact. Then their fingers touched, one of Tristan's hooked with his, and they both held it there. His skin was warm, smooth, and strangely Mateo liked the feel of it against his own. *One, two, three, four, five* seconds went by before they both pulled away.

"He's too good for both of us," Tristan said as they started walking again.

It was another thing they had in common. Another thing that somehow bound them together. And damned if he didn't wonder what else there could be that he didn't know about.

Chapter Eight

Tristan

It was like déjà vu, meeting with Mateo the same way he'd done with Josiah years before. Every instinct inside Tristan told him to pull back, to walk away, because he found it almost comforting having this routine with Mateo. Part of the comfort due to the reason he'd told Josiah—in a way it felt like Mateo had always been a part of them because he was such a huge part of Josiah.

Which pissed him off and made him wonder why he'd met with the man four days in a row. Yet, even the few times he tried to talk himself out of going, or into turning around, he never did it. And then there was that word again...comforting. He'd never really felt comfortable in his own life, even before Josiah turned it upside down. Tristan felt like he had everything he needed: money, stability, his own form of power. Even with that, he'd always felt restless. His mind was always going. He felt the only sort of calm he'd ever really know with Josiah, and yet he had a piece of it here, too. Walking with Mateo, and now feeding Josiah's birds.

It made his gut ache, his mind telling him to pull back. He'd already opened himself up to Josiah as best he could, and even he knew it wasn't enough. How the hell could he let himself get close to someone else?

He wondered if Mateo felt the same. They hadn't talked more about their individual pasts, which he was grateful for. They spoke a lot about Josiah. Mateo told him he'd taken a lot of his general education classes in prison. Jesus, how in the hell had he ended up spending time with an ex-con? Time he actually enjoyed.

Tristan watched as Mateo suddenly stopped, pulling a phone out of his pocket. He hit the camera button and aimed. Tristan followed where he pointed, not seeing whatever it was Mateo thought he needed to take a picture of. A few people walked around on the sidewalk. There was a homeless man wearing layers despite the heat, who was bent down, holding a cat who rubbed against his face.

Mateo took a few pictures before sliding it back into his pocket without a word.

Before he got the chance to ask him about it, Mateo spoke. "I should go, and I'm sure you have shit to do. I need to get to a Laundromat and wash some clothes."

Jesus, he'd forgotten the man was paying weekly to live in a hotel. He didn't let him think about what he was about to say. Just spoke. "Come to our house to do it." He'd only worked half a day this morning, and was supposed to be finishing up at home, anyway.

Mateo shook his head. "What are we doin', man? We don't fucking know each other. I'm a criminal, and you're a goddamned lawyer. We're both in love with the same fuckin' man, and I'm supposed to come and do laundry at your house?"

It wasn't anything he hadn't thought. Anything he still didn't think about. And he knew this couldn't be the first time Mateo did, either. Yet, they were both still here. "Veto."

"What?"

Tristan chuckled, surprised the word had come out. Instead of explaining, he said, "I don't know what we're doing." It was the only answer he had, but then he added, "It's something I used to say to Josiah."

Mateo let out a deep breath and swallowed. Tristan watched his Adam's apple move and wondered how many times Josiah had kissed Mateo there. Wondered what he tasted like.

Neither said anything else as they walked to Tristan's BMW, close enough that Mateo's arm brushed his as they moved. Neither of them pulled away.

They were quiet as he drove to Mateo's hotel. Obviously, he knew that Tristan had been the one to tell Josiah where he was staying. He waited in the car while Mateo went to get his things, wondering what they were doing just like Mateo had been. But it felt wrong walking away, leaving the man who had done so much for Josiah, even if all he was doing was giving him a free place to do laundry.

It only took a few minutes for Mateo to get back to the car. As he pulled onto the busy San Francisco street packed with traffic, his mind went back to what he'd thought about while he drove to Mateo's hotel. That Tristan knew where it was because he'd told Josiah. He'd sent Josiah to him. Sweat beaded on his brow, making Tristan turn up the air conditioner.

"What's wrong?" Mateo asked.

"How do you know something's wrong?"

"You get stiff as a fuckin' board when you get pissed about something. You also touch your wrist, but I'm guessing you didn't do that this time because you're driving."

Tristan frowned. There'd only been one other person who called him on counting his pulse, and that had been Josiah. "It calms me down," he found himself saying. His head spun; his world, too. Tristan never told people things like that, yet he was with Mateo. Even with Josiah, it had taken longer. *Because he's as broken as me.* It was different with Josiah, because even though he had his own painful past, it had always been about love for him. Just wanting the people he loved. He hadn't seen or done the kind of things Mateo and he had. And Tristan was glad for that.

"Makes sense," Mateo finally replied. "So why do you need to calm down?"

"I was thinking of when I told Josiah where you were staying." The pulse they'd just spoken about sped up. Questions—or one question—bumped around in his head.

"I know you're with Jay, and maybe it makes me an asshole, but I can't regret being with him."

There was his answer. Pain shot through his jaw he held it so tight. He couldn't find words. Didn't want to. It wasn't as though he didn't know. He couldn't even blame Mateo or Josiah. He would have done the same thing. Still, he couldn't bring himself to reply to Mateo, either. Jealousy rushed through him, strong and fast. Josiah was his. It made his chest ache to think of him with someone else, yet that wasn't all that was there. There was a part of him who was jealous that Josiah had Mateo, too… Those thoughts were wrong on so many levels, Tristan tried to ignore them.

The rest of the fifteen minute drive was spent in silence.

Mateo didn't bring it up again as they got out of the car at their house. Tristan looked over the top of the car at Mateo, who had his eyes firmly planted on the house.

"Good. He belongs in a place like this."

Just like that, some of the anger melted away. No, it hadn't even been real anger. He didn't know what it had been that he felt, but as he watched Mateo look at the house, it disappeared.

"Let's go inside." He didn't look behind him to know Mateo followed. Tristan unlocked the door and pushed it open for Mateo to step inside. He stopped dead in his tracks, making Tristan look up. Josiah stood in the living room beside the couch.

"You came home," Tristan said simply, even though he felt anything but calm.

Josiah didn't answer, his eyes dashing back and forth between himself and Mateo in confusion.

"We saw each other by The Warf a few days back."

Mateo dropped his bag to the floor.

Josiah's brow creased.

"Jay," Mateo said, stepping toward him. Tristan did the same.

Josiah shook his head. "I don't understand. I've been going crazy for over a week now. I don't know what the hell I'm going to do." He paced back and forth across the living room. "I felt like shit for walking away from you, Tristan, and going to Mateo. It's eating me alive, because I love you, but…do we even have a future? Will you ever really be able to give yourself to me?" Josiah's voice got louder and louder as he spoke.

"And Teo… It's been nine years. Nine *years*, and I've hardly gotten any answers out of you. You walked away. You did the one thing you promised me you would never do, and now that I've moved on, you're back? I've been a fucking mess for a week and you guys walk in here together…what? Friends now?"

He stopped walking. Stared at both Tristan and Mateo, breathing heavy. "I don't know what to do," he said again.

"Jay." Mateo walked straight over to him, putting a hand on either side of Josiah's neck, his thumb brushing his cheek. "No one will do shit if it's not what you want. And as for me, and Tristan, we both have pieces of you the other doesn't. We both missed you, and…"

And then Mateo turned to look at Tristan as though he couldn't finish. As though he had the same voice inside him that said their time together stemmed from Josiah, but that there was more to it as well.

Envy wormed its way through Tristan for the way Mateo could just walk up to Josiah, grab him and say whatever was on his mind. He just opened up in a way Tristan never did.

In a way, Josiah did, too.

It was with that in his head that Tristan walked forward. Took in the way Josiah and Mateo looked together, both of them sexy as hell, only in completely different ways. Saw the way they automatically leaned in to each other, and damned if it didn't make fire burn its way through him in a completely different way than he expected. He suddenly imagined what they would look like together in passion, touching, and it didn't make him jealous. It made him hot all over.

It was like he'd stepped into a foreign country he'd never been to, excitement, nerves and confusion twisting and turning inside him.

Tristan stepped up behind Josiah, his chest touching Josiah's back. Mateo tried to move his hands, but Tristan grabbed his right wrist, holding it in place.

Mateo's face… his eyes were hard as they stared back at Tristan, but he knew the anger would break. That it wasn't true anger to begin with.

"We have a future, Josiah." Tristan spoke into his ear while he still held Mateo's wrist, even though his hand was back in place on Josiah.

"Tristan?" Josiah tried to turn to look at him, but Tristan leaned forward, dropping his forehead against the back of Josiah's head.

"We have a future if you want it." It was the best he could do.

He thought before that Josiah and Mateo were beautiful together, but now a sudden craving built inside him. He wanted to see them together. Josiah didn't know what to do, because he loved them both and wanted them both. Like he and Mateo said, they'd both failed him. He didn't want to fail Josiah anymore. Wanted him to have everything he needed, even if it wouldn't be forever. He just wanted to take the pain away, and damned if he knew any other way.

Conflicting thoughts warred inside him. This was wrong. So fucked up, because though this was about Josiah, there was more to it than that, too. He didn't understand the desire stirring within him, but it was there. Jesus, was it there, and he wanted to explore it. Wanted to feel it, lose himself in it, if only for one night.

He locked eyes with Mateo, hoping to tell him what he felt without words. Wanting to see if they could give him this. Take care of him the way they'd both always wanted to do.

Mateo's jaw was still tight, but he gave Tristan a small nod, the anger in his eyes melting into desire.

That was all he needed before he pressed his lips to Josiah's neck. "Let us both take care of you tonight."

Then he hoped like hell Josiah said yes.

Chapter Nine

Josiah

Desire erupted inside Josiah, flames scorching him from the inside out. His erection throbbed behind the fly of his jeans as two hard bodies pushed against him.

Mateo and Tristan.

The only two people he'd ever wanted. Tristan's lips on the back of his neck, Mateo's hand on the side, his thumb brushing Josiah's cheek. He could feel the tension strung between the three of them—every movement careful in this new, unchartered territory.

Was this really happening?

As strong as that hunger busting through each and every one of his walls was, that anger was still there, too. Anger, hurt, confusion. He didn't even know who he was angry at or why. Maybe himself for wanting both of these men so much. A stronger man could walk away from both of them… but did he want that? No matter what that truth meant, he didn't.

But this? Lust lashed through him as Tristan gripped his waist, his hands sliding under his shirt.

"Let us make you feel good, Josiah." Tristan's breath was warm on his neck, and Josiah found himself leaning back into him.

He hadn't noticed his head dropped forward until Mateo's thumb dipped under his chin, tilting it up. "We got you, Jay. Forget everything else. Just feel good. You deserve that—to just feel good."

Those words shattered any mock resistance he'd felt. This would screw things up on so many levels. It would kill him in the end, but there was no way he could walk away from it. No way he could turn from having both Mateo and Tristan. He never imagined having them this way…but, hadn't he sort of wanted it? Wished that there was something to tie them all together so he wouldn't have to lose either of them?

"*We* deserve it," Josiah whispered. And they did. All three of them dealt with so much. Didn't they deserve just to feel *good*?

Mateo gave him a cocky half grin that he hadn't seen for way too long before his lips came down on Josiah's. Josiah gasped into his mouth at the feel of Tristan's teeth as they bit into the back of his neck.

Mateo kept kissing and Josiah got back into his groove, letting Mateo's tongue trace and taste every part of his mouth. It was so familiar. *He* was so familiar. His lips that were a little rougher than Tristan's.

Josiah wrapped an arm around Mateo, his other drifting behind him to wrap around Tristan's thigh. He needed them both closer. Needed to know they were both really there.

And they came. Came to him like he wanted. As Tristan's hand slid down, cupping Josiah's erection, Mateo moved in so their bodies touched head to toe. He felt Mateo tense up a little when his body came in contact with Tristan's hand, so Josiah held tighter, kissed harder, until Mateo rocked his hips in a movement that no doubt had his erection rubbing against Tristan's hand.

Then his lips were gone, but only for him to whisper, "Fuck," against Josiah's mouth as he continued to move against him, continued to keep the contact between himself and Tristan, too.

"To the couch." Tristan's voice was thick with lust.

Mateo, still with his hand on Josiah's neck, looked over Josiah's shoulder, locking eyes with Tristan. Josiah didn't have to see him head on to know the look in his eyes. No one told Teo what to do. Not like that, and he waited for it. Waited for the spell to be broken. Waited for this to all end. But Teo surprised him by pulling Josiah toward the couch.

"Get his pants," Tristan told Mateo as Tristan slid his hands under Josiah's shirt and pushed it up. He pulled it over Josiah's head as Mateo dropped to his knees, untying one of Josiah's shoes.

"I can do that, Teo," whispered past Josiah's lips as Tristan's tongue teased his nipple. Really, he wasn't sure he could do anything at all. This was about him. Logically, he knew that. His brain yelled at him that this was wrong. It would only screw things up even more than they were already screwed, but the more Tristan's mouth sucked at first one nipple and then the other, the less Josiah could think. As Mateo's fingers unbuttoned his jeans and pulled his zipper down, logic got more and more fogged over with pleasure.

Then Tristan kissed him. It was the first time he'd kissed him since the day he left to go to Mateo, and it went straight to his head. He moaned at the rough press of Tristan's kiss and the slight bite on his lip before he was sucked into Tristan's mouth. He loved being kissed by Tristan. Tristan was all passion and made him feel wanted in ways even Mateo had never made him feel.

Pleasure shot through him, making Josiah rip his mouth from Tristan's when his cock was enveloped in the heat of Mateo's mouth. His balls burned, wanting to explode right then.

And then Tristan's mouth was there again. On his neck, his ear, his chest, kissing, licking and sucking him everywhere. Josiah dropped his head back and felt. Felt good, the way Teo and Tristan wanted him to.

His eyes drifted closed as he tried to get his body under control. Mateo cupped his balls as he took Josiah all the way to the back of his throat before pulling all the way off to tongue his head. It was as if a million hands were on him and a million mouths were on him, making him feel good everywhere.

"Jesus, you are beautiful together. You are goddamned sexy taking your pleasure, Josiah."

Josiah's head snapped up to see Tristan watching. His eyes slowly traveling Josiah's face before dropping down to watch Mateo. He was transfixed, his eyes flaring with heat as Tristan took in Mateo blowing him.

Mateo peered up, and both he and Tristan watched as he sucked Josiah deep again. "Oh, God," Josiah mumbled, thinking Tristan was right. Mateo really was beautiful.

Then, as if he could read Josiah's mind, Tristan reached out. His hand lingered for a moment before he ran his hand through Mateo's hair, letting the black strands fall through his fingers, then doing it again.

They'd been wrong before. *That* was beauty. His orgasm slammed into him, threatening to pull him under as Josiah fought to hold it back.

Tristan's hand left Mateo's hair and wrapped tightly around the base of Josiah's erection. "Not yet. Don't come, Josiah." His voice was thick and gravely like it often got when they were making love.

Mateo's tongue ran the length of his cock one last time and then he pushed to his feet. He stepped close to Josiah, hands on both sides of his neck before covering Josiah's mouth with his. Tristan's hand wrapped around Josiah's prick, stroking it as Teo kissed him, so soft and tender. Just like Tristan made him feel desires on a different level, Mateo made him feel safe. Safer and more cared for than anyone else. Even in the way Teo kissed him, it was as if his only goal in life was to give Josiah everything he had.

The need to have both climbed higher and higher inside him. Flowed faster and deeper until that's all he knew. The way they both made him feel…he wanted that for them, too. Wanted to give that to them. Wondered if they could give it to each other.

Josiah slid one of his hands on the back of Teo's neck, and the other on Tristan's. He pressed another kiss to Mateo's lips before pulling away. Still holding them both, he kissed Tristan with all the strength and passion that Tristan gave him.

Hands on them, he pulled his head back, wanting them to find everything they gave him in each other, too.

Knowledge filled both their eyes as they shared a look between them. It felt like an eternity passed that Mateo and Tristan took each other in. *Kiss him. Love him, too.* He didn't know which he pleaded to. Both, he guessed, even though it was a ridiculous wish. How would that even work? He didn't know, didn't care. He just knew he would always want them both, and would always feel the ache of loss for one if he was with the other.

Teo raised a hand and Josiah's pulse skyrocketed. Mateo touched Tristan's hair, the way he always did with Josiah. The way Tristan had just done with Mateo.

Tristan's eyes closed for a few seconds longer than needed, and when he opened them again, Teo dropped his hand.

They couldn't do it.

Guilt swarmed like angry bees inside Josiah. "No. This isn't fair."

"Shh, *mi precioso.* Come here." Mateo grabbed his wrist and pulled him closer.

"It's definitely fair." Tristan ran his hand down Josiah's back and ass. "I'm right where I want to be." Then he pulled a condom and lube from inside the table by the couch. Tristan had them hidden all over the house for whenever they needed it.

Mateo pulled his shirt over his head and dropped it to the floor. He kicked out of his shoes, and his pants were gone next. His erection pulsed, veins running the length.

Josiah turned to Tristan, saw him watching Mateo, taking in his naked form as Teo laid on the L-shaped couch. The end they were at had a built-in ottoman, making it just like a bed.

"Come here, Jay."

Josiah made himself pull his eyes from Tristan and do as Mateo said. He straddled his hips and wrapped a hand around his cock. Teo sucked in a sharp breath. "Fuck. I'm gonna come if you touch me. You gotta hold off."

He wrapped his hand around Josiah's and kept it from moving as they both took in the sight of Tristan while he removed his slacks, then briefs, and then slowly unbuttoned his shirt.

"Dios…" Mateo rasped out. His dick twitched against Josiah's hand.

Josiah got it, because he'd felt the same way the first time he saw Tristan naked. Everything about him was always so incredibly sexy and put together, but naked, he was like a god. Fit, golden, and sculpted, almost as if he wasn't real.

Josiah felt a smile stretch his lips as Tristan cocked a grin, but then it slowly disappeared as he rubbed a finger over the bullet scar on Teo's shoulder.

"It's nothin'," Mateo told him.

"It's something," Tristan replied.

That's when Josiah saw it. Really saw it. There was something between them. He wasn't crazy enough to think it could possibility mirror what he felt for them, but there was a bond there that they'd somehow formed. It settled some of the fear inside him.

Tristan opened the condom and rolled it over his erection. Josiah didn't move, not sure what would happen next.

"Get on your knees, Josiah. Lean over him." Tristan got behind Josiah on the couch as Josiah leaned forward, his mouth next to Teo's and his ass in front of Tristan. "Lean forward a little more." Tristan pressed down on Josiah's shoulders so, he almost felt Teo's lips against his. The move put his ass higher.

He heard the lube open, then felt cold against his hole. Josiah moaned, loving the feel of Tristan's finger rubbing him, but needing Mateo, too. So he took him. Slowly he kissed Mateo, who opened his mouth, immediately letting Josiah in.

There was the sound of the bottle squeezing again, and he flinched as Mateo's cold, lubed hand wrapped around his erection again. A shiver went through him as he imagined Tristan putting lube in Mateo's hand so he could jack Josiah off.

Josiah's body seized, lurched forward as Tristan pushed inside him. The movement made him thrust into Teo's hand, their lips still connected.

And then Mateo's cock was there, too. His hand around both of them. They rubbed together, fucking Teo's hand each time Tristan thrust into him.

"So fucking good. Love being inside you." Tristan's hand rested on Josiah's back as he pumped harder and faster. Mateo's grip tightened as their tongues tangled together.

Josiah felt like he was in an incinerator. His orgasm already pricked at his balls, begging to burst free, but he fought it. Wanted this to go on forever.

Mateo's head fell to the side, making their lips pull apart. "Fuck... I love touching you."

And then he looked over Josiah's shoulder, watching as Tristan took him. He sped his movements, squeezing their cocks together. Rubbing his thumb over their heads before sliding down again.

"Make him come. If you don't, I will." Mateo winked cockily at Tristan, shocking Josiah.

"Yes. That feels so good," pulled out of Josiah's throat as Tristan slammed into him from a slightly higher angle, making both himself and Teo fuck Teo's hand harder.

He couldn't hold it back anymore. His body ripped apart. Come shot from him, landing on Mateo's chest. And then Teo joined him, a stripe of white erupting from him as well, mixing with Josiah's.

Tristan grabbed his hips and thrust one more time before his cock jerked inside Josiah as he emptied himself, too.

Arms and legs weak, Josiah collapsed, half on the couch, one leg over Mateo. A few beats went by before Mateo's arm wrapped around him. Then Tristan went down beside him, his arm around Josiah, too.

He had to be falling off the couch, or maybe not since he lay on his side, making as much room as he could. Josiah was too drained to look. All he knew was they were his. Both of them were his. After this, he swore he wouldn't give either of them up, no matter what it took. That was the last thing he remembered before he closed his eyes and his world went black.

Chapter Ten

Mateo

When Mateo's eyes slid open, the room was dark. Light from outside enabled him to make out the two figures in front of him. Josiah and Tristan. Holy fuck, how in the hell had this happened? Not that he hadn't enjoyed it—probably more than he should have—but damn… He'd shared Josiah. No, Tristan had shared Josiah with *him*. This was their home and their couch. They lay like this together every night; Mateo was the extra.

He fisted the hand that rested on Josiah, trying to calm the need to claim him, not just share him.

Mateo let his fingers ghost over Josiah's shoulder, some of the tension leaking from him with the touch. Could Josiah feel the roughness of his calloused fingers against his skin? In his sleep, did he know it was Mateo touching him, or did he think it was Tristan?

Josiah didn't move, his breathing deep and even, telling him he probably didn't feel shit. He'd come so hard, Mateo doubted he'd feel much of anything for a while.

Warm skin brushed against the back of his hand before sliding down Josiah's spine. Spontaneous heat flared inside him as he saw Tristan's hand float up Josiah's back and drift over his hand again.

His cock hardened against Josiah's thigh, a foreign voice asking silent questions in the back of his head: *Will he touch me again…? Do I want him to…?*

It wasn't as though he'd been a saint since he lost Josiah. He'd fucked men. Not a lot of them, but those had been quick, thirty-minute ways to get off. He'd never craved the touch of another man after it was gone, except with Josiah. So why did he want it from Tristan? From the suit who gave Josiah all the shit he never could?

Tristan pushed to his feet. Teo watched the man's firm, naked body move toward the chair, grabbing a blanket off the back before coming toward them again.

When he got close enough, Mateo noticed his cock was half hard, too. As much as that drew his attention, he also couldn't stop concentrating on the rest of Tristan as he straightened out the blanket. As he laid it over Mateo and Josiah. Over his man and Mateo, as though he was taking care of both of them. No one in his life had ever laid a blanket over him while he slept. No one except Josiah.

"Wait." Mateo slowly untangled himself from Josiah and stood.

"Top of the stairs, first door on the left. I'll be right there." Tristan grabbed his underwear and pulled them on before walking to another room. Mateo grabbed his pants and did the same, quietly making his way up the stairs while wondering what the fuck he was doing.

He opened the door, found the switch on the wall and turned it on, realizing Tristan sent him to his office. It was clean as hell, nothing out of place. No papers were out, giving the impression he didn't use it very often, though Teo somehow knew that wasn't true.

Mateo walked over to the tall window and looked out at the city below. At all the lights in the Golden Gate Bridge in the background, thinking everything looked a whole lot different from up here.

"Whiskey?" Tristan asked from behind him.

"Yeah." Mateo didn't turn around when he replied.

"I thought so." He heard the clank of glass against glass before Tristan stepped up next to him.

They both swallowed down the dark, brown liquid before Tristan filled their glasses again.

"Will he wake up with you gone?" Mateo asked, not sure why he thought it better for them to talk alone.

"No. I don't sleep well. He's used to me slipping out of bed." Tristan leaned against the opposite side of the large window from him.

"He never slept when I was gone. Guess that's because he was always wonderin' if I was dead somewhere." He didn't have to worry about shit like that here.

Tristan ran a hand over his short, dark hair before drinking the rest of his second glass of whiskey. He didn't flinch as it went down, setting the glass aside before crossing his arms over his bare chest. Mateo watched the movement, taking in the bend of all his muscles, the dark hair on his chest, trying to figure out how in the fuck Tristan looked just as put together standing there in his underwear as he did in a suit. Wondering why he liked it...

"What the hell am I doing here? This is some fucked up shit. I've always thought of Josiah as mine. I've always wanted him, yet now he's yours. But I just sucked his cock and then jacked him off while you fucked him."

Mateo turned, taking two steps to leave, before Tristan's firm grip wrapped around his arm. "You were taking care of him just like you always wanted to do."

He was. He knew he fucking was, but that hadn't been all it was about. He'd always want Josiah, but *Dios,* it had been about more than that. Flashes of Tristan and Josiah together filled his head. Tristan fucking him. Josiah relaxing into him like he knew Tristan would always be there to catch him. He'd never seen something that sexy, but again, it was more than just Josiah. He'd wanted...

"It makes sense that we'd both be intrigued by each other as well. Even before I knew you, I wondered about you. And now... It's not as if many men would turn down a chance at two lovers." He dropped his hand.

Mateo's muscles went rigid, unexplainable anger taking root inside him. He took a step toward Tristan, then another one. "So you figured you'd let me play with you guys. Let Josiah's piece of shit ex join you before he goes on his way?" His body lined with Tristan's as he boxed him in, hands on the wall. "Did I meet your expectations? You know, since I intrigue you and all. If that's the case, though, you should have let me fuck you so you'd get the full experience."

Tristan's eyes flashed with different emotions so quickly, Mateo couldn't get a read on any of them.

Tristan's mouth was tight when he replied, "Don't play games with me. I can promise you, you won't win them. And just so you know, no one fucks me."

Mateo stumbled backward, not expecting Tristan's mouth to come down on his. Tristan kept pushing, his tongue already in Teo's mouth as he backed him against his desk.

Mateo's hands cupped his face, his tongue battling Tristan's stroke for stroke.

It wasn't until he felt a tug at his hair that he realized Tristan's hands were on him, too, one on the back of his neck and the other digging into his waist.

Faster, harder, hands groping and squeezing, they warred with each other with their mouths and bodies. He kicked something and realized at some point he'd dropped his glass.

Tristan held him against the desk, but Mateo wasn't giving in to him. He pushed, too. The other man must not have expected it because his back hit the wall with a loud thump.

As quickly as it started, they jerked away from each other, facing off, both breathing heavily. His body, cock included, was stiff and rigid.

Tristan wiped his bottom lip with his thumb, and Mateo realized he'd bitten him.

What the fuck is going on here?

"You want me to want you." Tristan pushed forward so he didn't lean against the wall anymore.

"Fuck you."

"Because you want me, too."

The "too" pulsed through him like a never-ending echo. "I want *him*." Mateo pointed toward the door.

"You think this is easy on me? Jesus, half the time I can't even tell Josiah how I feel. Having a hard-on for you doesn't make this any easier, but at least I can admit it. I don't even know you and I know you have more balls than that."

Mateo unclenched his fists. Fuck, Tristan was right. But, "What good does admitting it do? We both love him, and we're attracted to each other." Saying that didn't feel right, though. Yeah, Tristan was sexy, so of course a part of Mateo desired him, but there was more to it than that. Some kind of bond he didn't understand.

Then, a piece of Josiah's conversation from earlier jumped into his head and he clung to that, because it was a whole lot easier to deal with than his own shit. "You love him, right?" Josiah had wondered earlier if they had a future, something Mateo didn't expect.

Tristan shook his head. "That's a stupid question."

And damned if he didn't know it was, even though Tristan still didn't answer. Mateo walked over to the chair on the other side of the desk and fell into it as Tristan leaned on the wall again. "It doesn't matter if we want each other. Jay feels a whole hell of a lot more for us than that, and fucking with each other, even with him, is just going to screw shit up even more than it already is."

Tristan sighed. "A little late for that, don't you think?"

That's when he knew he had to admit some things. His gut twisted into knots, the urge to vomit rolling through him. *Calm the fuck down.*

Mateo leaned forward, resting his elbows on his knees, his hands on his head. "There's shit I've done that could come back to haunt me. I mean, I don't think so. If they haven't by now they shouldn't, but they could. There's no promise my past won't come back and rip me out of his life, even if he didn't have you."

Self-hatred ate away at him, his insides filled with holes like wood infested with termites. *Dios,* he was such a piece of shit. Even so, he couldn't find it in himself to regret this.

"What did you do?" Tristan's voice was ice cold, detached.

"None of your fucking business."

He sighed before sitting in his chair at his desk. "Do I have to worry about someone looking for you who might hurt Josiah to get back at you?"

"Fuck you if you think I would put him at risk like that. Things were shitty between Javier and me, but it was even worse before I got locked up. I got outta prison early and just left. He doesn't give a shit where I am. He's probably thankful I'm gone." He sat up against the back of the chair, frustrated at himself for being an asshole to Tristan. All he did was try to protect Josiah. "No. It's the other side of the law who would come looking. You don't want to know any more than that."

Tristan nodded and Mateo pushed to his feet, feeling like he might lose his shit and puke all over Tristan's office. "I need to get outta here."

By the time he made it to the door, Tristan was right there, his hand on Mateo's arm again. "Don't disappear. We still have things to figure out."

He couldn't believe he did it, but Mateo nodded his head. A part of him knew Tristan was right. They did have shit to figure out, he just couldn't believe Tristan would want to. And didn't know what in the hell they could possibly do.

When Tristan let him go, Mateo jogged down the stairs. He had his shirt and shoes on in no time flat. He stopped by the couch and fingered Josiah's hair before grabbing his bag of clothes and heading out the door.

From the street, he stopped and looked up at the house, at the figure that stood in the window of the room he just left. A room that was now dark.

Reaching in his bag, Mateo pulled out the camera he'd bought at a pawnshop and took a picture before losing himself in the night.

Chapter Eleven

Tristan

He had no idea what the hell he was doing.

He'd never had a problem not getting involved before. His whole life he automatically kept himself at arm's length when it came to other people. Emotional attachments led to all kind of situations he'd never wanted to deal with…never wanted to risk. As long as he could take care of himself and his mom, that's all that ever mattered to him.

Now he'd fallen for Josiah. It was something that grew over the years, and even though voicing it aloud was still somehow trapped inside him, he'd accepted it. He could deal with it, because it almost felt like he wasn't putting himself out there, wasn't risking giving control to another person, if he didn't actually voice his emotions. He *wanted* to have Josiah in his life, no matter what, and that's all that he focused on.

Yet, now…hell, now he didn't know what to think of Mateo barging back into Josiah's life.

Tristan leaned back in the chair of his dark office. He knew what he should want. He should want the man out of their world. Not just because he didn't have room inside him to care about anyone else, or even because he'd hurt Josiah in the past, or because he could very well take the only man Tristan had ever really loved away from him.

Mateo threatened the one thing in his life that had always meant more to him than everything, except his mom. It meant more than his pride and dignity. He'd bent to another man's will, gotten to his knees for someone he didn't want, and let a man fuck him for money to secure his stability. Yet even being around Mateo threatened what he fought for. His career.

Mateo never played on the right side of the law. He knew that much from stories Josiah told him, but now he knew there were things that could come back for Mateo even now. Knowing about those things meant risking the control over his world that Tristan clung to so tightly. It was the only thing that made him feel whole…except for Josiah.

He closed his eyes, letting those thoughts absorb into him—thoughts of Josiah and Mateo both.

Josiah made him feel again.

He'd told Mateo not to run, even though that would have been the smartest thing for him to do.

Jesus, but he wanted Mateo around. That's the part that didn't compute.

Because he knew that whatever Mateo had done, he'd had a reason. It wasn't the right way to look at things. He fought to put people behind bars. To follow the law and to try and save people from dealing with the things his mother had. And yet, he would excuse Mateo's transgressions.

At least until he knew what they were.

For Josiah.

On reflex Tristan clicked the small lamp on his desk, picked up the phone in his office and dialed. Ben answered on the third ring. "What's wrong?"

The hollow feeling in his gut deepened that his friend knew something had to be wrong for Tristan to be calling him. It couldn't even be chalked up to the fact that it was the middle of the night. Ben would wonder regardless.

Still, Tristan found himself replying with, "Nothing."

"I've known you for over fifteen years, Tris, and can count the number of times you've actually called me, most of those being in college or law school when you needed a fuck. Don't lie to me. What's wrong?"

Damn, this was stupid. What had he been thinking calling Ben? It wasn't as though he could ask him to look into Mateo. The last thing he wanted was to let Ben or anyone else know that Mateo was in their lives at all. And it wasn't as though he didn't have the resources to look into Mateo himself.

"Are things okay with you and your boy?" Ben asked.

Tristan repositioned himself in the seat, as though that would make him feel less under the microscope. "He's not a boy, Ben."

"I see you still don't deny that he's yours, though."

He was Tristan's. Not just because Tristan wanted him to be, but because Josiah loved him. But he was also Mateo's. Probably always would be. He dropped his head back and let out a deep breath. "Things are so fucked up. I don't even know where to start."

Minutes of silence stretched between them, prompting Tristan to ask, "Are you still there?"

"Yes. I'm here. I just didn't expect you to actually admit you're not okay. You know my door's always open, Tristan. If you need to get away, you can always come here."

Those words softened some of the walls around his heart. Ben really was the only true friend he'd ever had. "I won't set foot into New York ever again. You know that. Plus, I don't need to go anywhere."

"Do you need me to come there? I'll get on a plane tonight."

There went another piece of the wall, this one caving in. Instead of replying to that, Tristan said, "Thank you. I know… Shit, I know I haven't been an easy person to be friends with—"

"An easy person to love," Ben interrupted.

He kept his fingers on his wrist but didn't count, just needing to know his heart was still going. "That, too. Thank you, and I'm sorry."

There was noise on the other end of the phone as though Ben was getting dressed. "You're scaring the hell out of me. You need to tell me something right now or you'll be telling me face-to-face in the morning."

There wasn't a second that Tristan doubted that. Still, what could he say? The man who risked his life for Josiah, the man Josiah had always loved, was back? That Tristan had actually talked to the man, and for some reason didn't want him out of their lives just yet? Even worse, that he'd let Josiah go to him, and then invited him into bed with them? It sounded like even more of a clusterfuck when he spelled it out like that.

But he also couldn't risk Ben coming here. "I shouldn't have called."

"But you did, and if you didn't want to, you wouldn't have."

Ben was right about that, as much as Tristan hated to admit it. So he gave Ben the only part of this whole situation that he could. "I just need to talk. Josiah's old lover is back. I didn't expect it, and I don't know how to deal with it."

"He still loves him?" Ben asked, his voice a little tighter than it had been before.

"He will always love him." There was a part of him that hated those words. That wanted them out of his vocabulary. That wanted them to be a lie. And another part…another crazy, fucked up, confusing part of him that felt okay with them. Josiah wouldn't be who he was without Mateo, and damned if Tristan could forget about him, either.

"That doesn't mean he doesn't love you. The lucky bastard worships the ground you walk on, Tristan. I can't believe I even have to say this to you, but you have nothing to worry about."

Tristan looked around the room, feeling eyes on him even though he knew there were none. Nothing to look at him, or inside him, the way he felt like they were. "I need to go."

Ben gave a humorless laugh. "Of course you do. Call me if you need anything, okay? I swear I will kick your ass if you don't. You owe me this much. You at least owe me a goddamned two-way friendship."

This time, he leaned forward, resting his elbows on the desk and his head in his hands. "I know." That was all he could give tonight. Josiah had already taken a part of him this evening. Mateo, too. And now Ben.

As if he knew, Ben hung up without another word. Despite the grit in his eyes, Tristan knew he would never be able to sleep tonight. Hours later, he still sat in his half-dark office when the door slowly pushed open. Josiah walked in with a blanket wrapped around him.

"Are you okay?" Josiah asked quietly as he stood next to the chair on the other side of the desk.

Some of the weight pulling Tristan under seemed to fall away. "As good as I ever am."

"You're not angry? Do you regret it?" His shadowed form shifted its weight from one foot to the other.

"No. That's not the first time I've done something like that, Josiah."

His lover didn't flinch, but said, "Yes it is. It might not have been the first time you were with two men, but I know it wasn't the same. You never fully come out and admit it, but I know you feel something for me that you've never let yourself feel. That makes it different."

Tristan sighed, almost cracked a smile. He loved that despite how quiet or shy Josiah was, there were so many things he didn't hold back.

He raised a brow at Josiah. "You decided to wake up before dawn just to bust my balls?"

"Tristan."

He wanted Josiah to continue but he didn't. Waited for him to come closer, but he didn't do that, either. Finally, Tristan spoke again. "You're right. It is different, but no, I still don't regret it. I'm not going to lie and say there aren't parts of me that aren't jealous. That hates knowing you were with him or that you want to be, but... Jesus, there's something about the way you look at him, Josiah. The way he looks at you. And even though it should piss me off, it doesn't, because you look at me the same way. It's like nothing I've ever experienced. I've seen people claim to love and care for someone, but it's nothing like what you show when you look at us. It turns me on, seeing you take your pleasure from him. From both of us."

Damned if it didn't show him things he always thought were a fantasy. People so in tune with each other, like they were a part of one another. In a lot of ways, love, or what she perceived as love, had been what caused everything to go wrong for his mom, yet he knew what she'd had wasn't in the same universe as Josiah's love.

"That's all there is to it?" Josiah came closer, but still the desk separated them.

Without Josiah continuing, Tristan knew what he meant. "I respect Mateo. Maybe I shouldn't. Maybe most people wouldn't, but I do. He protected someone he loved. He protected *you*. He's loyal." He fought himself to stop right there. Not to keep going because he was already raw, like someone had torn open his skin and left the wounds gaping. He made himself keep going for Josiah. "He's been through a lot, but he doesn't close himself off like I do. I envy him that."

"He told you things about himself?"

"Yes. We walked while you were gone. I..."

"You're a lot alike. You might not know it, and Teo might not, either, but you are. Both quietly noble, though neither of you will admit it."

That made Tristan shake his head. "No, I'm not, but thank you." What the hell was noble about letting his mom get hurt or being a rich man's whore?

"I kissed him, Josiah. Right up against the wall of my office, while you were sleeping."

Tristan held his breath while Josiah stood still and considered this.

"Damn. I missed it."

A surprised laugh fell from Tristan's mouth. He hadn't seen that coming.

"You're attracted to him."

"I think that's pretty obvious after how we spent our evening, don't you?" He shook his head. How did they get into this situation?

Tristan looked up at Josiah. More light bled into the room now. His knowing eyes zeroed in on Tristan, flaring with liquid heat. But there was more in them, too. Things Tristan was too tired to try and figure out right now. All he knew was, he needed Josiah. Needed to show him something he couldn't find the words to say.

"Are you naked under the blanket, Josiah? Drop it and let me see." His balls already thrummed with heat. His cock, already painfully hard, got even more so when Josiah tossed the blanket onto the chair.

His erection stood tall, hard, and so goddamned beautiful he needed to taste it. "Come here."

Without needing further prompting, Josiah walked over, stopping next to him. "His taste is still on my tongue, Josiah. I want yours there with his."

Damned if Josiah didn't smile before bending over and taking Tristan's mouth. Their mouths molded together, tongues tasting each other. It wasn't enough.

Tristan pulled back, ordering Josiah to sit on the desk in front of him. His veined shaft, right in front of Tristan's face. He took it into his mouth, loving the feel of the velvet-covered steel against his tongue. Josiah's hand went into his hair, little moans escaping his lips as Tristan's mouth moved up and down his length. And when Josiah came, Tristan swallowed down his seed before resting his forehead against Josiah's thigh.

Josiah's hand was in his hair again when he said, "I won't give you up, Tristan."

Hearing that calmed some of the storm inside him. "I know. And you're mine. I won't give you up, either."

Despite it all, he knew Josiah couldn't give up Mateo, either.

As they sat there, Tristan weaved his arms around Josiah's waist and wondered what they were going to do…or why he wasn't more upset that Josiah couldn't lose Mateo, either.

Chapter Twelve

Josiah

That morning, Josiah walked alone. Tristan had made an excuse as to why he couldn't go. Briefly he wondered if Mateo would show up but knew he wouldn't. He wondered if they both understood that he needed the time alone.

Despite being summer, the morning had a chill to the air that Josiah loved. The wind blew across the water, making him tremble as he took the path that he knew so well.

Thoughts of Mateo and Tristan filled his head, thick as the fog over the water. He struggled to settle on one thought—that Mateo was back, what they'd done, that Tristan and Teo had shared a kiss. The fact that they walked this very sidewalk together while Josiah kept himself locked in his hotel room.

Running.

Hiding.

He was good at that. After all these years, he still did it, still hid away waiting for someone else to protect him. How many times had he vowed not to do that only to fall into the same damn habit again?

Josiah stopped, slipped his hand in the bag and tossed some food for the birds. A flock of them descended on it, fighting and pushing their way through to get as much as they could. It was an instinct, automatic, the only way to survive. They took what they needed, and damned if he didn't want to do that, too.

Tristan and Mateo were worth fighting for. Worth fighting to *have*. If there was ever something in his life he'd scratch and claw to have, it was them. It didn't matter how unconventional it was. They were both a part of him, both always had been, and damned if he would let himself lose that. He knew he should probably be jealous that Mateo and Tristan had a quick bond he didn't completely understand, that they shared a kiss he wasn't a part of, but he wasn't. Because as much as Tristan said he thought Josiah and Mateo were beautiful together, he knew Tristan and Mateo would be, too. Knew whatever happened in that office didn't change how they felt about him.

With that in mind, Josiah emptied the bag and turned to head back toward Fisherman's Roast. He had no idea how he would pull this off, but he knew he needed to. For him, and for them, because he knew they needed him. Maybe they even needed each other, too.

Work was busy for most of the morning. The bell over the door jingled a few minutes before lunch. Josiah looked up to see Elliot step inside.

"Hey, man. Thought I would stop by on my lunch break today. How's it going?" Elliot stepped up beside him.

"Can you hang out a few minutes to talk?" He didn't realize he needed a friend until Elliot came in.

Elliot frowned a little as though he realized something was going on but nodded and said, "Sure. I'll wait outside for you."

Josiah told the employees he was heading to lunch, clocked out, and then met Elliot outside. Josiah smirked at him, tugging on his button-up shirt. "You look like Tristan. Feel good not to walk around smelling like coffee every day?"

Elliot laughed. "Are you kidding? It's still coming out of my pores."

They walked over to one of the benches by the water and sat down. Elliot waited quietly like the psychologists he saw in movies, letting Josiah lead the way. "Remember the guy I told you about? The one from when I was younger?" Elliot didn't know everything, or even close to everything, about Teo, but he knew some.

"Yes."

"He's back…"

Elliot didn't miss a beat. "He's been gone an awfully long time."

"Some of that was spent in prison. But he came for me. He came back earlier, but I didn't know it."

His friend sighed, his voice soft when he spoke, making Josiah realize how good he was at this. Elliott had found his calling. "I'm not sure if knowing he spent time in prison makes me feel any better about this. Does Tristan know?"

"Of course he does. I'm not going to lie to him. I need you to turn off shrink mode if we're going to do this. I need a friend right now. I love them both. I can't choose between them." Josiah met Elliot's wide eyes, seeing his friend realized what he meant. Maybe not completely, but in a way.

"Holy shit, I have never met anyone like you, Josiah. It took you forever to even talk to me. You keep to yourself, and are probably one of the nicest people I've ever met. Wouldn't hurt a fly. But I know there's more to your past, too, and now you're telling me…what? You want a relationship with your lawyer boyfriend *and* your ex from when you were a teenager, who just got out of prison?" He had no anger or disgust in his voice. Only shock and then slight laughter. "You've never done anything easily in your life, have you?"

No, he hadn't, and that hadn't always been his choice. "You don't understand. You don't know what Teo and I have been through together." Visions of red flooded his mind as he flashed back to Teo slitting the man's throat. "You don't know what he's done for me. He's not perfect, but he's a good man, and he loves me."

"If you love him, I'm sure he is. I don't doubt that, but I know Tristan, and I see how you guys are together. He loves you, too."

Guilt gnawed its way through but Josiah tried to ignore it. "I love Tristan. They've spent some time together, you know—Tristan and Teo. Even when I wasn't there. I think…" He let his words trail off, knowing there was no way Elliot could possibly understand. *He* didn't really understand it, but there had been something in the way Mateo and Tristan looked at each other. They were all so screwed up in so many ways; maybe this was another of them.

"Never mind. I can't do this."

"Hey." Elliot put a hand on Josiah's leg. "I'm your friend, man. Have been for a long time. You need to talk, and I'm here… And them, too, official capacity or not, with no judgment."

"Thanks. I—" Something caught Josiah's eye and he looked over Elliot's head. "Teo. Hey." He pushed to his feet. Mateo nodded at him, his eyes shifting to Elliot.

Maybe this shouldn't be his response, but he couldn't stop himself from grinning at the jealousy in Teo's dark eyes. "This is my friend, Elliot. Elliot, this is Mateo."

Elliot stood, the smile on his face sliding off when he saw Mateo. Recovering quickly, he held out his hand. "Hey, man. Nice to meet you."

Mateo's first finger and thumb rubbed over the earring in his ear, a slightly nervous gesture, before he shook Elliot's hand. "What's up?"

"I better get back to work," Elliot smiled at Mateo and dropped his hand before returning his attention to Josiah. "Remember what I said? No matter what, buddy." He clasped a hand down on Josiah's shoulder before walking away.

"He looked at me like he thought I would murder you in your sleep." The right side of Mateo's jaw ticked.

"He's just worried about me. He was the first friend I had here."

Sadness hardened Mateo's features even more.

"I didn't mean—"

"I get it. I sent you away. He's your friend. Hiding it won't change shit."

"It's over, Teo. I don't want to dwell on that."

Instead of replying, Mateo nodded his head toward the sidewalk. "Walk with me, Jay. I was supposed to do this with you. Wanna walk with you out here at least once."

"I only have about twenty-five minutes left of my lunch break."

For the first time today, Teo smiled at him. "I know. I went to your coffee house. Don't worry. I'll make sure you get back."

A thrill of pleasure swept through him at Mateo's promise. "I know you will."

They fell into step with each other, walking a few minutes before Mateo spoke. "Things are okay with Tristan? I didn't fuck shit up for you?"

"No." A flash of their night together hit him. Mateo on his knees in front of Josiah, Tristan's hand in his hair. "Everything's okay."

"Good. He said so but I wanted to make sure."

Warmth spread through Josiah's chest. "Of course you do. You've always done that. You always make sure things are okay for me, even if they're not for you." The knowledge that had always been there, buried so deep in Josiah, pushed toward the surface. Teo would always try and put Josiah first, even if it was wrong.

"That's why you sent me away. I was too young and scared to see it at first, then I was too angry, but I see it now."

"Don't do that. Don't try and make a hero out of me. You always tried to do that shit, Jay, and you don't know. You don't know all the things I've done."

Josiah grabbed Mateo's arm to stop him from walking away. "I know you. That's what matters. I'm not stupid. I'm not trying to turn you into something you're not, but you always tried to be a hero for me. You might not have seen it, Teo, but you did."

The tension in his arm disappeared but Josiah didn't loosen his grasp. Mateo lifted his other hand toward Josiah's face, toward his hair, but right before he made contact he dropped his arm. "*Dios,* I don't even have the right to touch you. This is so fucked up."

The tension was there again, and Mateo tried to pull free, but Josiah wouldn't let him. "I'm not letting you go. Not again. After last night… What if we can—"

"Last night doesn't mean I'm any better for you." He ran his free hand through his hair. "I've been in a gang or in prison every day of my life since losing you. That's not just going to go away, *mi precioso.* Do you get that? You don't need my shit. And I know I'm flipping back and forth with what I say to you, but… Seein' you with him…I get it. He's good for you, and you deserve that." He closed his eyes, his hand going to his stomach.

Josiah stepped closer. Grabbed hold of his waist. "I don't know what I'm doing. I'm not good at this stuff. All I have are words, and the truth is, I've never cared what you did because I know you. The real you. I know that you're fighting the urge to vomit right now. I know you hate everything bad you've ever done. That you wanted a different life with me. But we didn't get that. And maybe we weren't supposed to, because now there's Tristan.

"You try and purge the bad out of you, but he tries to drown it out. He holds his fingers to his pulse, trying to get lost until he can make things disappear. There are things in Tristan's past I may never know, just like there are with you. None of us are perfect, but we *all* deserve to be happy. Not just me."

Mateo rolled his eyes and let out a deep breath. Josiah thought he would pull away, but instead he dropped his forehead to Josiah's. "There's no way that can happen. It's just gonna be two outta three. You got a good life with him, baby. Take it."

"I want you there, too."

This time Mateo did try to pull away. "What the fuck would we do, Jay? One night in the big house with Tristan, and then you come stay in my shit-hole with me?"

Even though Mateo was in his arms, Josiah could feel him drifting away. Panic seized him as he fought the only way he knew how. "It worked last night. And I know you and Tristan kissed in his office this morning."

With that, Mateo jerked out of his grip, and Josiah waited for him to walk away for good this time.

Chapter Thirteen

Mateo

All these years and Josiah was still just as damned innocent as he'd been when they first met. And it hit Mateo in the chest, just like it always did.

Reaching out, Mateo cupped Josiah's cheek. "I've always loved that about you. Even after all the shit you've seen, you're still so damn pure."

Josiah pulled his head back but Mateo continued talking. "We both made love to you last night, Jay. He's an attractive man. Of course there's gonna be the urge to have him, too, but that's all it is. Attraction. Whatever thoughts you have going in your head right now, it's not going to happen." What he said was grounded in reality, but still tasted bitter on his tongue.

"You said I haven't changed, but you haven't, either. You tried to stay away from me because you didn't think you were good enough. But even when I couldn't admit it to myself, I saw how you looked at me. It might not be completely the same, but there are traces of it when you look at Tristan, too. I know that sounds crazy, but I also know it's there. I told Tristan I couldn't walk away from either of you, and now I'm telling you, too. If you can't handle it, it's going to have to be you who goes. As long as you're here, I'm fighting."

Mateo closed his eyes, concentrating on the feel of Josiah's lips as he pressed his mouth to Mateo's. Fuck, did he want Josiah to win this. Wanted what Josiah said to be possible. But what was he suggesting? They share him? That the three of them be together?

When Josiah tried to pull away, Mateo threaded his fingers through the back of his hair, holding Jay against him as he deepened the kiss. He couldn't touch Josiah without wanting all of him. They hadn't had nearly enough time to enjoy each other before.

Still, he pulled away. "Let's go. I said you'd be back to work on time, and you will be."

His body went cold when Josiah put a hand against his stomach to stop him. "You can stay. I can get myself back to work okay. But I meant what I said. I walked away last time without a fight, but I'm not doing it now."

Mateo watched until Josiah was nothing but a figure in the distance. He pulled out his camera and took a picture before he disappeared. It wasn't until he was gone that Mateo muttered a soft, "Thank you." He shouldn't, but he wanted nothing more than for Josiah to not be able to give up on him. And damned if watching that strength come out in him wasn't sexy as hell.

Every day he swore he would stay away, but still, at Josiah's lunch time, he always showed up by the water. They walked and talked, like he knew Josiah did with Tristan in the mornings. Jealously crept its way in but Mateo fought to hold it back. Yeah, that was supposed to be his and Josiah's time. They talked about it years before, but he threw that away when he fucked up with him. Now, it belonged to Jay and Tristan.

But this? Their hour together he damn sure took, even when he said he wouldn't.

"What are you doing tonight? I was thinking you could come over and have dinner with us or something?" Josiah asked on the fourth day.

Mateo shook his head. "Jay, you can't ask me to dinner to the house you share with your man."

"I'm pretty sure I just did."

Pride and irritation wrestled inside him. "What the fuck is up with you? You're pushier than you used to be."

"I might be not be as outspoken as some, but I go after something when I want it." He nudged Mateo's arm. "I kissed you first. I asked you to make love to me the first time, too. I went after Tristan as well."

Mateo groaned. "Do we have to talk about him?"

At that, Josiah stopped walking. "Does it bother you? I mean, really bother you, Teo?"

Mateo let himself remember the few walks he'd taken with Tristan. The similarities he'd seen in the man and himself that he never would have expected. Remembered the feel of his body as Tristan's lips had come down on his. The way he looked with Jay and the way he was there for him. Crazy as it was, no, it didn't bother him to talk about Tristan. He wasn't sure what that said about him. Maybe that he was even more fucked up than he thought.

"No. He's good for you." Good in a way Mateo himself had never been.

But that doesn't explain why I want him, too…

"Teo—"

"I gotta go."

Josiah opened his mouth to speak but Mateo cut him off. "I'm not giving you shit, okay? I really gotta go. I got a job and I don't want to be late."

Don't ask me what that means… Don't ask me why I'm putting down roots here when I need to get the hell out.

He could blame it on being on probation, having to be settled somewhere, but in reality, that had nothing to do with it.

Josiah smiled. *Dios,* that sweet, innocent smile still made him rock hard. Made his heart go crazy, when no one had ever been able to do that before.

"And I have to meet with my probation officer before I go, too."

The smile slid off Josiah's face, just like Mateo knew it would. "Does this make me an asshole? I don't want you to hurt, but I don't want Tristan to hurt, either. I just…don't we all deserve some kind of happiness? What if we can find it together?"

The pain in Josiah's voice ripped Mateo to shreds. "Come here." As much as he wanted to kiss him, Mateo just wrapped his arms around him. "You could never be an asshole. Not for tryin' to make people happy." With that, he pulled away. "See you tomorrow, yeah?" He threaded his fingers through Josiah's hair, faked a smile, and then left.

Mateo took the bus to his hotel before showering and getting ready. He really would be pushing it to make his appointment and get to work on time. Luckily for him, his PO didn't seem to give a shit about much of anything besides ushering them in and out so he was doing his job. In the grand scheme of things, Teo's drug charge wasn't shit compared to the things other people did. Wasn't shit compared to the other things *he'd* done.

He put on his work uniform of black slacks and a white shirt—which was pretty fucked up if you asked him. Why in the hell did a dishwasher need to wear a white shirt?

Anyway, once he was dressed, Mateo hopped on another bus to make it to his PO. When he got there, he went through the routine, pissing in a cup while some chick watched him, before meeting with his PO. He answered the same bullshit questions as he did every week before he left and walked to work.

Work was work. He got food and dirty water all over his clothes as he washed dishes for people whose meal cost more than he could ever afford. But considering he was twenty-eight years old and this was the first real job he'd had, it wasn't like he could shoot much higher.

By the time he got off, he was in a shitty mood that didn't get much better when he walked up to his hotel room to see Tristan waiting outside the door. He hated the fact that the first thing he noticed was the way Tristan's suit stretched across his firm body. That he knew what was underneath the suit, and liked it. That the man was everything Mateo wasn't, everything Mateo never thought he'd want, yet he couldn't stop his eyes from taking him in. From seeing the dark look on his face from over Josiah's shoulder when he'd been taking him.

"What do you want?" He turned from Tristan and unlocked the door to his room.

"For my car to still be outside when I come back out?"

He fumbled his key, not expecting the joke or the smirk on his own face. "Sorry about that, pretty boy. I'm only stayin' here till they finish building my house on your side of town."

Tristan followed him inside. "I wasn't thinking—"

"No. Don't do that bullshit. It's true. You're not the type to apologize for something like that."

Tristan quirked a brow at him. "You think you know all about the kind of man I am?"

Mateo let his eyes roam Tristan again. "I know enough. I smell like dishwater. What do you want?"

"You're jerking him around. I know you don't mean to but you are. I fucked him while he laid on top of you, and you can't bring yourself to come to dinner?"

Damn, he respected Tristan. Respected that he just came out and said what was on his mind without sugar-coating. Not many people did that. "You can't tell me you want me there. Blame it on me. Jay's used to me fucking up." As soon as the words were out of his mouth, he wished he could take them back. Still, he didn't.

Tristan stepped closer to him. "Do I strike you as the kind of man who does something if he doesn't want to?"

Those words hung in the air between them, heavy and suffocating because they were true for Mateo, too. *Dios,* did he want to be there with them. To somehow belong with Josiah. And in a way, with Tristan, too.

"But I'm also not the kind of man who wants someone there who doesn't want to be. It's dinner. Nothing more. I'll pull my car around front and wait fifteen minutes. If you're not out there, I'll assume you don't want to be. That you're done with Josiah."

If anyone else would've talked to him like that, he'd have knocked them out—or worse. But even though his hands clenched, even though his whole body was strung so tight he thought it would shatter, electricity thrummed through him, too. Because that? Having someone else take control like that, not in the way his dad or Javier had had control over him, but in a way that was commanding, yet gave him a choice, too, made his pulse go erratic. Made blood rush through him, quick and hot.

It released some of the pressure inside him to always know what to do.

Before Tristan got the door fully closed, Mateo was already on his way to the shower. Fourteen minutes later, he slipped silently into the passenger seat of Tristan's car.

Chapter Fourteen

Tristan

Tristan tried not to let himself think about what he was doing. That in itself was a rarity, but he didn't know what else to do.

He and Mateo were quiet the whole way to his house. It wasn't until he killed the engine and made the move to get out of the car that Mateo's hand came down on his wrist.

"Are you sure this isn't fucking stupid? That I'm not going to hurt him?" Mateo asked, kicking Tristan's respect for the man up another notch. He never stopped worrying about Josiah. Had anyone in Tristan's life ever cared about him that much? The answer to that was easy: Josiah did. The same way he did with Mateo, too.

"I'm one hundred percent sure what we're doing is stupid, but I'm not sure if it's right or wrong. As far as hurting him goes…we run the risk either way, don't we?"

From the corner of his eye, he saw Mateo turn to look at him in the dark car. Seconds later, he couldn't stop his eyes from falling on Mateo, too.

"What's your story, man? Who are you? On the surface, you have your shit together more than anyone I've seen. One of those guys I'd think had never been through anything. But that's not what's really there. Under the surface, you're just as fucked up as I am, aren't you?"

In that sentence, Mateo nailed down everything about him and made his heart race. He was just as Mateo said, but he wanted everyone to see that put-together man he tried to portray. "You know the answer to that question, so why ask? As for my story, you also know I won't tell it, so we're just wasting our time here."

Mateo's hand slipped off his wrist, and Tristan got out of the car. As soon as they stepped inside, the scent of Italian food bombarded his senses.

"It's almost ready!" Josiah called out from the kitchen. Tristan set his briefcase by the door and headed that way. He didn't fully get through the kitchen doorway before Josiah stood in front of him.

Tristan tilted Josiah's head up with a finger under his chin and pressed a kiss to his lips. "It smells fantastic."

"Thanks." Josiah kissed him again before pulling away. "I'm starved. It was a busy day at the coffee house, and then I had an appointment with the realtor after. She—"

His speech dropped off when Mateo stepped around Tristan. "Teo. Hey. I thought you weren't coming."

Mateo shrugged his shoulders, a gesture that contrasted the tense set of them. "Eh. Figured I couldn't pass up a home-cooked meal."

That had nothing to do with the reason Mateo was there, but Tristan didn't call him on it. Josiah turned to Tristan, his eyes saying so much. *Thank you... I'm sorry...*

But he had nothing to be sorry about. Tristan hadn't been lying when he said he didn't do things he didn't want to. If there was a part of him that didn't want Mateo here, he wouldn't be.

The buzzer on the stove went off, breaking through the silence in the room. Without a word, Josiah went to the stove, pulling a rectangular baking dish out of the oven. Tristan went straight for his wine. He withdrew a bottle then glanced over his shoulder at Mateo. Josiah would have one glass with him. He always did. Tristan held up the bottle. "Would you like some?"

Mateo's forehead wrinkled. "Do I really look like a wine kind of guy to you? Hell, I'd rather sell that bottle. It's probably worth a few days' pay. Got a beer?"

The room was silent for a moment as they both stared at Mateo. Josiah laughed first. Then Mateo. Tristan couldn't help the chuckle that fell from his mouth, too. When the laughter died down, he felt like he could breathe again. As though the tension that had filled the room all leaked out.

"Everyone can be a wine kind of guy, Mateo. Come here."

Mateo shook his head as though he thought Tristan was crazy, yet he still walked over to him. He slipped the bottle from his hand and back into the cooler, pausing before pulling out one of his favorite whites.

Tristan popped the cork, plucked a glass from the top of the cooler, and poured a little in. When Mateo tried to grab it from his hand, Tristan pulled back. "Don't be in such a hurry. Wine is something to be savored. Let yourself really taste it."

"You're crazy." Mateo shook his head.

"Trust me."

They both froze at that. Trust. The word wasn't something Tristan truly believed in. Or he hadn't. But then…he'd grown to trust Josiah, hadn't he? And Josiah had never done anything to betray that trust.

And damned if there wasn't a part of him that trusted Mateo, too.

As the pause drew out between them, his chest grew tight, because he realized this turned into something more than trusting him with the wine.

Slowly, his rough, beat-up hand reached for the glass. This time, Tristan let him take it. Mateo paused before he raised the glass to his mouth. Paused before taking a drink and lowering it, taking his time, just as Tristan had said.

And then he frowned. "How about that beer now?" Mateo asked. Damned if the three of them didn't start laughing again.

Tristan had never really been much of a laugher, but somehow when Mateo came to dinner the next night, they found something else to laugh over, too. And then the next, and the next. That didn't mean things weren't awkward, because they were. It didn't mean there weren't times the looks Mateo and Josiah shared with each other didn't rip Tristan up inside… But there were also those times when he felt Mateo's eyes linger on him. When Josiah would innocently touch him, and it took all the strength he had in himself not to fuck them both right then and there.

Sexual attraction was a potent feeling. When he added in his love for Josiah, and his…Craving? Respect? Need? for Mateo, he wondered how they'd made it this long without falling into bed together again.

A couple weeks went by, and every night that Mateo wasn't at work he had dinner with them. Each night Josiah asked him to stay. Offered the spare room. But Mateo always said no. And Tristan always found himself sad at the thought of Mateo going back to that small hotel room alone. The house felt quieter, calmer without him, and it suddenly felt a little lonelier, too. It was on one of those nights, as he and Josiah sat at the table, that his lover asked, "You like having him here, don't you?"

Yes, danced on his tongue, yet still Tristan struggled pushing admissions like that from his mouth. Instead of replying, he grabbed Josiah's chair and pulled it closer, until their legs touched. "It's been entirely too long since I've kissed you."

Josiah let Tristan take his lips. Let Tristan's tongue take over his mouth. Josiah released a deep-throated moan like he so often did when Tristan kissed him.

Tristan's cock hardened, but part of him wanted to just keep kissing, too. He loved the feel of Josiah's lips against his. Loved the tentative strength in which his mouth moved against Tristan's.

It was Josiah who pulled away first. "It's okay," he said. Before Tristan could ask him what he meant, he continued. "It's okay to tell me how you feel, Tristan. After all this time, I know you love me. I know you want me. I wish you could say it. Eventually I'll need to hear it, but right now, I know that you can't."

Guilt and self-hatred swallowed him whole. How fucking hard was it to say how he felt? Tristan was a smart man. He knew admitting something didn't make it more real than feeling it, yet knowing something didn't always change the emotions behind it.

It was Josiah who broke the silence. "And I also know that you like having him here. And that doesn't change how much I know you want me, just like my loving him doesn't change how I feel about you. That makes it doubly hard for you, doesn't it? You wanting both of us?"

Tristan's mouth clamped closed. He definitely wasn't in the mood to do this. Not that he ever was, but Josiah voicing his thoughts felt like him taking the reins, taking control over Tristan's world.

They also created a truth he couldn't sweep under the rug. Yes, he loved Josiah, and yes he wanted Mateo. He really did like having Mateo here, and Josiah knew it. And after all these years, he still needed Josiah to feel for him. To open up to things that Tristan could never do himself.

His phone rang, and more guilt churned in his gut because it meant he didn't have to respond to what Josiah had said.

Josiah leaned away as Tristan pulled his cell from his pocket, his heart stopping when his mom's number showed on the screen. "Is everything okay?" he asked.

"Of course it is, Tristan. Isabel isn't feeling well, though. I want to get her some of that soup she likes from Durango's, but…"

But she couldn't, because she didn't leave the house. Because years before, she'd decided she loved Oliver so much she had to see him again despite everything he'd done to her. He'd given her drugs that night, like he always did. Used her and sent her away, where she'd been attacked afterward.

"I'll get it. I'll be there within an hour."

"Tristan…I'm sorry," she whispered. "I know I'm a burden on you."

"No." He shook his head. He failed her, not the other way around. "You're not. I'll be right there." He ended the call. When he did, he noticed Josiah stood at the sink. He hadn't even noticed the other man walk away.

Tristan went to him, wrapping his arms around him from behind. "I'm sorry."

"I know." He didn't say it was okay, and Tristan knew it wasn't. "I want to meet her, Tristan. I deserve to meet her sometime."

Tristan nodded against Josiah's neck. "You will. I…I promise." He needed to do that for Josiah. For his mom. And maybe for himself, too.

It didn't take long for Tristan to get to Durango's. He ordered two bowls of the soup, to-go. He'd been there enough that even though he was probably one of the only people who came for to-go orders, they did it with a smile.

As he walked out the door, soup in hand, his phone rang again. Even without answering, he knew who it would be.

"Hello?"

"Isabel fell asleep. I'm tired all of a sudden, Tristan. So tired… You don't have to come tonight. We'll be okay until morning."

He pushed an annoyed breath out, trying not to take it out on her. "I'm already out. I might as well bring it over."

"I'm sorry. I'm always doing this to you. It's not right. Why don't you just bring it home for you and Josiah? Or you can bring it here if you want. I was just trying to save you the time…" Her voice got softer as she spoke, Tristan's protective urges going into overdrive.

"It's okay. I was actually supposed to grab something for Josiah, so this will save me another stop. He loves their soup."

"Good. I'm glad. When do I get to meet him, Tristan?"

He closed his eyes. "Soon. He asked the same thing tonight. We'll plan it, okay?"

"Okay. I need to go. I took my sleeping pill and I'm so tired. Goodnight, sweet boy."

His muscles seized up, hating that she had to take pills to sleep at night. Knowing he probably should, too. "Good night."

Tristan weaved his way through the people on the sidewalk as he shoved the phone into his pocket. As he rounded a corner, his feet rooted to the ground when he saw Mateo standing partway down the street. He watched as the man spoke with a woman and a little girl in torn clothes. She looked like so many people he passed on the San Francisco streets every day—homeless.

That had been him and his mom at different points in his life.

And if Mateo hadn't done some of the things he did to take care of Josiah all those years go, that could have been them, too.

For a good five minutes, he watched as Mateo talked to them. Watched as the man pulled something from his pocket, money he'd guess, and stuffed it into her hand. Saw his body stiffen as the woman hugged him…but then he hugged her back.

This from the man who spent time in prison. Who could get caught for things that could put him there again. Who lived in a run-down hotel and didn't have much. It reminded him of something Josiah would do. The kind of thing he'd never done.

When Mateo turned to walk away from the woman, his eyes locked on Tristan. He didn't let himself think. Didn't let himself worry. If Mateo could open up, and Josiah could, he had to find a way to be able to do it, too.

Tristan's steps were quick. When he reached Mateo, the other man didn't turn away. His stare was hard, defensive. Tristan handed the soup to the woman, who scurried away with her child.

Mateo didn't move when Tristan tried to back him against the building. He looked down, reached out, pulled his hand back, but then just went for it and grabbed ahold of Mateo's belt loop. "Don't ask me what it means. Don't ask me what will happen, or how long it will work. Just come home with me. Josiah wants you there... We want you there."

For an eternity, as people weaved around them on the sidewalk, Mateo didn't answer. Finally he grabbed Tristan's hand, untwisting his finger from his belt loop. "Fuck. Fuck if I don't want to be there, too."

Chapter Fifteen

Josiah

Josiah lay on his side already in bed, even though it was just after dinnertime. Tristan had only been gone about forty-five minutes when he heard him come home.

Josiah didn't move, just continued to lie there, waiting for Tristan to come up to him. Tristan would. He knew that. The man might struggle with words, but he was there for Josiah.

Heavy footsteps sounded on the stairs, and he didn't know why but his heart thudded harder with each one. His eyes didn't leave the door, a deep breath escaping his lungs as Tristan slowly pushed it open. He'd been nervous. Nervous and hadn't even realized it until Tristan's figure filled the doorway. What he didn't understand was why.

And then Tristan stepped aside, another person lingered behind him. This time his breath caught in his throat as he saw Teo standing there.

"What?" Josiah sat up. "How?"

Tristan's eyes didn't leave Josiah as he spoke. "I saw him outside of

Durango's."

"If you don't want me here, I'll go," Mateo said.

Josiah let his gaze drift from Tristan to Mateo when he spoke, but then let them go back to Tristan again. Yes, he wanted Teo there. They all knew that, but they couldn't keep going the way they were, either. Couldn't sleep together and then hardly talk. Or have Teo come for dinner but refuse to stay.

"This is the second time you've brought him home, Tristan. You kissed him in your office while I was sleeping."

At that, Tristan's brows pulled together and he came toward Josiah. "You know—"

"This isn't about jealousy." Josiah stood, his legs feeling weak. "It can't be like last time. It needs to be equal between the three of us, or we don't need to be doing it. I know you want me, both of you, and…and I know you want each other, too. That has to be a part of it or we can't do it."

Tristan stopped in front of him, questions in his eyes. Josiah looked over Tristan's shoulder, finding Mateo. The look on Teo's face said he knew exactly what Josiah needed from them.

His pulse pounded in his ears, but Josiah tried to stamp it down or ignore it. Whatever he had to do to make this happen.

"Come here, Teo. Please." How many times had Teo said those words to him? *Come here.* Every time he knew Josiah needed him, he'd use those words, except it was usually him who still went to Josiah. Or who pulled Josiah to him.

He waited, breath in lungs, counting the beats of his heart the way Tristan did, until Teo took a step toward them, then another. When Teo stopped beside Tristan, Josiah took them both in. The two men were opposites in so many ways, but so similar in others. It was more than just their dark hair and dark eyes. More than the fact that they were both his.

"I want to see you together." He looked at Tristan. "Will you kiss him?" It had to be a question, he knew that. Tristan didn't take commands or direction in the bedroom. Hopefully Tristan could give them all this much.

An electric charge zapped the air around them. The men faced off before taking a step closer to each other. It was Teo who moved first, his steady hands grabbing the sides of Tristan's face the way he'd done with Josiah too many times to count.

Josiah went hot all over, his cock hardened instantly as their mouths met. The kiss started out slow, but then it was a give-and-take battle between them, Teo's gentle hunger matching Tristan's fierce passion. He saw their tongues touch, saw Teo suck Tristan's into his mouth before releasing it. Saw Tristan nip Mateo's lip before grabbing his face the same way Teo held him.

Josiah's body burned in the most incredible way. His heart pounded as he watched the two men ravage each other's mouths. And then as if they planned it, they both reached out for Josiah. He went willingly, caught between the desire to taste them, too and enjoying seeing the two of them together.

When Mateo's lips drifted down to Tristan's neck, Tristan pulled Josiah forward, so their mouths met. The combination of Tristan's tongue in his mouth and the feel of both hard bodies against him made a jolt of pleasure shoot through him, then another, as though there were way too many sensations at once but also not enough.

"I want his mouth," Mateo said huskily, making Josiah's knees week.

It was like Teo somehow knew not to demand.

Tristan pulled away, his mouth going to Mateo's neck the way Mateo had just done with his. As he sucked Mateo's flesh, Teo's mouth crashed down on Josiah's, quick, urgent and needy.

Josiah moaned, kissing deeper when Teo's hand gently pulled at his hair. Visions flashed in his head, the three of them a tangle of limbs, a cluster of lips and mouths. It made his cock ache.

Josiah pulled back slightly, and that was all it took for Mateo and Tristan's mouths to meet again. Hands grasping, grunts and moans, and *ah fucks* filling the room. There was a part of him that wanted to do nothing but take it in. The sight of them pumped blood to his heart. Made it beat life into him. Filled his lungs with breath. And yes, made him feel like he was going to explode.

But he also wanted more, too. Wanted every part of both of them, and he damn sure intended to have them. "I want to taste you, Tristan."

Tristan gave him a nod, so Josiah went down to his knees. His hands went to Tristan's pants first. As they did, he saw Tristan working Teo's. With quick, shaky hands, he shoved Tristan's pants down, pushed his hands out of the way, and did the same thing to Teo. His heart slammed with fast, passionate beats against his chest, nerves and excitement creating a cocktail of feelings inside him.

He took them both in, Tristan longer, Mateo thicker. Tristan lighter,

Mateo darker. Tristan cut, Mateo not.

"Need your mouth on me, Jay. Wanna feel you." Mateo's words sent a thrill through him. He was so different than before, more vocal of a lover than he'd been when they were younger.

"You are so sexy, Josiah. Suck him, and then I want your mouth on me." Tristan's voice was all sex, silky and smooth.

When Josiah looked up, they were kissing again.

Josiah ripped his eyes from the show going on above him, taking Teo's erection into his mouth. With his other hand, he gripped Tristan's length, running his hand up and down it the same way his mouth did with Mateo's. Their scents mixed around him, different murmured curses coming from between their lips before they would no doubt silence each other with their mouths again.

Josiah let his tongue swirl around the head of Mateo's length before reaching over and sucking Tristan deep. His hand busied on Teo as he moved down, laving Tristan's balls the way he liked.

Back and forth, he sucked and licked and jerked off both of his guys. Still, it wasn't enough, so he wrapped his arms around them, pulling them closer so their cocks could touch and he could taste them at the same time.

"Ah, fuck, *mi precioso*. Just like that," Mateo said above him as Tristan's hand went into his hair, guiding his head as he pleasured them both.

"That's enough. It's our turn. Take off your clothes and get on the bed." There was a tension to Tristan's voice that spoke of how close to the edge he was.

With eager hands, Josiah shoved his boxer-briefs off, which was all he wore, and climbed to the bed. Tristan and Mateo ripped at the rest of their own clothes before they stood beautifully bare in front of him.

"I want to taste him now, Mateo. What do you think?" A blissed-out shiver ran the length of Josiah at hearing Mateo's name come from Tristan's tongue.

"Fuck yeah," Mateo replied before they lay on either side of him, their mouths meeting together, Josiah's cock between them.

He convulsed off the bed, the sensation so damn amazing. They didn't give him a reprieve, kissing and laving his erection at the same time, running their tongues up and down his length in unison. Tristan tongued his sac as Mateo sucked him deep.

The orgasm slammed into him so urgently he couldn't hold it back as he shot into Mateo's mouth. "Oh God. Holy shit." He spurted again, reveling in the feel of letting go, but knowing he'd go crazy if this ended.

And then Mateo's mouth was gone. Through hooded eyes he looked down his body, seeing Mateo take Tristan's mouth, knowing Tristan now tasted him on Teo's tongue.

Lust took the place of the feeling of completion he just had, and Josiah knew that if they kept going, he'd be able to get hard again. "Can Mateo suck you, Tristan? I want to see you in his mouth."

He waited for them to say no. Watched as they eyed each other before Tristan gave Mateo a simple nod. Excitement made Josiah's vision go blurry. Tristan hardly made it to his back before Mateo leaned over him, slowly taking as much of Tristan in as he could.

"Watch us, Josiah," Tristan commanded. "Watch him blow me. Do you like it?"

"Yes." He stumbled on the simple word, breathless. Mateo looked up at him and smiled around Tristan's erection before sucking him deep again.

He tried three times before he could find his voice, mesmerized by the erotic scene in front of him. "I love it. It's the sexiest thing I've ever seen."

One of Tristan's hands thread through Josiah's hair, and the other through Mateo's.

"I like seeing you with him, too. It's unnerving how damn much—oh yeah, just like that, Mateo." Tristan guided Teo's head down his prick again.

It was a start, but Josiah still wanted more. "Tell me how much you like feeling him, too, Tristan."

He expected a pause that didn't come. "His mouth is like silk, but then I feel the rasp of his hair or the roughness of his fingers, and damned if it doesn't almost send me over the edge. So goddamned sexy."

"Teo," Josiah prompted, but he didn't have to finish before Mateo responded.

"So fucking good." He tongued the slit on the end of Tristan's dick before sucking him again.

Josiah noticed instantly when Tristan froze up beneath Mateo. "No." He tilted Mateo's head up. Pain darkened his intense eyes, as though he hated what he was about to say. Josiah's heart stopped, fearing Tristan's words, too. "Not there. It's not you, but I don't let anyone inside me."

Mateo's hand slid up, and Josiah realized he must have tried to finger Tristan. The air in the room suddenly became awkward, but then Mateo's tongue went from the base of Tristan's erection to the tip before he said, "That's cool. This is enough."

Josiah couldn't stop himself from letting his mouth take Mateo's, their tongues teasing the head of Tristan's erection. It was part need, part a silent thank you.

"You fuck him this time, Mateo." Tristan eased away.

Josiah fought to find the right words, fear that Tristan was done, clinging to him. But before he spoke, it was Mateo's hand who grabbed ahold of Tristan. "Don't go. Let him finish you off while I take him."

Josiah somehow knew they weren't ready to have sex with each other, but he was glad for at least this. That was, if Tristan went for it.

Another nod from Tristan, and then he was reaching toward the drawer. He grabbed a condom and lube, giving them both to Mateo.

Josiah felt like he was overheating, his body going haywire, all-systems overload, and he'd never wanted anything more.

"Get on your hands and knees, Josiah." He did, and Tristan kneeled on his knees in front of him as Mateo positioned himself behind him. Tristan grabbed hold of Josiah's chin. "Make me come, baby."

"Tristan…" Josiah whispered. It was the first time Tristan had ever called him anything other than his name.

"I know." In typical Tristan fashion, he nodded.

Josiah heard the condom wrapper open behind him. All the muscles in his body relaxed, *finally* running through his head, when he felt

Mateo's lubed finger on his hole. Tristan's hand ran through his hair as Mateo pushed a finger inside, pumping, twisting and turning before adding another.

"Just take me, Teo."

"*Dios,*" whispered past Mateo's lips, and then his fingers were replaced by his cock as he slammed into Josiah from behind.

He grabbed hold of Tristan, trying to suck him off at the same time, but kept fumbling each time Mateo thrust behind him.

"It's okay. Just feel what he's doing and try and match his rhythm. Let him lead your body, Josiah." And then Tristan's eyes left him and landed on Mateo.

Josiah did as he said, letting Mateo lead him. Each time he thrust, Josiah let his body move forward, let his mouth suck Tristan.

They found a rhythm together, the three of them all taking their pleasure from each other.

Josiah was already hard again, his passion being kicked up to *oh God, I'm going to blow* when Mateo wrapped a hand around his erection each time he sank into him, jerking Josiah off.

"I'm so fucking close, *mi precioso.*" There was a pause, and then Mateo added, "You are so sexy fucking his mouth, Tristan. *Dios,* you guys are going to make me lose it."

With that, Josiah did. Semen shot out of him, running down Mateo's hand. Tristan pulled his hair, his salty essence spilling on Josiah's tongue. Mateo's other hand dug into his hips as he groaned, his erection jerking inside Josiah.

Josiah collapsed on the bed while Mateo got rid of the condom.

"Where can I get something to clean him up?" Mateo asked Tristan.

"No," jumped out of Josiah's mouth. "Don't clean up. Just lay with me, both of you."

And they did, Josiah in the middle of them. He laid on his back, his right leg over Tristan, his left arm touching Mateo. A mass of limbs, weary bodies, sex, and at least from where Josiah was concerned, love.

Chapter Sixteen

Mateo

The next day Mateo told them he had to go home, and Josiah asked him to come back. Before the nausea had a chance to grab hold of him, before he had the chance to say no when he really didn't want to, Tristan had offered to give him a ride to get a change of clothes.

And he'd said yes.

It went on like that for days. He told himself he still lived at the hotel. Most of his stuff was there, making it so he had to go back every day, yet when Josiah would ask him if he would be back after work, or from whatever he went to do that day, Mateo always said yes.

He didn't know what was going on but it felt good, and he hadn't had a whole lot in his life that made his chest swell the way Josiah did. And now…Now it was almost as though that feeling had doubled. Not completely, but Tristan made him feel in ways no one besides Josiah ever had, and he damn sure wanted to hold on to that while he could. Things could change in a fucking instant, and he already had enough regrets to last a lifetime. He wouldn't have any more.

They hadn't had sex again, and even though he could tell Josiah wanted to, he didn't argue when Mateo slept in the spare bedroom. He didn't want to take over their space. No matter what they shared, he knew that when it came down to it, Josiah belonged with Tristan now, and he'd be there with or without Mateo.

Made his fucking chest feel like it would crack apart, but that didn't make it any less real.

It was a couple weeks after he started staying with them that he lay in the small, dark room by himself. He'd had a shitty day at work and almost went back to the hotel, but then he'd stepped to the curb to see Tristan and Josiah waiting for him.

Despite all the shit he'd dealt with, getting yelled at by his asshole boss, and a dishwasher problem, his stupid fucking mouth had stretched into a grin when he saw them.

No matter what he'd planned to do, he realized at that moment he would have been miserable if he went to his dingy room alone. No matter what, he wanted to go…home, he guessed. It was more like a real home than he'd ever had. Even when he and Jay lived in New York, things had been so fucked up that he'd never been able to really relax.

He could now.

Reflex made him jump out of bed the second he heard the door to his room slip open. He'd told Josiah a million times to always listen for shit, and it was something he still did today. Half asleep or not, he heard someone step into his room.

But then the scent of coffee hit him, mixed with that expensive cologne Tristan wore, and he knew it was them as they stepped toward him.

He didn't have time to react before Josiah was kissing him, Tristan shoving a hand down his boxer-briefs.

They were nothing but hands and mouths, kissing, sucking, stroking. He felt like he would bust out of his skin. It wasn't enough. He wanted more, more, *more*, and as though they knew it, they gave it to him. He had Tristan's hot mouth on his cock. Josiah's gentle hands spreading his cheeks before his probing tongue played with his hole.

He groaned, cried out, but it still wasn't fucking enough. He didn't have to tell them because they somehow realized that, too.

Tristan pulled him to the edge of the bed. Josiah ripped his underwear down and then whispered, "Can I have you again, Teo? Will you let me inside?"

"Fuck yes," he rasped out, Tristan jerking him off. "Anything you want."

He thrashed under Josiah's touch. Pulled Tristan's hair when Josiah's lubed dick pushed into him. Jerked even harder when Tristan's mouth swallowed him whole.

He lay on his back, Josiah between his legs and Tristan bending over him. Mateo fisted Tristan's prick, pumping his hand.

They fucked fast and furious, all the tension of his day, of his fucking *life*, slowly finding its way out of him, or at least into hiding.

When he came, losing himself down the back of Tristan's throat, Josiah squeezed his hips hard enough to leave marks, plunging into his own orgasm as well. Right behind him, Tristan cursed, his creamy, hot seed spilling all over Mateo's hand.

Dios, this had been just what he'd needed. *They* had been. He opened his mouth to try and find the words to tell them, but Tristan spoke first. "You'll sleep with us from now on, that way we can have each other whenever we want."

He didn't argue. Didn't want to. Just got up and followed them to the other bedroom.

For the three weeks since that night, it's where he stayed. He knew their habits by now. Woke up automatically when Tristan left bed like he did so much, because the man didn't sleep for shit. Memorized the feel of Josiah's body molding against him, as though he was scared Mateo would leave.

Some days, they hardly saw each other. They still tried to walk together every morning, sometimes the three of them and sometimes two of them, but they still always went.

Walking alone today, Mateo raised his camera, watching the shadow of someone in the distance as they looked up at a graffiti mural on a big, brick wall. Two paintings, really. One of them was a fucked-up-looking heart, bruised, beat up and torn, resting an equally fucked-up-looking hand. But the way the hand held it, the way it looked like it wanted to protect the heart no matter how screwed up it was, made it beautiful.

Next to it was another heart…a perfect one, bright, red and untarnished, but alone.

He couldn't make out if the person looking at it was man or woman. Fuck, he wasn't even sure if it was real, just a black shadow, looking at the wall.

He clicked a picture. Then another. The person started walking, and he clicked a few more before they disappeared, and then he took one last picture of just the wall, strangely wondering which kind of heart the person had, and being okay with the broken one that was his.

When he knew Josiah would be home, Mateo headed that way. He always left when both Tristan and Josiah were gone. No matter where he slept at night, the house still wasn't his.

He used the key Tristan gave him to let himself in. He heard Josiah rummaging around in the kitchen, so he went that way. When he stepped inside, he saw him, standing in front of his coffee maker. He turned, grinning at Mateo, making the past slam into him so hard it ripped the breath from him. He forced words out.

"I remember comin' home in New York one day when you got a new coffee machine, and you would have thought it was fucking gold or something."

Josiah leaned against the counter. "To me it was better, just because it was mine. It was *ours*. Something I bought to go in our home. That's all that mattered to me, Teo."

Mateo tried to laugh off what he said despite the fact if he had nothing else, he could live off those words. "You're all heart. You always have been."

"So are you. You just don't want to admit it."

He looked down at his hands, remembering all the things he'd done. How he'd screwed up and everything in between. Just like before, Josiah saw shit in him that wasn't there. Calling him on it wouldn't change things, so he didn't.

Josiah reached for Mateo's hand. He let him take it, let him pull him so Mateo leaned against him, who still rested against the counter. "No matter what we went through, I was happy. It was hard, and I'm not saying that I wasn't ever scared or upset, but overall, I was happy. I'd never known what it was like to really belong until you, Teo."

No, *those* were the words he would live off of. The ones that would keep him going forever.

Mateo closed his eyes, leaned forward, and pressed a kiss to Josiah's neck. "Me too, *mi precioso.* I've only ever belonged with you." As true as those words were, they still sounded wrong to his ears, felt wrong in his chest. Being in this house, being with not just Josiah but Tristan, too…fuck if he didn't feel like he belonged with both of them. If he didn't *want* Tristan to own a part of him…the way he wanted a part of Tristan.

"I see the way you look at him. I see the way he looks at you, too. You guys are both so much alike, who knows if you'll ever admit how much you want each other. Even if…even if I wasn't around, and you guys met, you would have somehow ended up in this house."

Mateo jerked back at that. "What the fuck are you talking 'bout, Jay?"

Josiah held him, not letting him pull away. "How much in our lives has ever really made sense? We somehow ended up at the same home. Molly got sick, right after you turned eighteen, leading us to the city, and then here. Maybe most things, the important things, don't really have to make sense. Maybe they just *are*.

"Feeling something for Tristan, no matter how new it is, doesn't change how you feel about me. I know that because no matter how much I love him, I love you just as much. I know there are things you guys have both been through that I probably won't ever understand, or that maybe you won't ever tell me, but if you can share it with anyone, I want it to be each other. There are things I have with you that I don't have with Tristan, and things I have with him that I don't have with you. It's like, for the first time in my life, I feel like I'm really whole, Teo."

Words got stuck in his throat. Damned if he didn't know everything Josiah just said was true. And… "Me, too. *Fuck,* me too, Jay."

Mateo left no space between them, Josiah tightly squeezed between his body and the counter before kissing him. It was a slow kiss, full of everything he had.

"I don't carry them anymore, my queen and my bird. I don't have to carry them, because I don't need them when I have both of you."

Mateo's chest swelled, feeling full. "You always make me get so fuckin' emotional. I'd get my ass beat if anyone saw me the way I am with you." He laughed, and Josiah did the same before pulling back.

"What's with the camera?" Josiah asked. "You have it with you a lot."

He reached for it, and Mateo almost pulled it away but he didn't, instead letting Josiah into this new part of him. "It's nothin', really. Just something I started doing. Things look different to me when I look at them through a camera. I try to capture it but it doesn't always work."

Josiah turned it on, flipping through all the images. Mateo's skin started to feel tight as though Josiah was dissecting him.

"Holy shit. Do you know how incredible these are? They're beautiful."

Suddenly, he didn't feel so on display anymore. Or maybe it was that he didn't mind. "Here, lemme show you the one I took today."

After they moved to the table, Mateo showed Josiah the picture of the hearts. Then they went through all the images again, and he told Josiah stories about a lot of them. When they were finished, Josiah said, "You should try and do something with these. I've never seen you so passionate about something."

He didn't know what he could ever do with them, but still he said, "Yeah. Maybe. When does Tristan get home?"

Josiah smiled. "A little over an hour, I think. I was about to start dinner. Want to help me?"

Yeah…Yeah, he actually did.

Chapter Seventeen

Tristan

Tristan got off work early and decided to stop in to see his mom before he went home. He'd been going more often since she called about the soup over a month ago. He couldn't imagine never leaving his home, being so afraid of the world or afraid of what you'd seen that you couldn't face it. His whole life he'd felt lonely, but it couldn't compare to how she must be feeling. He should be seeing her every day. Maybe the depression would go away if he visited more often. Maybe she could get better.

When he stepped into the house, his mom sat in her favorite chair by the window. His insides seized up watching her look out at the city she hadn't ventured into in years. She'd never seen much of San Francisco at all.

The heavy weight he always carried around in his chest doubled. The urge to reach over and look for the beat in his wrist was there, too, but he fought back.

"The lights are pretty," he said as he walked over. She didn't turn to face him.

"They are."

"Nighttime used to be my favorite time in the city," he told her as they stood shoulder-to-shoulder, her cotton robe against his suit.

"And it's not now?" she asked.

"No. Now I'm quite fond of early mornings." And then, because he knew it would mean a lot to her, because it would mean a lot to him, too, he forced himself to add more. "Remember when I told you Josiah likes to walk? Well, he does it every morning. I like to go with him. We have someone else living with us, too. His name is Mateo. Sometimes the three of us go together." Even though he knew she didn't really get what he meant about Mateo, it was important for him to say.

She looked up and smiled at him, suddenly the woman he knew as a child standing in front of him instead of the scared, broken one she'd become. She hadn't smiled like that in years.

"You're happy. I said that a while back, when Josiah came into your life, but it's even more apparent now. You're happy in a way I've never seen you."

Those words broke through his barriers. Had he really never been happy? No, that wasn't true. Things had never really been great, but they'd had their moments. They'd laughed together and decorated Christmas trees, even if it was only a cheap, two-foot tree they got at a secondhand store.

But there had always been the underlying sadness, too, waiting to get its claws into him when it inevitably grabbed her. "I'm trying. I want to be." And he did, but he also wanted that for her, too. "Maybe we can try sometime? To walk together? We wouldn't have to go far."

She shook her head. "Oh, Tristan. I don't know. It's been so long. I don't think there's anything out there for me anymore. Sometimes I don't even remember what it's like… or how this all happened."

Slowly and painfully. She left less and less after the attack. Struggled in crowds and being around people. He'd come home to find her crying, or even see her sitting outside the apartment, arms wrapped around her legs, scared about something she would never voice.

And then things would seem to get a little better before they'd get worse again. And when they did, Tristan sold himself to ensure he could always take care of them, the same way she had done to take care of him.

He'd thought things would get better when he managed to get her out of New York, but she slipped even farther way.

A good son would reach out and grab her hand, maybe even hug her, but hell, he didn't know how to do that anymore.

"There are things out there for you. I can show you. Your doctor comes to see you tomorrow. Maybe it's something you can talk to him about."

She gave him another smile, threading her arm through his since he would never do it. "I don't want to talk about that. I want to talk about you. You're in love, and that's all I've ever wanted for you."

He couldn't say much, but Tristan found a way to say what he could. He started with, "Did Josiah ever tell you his dream is to have his own coffeehouse? I don't get it, but it makes him happy," and then continued to talk from there.

It surprised him when toward the end, he added, "And pictures…He likes to take pictures, too." He meant Mateo, not Josiah. He still hadn't sorted out exactly what his feelings for Mateo were, but leaving him out didn't feel right. Neither did trying to explain it to his mom.

A little while later, Tristan let himself into the house, Mateo and Josiah's laughter coming from the kitchen. After setting his briefcase down on the table by the door, he stopped in the doorway to the kitchen and leaned against the frame.

"What the hell, Teo? How much salt did you put in this?" Josiah wiped his mouth as he stood next to the stove, a big pot in front of him.

"I don't fucking know. You said to put salt in it, so I put salt in it."

"The whole bottle?" Josiah replied, and Mateo playfully pushed him.

This time when Tristan put his finger to his pulse, he welcomed the rapid beat—the reminder that he was, in fact, alive. They were just as beautiful like this, laughing and having fun, happy, as they were making love.

Maybe he should feel some kind of jealousy but he didn't, because he could be a part of that. They wanted him there.

Josiah caught his eye. "Hey. I didn't hear you come in. What are you smiling at?"

He was smiling? News to him. "You guys, I guess." He walked over to them, kissing Josiah. He paused before pressing a kiss to Mateo's lips, too. They sat at the table and ate overly-salted spaghetti but no one complained. They talked about their days and Josiah showed him Mateo's pictures.

Afterward they cleaned the kitchen together and, just before they left the room, Tristan ignored the lump in his throat and spoke. "Next weekend, we're going to have dinner with my mom." He looked at Mateo. "All of us."

Josiah pulled him into an easy hug, whispering "thank you" in his ear. Over Josiah's shoulder, he returned Mateo's nod.

Chapter Eighteen

Josiah

They walked around the small, empty building. It wasn't in The Warf, but it was very close. It was also a little over what Josiah had been approved for, but Tristan had insisted they come.

And he was right. The place would be perfect. It was almost everything Josiah had dreamed of. The building had an older feel, and, he couldn't explain it, but it just felt right.

"It needs a little work," Tristan said as he stood where the main counter would go. Josiah pictured it being a warm, chocolaty brown.

"I could do it," Mateo said at the same time Josiah said, "That's okay. I want to work for it." He looked over at Teo, who grinned. "Okay, help *you* work for it." He wasn't going to pretend he could work with his hands as well as Teo could.

"Mmm. I wanna see you all covered in sawdust. Dirt smudged under your eyes after workin' hard all day. That'd be sexy…" Mateo looked at Tristan before adding, "Wouldn't it, Tristan?"

Josiah watched fire blaze in Tristan's eyes. "Yes, it would be."

"Ah, the suit likes things dirty. I never would'a guessed," Teo teased. With each word that they spoke, Josiah fell in love with them more. Watched them falling for each other, whether they realized how much they were or not.

"I can show you just how dirty I like it." Tristan stepped closer, but his phone beeped in his pocket. He pulled it out, no doubt making sure it wasn't his mom before putting it away again. Unfortunately, it had broken the spell, something he figured Tristan and Mateo were both kind of okay with. They wanted each other. They all knew that, and they touched and kissed and sucked each other, but Tristan had yet to fuck Mateo, and they all knew Tristan would never let any of them fuck him.

But Josiah wanted that. Wanted it so much he ached inside. He would do anything to see them together, and he could only hope one day Tristan trusted one of them enough to let them have him. It wasn't the sex part that was important, though he would definitely enjoy that, but no matter how close they were, something painful kept Tristan from fully giving himself to anyone.

"Jay, we could make this pretty incredible. Look at the view from the windows. It might not be right on the water, but you can see it." Mateo nudged him and Josiah went over, looked out at the water they'd spent so much time walking by.

"It's too much, though. You know I can't afford this." He didn't realize how much he wanted this, *this* exact place, until those words left his mouth.

"I can."

Though Tristan's words meant everything to him, they left him feeling hollow, too. He would give Josiah the world. There was no doubt in his mind that Tristan loved him, yet he'd still never said the words. He still couldn't put himself out there, and take from Josiah or Mateo the things he would give. "I can't let you do that, Tris. You've already done too much."

Tristan wrapped his arms around Josiah from behind. "I want to do it. We both know I haven't given you enough."

"You know this place isn't what I want from you."

Tristan sighed and let him go, but it was Teo who spoke. "Actions speak louder than words, Jay. You deserve this."

That was easy for Mateo to say. Each day closer to meeting Tristan's mom, he withdrew further. Josiah wasn't stupid. He knew Teo well enough to know what was going on. He knew him well enough to know that he wouldn't be going with them when the day came.

"Tristan can help you get your dream, and I'll help you build it."

It was that statement that almost pushed the word *yes* from his mouth, made him go weak in the knees. As far back as he could remember, he'd never known what love was, but now he had both of these men who, despite their faults, he knew both loved him.

"I'll think about it," Josiah replied.

"Good." Tristan opened the door, letting Josiah and Mateo out before he followed behind them, toward the realtor who waited outside.

Things were busy for them after that. Summer had started coming to a close. Tristan was busy on a case. Mateo picked up extra hours at the restaurant, wanting to make more money to help out. He had to check in with his PO often, and with Josiah's busy work schedule, they hardly saw each other over the next week.

Mateo came in later than the rest of them most nights, and it seemed the only place the three of them met up was in bed.

Tonight Josiah was in the room alone, Mateo still at work and Tristan in his office, working. Tomorrow was the day they were all supposed to have dinner with Tristan's mom.

When he heard the door downstairs, he waited, wondering how Mateo would tell him that he wasn't going, wondering if Tristan already knew it. It took a few minutes before there were footsteps on the stairs and in the hall, but he never came in.

Josiah waited a few seconds before jumping out of bed. He'd kill Teo if he tried to go back to his old room, and he'd kill him if he tried not to go tomorrow. Maybe he didn't realize how big a deal this was for Tristan to invite them, how much Josiah wanted them both there, and he refused to take no for an answer.

It wasn't until he stepped into the hall that he realized Teo hadn't gone to the spare room, but to Tristan's office instead. The door was cracked, their soft, mumbled voices inside.

He reached for the handle, almost grabbing it, before pulling back. No matter how much he wanted tomorrow to be right for all of them, he realized now that it wasn't his place to make it that way. He could love them both, want them both, but Teo had to want to be there. Tristan had to show him he wanted him there. They both knew how Josiah felt about everything. The rest was up to them.

He closed his eyes, let out a deep breath, and then turned back for their bedroom, quietly closing the door behind him.

Chapter Nineteen

Mateo

"You didn't come in here to talk to me about work, Mateo. You're too brave to pretend you did. What is it?"

Mateo watched as Tristan closed his laptop and leaned back in his chair. He didn't look smug, or annoyed, just curious and honest. Tristan was also right. Well, about the not coming in his office to talk to him about work, at least. "I'm not fuckin' brave. How do you get that?"

Tristan's eyebrows pulled together, as though he couldn't tell if Mateo was serious or not. He must have realized he was because he said, "A long list of reasons that will only go in one ear and out the other unless you want to believe them."

Mateo let those words percolate for a minute. "In the beginning, I didn't think we could be, but we're not so different, you and me. The difference is you made something of your life, regardless. You're a goddamned attorney. What the fuck am I?"

Tristan didn't reply, and Mateo somehow knew he wouldn't, that he would just wait for Mateo to continue. "With Jay, I didn't have to worry about shit like this. I just had to be good enough for him. We both knew I never would be, but we still made it work. I'm not the guy who meets someone's family. I'm an ex-con. An ex-drug dealer. I…" He shook his head before he and Tristan met eyes. Now the anger, the frustration, set in Tristan's features, because he didn't get it. He never would.

"Did Josiah tell you everything about the day he almost got hurt? That I was an asshole to him, and then went to sell drugs to crack heads, hookers, and fucking *moms*? That I was so fucking busy I was late to pick him up, and that's when they attacked him?"

Tristan's eyes were closed when Mateo looked at him again. He held his fingers to his wrist, something Teo hadn't seen him do in a while. *Finally.* Finally he saw who Mateo was…and it fucking hurt. But it was important, too.

Mateo didn't try and block out the visions in his eyes, the picture of that motherfucker on top of Josiah, because he figured he deserved to live with it. "I didn't even try and use my fists. I didn't even try to pull him off. I took out my knife, and as he lay on him, I slit his fucking throat. *That* is who I am, and I will never regret doing it."

Dios, if he didn't suddenly feel the urge to count his pulse, too, to remind himself that he was really there. Who knew how much longer he would be.

"So, you saved him. You killed a man who would have raped Josiah. You should have!" Tristan's fist came down on the desk. "Hell, you probably saved more than just Josiah by doing it!"

"Maybe I did save him, but it doesn't change what I did. That it was my fault he was out there in the first place. That I left him. It doesn't change the fact that years later, after Josiah was safe here, I was so angry at myself, so pissed at the fucking world, that I found out who helped that night, the one I missed. That time, I didn't let him get away."

That's when the nausea he hadn't felt in so long hit him, almost took him over. That hadn't been about protecting Josiah. It had been about revenge…And anger at himself for losing Josiah. He brought his hand up to cover his mouth.

Tristan was silent for what felt like an eternity before calmly, in a monotone voice, speaking. "That's what could come back to haunt you?"

"Either of those incidents can. People on the streets talk, especially to save their own asses. There's no guarantee I didn't piss off someone else with a big mouth that will happen to find out. And Javier's the one who got rid of the first body."

Silence again, except for the sound of his heart slam-dancing in his chest.

"Are those the only two lives you've taken?" There was a tenderness to Tristan's voice he hadn't had moments before.

"Directly. I still sold drugs to people, Tristan. I knew the people I associated with were taking people out every day. When I was a kid I watched my father string a man up, let him force me to beat him before he blew his brains out in front of me. I'm far from fucking innocent."

And he hated himself for it. Hated what he did and the fact that Tristan knew, or the things Josiah knew. As much as he'd wanted to pretend he belonged here with them, he didn't. If Tristan was smart, he'd kick him out right now, because as weak as it made him, he wouldn't leave unless Tristan asked him to.

Tristan leaned forward, elbows on his desk. Deep breaths filled the room as he looked down at the table, hands on the back of his head.

"I'm okay to fuck around with, but you don't want me in your life that much. You don't want me to go into your *madre's* home and sit at her table knowing who I am. I'll make an excuse to Jay."

Mateo pushed forward, only getting halfway to his feet, when Tristan's voice stopped him. "I grew up on those same streets you did." He didn't look up, still with his hands on his head, staring down at the table as he talked. "When waitressing didn't pay the bills, my mom fell in love with a man who she thought would. It wasn't long before she was turning tricks. Before people fed her the same kind of drugs you were probably selling."

Fuck. Mateo fell back into the chair, feeling as though he would disappear at any second.

"I prayed every fucking night for the balls to take her away, to kill the man who did that to her, the same way he was killing her, but I never had them. I know she did what she did to try and survive, just like…just like you did. You survived and you protected and defended what was yours. Josiah. Do you want to know what I did?" He spoke more softly than Mateo had ever heard him speak. With more pain in his voice than Mateo knew was possible.

He didn't know if it was the right thing to do, or if it would help in any way, but he pushed to his feet again, this time walking over to Tristan. He thought Tristan would fight him when he pried his hands away and tilted Tristan's head up. "What did you do?"

Tristan gave a humorless laugh at that. "Nothing. I hid in closets as a child, counting my fucking pulse because it gave me something to concentrate on rather than what I heard. And when I got older, I did nothing to find the people who had hurt her. I went to fucking college, telling myself money would save us. I…" His voice broke before he jerked away from Mateo's grasp. Mateo grabbed for him again, but Tristan shoved to his feet, breathing heavy.

"What? What did you do?" Mateo grabbed Tristan's arm when he tried to walk away, turned him and pulled Tristan against his own body. "I told you my shit, you give me yours. What the fuck did you do?"

Mateo grunted as Tristan shoved him backward, into the wall. But then his body was there, too, lined up against Mateo's, holding him against the wall.

As though someone flipped a switch, the rigidness in his body evaporated. He sagged against Mateo with his face in Teo's neck. "I sold myself to the highest bidder," he whispered. "I made money for school and to take care of my mom by letting someone fuck me. I was his paid whore for years. A whore to his friends, and then I would take that money and buy her food. I'd spend it on my stupid fucking education, because I somehow made myself believe that if I could take care of us, everything else would go away."

When Mateo wrapped his arms around Tristan, he realized Tristan wasn't just slack against him anymore…they were holding each other up. His eyes stung. His gut ached. Bile rose in his throat. And fuck if his heart wasn't somehow matching Tristan's beat.

Tristan didn't move, kept his face in Mateo's neck, breathing heavily, and despite everything, he realized he loved this man, too. That he wanted him with the same fierce need that he felt for Josiah. "You survived." Mateo ran his hand through Tristan's hair. Held his waist tightly with his other. "You survived, and you protected what was yours the best way you knew how."

Then he lifted Tristan's head and took his mouth. Slowly he eased into the kiss, letting his tongue try and soothe them. Pulling back, he let Tristan take over. Wondered if Tristan knew how each stroke of his tongue calmed Mateo.

When they ended the kiss, Tristan dropped his forehead to Mateo's. "He's the light to our dark." And that was true. Josiah softened both their rough edges.

"He makes me want to shine, too."

Tristan nodded as though he agreed with Mateo.

"I want you to come with us tomorrow. It wouldn't be the same without you, just like…Just like *we* wouldn't be the same without you. I'd be honored to have you there."

Nothing in this world was completely black or white. Wrong or right. Or if it was, what mattered was whose eyes it was being seen from. He realized then they all saw things differently, and what mattered was how the people involved felt about it. He understood Tristan's choice, but hated his own. Tristan somehow understood Mateo's, but couldn't stomach his own. Maybe they just needed to believe for each other.

"Yeah… I'd be honored to go."

Chapter Twenty

Tristan

Josiah grabbed Tristan's arm as they walked down the hall toward his mom's apartment. Stupidly, it frustrated him that the touch soothed him. Josiah pulled Tristan's fingers away from the wrist that he hadn't realized he held, looking for the pulse point. Mateo lingered behind them, as though giving them a minute.

"It's going to be okay," Josiah whispered. He leaned against the wall, pulling Tristan so he boxed Josiah in. "I know you've never let anyone in like this, and I know it scares the hell out of you, but it's just us. Everyone here tonight loves you."

This is where he should say it back, but instead he leaned forward, resting his forehead against Josiah's. "I know, but it's not just that. It's hard having other people see her like this. Having to bring the world to her because she will never venture into it." And yes, the guilt that came along with that.

Before Josiah could reply, Tristan kissed him, pressing him tightly against the wall because this was so much easier than words. Because this was the only way he fully knew how to express himself.

When he pulled away, Josiah sucked in a deep breath as though Tristan had stolen it from him. Reaching for Mateo, Tristan wrapped his hand around the back of his neck. Mateo nodded, showing Tristan he knew what was in that simple touch. *Thank you* and *let's do this.*

They finished the short walk to her apartment door and Tristan let them inside. His mom stood in the kitchen, wearing a dress he'd never seen, covered by an apron. She looked so damn normal. Looking at her now, there were no traces of the shadows she always had in her eyes. Of the sadness that showed in everything she did. Looking at her, you'd think she went out shopping for that new dress rather than having Isabel do it for her. How he wished that were true.

But then a truth she tried to hide did show in her eyes: shock. She hadn't thought he would really come. That added another layer of guilt to those Tristan already carried.

"It's so good to finally meet you." Josiah broke the heavy silence in the room, stepping toward his mom.

He held out his hand, but Tristan's mom pulled Josiah into a hug instead. She squeezed her eyes tightly shut as she embraced Josiah. His mom and the first man he'd ever loved. Fear climbed his spine, only settling with the feel of Mateo's hand as he touched his lower back.

"I never thought..." she started to say but then didn't finish, just held Josiah another moment before adding, "It's so good to meet *you,* Josiah." She placed her hand at the back of Josiah's head the way she used to do with Tristan when he was a kid.

When they finally separated, Tristan put a hand on Mateo's back and eased him forward. "This is Mateo."

The corner of her eyes wrinkled and Tristan added, "Remember, I told you about him." As much as he could, at least. They'd decided not to tell her who Mateo was to them. Well, Mateo had decided, and Josiah and Tristan finally accepted it. He didn't like it, but he had to admit that it was probably for the best. How could he expect her to understand it when he hardly did?

She waved a hand at him. "Of course I remember. I'm agoraphobic and depressed, but my memory works just fine."

Tristan tensed up but she smiled. "I'm kidding, son. Lighten up." Turning to Mateo, she continued, "I'm Rhonda. It's so nice to meet you, too."

Just as she'd done with Josiah, she pulled Mateo into a hug, only it didn't linger as long. "Nice to meet you, too, *senora*."

"Oh, don't call me ma'am. Please, use Rhonda."

Mateo stepped back. "Rhonda."

She eyed Mateo again, then Josiah, before her eyes landed on Tristan. She didn't pull him into a hug like she had with his guys, but smiled instead.

"I made roast and potatoes. It should be done any minute. Make yourselves at home and I'll get it finished."

Mateo finished washing his hands first before asking, "Need some help? Setting the table or somethin'?"

She nodded once, reminding Tristan of himself, before she showed

Mateo where the plates and silverware were. Mateo set the table while Josiah spoke with his mom as she finished dinner. Even if he'd wanted to, he wouldn't have been able to get a word in. Tristan wondered if this was how they spoke when on the phone, each of them rambling on and on about anything they could think of.

His chest somehow felt both tight and relaxed at the same time. He couldn't describe the mixed emotions going through him, so he excused himself to the bathroom.

He splashed water on his face as though that would wash away the feelings he didn't want to focus on. The fact that Josiah and Mateo were standing in his mother's house.

The fact that he was glad they were.

When he went back into the other room, his mom had just pulled the roast out. "Here, Mom. Let me cut it for you."

She handed him the knife. Less than five minutes later, the four of them sat at her too-large kitchen table. The most it had ever sat was three, on the rare occasions Tristan ate with his mom and Isabel, who had gone out for the evening.

"So, Mateo. Tell me a little bit about yourself?" she asked as they ate.

From across the table, Tristan saw Mateo seize up. It was such a simple question, but one Tristan knew Mateo wouldn't want to answer. The urge to protect Mateo surged inside him, though he knew Mateo didn't need it. Not him. Mateo protected people, not the other way around. Still, Tristan found himself cutting in. "He's known Josiah since they were teenagers. He's…very important to us both." And then before his mom could question him on it, Tristan added, "He takes incredible photographs. Maybe he'll show you sometime."

"Nah, it's nothin'. I'm not that good." Mateo glanced at him out of the corner of his eye.

"Yes you are, Teo. They're beautiful. I keep trying to tell him he should do something with them, but it's not working. Maybe you can talk him into it," Josiah told her.

"You should," his mom said. "My son isn't easily impressed, and I have a feeling Josiah might not be, either. No one ever thinks they're good at something, but if these boys say you are, well, I'd bet you are." She reached over and patted Mateo's hand, then grabbed Josiah's. Tristan's breath caught. His heart thudding to a wild, almost happy beat as he watched them.

"I'm so glad to meet you guys," she said again.

In that moment, Tristan knew he'd done something he'd always wished he could do. He'd made her truly happy.

Two hours later, they all sat in the living room. Josiah sat next to his mom on the couch, Mateo in a chair next to it, and Tristan on the other couch. He couldn't remember the last time he'd heard his mom talk so much, if ever.

"Was Tristan as quiet as a child as he is now?" Josiah asked her.

She laughed. "Oh, God yes. It's always been work to pry words out of his mouth. I used to tease him and say it was like he'd swallowed an old man."

"What?" Josiah laughed.

"Maybe you should have that checked," Mateo teased.

Damned if Tristan didn't find himself chuckling, too. "If either of you give me hell about that, I won't hesitate to take action."

"I think I'm going to need you to explain that one to me." Josiah still laughed.

"It's like he's an old soul," his mom said. "Tristan has always been older than his years. He's always been serious and quiet." The air in the room thickened. "He's always taken responsibility for things he shouldn't."

A fist grabbed Tristan across his middle, tightening more and more each second. No, he very much needed to take responsibility of things he hadn't protected her against.

"Even though I wish he didn't do it, I respect him for it, too. You have to have an awful big heart to care that much." The strength in which she spoke told him how much she believed it. It made the fist holding him tighten even more.

"If you'll excuse me for a second. I need to check my phone. I forgot it in the car." Tristan pushed to his feet and headed for the door. He didn't have to turn to know Josiah was right behind him.

Still, Tristan didn't stop until he stepped onto the street. "Tristan."

He kept walking, kept going until they got to the car because he didn't want to do this in public. He made it as far as his car in the parking structure before Josiah reached him.

"Don't do it. Don't tell me it's not my fault and that I do have a big heart. I can't deal with that right now."

One, two, three, four, five, one, two, three, four, five.

Josiah pried Tristan's hand off his wrist. "Okay. Can I tell you I love you?" Josiah didn't stop there. He stepped closer to Tristan, just like Tristan had done with him in the hallway. "Or that I know it took a lot for you to bring us here tonight, and I'm glad? That I love your mom, and that you, no matter what, made her really happy tonight?"

He raised Tristan's hand, pressing his lips to his pulse. "You make me happy.... And Teo. One day I hope you'll let us make you happy, too."

In that moment he realized how much he wanted that, too, how much he wanted to find a way to give them both what they gave him.

When Tristan bent forward and kissed him, his body sang with pleasure, like it always did. The pulses of his heart became Josiah, like they always did, but there was something missing. Someone.

Tristan eased back. "You feel so damn incredible, but it like there's an empty space, too."

Josiah's hands tightened in his shirt as he pressed his lips to Tristan's again. It was in the way Josiah held him, the way he kissed him, that, as much as they loved each other, Josiah felt the same.

Tristan pulled back, grabbing Josiah's hand, before nodding toward the building. "Come on. Let's go get Mateo and go home."

Chapter Twenty-One

Josiah

Josiah handed a latte to the woman before she walked out of Fisherman's Roast. He hadn't had a drop of caffeine today, still riding the high of meeting Tristan's mom the night before. Still thinking about the way Tristan had touched he and Mateo when they'd gone home. The looks he gave as he'd told Mateo to touch Josiah, as they made love the way they had so many times lately.

A week ago, Tristan would have pulled away after opening himself up. No, he still hadn't given Josiah or Mateo free rein over his body, and he had yet to take Mateo himself, but he hadn't walked away after letting them into this life. To Josiah, that was huge.

It was progress, and that's what mattered to him.

A flood of teenagers came through the door. They'd had waves of people all day, not having much downtime.

As they made their way to the counter, his cell vibrated in his pocket. While the employee at the register took their orders, Josiah slipped his phone out of his pocket to glance at the number.

His heart stuttered slightly when he saw that it was Rhonda calling, but then figured she just wanted to talk about last night.

"April, can you come up here and help Holly? I'm going to take five minutes real quick." The woman nodded at him while Josiah headed toward the back office. He hit talk, raising the phone to his ear as he went. "Hello."

"Josiah? This is Isabel. I'm sorry to bother you, but Tristan isn't answering. It's driving me crazy sitting around and waiting. I wanted to see if you guys have heard anything yet."

His heart filled with concrete, dropping to his feet almost like weight, making them too heavy to move. Josiah gripped the phone tighter, firmly planted in the same spot. "What do you mean heard anything? What happened?"

There was a pause on the other end of the line before she spoke again. "I'm sorry. I just assumed you knew because Rhonda said you and Tristan—"

"What happened?" he asked again, finally able to move, but instead of toward the office, he went for the door.

"When I woke up this morning, Rhonda wasn't up yet. That's not unusual, so I wasn't really worried about it. After a while, I figured I needed to check on her. When I went into her room she was gone."

Josiah's blood ran cold. "I have to go!" He yelled over his shoulder as he walked out of Fisherman's Roast. "How long ago?"

"I got up at seven. She sleeps in sometimes, so I didn't check on her until eleven. She had to have been gone before I woke up."

And it was three now.

"Tristan?" Josiah was running now, running for the bus, home, hell, he didn't even know where. He just knew he had to find Tristan, and Rhonda…holy shit, he couldn't imagine her out here alone.

"I called the police before calling him. They were all here this morning. They're out looking for her now. I'm so sorry. I should have looked in on her earlier. I thought you would be out looking with them. I thought Tristan would have told you."

Josiah's chest squeezed at that. Yeah, him too. "If you see Tristan tell him to call me, tell him I'm looking too, okay? And if they find her, let me know."

With that Josiah hung up the phone. He called Tristan three times before he answered. "Have they found her?" he asked before Tristan could say anything.

"No." His voice held no emotion.

"Where are you? I'll help you look. Teo will, too. We'll find her, Tristan. I don't care what it takes, we'll find her and she'll be okay." She had to be.

"The police have a few squads out looking for her, but it's not enough. Goddamn it! I can't believe I told her…" Tristan took a deep breath. "I have to go. Jesus, I don't even know what the fuck to do besides drive around the fucking city looking for her. They've contacted all the hospitals, shelters and everything else they can think of, we just… I need to go. I have to find her."

"Let us come and search with you. You shouldn't be alone, Tristan. Don't block us out."

"Don't. I don't have time for that shit right now. I have to find her." Tristan hung up the phone.

Josiah stopped and leaned against the wall of a building. The city was loud with cars, people and construction work around him. His throat nearly closed up when he thought of Rhonda out in the city alone after not leaving her house in who knew how long. His chest ached at the thought of possibly losing her, and knowing Tristan would be lost to him, too, if they did.

Maybe they never really had him.

Chapter Twenty-Two

Mateo

Mateo and Josiah combed over the same streets they'd looked through two days before.

Today marked Rhonda's third day gone, and no one had seen a trace of her. And they'd only seen Tristan once. He rarely answered their phone calls, and it had been an accident they'd even run into him when they had. He hadn't been at home because as far as they both knew, Tristan hadn't gone back since she came up missing.

"What if we don't find her, Teo?" Josiah asked.

"We will." He turned down an alley before looking in and around the dumpster.

"It's been three days. God, what if something happened to her? She was so happy the other night. And Tristan."

"We'll find her, Jay." Fuck, he hoped those words were true. He ignored his brain that wouldn't shut the fuck up with the fact that she'd been gone a long time in an unsafe city. That she's probably been freaked out, scared, and there were a whole hell of a lot of people who would take advantage of someone like that. "We'll find her," he said again, because he needed to hear it. Because he owed her that much and more after the other night.

"Rhonda!" he called, not knowing what else to do.

"Rhonda!" Someone else echoed him, and it took everything in him to unclench his fists and not find the motherfucker and show him just how funny that wasn't.

"My phone's dead," Josiah said as he peered around a corner.

"Yeah, mine died a long time ago." He pulled it out of his pocket. "Why don't you take them home? We need to have them to keep in touch with Tristan and Isabel. Hell, for all we know they could've found her. Get some rest. Try to get ahold of Tristan or somethin'."

Josiah was already shaking his head before he spoke. "It's not right. While you guys are out here looking, I will be, too."

Mateo grabbed Josiah's waist and pulled him closer. "I know you want to be out here helpin', Jay, and you will be, but we need our phones, too. What happens if we find her and she needs help? We gotta be able to call someone."

Mateo felt Josiah's warm breath across his cheek when he sighed. "You're right. I know you are. I won't be able to get ahold of you, though. Meet me at Fisherman's Roast at six, and we'll start looking again."

Because they needed all the eyes they could find. He doubted the cops were doing much anymore. Not after this many days. "Okay."

Mateo watched until Josiah disappeared around the next corner before he started walking again, walking and looking, ignoring his head and listening to his heart, because they needed to fucking find her. There wasn't much he could do for Tristan or Josiah, but he damn sure could stay on these streets until they brought Rhonda home.

***

Mateo had walked around for hours. As soon as Josiah left for home, he'd gone down to one of the parks where a lot of the transients and gang bangers spent time. It was a long shot, but he knew he'd get a whole hell of a lot more information down here than the cops would, or even than he would have gotten if Jay had been with him.

Still, he didn't have much luck. He'd pulled his camera out of his bag and showed the picture he'd taken when Josiah and Tristan had gone to the car the other night to any and everyone who would look. The picture he'd taken of Rhonda for Tristan.

No one had seen her. He'd even told people he'd give them the fucking camera if they knew where she was. It wasn't worth much, but a couple hundred bucks was like gold to the people down here. Still, no one said shit.

After that it was back to alleys and quiet, lonely streets, because he figured if she freaked out, she'd probably be running away from people instead of toward them.

He asked a random man the time and realized it was almost time to meet Jay when he saw a space about five feet wide between two buildings. He didn't know what the hell it was there for, but turned and made his way down it, stepping over weeds growing between broken pieces of concrete.

It was probably a waste of time but he didn't stop going. Didn't want to acknowledge the fact that anything could've happened to her out here.

Cars sped down the streets in front and behind him as Mateo made his way through the thin space.

The streets were quiet for a second, and that's when he heard the soft moaning that sounded like a woman. The hairs on the back of Teo's neck stood on end, chills running down his arms.

Did he say her name or not? He didn't fucking know. He needed Jay for this kinda stuff.

Hell, it might not even be her, but somehow he knew it was, and that made his heart want to speed up and slow down at the same time. Who knew what happened to her while she was out here.

"Rhonda?" he said softly as he kept going. Mateo stopped when he got to another open space between the front building and the back. It was even smaller than the one he was in now, leaving the figure huddled on the ground hardly enough room to squeeze in.

"Rhonda?" he said again. "It's me. Mateo. I'm Tristan's…friend. We met the other night." He bent down and she cried harder, trying to shove her way deeper into the space.

"It's okay. I won't hurt you." He reached for his phone before remembering he didn't have it. *Dios,* what the fuck was he supposed to do?

"If you come out here, I can take you to Tristan. He's been real worried. He misses you."

Her arms were around her knees as she started rocking back and forth. Teo looked down toward the street. The street was pretty quiet, with not a lot of people walking around. He sat down, not sure what else to do. Damn, he wished Tristan or Josiah was here. "We gotta get you outta here, Rhonda. You can go with me. I won't hurt you. I promise."

She was shaking so bad he could have sworn he heard her bones rattling together. She'd been attacked before, he knew that, and it scared the hell out of him to think about trying to reach for her to get her to come out.

"Hey!" he yelled when a woman walked down the sidewalk at the end of the path.

She passed but then peeked around the corner.

"Hey! I need your help. You got a phone…" he let the last word linger when she walked away. Not that he blamed her. What woman wouldn't be nervous seeing him ducked down back here in this neighborhood?

Mateo leaned against the wall. "It's okay if you can't come out. I'll stay here with you as long as you need, but you gotta remember, we have Tristan waiting for us. Josiah, too. They're worried about you."

She had to be scared to death, and who knew what else. What if something happened to her out here? How would they deal with that? It would kill Tristan.

"You were right, you know? I don't know if you remember when I came to your house the other night. Remember when Josiah and Tristan went outside. I took a picture of you for Tristan, and you said I loved him, too. I don't know how in the hell you knew that, do you remember?"

When she didn't answer, he kept going. "I didn't admit it. Hell, I don't know if Tristan would want me to. I know it's kind of a fucked up situation. You said he loved me as well, though." Mateo shrugged. "I don't know if that's true. Don't really see how it can be. He loves Jay. Still hasn't told him, but he does. Anyway, I wanted you to know you're right. That I do. I should have just told you that night."

Because as fucked up as the whole thing really was, he felt whole when he was with Josiah and Tristan, in a way he never had. He'd never known what it felt like to truly feel whole until them.

It was then that Mateo realized she'd stopped crying. Mateo glanced over at her, and for the first time since he'd found her, she looked up at him. She was dirty, her hair a mess, as though she'd been on the streets forever.

"Tristan. Tristan, Tristan, Tristan, Tristan," she whispered his name over and over again.

Slowly, Mateo pushed up to his feet, but still kneeling. "That's right. I can get you to Tristan. Come with me, Rhonda." He said her name, hoping that would help. That if she was confused, she would at least recognize she should know him since he said her name.

"Tristan, Tristan, Tristan, Tristan," she continued quietly, mumbling Tristan's name. But she moved forward a little, too. Then a little more. He felt like putting his finger to his wrist like Tristan did, like that would somehow help or something.

"Let's go. Let's go find Tristan." His hands shook a little, scared he wasn't doing the right thing. Nervous of how she might react on the busier street.

She kept crawling forward, until she kneeled at the corner where it opened up to the space Mateo was. Slowly, he stood up. "Let's go see Tristan, Rhonda."

She looked up at him again, her eyes so damn lost. But still she pushed to her feet, took a step forward. But when she did, her foot caught on something and she stumbled. Mateo jerked his hands out to catch her, and the second he did, she screamed and jerked away. "No! No! Don't touch me!"

Rhonda ran between the buildings, Mateo right behind her. What the fuck should he do? If he caught her again, she would freak out, but he couldn't let her take off, either.

When she hit the sidewalk, she turned and kept running, still yelling, "No! No! No!" as she went. Mateo kept after her, people looking at them as they ran, probably wondering how he'd hurt her.

"What the fuck are you doing to her, man?" A guy grabbed his arm. On reflex, Mateo punched him in the face so he could get free and took off after her again.

She took another corner, screaming and stumbling as she went. Mateo turned it, too, noticing a cop who stood on the sidewalk.

"Hey. What are you doing?" The cop grabbed ahold of him just as the man he'd hit came up behind them.

"He's after that woman. He fucking hit me." Blood ran down the guy's face.

"She needs your help, man. Forget about me. We need to get her." He fought to pull away. "She's missing. She's my…" What was he supposed to say? She's my boyfriend's mom? Yeah, he's one of the state prosecutors and I'm an ex-gangbanger.

Mateo tried to jerk out of his grip again, his heart slamming. "That's Tristan fucking Croft's mom. She's been missing and she needs our help."

As soon as those words left his mouth, he heard the tires screech, heard the horn blare, before Rhonda screamed.

Chapter Twenty-Three

Tristan

One, two, three, four, five, one, two, three, four, five.

ONE, TWO, THREE, FOUR, FIVE.

Tristan stood outside the Emergency Department, counting. His pulse echoed loudly in his ears.

Open the door. Open the door, walk in, and look at the dead woman they think is my mom.

He owed her that, at least. He couldn't save her, but he damn sure needed to be strong enough to look at her, look at her and *know* he couldn't save her.

He stopped for a minute, leaned against the wall, and fingered his cell phone. *Call them.* They should be here with him. He *needed* Josiah and Mateo here with him, and that made his heart rate go even faster. Needing left people vulnerable, and he'd sworn never to need anyone.

They hadn't even moved her yet. She wasn't supposed to still be in the ER, but since the hospitals knew his mother was missing, they kept her here. In the loud, busy ER, which she would hate.

Tristan palmed his cell, pushed away from the wall and opened the door to the small room in the back of the department.

He didn't look up, didn't look at the bed until he stepped up to it. His hands shook. His throat hurt, though he didn't know why.

When he almost ran into the bed, he stopped. Stopped and forced himself to look at what had happened because he hadn't protected her when he was younger, because he told her that she should try to go outside again.

Tristan's legs went weak, his knees buckling. *Thank God.* It wasn't her.

He couldn't believe it wasn't her. The tightness in his throat eased up, the shakiness in his hands still going crazy. It wasn't *fucking* her, which meant she was still out there…but at least she could still be alive.

I can make it up to her.

And if he could make it up to her, maybe he could really have Josiah and Mateo, as well.

"Mr. Croft?" A doctor walked into the room.

"It's not her." But she was still someone's mother. Someone's daughter, sister, or friend.

"Good. I'm so glad. We—"

"Dr. West, I'm sorry to interrupt, but we just had an ambulance come in. Woman in room two. They had to strap her down. Doesn't seem to be drugs, but she's combative."

Dr. West left the room, Tristan right behind him. He didn't know why, but the faster the doctor went, the faster he did. He followed right behind the doctor, stopping in front of room two.

"Tristan! Help!" His mom thrashed around on the bed.

"Watch out! Be careful with her." He shoved his way into the room. His mom's eyes locked on him and he saw the shock there, realized she called for him before she even knew he was there.

Tristan shoved his way over to her. "Shh. It's okay. I'm here."

"We're going to have to give her something," Dr. West said.

He watched as they stuck a needle into her arm. She looked up at him and whispered, "Tristan. I knew you'd come."

***

Tristan was still sitting by her bed two days later when she turned her head to the side and smiled at him. Her voice was low and broken when she spoke. "Well, I left the house. It would have helped if I didn't get lost. Would also help if they took these straps off me."

"That's not funny."

She sighed. "I know."

"What were you thinking?"

It took her a minute to reply. "That I wanted to live. I haven't lived in so long, Tristan. I don't know if I ever have, and I want that. I didn't realize how much until I saw you with Josiah and Mateo."

He pulled back at her words.

"Yes. Him, too. I don't care who you're with, as long as you're happy. That's all that's ever mattered to me, and screw anyone else who might have a problem with it. One look at you boys and I knew. But, sweetheart." She tried to reach for him but couldn't because her arms were strapped down. Tristan grabbed ahold of her hand.

"You're still not fully living, either. You might be going through the motions. You might be happier, but I realized at dinner you're still not fully living. You don't let them in, and I thought..." Tears rolled down her face and he wiped them away for her.

"I thought that if I could do it, if I could get past all my problems, it might make it easier for you. You're still holding yourself responsible for all my mistakes, and you can't do that. Not anymore. If you don't let go of your past, you're going to lose them, and yourself, too."

She tried to smile again. "I guess I didn't think my plan through very well."

Tristan couldn't stop thinking about what she said. Hearing her words repeat over and over in his head. *Let go of your past. Lose them.*

He couldn't let himself lose them.

"I don't understand it," he said, elbows on her bed, looking down. "How I can need them both. Mateo...I haven't even known him for long."

"So?" she said sleepily. They were keeping her heavily medicated. "There aren't laws for emotions, Tristan. There isn't a magical timeframe where it's okay to fall in love with someone or okay to fall out of it. Emotions don't play by rules. That's what makes them so incredible."

Her chin quivered. "Don't let your life pass you by. Don't be like me. Even now, I'm scared. So scared, Tristan. I don't want that for you. I couldn't live with that."

For the first time since he was a child, Tristan leaned forward and kissed his mom's cheek. He wanted to do just what she said. Wanted to live…Wanted to let go and trust them. Trust them to catch him. "I'll do my best," he said, and she smiled at that.

"I can't ask for anything more than that. Mateo…I have this faint memory about him."

"He found you," Tristan told her. His heart sped up thinking of that. He could never repay Mateo for that.

"He's at home, waiting. When you're ready, he can come and see you. Both Josiah and Mateo want to come."

He didn't tell her she'd run from him. That she'd almost gotten hit by a car. That Mateo had almost gotten arrested.

"Good. That's good." Her eyes fluttered. "You go see your guys. I'm not going anywhere. I'll be here when you come back."

Her eyes closed. Tristan kissed her cheek one more time before he did what she said…before he went home to his men.

Chapter Twenty-Four

Josiah

"I'm not giving up." Josiah stood next to Mateo, who leaned against the back of the couch. Tristan had understandably been at the hospital with his mom since she'd been brought in. He'd called to let Josiah and Mateo know what was going on, but that was the extent of it.

Josiah got it. He really did. Tristan was where he needed to be. But that didn't mean he didn't understand what Tristan was doing.

"What are you talkin' about, Jay?"

"I'm not giving up on this. On us. Tristan's already pulling away. He doesn't know how to handle things emotionally, so he cuts them off. I'm not going to let him do that, and I'm not going to let you, either."

Teo wrapped a hand around the back of Josiah's neck, letting it rest there. "I'm not doing that."

He may not realize it, but he was. Even the detached tone of his voice said so.

"It wasn't just because of who you are that they thought you were attacking her. It would have happened to anyone. You have to admit that."

Mateo humorlessly chuckled. "But the rest of you wouldn't have had a record to go with it. You wouldn't have gotten held up because they had to call your PO, and shit like that. Tristan's a fucking lawyer. A prosecutor. How does it look for him to have someone like me around?"

Josiah jerked away from him. "When have you cared what other people think? Do you love him?"

Josiah knew he did, but he also wanted Teo to say it. Thought Teo himself needed to.

One thing about Teo he'd always loved, he didn't back down to admitting how he felt. He didn't let Josiah down when he said, "Yeah…Fuck it, but yeah, I do. Who the hell woulda thought? He's a suit."

"That doesn't matter. Look at all three of us. We're all different. Maybe that's why we work. Loving us isn't enough, though." Josiah moved and stood in front of him, grabbing hold of Mateo's waist. "You loved me but you didn't fight for me. For us."

Mateo tried to speak but he cut him off. "I know why you did it. You didn't think you deserved me and you wanted to protect me but that doesn't change the fact that you did it. You have to want us enough not to let the other stuff get in the way. You have to want us enough to stick around no matter what. Can you do that, Teo? Can you stop using your past as an excuse? Do you want a life with us enough to do that? To fight with me?"

Chapter Twenty-Five

Mateo

On the outside, Josiah looked like the weakest of them all. Mateo had always known how strong he was, but looking at him right now, hearing him, it slammed into his chest just how much more strength he had. More than himself. More than Tristan, too. He was the rock, and not just because he drew them together. No, because he *held* them together. He was the glue that made all their broken pieces fit to make them whole.

"I want it," hardly brushed passed Mateo's lips when he heard the twist of the doorknob.

Josiah turned, and Mateo took one step forward when Tristan came into the house. He was pale, his eyes tired, his body looking even more exhausted. Josiah didn't hesitate before rushing over and wrapping his arms around Tristan.

Mateo watched Tristan's hand knot in Josiah's shirt like someone would have to physically pry it free.

Mateo turned to walk away, but then Josiah's words, *his* words from just a minute before, repeated over in his head. He was fighting.

Before he got the chance to turn back toward the men, Tristan said, "No. Don't go. I need you, too."

Mateo wasn't even sure how he got there, but suddenly he stood next to them. Suddenly it was the three of them in an embrace, clutching and squeezing, daring anyone to try and pry their hands free.

"You're still here. No matter how many times I've pushed you away." Tristan touched Josiah's cheek, and Mateo knew that part was mainly for him. "No matter how much I fought it, you never turned your back on me." He turned to Mateo. "And you wouldn't, either."

Josiah led the way, taking Tristan's mouth. Mateo watched their lips move together, their tongues give and take, and damned if he didn't feel like he was a part of it, too. If it wasn't them acting on not only how they felt, but how he felt. And when it was his turn, when his tongue wrestled with Tristan's, he knew Jay was seeing the same thing.

"I'm tired. So damn tired of doing it alone. Tired of not living." Tristan looked them both in the eyes as he spoke. "I want to give myself to you both, every part of me, but I don't know how." And then he looked down. "Show me how."

Mateo's whole body buzzed with electricity, swelled with hunger and so much fucking honor.

"You don't have to. It's okay—"

"Go upstairs." Mateo cut Josiah off. "Go into the bathroom and start a shower. Don't get undressed yet. We'll be right there to take care of you."

Tristan took a couple of deep breaths before stepping back and toward the stairs.

As soon as he was gone, Mateo cupped Josiah's cheek. "I know you want this, Jay."

"That doesn't mean it's right. I don't want to push this on him."

"You wanna take care of him, this is the way. He'll tell us if he can't do it. We owe it to him. He deserves for us to give him what he needs."

Josiah nodded, and they both went for the stairs. Teo's body thrummed—lust, need, want, fear and love mixing together, carbonation in a shaken-up can that could burst at any second.

Josiah closed their bedroom door before they both stepped into the oversized bathroom, steam already fogging the mirrors, drifting over the glass doors of the standalone shower.

Mateo stopped in front of Tristan, trying to tell him with his eyes that he got it. He knew what Tristan had been through, and what this meant to him—and what it meant to Teo and Josiah, too.

"If you don't want something, you tell us, otherwise we have control." He stepped closer, their bodies aligned. "Tell him, Jay. Tell him what we want."

And then Josiah was there, so damn close, too. "We just want to take care of you."

Not take advantage of you… Take care of you.

Teo moved backward, signaled for Tristan to step away from the counter. "Keep your hands to yourself." He winked, trying to lighten the mood. Trying to do whatever he could to heal Tristan, to heal them all.

Chapter Twenty-Six

Tristan

Tristan's body vibrated from the inside out. He wondered if they could feel him, but then realized it didn't matter. They knew the parts of him no one else did, yet they were still here.

He closed his eyes, recognizing the feel of Josiah's cold hands as they pushed under his shirt, taking it up higher and higher, until Tristan had no choice but to raise his arms and let Josiah take it off.

He dropped his head back, trying to concentrate of the feel of Josiah's lips on his chest, his tongue tracing one nipple and then the other.

On the feel of Mateo's fingers unbuttoning and unzipping his pants.

Tristan tried to toe out of his shoes, but then Mateo's hand was there. "No. We're doing this for you. You're letting us lead the way, remember?"

Tristan fisted his hands, fighting not to pull away, not to count the rapid beats of his heart.

One shoe was gone, then the other, before Mateo pulled his pants and boxer briefs down. His cock flexed against his stomach, painfully hard and needy.

"Get in the shower and wait for us," Mateo commanded.

Tristan bit back the urge to say no. He fucked who he wanted, he controlled things in the bedroom…But then, he wanted to be here with them. Wanted to give whatever he could to both of these men.

So he went. Walked to the glass doors, opened them and stepped inside. Watched as they undressed before joining him—Josiah behind him and Mateo in front of him.

Water slid down his body, slid down theirs, too, as Mateo soaped his hands before handing the bar to Josiah. And then they washed him, and fuck if it didn't feel like they were cleansing his past. Washing it away with the water, Mateo's soapy hands ran up and down his chest, his arms, and down to his dick, his sac, before he went to his knees, washing Tristan's legs, too.

And then it was Josiah's turn, his shoulders, his back. Tristan tensed when Josiah touched his ass.

"It's just me. Only us, Tristan," Josiah said.

"I know. Keep going."

And he did. His finger drifting down Tristan's crack before he went to his knees to clean the backs of his legs as Mateo had done with the front.

They were both to their feet after that, leading him under the spray, bubbles disappearing down the drain.

"Now to the fun part," Mateo said, and damned if Tristan didn't smile. He leaned forward and sucked one of Tristan's nipples into his mouth.

"*Fuck.* Yes. Give me more." Fire burned its way through Tristan's insides, making him hotter, more urgent, as each second went by.

Mateo's teeth bit into his nipple. Josiah's arm wrapped over his shoulder, holding Tristan's back close to his chest, and keeping a hand on Mateo, too.

Josiah kissed his shoulder, Tristan struggling to keep his arms by his side. To not take the lead and push Mateo to his knees, or to take one of them into his mouth himself.

He was completely at their mercy, their command, and suddenly that knowledge made a new rush of desire flare inside him.

He leaned his head back against Josiah, letting his men take care of him. Letting them love him.

"I'm going to suck your cock now, Tristan. Gonna take it all the way to the back of my throat. Love suckin' your dick. But I think Jay wants to taste you, too, don't you, Josiah?"

"Yes…" He kissed Tristan's shoulder again. Ran his tongue from behind Tristan's ear, down to his shoulder.

"Jay's gonna go real slow. He wants to taste that sexy ass of yours. He's gonna love you so fuckin' good."

The heat in Tristan's body flooded out, as he tried to pull away. But Josiah was still at his back, Mateo at his front, neither of them moving. It was Mateo who spoke. "You don't want it, and he won't give it to you, but I think you do. Let him replace the bad shit. Let us both. We just want to love you."

And that's what did it. They both wanted to love him. They both did. This was his life, his fucking choice, and he chose to live it. Chose to share it with them. To give himself to them.

As if they heard his silent confirmation, Josiah pulled him back slightly, moving them out from under the spray of the shower.

Josiah went down to his knees behind him.

Mateo went down in front of him.

Mateo didn't waste any time, wrapping his hand around Tristan's erection before taking him into his mouth.

Tristan's hands itched to grab his hair, to lead him, but he held back, wanting only what his men wanted to give him.

Josiah's lips pressed to the small of his back, lavishing kisses down it, on one cheek and then the other.

His instincts to pull away went crazy, but he held them at bay. *I want this. I choose this. I love them...*

Mateo sucked Tristan's sac as his hand worked his dick. His balls already burned with the need to explode, but Tristan fought that off, too. He grabbed the top of the shower door, and then a lip on the wall, squeezing to keep his hands busy.

"I've wanted to touch you here for so long, Tristan. Wanted my finger and my tongue in your hole. Wanted to make you feel like you're coming apart, the way you do with me." Josiah's breath brushed across his ass.

"*Dios,* that is so goddamned sexy hearing you talk to him like that, Jay." The words just passed Mateo's lips before he swallowed Tristan's cock down again.

"Please. Bend over for me a little, Tristan. Let me taste you." Josiah gently pushed on his back…But he didn't need to. Tristan leaned forward, spread his legs, offering himself to Josiah. Fucking wanting him.

One of Josiah's hands went to each of his cheeks, spreading them wide before his tongue rasped over Tristan's asshole. "Fuck!" He couldn't help but pump his hips forward, making himself fuck Mateo's mouth.

Again and again, Josiah kept going. His tongue licking and rubbing at his ring.

They didn't ease up on him. Both of his men, torturing him in the most incredible way.

Mateo kept sucking, his hand palming Tristan's balls.

When Josiah's mouth was gone, Tristan almost called out. Almost grabbed him, forcing him back where he wanted him. But then there was pressure as Josiah's finger worked its way inside.

He seized, about to jerk back, but then heard Mateo's voice through the fog in his ears. "Told you he'd love you so fuckin' good. That's what he's doing."

The tension in his body evaporated, replaced with pleasure, with the feel of Josiah's finger pumping inside him. Of Mateo's mouth working his cock.

"Jesus, I'm going to come," Tristan managed to groan out.

Mateo's lips were suddenly gone. "That's enough."

And then Josiah's finger was gone, too… And he wanted it back. Wanted them both back so badly he could hardly stand it.

Mateo stood. "You're going to fuck me tonight, Tristan."

"God, yes." He grabbed Mateo and tried to pull him toward him, but his next words stopped him.

"While Jay fucks you."

He closed his eyes, fighting back memories of the past. Fighting back choices he made, and choosing now to move forward. To make himself whole—make them all that way.

"Yes."

It was almost as if he stood on the outside watching things from there. The water was turned off and they dried him off. Then they were in the bed, a mass of hands and mouths, kissing and touching.

For the first time, it was someone other than Tristan who grabbed the lube from the drawer, without being told. Mateo bent forward, rubbing a lubed finger over his own hole before handing the bottle to Josiah.

He scooted toward the edge of the bed, shoving a pillow beneath him. "Stand up and lean over me. Get behind him and lube his cock, Jay."

Josiah's wet hand wrapped around his dick before Tristan positioned himself above Mateo…Josiah behind him.

Then Josiah's lips where there again, on his shoulder, before he whispered, "I love you. I can't wait to make love with you." He looked at Mateo next. "I love you, too, Teo."

Teo whispered, *"Te amo."* His eyes caught Tristan's next. "Josiah is the only person who has ever been inside me. It will only ever be Josiah or you."

Tristan knew exactly what he was saying. That he loved Tristan, too. He ran his hand through Mateo's hair. Mateo, who nodded, not needing any other response right now.

Tristan leaned over him and rubbed his finger on Mateo's asshole. Prepared his body and then pushed his way inside.

"So good. So fucking good," Mateo groaned.

When Josiah's cold, wet finger breached his ring of muscles, Tristan didn't flinch.

He wanted more.

And Josiah gave it to him, slowly easing his erection inside Tristan. He was full, so fucking full, in a way he hadn't been in so long. No, in a way he'd never been.

His balls begged for release already, and they hadn't even moved yet.

But then they were. It took a minute to find a rhythm, Josiah's cock slamming into him from behind as Tristan worked his way in and out of Mateo.

The room was filled with the sounds of bodies slapping together, and breaths.

Tristan wrapped his hand around Mateo's cock, jerking him off while he made love to him. While Josiah made love to Tristan.

As soon as he felt Mateo's hot, sticky fluid slide between his fingers, curses flying from his mouth, Tristan let go. Pumped every ounce of what he had inside Mateo as he exploded.

Another wave of pleasure hit him when he felt Josiah's dick jerk inside him. As Josiah's fingers dug into his hips as he filled Tristan.

They went down to the bed together, a pile of bodies wrapped and intertwined with each other. Like a solid, a whole.

And somehow, he couldn't keep the words back anymore. They fought to break free from the walls he'd locked them behind. "Years ago, you thought I was trying to save you, Josiah. I assume the same way you probably thought Teo wanted to save you. You were wrong. It was you who saved me, the same way the two of you saved each other. And now…And now you brought me Mateo, too. I want you both. I love you both."

Even after the words left his lips, everything felt okay. It felt fucking amazing.

Josiah buried his face into Tristan's neck, but it was Mateo who spoke. *"Nunca nadie me ha amado en mi vida excepto ustedes dos. Yo nunca amare a nadie en mi vida solo a ustedes dos."* He took a breath and then repeated himself in English. "There has never been anyone in my life who loved me except the two of you. I will never love anyone except the two of you."

Mateo ran a finger down Tristan's jaw. "*Mi pieza perdida.* My missing piece." And then his hand ran down Josiah's back. *"Mi precioso."*

Josiah leaned up, taking Mateo's mouth first. Then Tristan's. "We might be broken in so many ways, but together, we're whole."

That's all that mattered to Tristan.

Life was so damned uncertain. Mateo had a past that was uncertain, and Tristan sure as hell wasn't perfect. He still had his mom to take care of, and Josiah had his dream to fulfill, but for the first time, they were moving forward. All of them. And somehow, Tristan knew it would be okay, that they would fight for each other and take on the world for each other. The only thing that mattered was that they were together.

```
                    The End
```

```
Josiah, Mateo and Tristan's story

       continues in late 2014.
```

Acknowledgement:

Big thanks goes to Jamie. I don't know what I'd do without his input. Thanks for the help. Also to Evie, Ellis, and another very close friend for the early reads. Thanks to Jackson Photographix for the incredible image. He is a master behind the camera. To all the readers, bloggers and reviewers for giving these men a chance. I know this story is completely different than COLLIDE but I appreciate the trust and hope they enjoyed the journey.

ABOUT THE AUTHOR

Riley Hart is the girl who wears her heart on her sleeve. She's a hopeless romantic. A lover of sexy stories, passionate men, and writing about all the trouble they can get into together. If she's not writing, you'll probably find her reading.

Riley lives in California with her awesome family, who she is thankful for every day.

You can find her online at:

Twitter
@RileyHart5

Facebook
https://www.facebook.com/riley.hart.1238?fref=ts

Blog
www.rileyhartwrites.blogspot.com

Tumblr
http://rileyhartwrites.tumblr.com

Made in the USA
Lexington, KY
31 January 2015